TEMPTATION

"Let Strong Bear kiss you again," he said, drawing her closer.

Pamela shut her eyes, having waited oh-so-long for a man who could send her to such heights of wonder. Desire welled and surfaced when he kissed her with a fierce, possessive heat.

Even when his hands moved lower and cupped her breasts through her dress, she did not refuse him. She was beyond coherent thought. She wanted him now, more than...life itself.

Pamela drew a ragged breath as Strong Bear's lips lowered and kissed the hollow of her throat. "Yes, oh, yes..." she whispered. "Love me, Strong Bear. Make love to—*with*—me."

D1173149

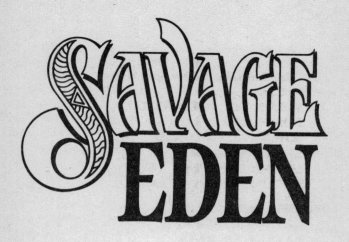

SAVAGE EDEN

CASSIE EDWARDS

LOVE SPELL ◆ NEW YORK CITY

LOVE SPELL®

June 1996

Published by

Dorchester Publishing Co., Inc.
276 Fifth Avenue
New York, NY 10001

Cover art by John Ennis

The name "Love Spell" and its logo are trademarks of Dorchester Publishing Co., Inc.

Printed in the United States of America.

With much affection I dedicate
Savage Eden
to Debbie Oxier and Janet Kraemer
my two faithful friends
and romance advocates from
Marion, Indiana

THE CRY

The cry of the Indian was of little use,
To them the white man turned a deaf ear,
The proud Indians were tired of their abuse...
In this, it seemed their final year.

They once rode with great pride and glory,
These Indians with honor and courage.
Now from the white man they must hide,
Their life's blood slowly draining away...
In this, it seemed their final year.

They once were trusting people,
A man's word meant everything.
But the white man thought them ignorant savages...
In this, it seemed their final year.

Some white men were honorable,
But of them, the number was few,
On the Indian was put the blame for everything...
In this, it seemed their final year.

If you listen closely,
You can still hear their mournful cries,
Cries for peace and respect...
In this, it seemed their final year.

The Indians wanted to live peacefully,
White men would not let them.
They no longer could stand by and be silent.
If they died, it would be with honor and courage,
    not shame...
In this, it is their final year.

—Dawn Luck
    Romance reader and devoted fan

Prologue

The Wilderness of Kentucky: 1779

Bordering on the Ohio River, the land exceeds description. The soil is astonishingly rich. Leaving the rivers, a high hill skirts the low ground. Here the land is also amazingly fertile, covered with a heavy growth of timber, such as white and red oak, hickory, ash, and beech.

A number of small streams take their rise, then gently creep along through the winding valleys, and in their course these winding streams form a great quantity of excellent meadowland. The meadows enlarge and extend themselves till they discharge their crystal streams into the rivers.

White clover and bluegrass grow in spontaneous abundance. The air is so still one can hear the clear call of the bobwhites . . . and the mellow chorus of the turtledoves, for miles around.

Hogs fatten in the woods. . . .

One

❦

Her eyes as stars of twilight fair;
Like twilight's, too, her dusky hair.
                    —Wordsworth

Kneeling down on the rough hearth, Anthony Boyd laid on kindling and encouraged a blaze by waving his hands over the crackling bits of wood. The fire began to eat away at the backlog and soon the whole room was lit with its gentle glow.

But Anthony felt none of the same sort of glow warming his insides, for a body-wracking cough reaching from the far side of the one-room log cabin was a rude reminder that his father was no better this morning, and perhaps even worse. The fever, chills, and severe headache caused by the dreaded disease, malaria, were fast taking their toll.

Anthony's sister, Pamela, spoke abruptly from behind him. "Papa's worse this morning, isn't he?"

Startled by her sudden presence, Anthony rose quickly to his full height. He turned and smiled at his sister, experiencing afresh the relief that nothing had happened to her on the long and grueling journey from Williamsburg to this Kentucky wilderness. All but one member of the Boyd family had survived. Anna Boyd, the beloved wife and mother, had passed away along the trail. Her frailties had slowly consumed and claimed her.

"My, but aren't you looking pretty this morning," Anthony said from his towering six-foot frame, evading Pamela's question about their father. She would see his weakened condition soon enough.

Anthony's gaze swept over her admiringly, marveling anew at how his sister awakened each morning looking so fresh and vibrant. This morning her crystal blue eyes could never sparkle more vivaciously, nor could her cheeks be rosier. Her hair was already freshly brushed, tumbling in an auburn sheen down her straight and perfect back.

Her cotton dress looked comfortably soft and was delicately printed. Its skirt was gathered, its sleeves puffed, and a V-shaped bodice revealed the uppermost lobes of her pale, yet quite womanly breasts. Now twenty, she was a vision of loveliness.

"Papa?" Pamela said, looking past Anthony to the far dark corner where she could barely make out a slight figure sleeping on a bed arranged between two others. She had been assigned the overhead loft where she could have more privacy. "I heard Papa coughing most of the night. Is he worse, Anthony?"

Anthony nervously raked his fingers through his rusty shoulder-length hair. "I'm afraid I must go for help soon," he said hoarsely. "We may have no other choice. Papa needs medicine. Without it . . ."

Pamela's face paled with the thought of what Anthony had in mind. "But, Anthony, the only others close enough to seek help from are the British. And you know the dangers in *that*. Even the journey there could be perilous. There's the constant threat of Indians."

She always worried about her brother, who was five years her senior. Though he displayed such a magnificent height and broad shoulders and was, even himself, dressed as a savage in heavily fringed breeches and shirt sewn from buckskin, he was only one man. The British and Indians were *many*.

Anthony shook his head contemplatively. "Yes, I know," he said. He knelt before the hearth and began feeding wood into the flames. "Perhaps I'll wait a couple more days. While I'm out hunting today you and Robert can take turns bathing father's brow with cool compresses. If we can just get some kind of hold on his temperature . . ."

Pamela moved to her father's bedside. Seeing him in this weakened state made her heart ache. She looked down at his body, a body that had at one time boasted strength and robust health but which was now reduced to skin and bone. Anthony had wanted to go for medical assistance but Aaron Boyd had forbidden it. He had reminded his son that, although the British were the only civilized people within riding distance, they were, for the most part, less civilized than the Indians. It was common knowledge that the British compensated the Indians for scalping American settlers, to discourage other settlers from traveling to Kentucky. Though America had won its independence from the British, some British forts were now illegally in this area, continuing their brutal practices against those Americans who dared clear the land for settling.

But with her father's health still failing, Pamela knew that one day soon Anthony would most surely have to travel to the nearest British fort to plead for some sort of medical assistance, if there was even any available for malaria. Surely differences could be cast aside this one time between the British and one family of settlers. Their skins were of the same color, were they not . . . ? It was only their hearts that bore a difference.

Pamela turned and smiled weakly at her other brother, Robert, as he rose from his bed and ambled toward her, slipping suspenders over his shoulders, yawning.

"Papa's no better, is he?" Robert asked, now reaching for his gold-framed spectacles left on the kitchen table the previous night. "I heard you say something about the British. Anthony, are you going today, to ask for their help?"

"Maybe Anthony *should*," Pamela interjected, stepping away from the bed so that her voice would not awaken her father. "What do *you* think, Robert?"

Robert slipped his spectacles on, and blinked his vision clear. Without his eyeglasses he could only make out a blur of movements and colors. He had brought a spare pair from Williamsburg in case the other broke.

"You're askin' me for advice?" Robert said, laughing low. "Does that mean that I've graduated from being a brother who should be seen but not heard, into someone whose opinion actually matters?"

"You *are* eighteen, you know," Pamela said, casting a pleasant grin his way.

"Eighteen is so much older than seventeen?" Robert taunted. "Or is it because you want to get on my better side so that I'll be more eager to help Anthony build that fence he spoke about all the way from Williamsburg?"

"Well, perhaps." Pamela giggled. She went to Robert and hugged him, laughing to herself when she felt muscle instead of the bone of only a year ago before the youngster had blossomed into a man.

She eased away from him and searched her younger brother's face. Though freckled and forced to wear eyeglasses, he was a handsome fellow who boasted golden-brown eyes and rusty hair. The women of Williamsburg had lost a prime catch in both him *and* Anthony, as had the men because *she* had left, or so her brothers constantly scolded. Would they ever leave her be where men were concerned? It was her life, and she had the right to make her *choice*. So far, no man had spoken to her heart in the way she would expect, when in love. If she was even forced to live the life of an old maid, it was better than marrying a man, just to be married!

"You think you can build me one damn good fence,

huh, Robert?'' Anthony said, looking from Pamela to
Robert.

"You bet I can," Robert said, squaring his shoulders.

Anthony patted Robert fondly on the back, then walked
away to get a leather string from a peg on the wall. "We'll
begin that fence one day soon," he said, securing his hair
into a pony tail with the leather. "But let's first see what
we can do to make father more comfortable. Robert, you
go down to the creek and fetch a bucket of water. Pamela,
you—"

Pamela stepped between her brothers and flashed her
most winsome smile. "It's *my* turn to fetch the water,"
she argued softly. "Anthony, you haven't let me out of
your sight for months now. Don't you think it's about
time for me to do something on my own? Let *me* fetch the
water. Please?"

Anthony scowled. "Maybe next time. We haven't been
here long enough to know how safe it is. Indians could pay
us a surprise call any day now. It *was* the chance we took
by decidin' to settle here," he said, pausing to rake his
eyes over his sister. "And with a lovely lady a part of our
household? That could attract Indians to us like bees' are
attracted to *honey*." He gave her a harried look. "Pamela,
it would've been best had you stayed in Williamsburg,
married to a caring man. This isn't a suitable place for
you. You saw what happened to Mama. She didn't last no
time after leavin' Williamsburg. Why couldn't you have
said yes to one of those fine gents who tried to court
you?''

"Anthony, I'm not like Mama. She was frail. I'm strong.
And had I married someone in Williamsburg I wouldn't
have been able to come with you. I wanted to come to
Kentucky and settle here as bad as you did. I wanted
adventure, a new way of life, not days wasted caring for a
husband and children. And I didn't want to marry someone
just for the sake *of* marrying," she argued. "I want to *love*
first."

"And you expect to find someone to love out here in

this godforsaken land of Indians?'' Anthony tormented. ''That's not likely, Pamela. Not likely at all.'' He waved a hand toward Robert. ''Fetch the bucket. Get on down to the creek like I told you, Robert. Pamela, get the corn mush ready for cooking.''

Pamela's eyes blazed in exasperation and anger. She lifted the hem of her dress and stomped to the water bucket, grabbing its handle before Robert could reach it. ''You can't keep me in this cabin like a prisoner,'' she fumed. ''I intend to get some fresh air as well as you and Robert. I *shall* go for the water.''

Frowning darkly, Anthony took long strides toward her. ''No you're not. Not now,'' he argued, seeing that she was as pigheadedly stubborn now at twenty as she had been at ten. Could any other sister be as feisty or mule-headed?

''Just you *see*,'' Pamela said, flouncing toward the door, which she flew open.

Anthony shook his head and sighed. He was in no mood to argue. Pamela *wasn't* ten. He *couldn't* spank her to get her to mind. And if he continued to make a scene with her, it could disturb their father.

Knowing when a battle was lost with his sister, Anthony grabbed a flintlock rifle, primed it, then hurried after Pamela as she continued down the pathway toward the thick woods.

''One day your stubborn ways are going to get you into a peck of trouble,'' Anthony growled, grabbing Pamela's wrist, stopping her. He thrust the rifle into her hand. ''Now you fire upon anything that moves in the forest. Do you hear? If you wait to check to see what's making the noise, it might be too late.''

''Do you even think me capable of firing?'' Pamela taunted, stubbornly lifting her chin in defiance of her brother's continued agitated state.

''You'd damn well *better* know how,'' Anthony spat, placing his hands on his hips. ''I hope I didn't spend all those many hours teachin' you for nothin'.''

Pamela's stubborn stance softened, and she cast her eyes downward. She was choosing a bad time to argue with her brother. Their ailing father should be her main concern.

"I'm sorry," she whispered. Then her eyes shot upward as she squared her shoulders. "But that doesn't mean that I don't still want to go to the creek."

Her searching gaze absorbed the loveliness of the setting. The sky was clear, there was a gentle warmth in the air that soothed her frayed nerves, and all the world of vegetation was shaking off the winter lethargy as buds burst forth and leaves and blossoms unfurled. Butterflies flitted about, insects buzzed and frolicked, and lively lizards scurried through the dry leaves, their rushed passage marked by a scraping noise.

All of this—the pure, bracing air, the puffs of apple bloom in the nearby forest, so beautiful, so sweetly aromatic—went far to compensate for the wilderness.

"I want to *feel* the setting, not only *see* it," she said, again imploring Anthony with a daring look in her bewitching blue eyes. "And so I *shall*."

Laughing softly, she turned and hurried toward the shine of the water beyond some saplings, afraid of no one, or anything.

But too soon her smile faded when she pictured her father as he had first described this land of Kentucky to her. He and Anthony had chosen this plot of land for homesteading after they and a group of surveyors had spotted it while surveying. Her father had said that the land and its beauty had seduced him, as a lady seduces a man with a flirting eye. His eyes had sparkled as he had talked about fish that were so a'plenty in Kentucky they plumb jumped from the water!

Bringing his family, giving them an opportunity to make a permanent home in this new land of promise, had become more important to her father than his surveying career. Perhaps even his *life*.

Too, they were the first of a contingent of setters swarming over these lands, though so far, other families and their cabins had not been put up too nearby.

Shaking thoughts from her mind that were spoiling her outing, Pamela began to run. She would enjoy her rare moment of freedom. Surely her father's health would improve. It *must*. He was the backbone of the Boyd family. Without him . . . ?

Anthony sighed, letting Pamela have her way this time. Of late he *had* been too demanding of her, too domineering. She needed freedom, too. This time he would allow it. But trips to the creek *would* be few and far between. He would see to that!

Turning, he looked at the cabin. This was home. While Pamela had kept food warming over a nearby campfire, the male members of the Boyd family had worked together day and night splitting logs for the walls, floor, and roof. Wooden pins had been used for nails, leather straps for door hinges. Latches for the door were wooden, and a string had been hitched onto the latch and run out through a hole above so that when anyone wanted to come in, they yanked the string and that lifted the latch. They only needed to pull in the string and the door was locked.

Bit by bit, stone, mud, and sticks had been formed into the wide fireplace chimney. The furniture was all hand-made. Though plain, he was proud of the table and chairs, the bedsteads, and the mattresses made from the feathers of ducks and the soft down of cattails.

Worry of his father drew Anthony back toward the cabin. Lost in thought, he walked in a slow gait. If his father didn't make it through the traumas of this dreaded illness, so many dreams would be taken to the grave with him. This land had opened its arms and enfolded the Boyd family as though they'd been born of its womb. But now the land was like a parent denying birthright to Anthony's father in his grave illness.

Anthony stepped inside the cabin, to be met by a weak and quivering voice. Aaron spoke again. "Anthony . . ."

The weakness of his father's voice tore at Anthony's heart. His buckskin clothes smelling new and fresh, he went and knelt down on the floor beside Aaron's bed. He touched his father's brow, yet already knew that his temperature was soaring. His father's sunken cheeks were flushed scarlet, and his eyes were bloodshot. Another day of cool compresses to his brow lay ahead of him.

"Anthony, son . . ." Aaron said in a shallow rasp, grasping Anthony's hand, his bones digging into his flesh. "Don't let our dreams die with me." An escaped tear silvered his flushed cheek. "This land we've settled on. It's now ours." His parched lips quivered into a weak semblance of a smile, and then his feverish eyes closed and he fell into another deep sleep.

"Damn," Anthony whispered. Feeling helpless, he rose slowly to his feet, his head hung low.

"Well? How is he?" Robert asked, stepping to Anthony's side.

"Not so good," Anthony said. With Robert trailing along beside him, Anthony went to stand before the hearth. "But we must keep faith, Robert. Prayer sometimes works miracles, you know."

Robert knelt and tossed a log on the fire, casting Anthony a sidewise glance. "Then you aren't going for help just yet? You're not going to the British fort?"

Anthony leaned an arm against the fireplace mantel, his golden eyes flecked with worry. "Soon, perhaps," he murmured. "But first I must replenish our food supply. If I travel to the fort and the British should choose to imprison me . . ."

Pamela lifted the hem of her dress and bent to her knees on the grassy knoll beside the creek. She wanted to savor this moment alone. If Anthony had his way, she would *never* leave the drab cabin to explore the wonders of this lush world. Didn't he know that she longed for adventure? She didn't want to be stifled, stuck away in the cabin doing womanly chores. Perhaps she *should* have married someone in Williamsburg after all. At least she could have come and gone as she pleased.

Taking more time than she knew her brother would allow, Pamela cupped her hands onto her lap and relaxed. She watched the swirling life in the water, smiling. Tadpoles were darting about, miniature specks of black wriggling in the path of the sunbeams. A bullfrog's deep, resonant voice bellowed at intervals from the nearby rock formations. Mud turtles were sunning on the snags that rose above the level of the water.

Leaning, Pamela saw her reflection in the clear mirror of the water. Her fingers wove through her waist-length hair, twisting and shaping it first one way, then another, trying to decide which style she liked best.

Then, tiring of this, she tilted her head backward and let her hair tumble across her shoulders. She closed her eyes for a moment and enjoyed the sun's warmth on her upturned face. She had never been as free as now. Inhaling the sweet fragrance of the unspoiled air, she coiled her fingers through the cool grass on either side of her.

But her moment of total serenity was suddenly shattered. Her heart skipped a beat and her eyes flew open when a rustling sound alerted her stirred senses that someone lurked nearby, observing her. Anthony's warning quickly came to mind. Hadn't he told her what to do if she should hear a noise that alarmed her . . . ?

Her fingers crawled toward the rifle on the ground beside her, and she scarcely breathed. It was as though time were standing still, and even her surroundings, which had teemed with life moments before, had suddenly become eerily quiet! Someone *was* near. But she was afraid to look to discover *whom*. Her eyes were firmly fixed. She swallowed hard. But the cold touch of the rifle made her realize that it and her courage were the only two things that perhaps stood between her and possible death.

Clamping her fingers about the rifle, Pamela jumped to her feet. Swinging around, her eyes searched through the forest vegetation. Then her breath momentarily caught when she spotted the intruder on her privacy.

Her knees grew so weak they nearly buckled, and her heart lurched as she peered into eyes as black as a starless midnight as they, in turn, focused on her through a break in the trees only a few footsteps away. It was an Indian brave! Never had she stood so closely to an Indian as she did now!

She tried to force herself to fire upon the Indian but she couldn't, for he did not seem at all threatening. His bow was slung casually across his shoulder, his arrows held within a quiver at his back.

Pamela's gaze swept over him, seeing how he was so minimally clothed in only an Indian breechclout. It revealed more of his copper body than she felt civil to behold, and her reaction to the length of his long, lean body was disturbing in the extreme. She suddenly had no control over her heart. It thumped wildly. And the pit of her stomach was filled with an even stranger quivering! She had never before been so affected by a man. And this wasn't just any man. This was an *Indian*.

Trying to capture control over her feelings, Pamela studied the Indian even more intensely. He was at least six feet tall. His body was solidly built and muscular. His large and piercing eyes expressed intelligence and firmness. His forehead was high and broad, his nose straight. Full sensual lips enhanced what Pamela already found to be an extremely, if primitively, handsome face.

Pamela had read in her studies of Indians that most rubbed their hair with certain kinds of herbs and bark to give luster and strength to it. This Indian showed evidence of this practice. His hair was luxuriantly black and long, decorated with several feathers in a coil at the back. And the way he held himself so proudly erect, it was surely a posture of a person of stature, perhaps even a powerful *chief*.

"Pamela!"

Pamela was drawn from her reverie by Anthony's shout.

She saw that the Indian also had heard, for he started and grabbed an arrow from his quiver and notched it quickly onto the cording of his bow.

Pamela was horrified at his behavior but restrained her instinct to fire. For a moment it had been as though they had been exchanging some wordless dialogue, their behavior awash in mutual admiration.

But then the Indian's threat grew too real as he drew the cord of his bow back, readying to fire his arrow.

She brought the rifle up without taking the time to aim. Closing her eyes, she pulled the trigger, the jolt of the discharge unsteadying her.

When she regained her composure and opened her eyes, she was afraid to see if the Indian was lying lifeless on the forest floor. She had never killed a man before. And though most did not consider an Indian human, but rather a heathen savage, the brief flicker between them had proved to Pamela that he was perhaps more man than any other she had ever met, or would ever meet again.

Lowering the rifle to her side, Pamela looked hurriedly into the brush where the Indian had been standing. Her gaze moved to the ground, then she glanced quickly in all directions, seeing him nowhere.

"I . . . must . . . have missed," she whispered, silently thanking God that she had. She didn't want her restless dreams to be haunted by the Indian's dark, compelling eyes. And if he had been a true threat, would he have turned and fled after she had fired upon him and missed? Wouldn't he have killed her?

Anthony ran toward her carrying another primed flintlock rifle. He was breathless when he came to her side, his eyes roaming about anxiously, and peering deeply into the forest.

"Why did you shoot?" he asked raspily.

"Why does anyone fire a rifle?" Pamela taunted, seizing this opportunity to prove that she *could* defend herself in this Kentucky wilderness. "To protect one's self. I saw an Indian watching me. I didn't give him a chance to fire upon me *first*."

Anthony looked down at Pamela, his eyes wide with surprise. "You? You shot an Indian?" he asked, shifting his rifle to rest in the crook of his arm. He let his gaze linger from place to place as he probed for the fallen Indian. "Well? Where is he?"

"Anthony, I didn't say that I *hit* him," Pamela said, sighing. "I scared him off, that's all." She rocked playfully on her heels, smiling mischievously up at him. "Aren't you proud of me?"

Anthony's eyebrows narrowed into a straight line. A part of him wanted to grab Pamela up and hug her, thankful that for some reason the Indian had decided not to kill her when she had apparently missed him. Another part wanted to turn her over his knee to spank her for so stubbornly coming to the creek in the first place. Another still doubted her story, convinced her imagination—influenced by a bout of cabin fever—was responsible for the wild tale.

He followed his first instinct. He grabbed her hand and began running her back to the cabin.

"But Anthony, I didn't get any *water*," Pamela fussed, panting to keep up with him.

"To hell with the water," Anthony growled. "Don't you have any sense about you? If that Indian existed, he couldn't have gotten far. I'm going to get you inside the cabin and, damn it, you stay there until I return. Do you hear?"

Pamela turned her eyes to him. "What do you mean 'if,'" she flared, almost tripping through the door of the cabin as he brusquely drew her past Robert, who had witnessed everything from afar but her firing upon the Indian.

"Never mind," he said, already regretting voicing his skepticism as he dragged his sister inside. The least he could give her in these tumultuous days was some belief in her crazy notions. He began to rummage about the room for his hunting gear.

"Then you've decided to go to the fort to speak with the British after all?" she asked, wiping a pearly bead of perspiration from her brow as Anthony readied himself for his trek into the forest for game.

If what his sister said about the Indian were true, the thought of the Indian roaming about so close to the cabin made Anthony's insides turn cold. This was a hell of a time to have to replenish a food supply. He might lose his *scalp*, instead of gaining a fat venison for the supper table!

"Not today," he said sourly, sheathing a knife to his waist. "I've got to get some food for the table. I've allowed our supply to get too low as it is."

Pamela smoothed wrinkles from the skirt of her dress. "But, Anthony, the Indian . . ." she said nervously.

"Don't worry your fool heads off about Indians," Anthony said, looking from Pamela to Robert. "If you two stay put, you'll be fine. Just tend to Papa until I come back. I should have us something fine and tasty for the supper table."

"What about the fence, Anthony?" Robert asked, eyeing his box of books on the floor, favoring reading one of them over another day of hard labor. He silently thanked the possibility of Indians nearby offering a reprieve from the backbreaking chores. It wasn't that he was lazy. He just loved books almost more than life itself.

"Perhaps we can get to the fence tomorrow," Anthony said, heading toward the door. "It's waited this long to be built. It won't hurt none to let another day pass without it."

Pamela ran to Anthony and whirled around to stand in front of him. On tiptoe she kissed him on the cheek. "Be careful," she murmured.

"Be*have*," he said, his lips quivering into a nervous smile. "Pass the day by caring for Papa. He depends on us, totally."

Pamela stepped aside, her hands clasped behind her. "Don't I always?" she teased, her eyes twinkling.

Anthony shook his head and sighed as he stepped outside into the sunshine, his muscles coiled with tension. He looked into the dark shadows of the forest. If an Indian saw him leave the cabin, would the savage take advantage of his absence? Or had Pamela frightened him off by shooting at him? Or had she alerted a tribe?

Shaking off his burdensome thoughts, he steeled himself for the task at hand: the Boyds' food supply must be replenished today. Or they'd all perish, Indians or no Indians.

He turned and glared at Pamela. "Lock the door as soon as I leave. Understand?" he flatly ordered, yet realizing that no amount of locks on a door would stop Indians from penetrating their home. And no amount of brothers present could protect a sister, either. In this wilderness, all settlers were at the mercy of the Indians.

But so far none had ventured closer than the forest that rimmed their land. Perhaps there was hope after all that they could coexist with the Indians; that is, if the British didn't order the Indians to run the Boyds off the land they now claimed as theirs! Anthony had thought that perhaps this had been the fate of others who had rooted in this particular spot, for no other cabins had been sighted either earlier, or *now*. The Boyds were alone, truly isolated from the sort of life they had always known, until now.

Pamela nodded a silent response to her brother's orders. She stood at the door and watched him ride away on his horse until he was out of sight. Then her gaze was drawn hypnotically to the spot where she had last seen the Indian. A strange sort of thrill coursed through her veins as she recalled the Indian's primitive handsomeness, his magnificent physique, his compelling dark eyes. Strangely enough, not understanding herself at all, she could not deny that she desired to see him again. His difference magnified his specialness in her eyes.

Then she paled, recalling the moment she had fired the rifle at the Indian. Why hadn't she thought earlier to wonder if she had possibly injured him? He could have fled into the forest mortally wounded! Should she go and search for him?

Pamela was torn, not knowing if it was because of his welfare that she was deliberating over him in her mind, or because she would chance everything to see him again? He *was* the only man, ever, to stir her senses so much, she felt totally, unabashedly alive! And he had yet to even touch, her, except . . . with . . . his eyes.

Strong Bear winced as he slumped into the shadows of the cave that he had found many moons ago upon his earlier explorations of this land. The wound at his temple inflicted by the white woman's firestick burned as though his flesh had been seared by tongues of flames. Though he hadn't lost that much blood since the wound was no more than a grazing, it was the location of the wound that had rendered him light-headed. Never had his temples pulsed so fiercely!

But before becoming too lethargic he had managed to find the proper ingredients for which to treat his wound. With long, lean fingers, he had dug out sumac leaves and roots of the pallaganghy from the forest floor as he had followed the cave trail, then crushed them into a powder. He smoothed this mixture onto his bloody flesh; then, breathing hard, he closed his eyes and leaned back against the moss-covered wall of the cave.

Slowly he began to drift into unconsciousness, his thoughts troubled by visions of a white goddess who possessed the courage of a bear, and whose eyes were the color of a summer sky. How *could* he eventually kill anyone as beautiful . . . as courageous . . . ?

But he *must*, mustn't he? She and her family were intruders, a threat to Strong Bear's people! If he let them stay on the land that the Great Spirit had chosen for the new site of his Miami village, wouldn't other white settlers follow?

Now boasting twenty-five harvests, and a powerful chief of a proud tribe of Miami Indians, Strong Bear *must* protect his people above all else!

But Strong Bear had not yet turned to violence against the white settlers. How could he now? Only the Delaware were guilty of this, and more oft than not because they were paid by the British. Strong Bear did not like the British or their ways. He tried to avoid bloodshed at all cost. Raised by a warring father, Strong Bear had seen enough bloodshed and heard enough cries of his people during the reign of his chieftain father! And now that Strong Bear was chief he wanted to settle his affairs by peaceful methods.

But how could he now? This land these settlers had claimed as theirs was sacred, a land promised for Strong Bear's people. The Great Spirit had led Strong Bear there while experiencing his special vision after smoking the sacred pipe filled with traditional Miami herbs only a few knew how to blend.

Perhaps he could take the white woman as his hostage. Could that be the answer to how not only she, but also her family, could be spared? Strong Bear would use her for bargaining! Wouldn't her family willingly leave this land if they knew that her life would be spared only if they agreed to flee? But he would never let her return to them. She would be Strong Bear's, not theirs! This, too, they would have to accept or every one of them would be killed, even *her*.

Unable to fight off the black void of unconsciousness any longer, Strong Bear felt himself drifting, drifting, drifting, escaping the responsibility of decisions for the moment. . . .

Two

❧~❧

I want you when in lazy, slumbrous fashion
My senses need the haven of your breast.
— Gillom

Pretending to be the dutiful sister who always obeyed her brother, Pamela closed and locked the door, knowing darn well that she would be opening it again very soon, to leave. She must make sure the Indian wasn't lying somewhere in the woods slowly bleeding to death like a wounded animal. He *wasn't* an animal; he was quite human and, to Pamela, the most handsome and intriguing man she had ever seen!

Though she knew the risks of wandering outdoors alone again, she did not alter her decision. Everyone knew that living in this wilderness was a risk in itself. The presence of Indians was only one danger. And this Indian who was troubling her thoughts had not appeared to be all that dangerous. Although he had aimed his weapon at her he had only done so to protect himself, the same as Pamela when she had *shot* at *him*. In both cases their instinct for survival guided them both into a hasty decision.

She was alive. But what about him?

Envisioning his handsome face twisted in pain, even in her mind's eye seeing him nearby, lying on the ground in a pool of blood, Pamela rushed across the room, setting her plan in motion. She must leave the cabin soon and search for the Indian. If she were too late and he were to die, wouldn't many Indians arrive to search for him? If they discovered who had caused his death the Boyd family would not have a prayer of a chance for survival!

"You really saw an Indian, Pamela?" Robert asked, yet he didn't appear all that interested as he sorted through his books, eager to choose one to read. Very rarely had he had the chance to settle down to read since they had arrived from Williamsburg. Chores were too plentiful when trying to establish a new home and farm. Too many conveniences had been left behind. Everything had to be made by hand here in this damn wilderness.

"Yes. I saw an Indian," Pamela murmured, fussing with her father's bedding, tucking the blanket beneath the edges of the feather mattress. "And as you know, I fired at him. But I'm not truly sure whether I hit or *missed*."

She turned to Robert, her hands clasped nervously together behind her. "He just seemed to disappear into thin air, Robert."

"Poof! Just like that, huh?" Robert teased, flipping his chosen book open, sorting through the pages to find the last passage he'd read.

Seeing his total disinterest in what she was saying, angry at how he was taking all of this so lightly, Pamela stormed to the table and slammed the book shut. "Robert, we've things to do," she spat, her eyes flashing angrily. She nodded toward their father. "We must see to Papa's comfort. *We*, Robert. You and I. You can read some other—"

She broke her words off deliberately, suddenly seized with an idea. It would be *much* better than asking Robert to guard their father's bedside while she fetched the water. If Robert were dying to lose himself in a book, so be it! He could read to their father. That could not only occupy her brother while she did her snooping in the forest, but her father could also benefit. Though her father was sleeping, a steady, comforting voice beside his bed could possibly reach into his unconsciousness and somehow lift him into a more pleasant state.

Pamela's heart soared with excitement. Yes! It *would* work! And Robert would be so absorbed in reading he wouldn't even notice that her absence might be longer than necessary for fetching water.

But she *would* have to convince him that she would be safe alone outdoors. Hopefully the lure of literature would lessen his fears for her.

Lowering the pitch of her voice, amused even at Robert's expression caused by her sudden flurry of activity, Pamela reopened the book. Thumbing through it, she was glad this was a story that her father liked. He had so often read it to her as a child at her bedside. It was time to repay such a kindness.

"Robin Hood," she said softly, yet purposely loud enough for Robert to hear. "Papa's favorite." She swung around and faced Robert, her eyes innocent. "You wish to read today, Robert? Read aloud to *Papa*. He would so enjoy it. I just *know* that he would somehow hear you." She grabbed Robert's hands. "Will you? Please? Do it, Robert. You put such feelings into reading because books mean so much *to* you."

"But, sis . . ." Robert said, his eyes wavering. "It would be awkward. Papa's *asleep*. I would feel as though I'm reciting aloud to the floor and *walls*."

"Hogwash!" Pamela said, rushing away from him. She took a candleholder and its tapered candle from the fireplace mantel, leaned the candle's wick into the flames on the hearth until it began flickering with light, then determinedly carried it to her father's bedside and sat it on the floor.

Scooting two chairs beside the bed, she placed the candle on one for Robert's benefit, then patted the seat of the other chair, smiling toward her younger brother. "See? You have a chair for sitting and enough light for *seeing*," she encouraged. "Need you ask for more? Come on. Read to Papa. It would be *so* sweet of you, Robert."

Robert laughed. "Sweet?" he said in a half groan, grabbing the book up from the table. "Good Lord, Pamela, call me anything but sweet. Only *girls* are sweet!"

His spectacles already nestled on the bridge of his nose, Robert settled down on the chair beside his father's bed. "Robin Hood it is," he said, opening the book. "But I'm going to feel foolish."

Foolish or not, he had always enjoyed reading the adventures of Robin Hood, having often envisioned himself experiencing the same sort of exciting life. His life had been boring as hell. And now, even in this wild land of Indians and bears, Pamela was experiencing more exciting challenges than he. *She* had been given the opportunity to fire upon an Indian, not *he*.

Pamela leaned and hugged Robert fiercely and gave him a quick kiss. "What you are about to do could never be defined as foolish," she whispered. "And whether you like it or not, I think it's *sweet*."

Gently shoving her away from him, Robert tried to hide his blushing face by looking down at the book. "Aw, go on, sis," he fussed. "Do your chores. Leave me be. All right?"

"Yes, I *must* do my chores," Pamela said, squaring her shoulders as if preparing for battle. "I must *still* fetch the fresh water from the creek for bathing Papa's brow."

She awaited Robert's explosion, expecting him to order her to remain in the cabin. But her words had gone unheard for Robert was already absorbed in the book, his voice soft and soothing as he began reading aloud. Pamela stood for a moment and listened to the familiar tale. Robert was reading a passage about Robin Hood's most frequent enemy, the sheriff of Nottingham, who was swearing to find and kill Robin Hood. Robin Hood had just robbed and killed another representative of authority and had given the small fortune to the poor.

Pamela began inching backward, wondering if she left now, would Robert truly even miss her? He was absorbed in the tale of a time when a good deal of the rebellion against authority stemmed from restrictions of hunting rights. The story of Robin Hood revealed the cruelty that was an inescapable part of medieval life.

Pamela had often been struck by the parallels between then and now; things were not all that much different. The Indians were a prime example. She and her family were even guilty of taking land that the Indians had staked out for themselves. Just how right could that be? Weren't the Indians, in a sense, losing their hunting rights wherever settlers cleared land and built their houses?

"Where are you going?" Robert said, breaking through Pamela's thoughts, peering at her with squinty eyes through his eyeglasses. "You've got a mighty mischievous gleam in your eyes, Pamela. Why are you walking backward looking at me so funny? What kind of scheme do you have up your sleeve anyhow?"

Pamela stopped abruptly, smiling sheepishly at Robert. Then she squared her shoulders and set her jaw firmly, determined to do as she had planned. "As I told you," she said dryly, "I've my chores to do. I'm going to fetch some water." She grabbed the flintlock rifle that she had taken with her to the creek earlier and went to the door, avoiding Robert's watchful stare. "I shan't be long, Robert. Just you keep reading. When I return you can still continue reading to him while I bathe his brow."

Pamela's fingers froze on the door latch when Robert's voice boomed close behind her. She grimaced when he grabbed her wrist and whirled her around to face him. "You're not going anywhere," he growled. "You know what happened the last time you went to the creek. I can't allow it to happen again. Anthony would skin me alive if anything happened to you."

Pamela glared at him. "Robert, I think you forget that you don't have much say about what I do," she argued. "I'm older than you. By rights I tell you what to do, not the other way around. And, by damn, Robert, I know what I'm doing. I'd be as safe as you out there and you know it. I bet I can fire a rifle even *better* than you. While in Williamsburg you chose reading over shooting."

She smiled smugly. "Now what do you have to say? Tell me *now* that I can't go."

Robert released her wrist. "Pamela, you might be older but, by damn, you aren't *wiser*," he argued hotly. "Don't you know that any man can whip a woman in gun shootin'? And about my practicin'—I didn't need all that much to hone my skills at shootin'."

Pamela's face grew hot with anger. She hated it when her brothers spoke down to her, so often labeling her a "mere" woman. Just because women were expected to do house chores and raise babies did not mean they were weaker or less skilled at defending themselves! Especially Pamela. And she would show Robert that he was wrong if it was the last thing she did on this earth.

Unlocking the door, she yanked it open, letting a burst of sunshine into the dreary cabin. Carrying the rifle, she stepped outside and inhaled the crisp, clean air. "Robert, how could anything truly bad happen on such a beautiful day as this?" she said, turning to smile at him. "Honey, just you go back to reading. I *can* take care of myself. The rifle is primed and ready for firing. Nothing will be allowed to get near me. Honest!"

"Sis . . ." Robert said, yet knowing that he had lost this battle, as he did most of the time with his stubborn, willful sister.

"Robert, go back to Papa's side," Pamela said, smiling softly at him. "He *will* sense your presence, and when he awakens, he'll need you."

Robert swung the door open more widely. "I'll leave the door open and keep an eye on you while you fetch the water," he said thickly.

Panic rose inside Pamela. If he should watch her, then she wouldn't be able to search for the Indian. "No, Robert," she encouraged softly. "Though I'm sure you welcome the chance to have fresh air flow into the cabin, the draft might be bad for Papa. Now just go on. Close the door, read to Papa, and let me get the water at my own leisurely pace. I want to enjoy the sunshine and air for a little while. Please understand?"

Robert nodded. "Yes, I guess I do," he said. "You are cooped up with three men in this cabin. Well, enjoy yourself. But keep a watch, do you hear?"

"Yes. I'm no ninny," Pamela sighed in exasperation. "I don't want to lose my hide to an Indian any more than you want me to. I *will* be careful."

Impatiently, she watched until he closed the door. And then with a wildly thumping heart she turned and let her eyes slowly search the dark depths of the forest. An anxious tremble coursed through her. Was she being foolish to think that the Indian was still near? Would she find a trail of blood that might lead her to him? Or was he probably already halfway back to his village?

Running more than walking, Pamela searched for the spot where he had stood observing her. The trees shadowed her; the pungent smell of the dew-dampened leaves covering the ground beneath them made her nostrils flare.

And then she gasped softly and stopped with a start when she looked down and saw a smudge of blood on the ground at her feet. Her nerves tightened. She paled. It had to be the Indian's blood, for Pamela was standing almost exactly where the Indian had stood. Her worst fears had been confirmed. Her aim had been more accurate than she had thought. She *had* shot the Indian.

At least Anthony would have believed her story about the Indian, instead of looking at her as if she'd been half-crazed. She gasped, lifting a hand to her mouth as she chided herself. If they had spotted the blood before, Anthony might have tried to track the wounded man down. It was good she hadn't insisted on finding signs of the Indian's presence.

Her gaze sweeping the land, she was afraid to see how exact her aim had been. Was the Indian wounded or dead? If he was wounded, would he be even more dangerous? Pamela had been warned by her father never to go near a wounded animal if she came across one in the forest. Animals, he had said, were more deadly wounded than well.

"What am I *doing*?" Pamela gasped. "I'm comparing the Indian to an *animal*. And he's *not*. He's not."

Kneeling, she felt a keen anxiousness rising within her. She studied the size of the bloodstain, then saw a few others farther ahead spotting the forest floor and undergrowth. The stains were hardly more than the size of a coin. It was easy to see that it had not been a mortal wound, or he would have lost more blood.

"He *is* only wounded," Pamela whispered, a strange relief flooding her. She pushed herself up to a standing position, again looking in the direction of the trail marked by bloodstains. She must find the Indian. She couldn't chance that he might bleed to death. Though bleeding slowly, any loss of blood could eventually prove fatal. And if *he* died, she and the rest of her family surely would as well. Once his body was found so close to their cabin by other Indian braves, there would be no doubt in their minds who was responsible.

But if she found him wounded and offered him assistance, couldn't her sincerity persuade him not to return later with other braves to kill her?

Fright and excitement fusing as one emotion within, Pamela began moving cautiously onward. Her fingers, clamped tightly to her rifle, trembled as she held it unsteadily before her. If she were forced to fire it again, she would most surely miss this time. She had never felt so unsure of so many things about herself as now, in not only her aim, but also her ability to make rational decisions. Should she retreat and hurry back to the safety of the cabin? Or should she do as her pounding heart urged her—continue searching for the Indian?

Even if she found the Indian wounded and in need of assistance, would he accept anything that she offered? It was not a common thing for an Indian to trust a white man *or* woman, especially one who had shot him. It was foolish, even, for a white woman to believe she could ever trust an *Indian*.

Yet, a thrill pulsed through her veins like wildfire when she recalled how she and the Indian's eyes had met and held. There had been something beautiful exchanged between them in those few wondrous moments. If it was at all possible, Pamela wanted to find out *what*. She had received many looks of admiration from men in her life and none had ever touched her heart in this way.

Strange that it would be an Indian who would awaken those feelings inside her, feelings that were surely meant to lie dormant from birth until she found the man who would become that missing link in her life, to make her whole . . . to make her a *woman*.

Shaking her head to clear her thoughts, amazed at how her mind could conjure up such ideas about an Indian whom she should be fearing, not fantasizing of *loving*, Pamela focused more on the trail of blood, which had now led her to the creek.

Walking cautiously along its embankment, she continued following the bloodstains, only vaguely distracted by the activity around her. A kingfisher was a natty arrow as it hustled upstream on some busy errand. Bluejays scolded from the trees along the stream bank. Purples of thistle in giant clumps were flanked with beds of black-eyed susans, a riot of orange and yellow. From his perch on an old snag a red-tailed hawk surveyed his hunting territory, alert for a morning snack. The sun breaking through the overhead foliage was lighting the water in great shafts of golden light.

The soft whinny of a horse from somewhere close by caused Pamela's steps to falter and her heart to skip a beat.

The horse couldn't be Anthony's. Though Pamela had walked farther into the forest than she had ever before dared, she was still too close to the cabin for the horse to be Anthony's. He didn't make it a practice to hunt for game so close to their cabin. He always rode deeper into the forest to do his shooting. Not only did he worry about stray gunshot, he worried about whom the gunfire might attract. If either the Indians or British followed the sound, he would be the only one to be abducted or killed. Not the entire family.

"It *must* be the Indian's horse," Pamela whispered shallowly. "He didn't leave for his village after being wounded, he just moved farther into the forest."

Her pulse racing, Pamela began to scan the vegetation ahead with her searching eyes, tensing when the horse whinnied again, but this time giving her a sense of direction because she was more alert and was expecting it.

But she found herself too afraid to move. Her feet seemed frozen to the ground. Before, she had only to think she might actually come face-to-face with the Indian. Now she *knew* that she would. Her courage was waning, replaced by a growing chill. How could she have been so foolish to think that this was a sane thing to do? Was her hunger for adventure this great? Had she become so bored with her daily routine that she was ready to risk death to feed her dangerous impulses?

"Who's there?" she found herself crying, without another thought. Her hands now trembled fiercely as she kept the rifle leveled for firing.

When she didn't get a response, she felt a desperate need to look more courageous than she was feeling. She shouted again. "I know someone's there! Make yourself known, or are you a yellow-bellied *coward*?"

When again she received no human response, her earlier fears for the Indian raced back into her mind. He was wounded worse than she thought! Otherwise he would have made himself known to her!

Pamela blanched. His silence could also mean that he

was playing games with her. He could be leading her into a trap.

She began to inch backward. She wouldn't go any farther. She was wrong to come this far. If she returned safely to the cabin she would never be this foolish again. Even though she hated the thought of being cooped up in the cabin both day and night, she vowed she would never leave it again! Never had she been so engulfed by fear as now!

A groan laced with pain, surfacing from somewhere just ahead, grabbed Pamela's keen attention. She stopped abruptly, her eyes wide. Another groan sounded, spearing directly to her heart. No one could pretend the pain that she had witnessed twice now. Someone was in agony. Not just *someone*. It must be the Indian. And surely it wasn't a way to trick her. The cry of pain was genuine.

Lowering her rifle to her side, Pamela was once again determined to find the Indian. She couldn't let him suffer. She must find him and see if she could help him. It was the only Christian thing to do!

But deep within, where her womanly desires had found birth, Pamela knew that she must find and help the handsome Indian for other reasons than being a good Christian. He was like a magnet, drawing her to him. No fears, nothing could stop her now that she knew he was in pain . . . pain inflicted by her!

Following the sound of both the Indian and the horse, Pamela left the creek behind and made her way through thick brush. Briars reached out like vicious fingers, tearing the skirt of her dress, piercing her legs.

. But these troublesome obstacles left her feeling undaunted. She pushed her way onward, then stopped when she saw a magnificent strawberry roan reined at a cave's entrance. Its lovely head hung, leisurely feasting upon ankle-deep bluegrass. When it sensed her, it raised its head and shook its magnificent mane, only emitting a soft snort, then resumed feasting upon the grass.

Pamela's pulse raced when she noticed the Indian blankets folded neatly on the horse's back, where normally a saddle would lay if it were a white man's horse. Indians sometimes substituted blankets for saddles. This *was* the Indian's horse. The handsome Indian *was* only a few footsteps away!

Having found the Indian's hiding place, Pamela felt her insides becoming strangely soft. In only a matter of minutes she would see him again. His groans had proved that he was alive. But just how much . . . ?

Concern for him made Pamela cast any doubts aside that she may have had earlier for her safety. For many reasons now she felt she must do everything within her power to keep the Indian alive!

Creeping toward the cave's entrance, she scarcely breathed, her heartbeats almost swallowing her whole. . . .

Three

✦❦✦

My heart beats loud and fast.
Oh! Press it close to thine again.
                                  —Shelley

The roan's tail swooshing in the air, snapping at an occasional fly, was the only sound that Pamela was aware of except, perhaps, for her rapid breathing as she stepped to the cave's rugged, squat entrance. Vines trailed along the tops and sides of the rocky opening, morning glories blue in their brilliance peeking from their folds.

A musky odor met Pamela's nose as she stooped to peek inside the cave, her fingers so tight on the rifle her knuckles were white. Squinting her eyes, trying to adjust them to the darkness within, she could only make out moss-covered walls on each side, unable to see farther than the circle of outdoor light would allow.

Glancing over her shoulder in the direction of her beckoning cabin, Pamela frowned. What should she do? What was the right thing to do? Her brothers would be appalled if they knew she was placing herself in jeopardy. Surely they would urge her that if she did find the Indian she should shoot him dead, *then* run for her life or cover!

But she could do neither. Her heart had won in this decision. It had led her into wanting to know the Indian better. Perhaps she would never get another such opportunity. And the thought of never seeing him again made her heart ache dully.

A soft moan crept from the cave's interior, startling Pamela anew. She inched forward, entering the cave with stooped shoulders. Once inside she found that she had room to stand fully erect. She peered anxiously in all directions, unable to make out the source of the noise.

And then, as her eyes finally adjusted to the dark, she flinched when she saw the Indian. He was sitting with his back resting against the moss-lined wall, his head bent low. His breathing seemed even enough as his chest moved easily in and out. But he was in an unconscious state. Would Pamela's approach quickly awaken him? Where was his wound? Did he have much pain? More than once he had emitted the sounds of one who was in pain.

Pamela's heart lurched when her vision improved as her eyes continued to adjust to this vague, dimmer light. Though the Indian's head was bowed and he was slumped against the wall, she could now see his wound. Blood had dripped from his temple to his broad, copper chest.

Pamela sighed with relief. From what she could see at this distance the wound did not look that severe. Thank God it looked as though it were a mere graze treated with some sort of medication. That it was a head wound explained why he had lost consciousness.

But he could awaken at any moment and discover her there!

Panic seizing her, Pamela looked and with her searching eyes found his weapons. His bow and quiver of arrows were on the ground close beside him. His knife had been removed from the leather sheath at his waist and now lay close to his hand, from where in his sleep it had fallen.

She must get his weapons away from his reach. That would leave him defenseless, since she would have them all at *her* disposal!

Tiptoeing, cringing when she accidentally scattered loose rocks as her feet caught some crags, Pamela went to the Indian's side. Her breathing raspy, she knelt and reached a hand to his bow. When her fingers were circled about it she crept to the cave's entrance and placed the weapon outside. She repeated this until all of his weapons were outside, away from him.

On her third return Pamela's stance faltered when she found him fully awake, standing, his eyes two dark pits of fire as he glared down at her from his magnificent height. The Indian having fully revived so quickly, he was now a true threat to Pamela, whose stomach and knees now quivered.

"You . . . you're . . . awake," she gasped, taking a step backward, her hold on the rifle quite unsteady within her trembling fingers.

When he didn't make any threatening gestures, but instead stood immobile with his arms folded stiffly across his chest, Pamela's nerves settled a bit. But he hadn't uttered a sound. Didn't he know the English language? Would they not be able to communicate? Would their ways of defending themselves be the only things between them that they would be able to understand?

Unable to stop herself from seeing his utter handsomeness, his uniqueness, Pamela seized this moment of silence between them to quickly sweep her gaze over him. Ah, didn't he cut a striking figure standing there with his strong, determined face, his hard, high cheekbones, and luxuriant black hair? It was as though this Indian who was a six-foot stretch of sinew and muscle had forgotten his wound.

Everything about him made Pamela's heart go strangely wild. Was it because his eyes were now touching her all over, awakening in her the same feelings as before, when they had looked upon each other with wonder? She *had* wanted to feel something for a man earlier in her life, but none had made her insides come alive as this man who now stood before her only scarcely clothed in a breechclout. She could not deny that he had triggered a fire within, and such feelings were wrong, were *dangerous*. He was an Indian. No Indians had good feelings for white men *or* women. He had surely not fled farther than this cave not only because of his wound, but because he planned to kill her!

Though his weapons had been removed from within his reach, his dark, fathomless eyes were now his prime weapon. They were drawing Pamela's to lock with them. It was also as before, when she and the Indian had looked at one another. Much was being exchanged without the need of words. It was as though they had known each other previously, perhaps in another life, and were getting acquainted all over again in this lifetime.

"You have come to search for Strong Bear?" he said suddenly in a rich and vibrant voice, which seemed to seep into Pamela's soul, startling her with its soothing effect. "Why *did* you?"

Strong Bear's heart was reacting strangely to the white woman's nearness. As he had seen before, when he had watched her from afar, he noticed how everything about her was perfect. Her supple waist was narrow, her hips invitingly rounded. He could even see the outline of her nipples pressing against the softness of her low-swept bodice.

Yes. With her standing so close to him with her ripe, curving breasts and eyes the color of the sky so filled with mystery and innocence, Strong Bear was finding it hard to control his breathing. When one's heartbeats became erratic, breathing became the same.

As the white woman returned his gaze openly—fearlessly—Strong Bear found himself comparing her face to that of a quiet meadow. There were no signs of hatred in her expression or in her eyes. He was finding it increasingly disturbing to look into her eyes, yet to look upon this slim, dark-haired beauty *anywhere* made longings never felt before stir within him.

It was at this moment that he knew he could never kill her. He *would* take her hostage. He would then have not only this land of his vision for his people, but also *her*. . . .

"Why did I come?" Pamela said, blushing after having felt herself being openly scrutinized by this Indian, whose name she now knew to be Strong Bear. But her knees were no longer weak. Her heart was the only part of her that still reacted to his presence. His lean, handsome bronze visage unnerved her, trapping feelings quite new to her inside her heart, perhaps never to escape.

"I began worrying about you, fearing that I may have wounded you," she quickly added. "I couldn't just let you die slowly of a wound. It . . . it wouldn't be Christian."

She was in awe of how he had spoken so succinctly in English and that he was actually there, talking with *her*. Surely this wasn't happening. It was a fantasy, one dreamed up inside her head to feed her compulsion for excitement! Or was it a fantasy come to life because she had willed it to?

Then something grabbed at her heart. Though he had said only a few words, he *had* spoken them *well* in English. Perhaps *too* well. Did that mean that he had already made the acquaintance of many white men and women? Did he, perhaps, even have white slaves in his village? Slaves *were* taken by Indians every day along the Ohio River. Was he even now playing a game with her, all the while planning to abduct her, to take her back to his village to become her personal slave?

Pamela's hand tightened on the rifle. Had she chosen to let her guard down too soon?

"Why did you shoot the ugly firestick that speaks of thunder and fire if you did not wish to kill me?" Strong Bear said in a stiff reserve, wincing when a sharp pain pierced his wound. He forced himself not to react further to the pain. Instead he stared down into Pamela's limpid blue eyes, seeing a vibrant spark, a bold daring in their depths.

Pamela stood her ground, looking defiantly up at him, yet melting inside beneath his hypnotic stare. "I fired upon you because you threatened me with your bow and arrow," she said dryly. "Why didn't you kill *me*?"

Not used to women openly challenging him, Strong Bear shifted his feet nervously. "Strong Bear chose to restrain himself for reasons best not spoken," he said, his eyes no longer dangerous and flashing, instead increasingly clouding with pain. He placed his hand to his brow, which was suddenly laced with pearly beads of cold perspiration. "You have come? You have come to help *me-to-san-ah*, a red man? Strong Bear still does not understand."

"As I said before, it is because I am a Christian," Pamela stammered, knowing that she couldn't tell him the true reasons she had decided to come and offer her assistance. She especially couldn't tell him that one of those reasons was because her heart had led her back to him.

She lowered her eyes and focused on the toe of her shoe as she nervously dug it into the loose rock beneath it. "A Christian offers assistance when one is in *need*," she murmured.

"Even when this person's skin is of a different color?" Strong Bear tested, his eyes once more locked with hers as she jerked her head upward to look wonderingly at him. "Isn't this unusual?"

"Perhaps for some," Pamela said, the rifle becoming obtrusive as it weighted down her arm. "But not for *me*."

"Before, you used your firestick for protection," Strong Bear grumbled. "Why do you feel differently now?"

"I no longer feel that you are a threat to me," Pamela said, flinching as Strong Bear's jaw tightened and his gaze fell upon the spot where he had left his weapons. She took a step backwards when he jerked his head and eyed her vehemently, his fingers coiling into tight fists held at his sides.

"Without *weapons* Strong Bear is no threat to you. Is

that what you mean?'' he growled, the haze in his eyes momentarily replaced by fire. ''What have you done with my weapons?''

Pamela's eyelashes fluttered nervously; her fingers tightened on her rifle, yet she could not lift it to aim at Strong Bear. They had made too much progess in their acquaintanceship for her to show that she trusted him less now than moments before. She was torn with conflict. A part of her wanted to trust him, yet a part of her warned her about pursuing this with him any further. She did not know his intentions. Nor did he know hers.

She squared her shoulders in an effort to show him that she would not be intimidated. ''Your weapons?'' she said, her voice firm. ''I took the liberty of removing them from the premises.''

Strong Bear took a step toward her. ''While Strong Bear slept you stole weapons,'' he growled. ''You make me defenseless, then speak boldly to this Miami chief? This is true reason you come searching for Strong Bear. You wish to finish what your poor aim did not allow earlier. So when will you discharge firestick to kill Strong Bear? Now?''

''Chief?'' Pamela said in a shocked whisper, yet recalling the first time she had seen him, thinking that he reflected one of power, perhaps an Indian chief. ''You . . . are . . . a chief?''

Strong Bear had seen how this statement of fact seemed so incredulous to her, and he was appalled. Did he not have the appearance of a powerful chief? In her eyes, how *did* he appear to her? His heart was betraying his body because of her closeness, its wild thumps telling him over and over again that he had sensual feelings for this woman of blue eyes and pale skin. Though she was beautiful beyond words, he was also attracted to her courage, her willful ways. Always before, whenever white women had seen him—a red-skinned savage as he was labeled by most white people—they had run away, screaming and hollering like someone gone mad.

But this woman standing before him now, with liquid curves and a vibrant, glowing face, had daringly stood her ground when she had earlier discovered him there, watching her. She had even displayed the courage to fire upon him!

It was then that Strong Bear had realized that he had to know her better, understand her ways. But what of her feelings toward him? Though he saw so much in her eyes that spoke of passion, was she ready to kill him now, rid her life of this person whom most white people not only despised, but *feared* . . . ?

Strong Bear began to speak, to defend himself and his title, but renewed pain shattered his senses. He gritted his teeth and grabbed his head as he swayed. His temple screamed with fire as he tried to balance himself. When cool, soothing hands stroked his forehead and a protective firm arm wrapped about his waist, he leaned fully against her.

"I *have* come to help," Pamela reassured him, dropping her rifle to the ground. She guided Strong Bear downward, to the exact spot where he had been resting before. "Please let me."

Through the incessant throbbing pain, Strong Bear was aware of how she spoke in a quiet, gentle tone. His heart was touched by this, for he understood now that she was sincere in her concern for his welfare. She had not come to assure herself that he was dead.

Pamela knelt before Strong Bear as he sagged against the wall with closed eyes, perspiring brow, and clenched lips. Her gaze swept his handsome visage, aching so for having been the one who was causing him such pain.

Her eyes locked on his wound. Blood was seeping through the homemade medication that he had applied. The raw skin encircling the wound pulsed, sure proof that his head was throbbing unmercifully.

"I'll go to the creek and get some water to cleanse your wound," Pamela murmured, her heart lurching when Strong

Bear suddenly opened his eyes and looked at her with an intensity she did not—was afraid to—understand.

She tensed as his hand grabbed her wrist and held her in place. Though he was in pain, his strength was far from gone. His grip was like nothing she had ever felt before. It was like steel encasing her flesh and bone.

"No. Do not go," Strong Bear said thickly. "My wound is unimportant. It is only a flesh wound. When the sun rises on a new day, all pain will be gone and the skin will be healing. I have medicated my wound in my own way. It is the *best*. Strong Bear suffers only briefly."

"Isn't there anything I can do at all?" Pamela asked. His grip loosening on her wrist, now felt almost pleasant in its gentleness. His flesh against hers in any capacity was a threat to Pamela's sanity, however. If his eyes touching her had affected her so strangely, how could she expect anything less from being touched by his body?

"My weapons," Strong Bear said. "You can return my *weapons*. A Miami warrior is stripped *naked* without his warring gear!"

He studied her, trying to weigh her behavior. What could she want from him, unless it was the same as he wanted from *her*? Didn't he see it in her eyes even now? He could feel the racing of her pulse where his fingers grasped her wrist. Should he put her to a test, to see . . . ? Should he kiss her?

His wound pained him, but not so much as his loins where his desire showed so tangibly. He wanted to possess the white woman. Fully!

Pamela blanched and the pit of her stomach rolled when he bluntly demanded his weapons back. Was he pretending to be in pain to trick her, to purposely draw her into being sympathetic, to encourage her to return his weapons? Once he had them, would he swiftly kill her and be on his way?

Oh, Lord, what should she do? She wanted so to trust him. He seemed gentle, and genuinely friendly. Surely he could be trusted. But why should she? He had given her no reason to, except that he hadn't killed her before when he'd had the chance. He was an Indian chief, surely most accurate in everything that he tried!

Remembering that he *was* a chief and that she was attracted not only to an Indian, but to a *chief*, sent her awe soaring . . . She decided to, yes, trust him. . . .

"All right," she said, her voice weak. "I'll return your weapons. But you must understand something. I will keep possession of my own, also."

Strong Bear's eyes twinkled. His insides grew warm. He was right about her. Everything she felt about him was good! "You keep weapon, Strong Bear has his," he said, gesturing with a hand toward her rifle. "Strong Bear not use his. White woman not use hers. We share mutual trust between us."

"Yes. Trust," Pamela said, her insides trembling, praying silently to God that she wasn't being too hasty in this decision. One plunge of his knife and she would take her last breath. It would be all over quickly! And yet there was so much about Strong Bear that made her believe that she *could* trust him!

Scooting her rifle aside, Pamela went outside and filled her arms with Strong Bear's weapons. Then, with a pounding heart and an awkward sort of smile, she returned to him and knelt before him, laying his weapons at his feet.

Her nerves tight, her breathing short, Pamela watched to see what Strong Bear's next move would be. And when he only scooted the weapons close to his side, failing to pick any of them up with which to threaten her, only then did she know that her prayer had been answered and that she was safe enough in Strong Bear's company.

A sigh trembling on her lips, Pamela relaxed with a slump of her shoulders. "If there's nothing else I can do for you, I must return to my chores," she said, truly not wanting to leave him. More than likely she would never see him again. "If my brother, Robert, becomes alarmed by my continuing absence, he'll come searching for me. If he were to find us together, I'm afraid to say what might happen."

"Brother?" Strong Bear asked, his eyes narrowing. "How many do you have? Also do you have a *husband*?"

His question of family came as a surprise to Pamela, but why should it? She could tell by the way he looked at her, by his gentleness, that he would want to know especially about a husband.

This thing that was weaving between Pamela and the Indian frightened, yet thrilled her. The sort of love shared between an Indian and white woman was forbidden in the eyes of all who declared to live in what was termed the "civilized world."

And the word *love* could well define Pamela's growing feelings for this man who had mesmerized her with his different ways and haunting dark eyes. There was no pretense to him. He spoke from the heart. Pamela doubted if he had ever spoken a nontruth. He was refreshing, after her stuffy gentlemen callers in Williamsburg!

"My family?" Pamela said, forgetting her worry of Robert for a moment longer, hoping that he was still reading, and enjoying it. She clasped her hands in her lap and smiled at Strong Bear. "I've no husband, only two brothers." Her smile faded when she spoke her father's name. "Also my father. But, he's . . . so . . . ailing." She rose quickly to her feet, her face flushed with the realization that she was neglecting her father's needs while caring for a man she had only met. "I must leave. I was to fetch water, to bathe my papa's feverish brow."

She cast her eyes downward in sudden shame. "I am a neglectful daughter."

Strong Bear grabbed his head as he pushed himself up from the ground. He teetered momentarily, then steadied himself and took Pamela's hands in his.

Her gaze jerked up, startled. She found eyes midnight dark with passion peering down at her. Suddenly she was afraid. Not of Strong Bear, but of emotions crashing through her like waves against rocks on a seashore!

"In the white man's language what are you called?"

Strong Bear said, his voice laced with emotion. "What is your Christian name?"

"Pamela . . ." she said, gulping. "Pamela . . . Boyd." Then she questioned him, trying not to react so blatantly to him as he clutched her hands so possessively in his own warm pair. "You use the word, Christian. How do you know of it? I mentioned it to you in another capacity other than with the use of my name."

"That word is very familiar to Strong Bear," he said hoarsely. "It was a man of *Ma-nat-too*, God, who many moons ago came to my village and spoke to my people of being a Christian. He called himself a Jesuit missionary and he was dressed in a peculiar black robe and wore an even more peculiar hat. And even his face was not ever plucked of hair. He wore what he called a beard."

Strong Bear looked past her, as if deep in thought. "My people have the Great Spirit for worshiping. No other gods were welcome in my village of Miami then, nor are they now."

Again he looked at her. "After a while this man was sent away. My father, who was then chief, allowed him to stay long enough for us to learn the white man's language from him."

Strong Bear smiled then, as though recalling something pleasant. "He was the first white man to be Strong Bear's *friend*. It was because of him that I never wanted to spill any white man's blood."

His eyes narrowed. "Unless when it is necessary to protect Strong Bear's *people*."

Having seen so much suddenly enter Strong Bear's eyes, and having heard the tone of his voice when he spoke of protecting his people, Pamela's insides took on a strange coldness. Knowing that he would kill if he was forced to by circumstance, she wondered anew about her sanity for being here with him. She was even letting him hold her hands!

Yet *she* posed no threat to him in any capacity. She was

foolish to be threatened by him merely because of his words.

"Why were you watching me this morning while I sat beside the water?" she blurted. "I've never seen you before. Why were you there then?"

Strong Bear looked away from her momentarily. If she knew that he had found her and her family a threat, she would understand that they were just the sort of circumstance that could cause him to kill. And he could never let her know this truth.

He moved his eyes slowly back to hers, meeting the questioning wonder he found there. "This land drew not only you to it," he said dryly. "But also Strong Bear. Many moons ago, before you were here, Strong Bear came to this land you built your dwelling on."

He would not tell her that the Great Spirit had led him to the land She would not understand visions or the Great Spirit who willed them. "It is a land of richer soil and more plentiful game. After the gathering moon, after all my people's crops are harvested, Strong Bear planned to lead his people here."

A coldness he could not stop glazed his eyes. "But your dwelling now stands in the way of the progress of my Miami people."

Guessing the meaning behind his words, Pamela felt fear ebbing its way back inside her heart. She slipped her hands from his. "I really must be going," she murmured, bending slowly, cautiously, to pick up her rifle. "My father needs me. I'm sure you understand the needs of an ailing member of one's family."

"Yes. Strong Bear understands."

"Then . . . I'll be going, Strong Bear."

"Yes. You must go."

Strong Bear hesitated and then swept Pamela into his arms so quickly it snatched her breath away. When his lips bore down upon hers in a savage kiss, at first she felt faint from the suddenness of his actions; then she began to answer his meltingly hot kiss with a need of her own. The euphoria that filled her was almost more than she could bear. Fear of him and his kiss and the ecstasy that it had evoked within her was only a faint whisper at the far recesses of her mind. His torrid embrace was robbing her of all her senses.

And then suddenly he released her, yet looking down at her with searing passion in his eyes.

"Return tomorrow," he said huskily. "I will wait for you."

Pamela drew a ragged breath, trying to bring her senses under control. She was momentarily rendered speechless not only by his kiss, but by her shameless reaction!

"Do not fear what just happened between us," Strong Bear said, seeing the questioning in her eyes. "Our hearts drew us into such an embrace. Our minds and bodies obeyed the will of our hearts. It was not wrong. It was even *good*."

Pamela was still speechless. Her lips still throbbed with his kiss, and her insides trembled from awakened pleasure.

"I . . . must . . . go . . ." she murmured. "Truly. I've been gone for way too long already."

Strong Bear placed a hand gently to her elbow and walked outside with her. A renewed pain in his wound made his body jerk and his hands grab his head. He bowed his head, closed his eyes, and groaned.

"Strong Bear!" Pamela gasped, quickly forgetting everything but that he had folded over again in pain. "You're not at all well. You're *not* going to be all right. I *know* it."

She set her jaw firmly. "Yes, I'll return tomorrow. I'll bring something from our cupboard for that wound. I don't know what, but I'll find something."

Never wanting to use white men's medicine, Strong Bear began to object; but he realized this was a sure way to bring her back to him, so he nodded, pretending to agree.

"Yes. Bring medicine," Strong Bear said thickly, hiding the beginnings of a mischievous grin as he kept his head ducked. Already the pain was lessening. By tomorrow it would be gone.

Pamela's eyes wavered. "I wish that I could return today with blankets and medicine so you could be more comfortable tonight," she worried aloud. "But I cannot leave again today once I return to my cabin. It will be hard to get away from my brothers again even tomorrow. But I'll manage. *Somehow*."

Placing a hand on Strong Bear's arm she coaxed him to look at her. "Will you truly be all right until I can return with medication?" she murmured. "It will be such a long time. You will have to spend a full night suffering!"

Though the pain was again only a memory, Strong Bear was compelled to clasp Pamela in his arms. Her eyes—her words—were full of genuine concern for him. Drawing her into a total loving of him would not be all that hard. But still, he had to hear her actually say what he so badly needed to hear.

His dark eyes devoured her, then he said, "Do you regret that your aim was not exact . . . that I am still alive?"

"How can you ask that?" Pamela said in a quivering sigh. "I am, oh, so relieved that you *are*."

Twining his long, lean fingers through her hair, Strong Bear guided Pamela's lips to his, her body pliant in his arms as she eased up against him, responding. He anchored her fiercely still, aware of the press of her breasts against his bare chest. Her mouth was sweet . . . sensuous. He kissed her hungrily; then, realizing that now was not the time to possess her fully, he released her.

"Go. Now," he said huskily.

Eyes wide, rendered breathless once again by Strong Bear, Pamela nodded. Then she threw herself back into his arms and clung to him a moment more. But fear of what staying with him any longer might create between them made her turn and flee without even a backward glance. If he should beckon to her with his dangerous eyes to return to him, she did not know if she would have the willpower to refuse him. Would she even tomorrow, if the same transpired between them, as it had, today?

Shameful feelings assailed her. A soft sob tore through the silence of the forest. Her desires were out of control, making her become a stranger to herself. . . .

Strong Bear watched her flight away from him, his shoulders proudly squared, his jaw set. He would not be forced to take her hostage after all! He would win her love, then *she* would persuade her family to leave this land that was Strong Bear's!

Four

⊰⊱

Blessing She is! God made her so!
                              —Lowell

Pamela lay snuggled beneath her patchwork quilt, her eyes
fluttering open from a night that had been less than restful.
She had dreamed forever of Strong Bear and how his kiss
and embrace had affected her. Shamefully, she was willing
to let him fill the void in her life. She was finally finding
the excitement that she had come to this wilderness for!
But never had she thought that excitement and adventure
would come in the form of a man. Not only a man, but an
Indian.

Pamela's eyes grew suddenly wide with remembrances
of how she had left Strong Bear, of how he had been in
such pain, and of promises that she would return to him
today. She looked through a crack in the rafters overhead
for signs of daylight. Her brow creased with disappoint-
ment. The night had been endless and it was still dark.

But even when daylight arrived with its usual brilliant

blue skies and sunshine, she would have to wait until Anthony left. Robert was her only obstacle. She must be sure that he didn't go outside to work on the fence, but stayed at their father's bedside during her absence.

She already knew what her strategy would be, but she had to plan around Robert and *his* activities! When Anthony had returned yesterday with no more than a mere turkey for the replenishment of their food suppy, he had vowed to leave again today to try his luck at shooting a fat venison.

Snuggling more beneath her quilt, trying not to feel guilty by knowing that Strong Bear was less comfortable than she, Pamela smiled mischievously to herself. While Anthony was gone today in search of his prized deer, she would tell Robert that she had her own ways of supplying the table with food. She would remind him again of the hundreds of mushrooms she had seen in the woods and of the luscious patch of greens just waiting to be picked! She had already told him upon her first arrival yesterday after seeing Strong Bear that her dress had become ripped because she had been lured into the woods by the presence of these greens and mushrooms, not thinking at that time it would be an ideal excuse for returning!

Yes, it would be so easy! It would be so convincing! Her wicker basket was sitting at her bedside even now, where beneath a checkered linen napkin lay a bandage spool and the only medication she could find in their cupboard to take to Strong Bear.

"Even *horehound* . . ." she whispered, in her mind's eye seeing the apothecary displaying his wares in the pharmacy in Williamsburg.

She had always enjoyed going into the pharmacy just to look around. A well-equipped apothecary was supposed to have in stock scorpions, ants, earthworms, and even *mummies*, and the pharmacy she had frequently visited in Williamsburg had them all!

She had also seen jars of drugs; gallipots, which were medicine containers; draft bottles; herb cabinets; and calf-bound books on alchemy and tomes instructing the pharmacist in the art of ridding his patient of "pecculant humours and morbific matters."

Always ranged along the counter for sale were containers of bay leaves, nutmegs, cinnamon sticks, licorice root, lavender, boxes of twist tobacco, even twigs labeled "A Good Wintergreen toothbrush, five cents lawful money."

But the one thing that Pamela always bought when she had a few spare cents was the sweet horehound drops. Horehound was advertised, everywhere commended, for those who were bruised, burst, or fallen from high places. But Pamela had enjoyed it merely for its different taste.

She had brought several horehound drops from Williamsburg and would this morning offer some to Strong Bear not only for what was ailing him, but also for enjoyment as well. She had also slipped a jar of some strange ointment her mother had always prescribed for snake bites into the basket. Since no anesthetics were available, surely this ointment could benefit in some way, instead.

Late last evening, after everyone had gone to bed, she had sneaked a blanket outdoors and hid it so no one would know that she was also taking it to Strong Bear this morning along with the bandage and medication.

Hearing a stirring beneath the loft, Pamela tensed. Anthony was already up and preparing to leave. He was determined to bring home fresh meat this day besides a mere turkey. He was getting an early start and would probably be gone all day.

Slipping from her bed, Pamela peeked down from her overhead loft and watched anxiously as Anthony built the morning fire, even placing a pot of coffee in its coals. He would expect her up shortly after he left, for he knew that she was a light sleeper and would have heard him puttering around in his preparations for leaving.

A hacking cough broke through Pamela's consciousness, paining her as though she were the one afflicted by the disease causing it. Guilt spread through her like wildfire for having become so caught up in the intrigue of

Strong Bear, when all of her thoughts should be on her ailing father.

But nothing would ever cause her to forget Strong Bear. He was now a part of her existence, just as her father had always been. Both were now important to her, but in a much different way. Should her father survive this terrible scourge of malaria, Pamela would hope that he would understand her feelings for an Indian. He had never been one to separate feelings for anyone just because of the color of their skin. He respected everyone's right to life . . . to love.

Hearing Anthony open the door and leave, Pamela waited to hear the horse carrying him away. She would then dress and get her day started. By mid-morning she should have convinced Robert of how nice it would be to have a pot of greens and fried mushrooms to compliment the venison Anthony would bring home for supper. Their meals had been so colorless, so tasteless, of late. How could Robert refuse this opportunity to have something different for a change?

Smiling, Pamela drew her cotton nightgown over her head. It wouldn't be long now before she would see if she had been made a fool of. So much depended on whether or not Strong Bear truly awaited her return to him.

Spreading dirt onto his campfire to kill its flames, Strong Bear was feeling an anxiousness never felt before as the time for the planned rendezvous with Pamela drew near. Though she thought he had stayed the full night in the cave, he had not. He hadn't wanted to build a campfire that close to her dwelling, fearing that the scent of smoke might alert her family that he was nearby. Instead, Strong Bear had traveled some distance before stopping to build his campfire for the night.

But now the black cloak of night was being replaced by the faint shimmerings of light along the horizon. He must return to the cave before Pamela discovered that his traveling to another distant place for his campsite would prove that he had not been as ill as she had assumed. It was important that she wasn't given cause to doubt him. Today he wanted to let her know his true intentions for her. Today he wanted to claim her as *his*. She must be persuaded into wanting the same. And the only way he knew how to get the desired result was to lead her into sensual moments with him again. She had responded before. She would again. The passion in her eyes and kiss were proof of her feelings for him.

Kicking more dirt onto the last glowing embers of the fire, his stomach comfortably filled with rabbit meat, Strong Bear felt only a faint twinge of pain from his head wound. He had cleansed the last of the blood and his medication from it only moments ago and there was only a puckering of the skin around the wound. Even that would soon be gone, and he would no longer have signs of ever having let the firestick shame him! And it would never happen again. He understood the voice of the weapon now, more than before.

A sudden blast of gunfire followed by a thunderous roar and an ensuing loud thud behind Strong Bear drew him quickly around, startled. He looked in disbelief at a bear that lay on the ground at his feet, lifeless, blood spreading on its great mat of rusty-brown fur.

And then with his eyes jerking upward, Strong Bear discovered a white man on horseback with a smoking firestick in his one hand, staring back at Strong Bear without a trace of fear in his eyes.

Recognition of the man seized Strong Bear as though a bolt of lightning had struck him. Before Strong Bear had left yesterday to find a campsite for the night, he had gone and again viewed Pamela's cabin from the shadows of the forest. There he had seen this man returning. This had to be one of Pamela's brothers.

Strong Bear's gaze moved from the white man, back to the dead bear, then back to the white man. This white man had saved his life! Had the white man not come along, the bear would have attacked Strong Bear from behind. Strong Bear would not have had a chance to defend himself.

This family of paleskins were a complex people. One shoots at Strong Bear and then worries about his welfare . . . the other boldly saves his life from the devious claws of a grizzly bear! Was it their God who made them so caring? Surely so! And if they believed in their God as much as Strong Bear believed in his Great Spirit, it was easier to understand them and know that they were totally good people. Strong Bear was glad to have chosen to spare this white family. He was happy that he had chosen the women to be *his*!

Strong Bear's heart was filled with thanks, with a keen humility. Yet he was too cautious to approach the white man to thank him. Perhaps he was not all that kind after all. He still held the smoking firestick! Had he planned to kill the bear first, the man with the red skin second?

Tense, Strong Bear lifted his chin proudly and folded his arms across his chest, awaiting his fate. He would not be shamed twice in two days. He would not turn his back to the white man to reach for his bow and arrow, which had been left so carelessly on the ground, to allow himself to be shot in the back. If he was to be slain by the stick that spoke of thunder and fire, Strong Bear would die as a brave chief dies, not as a coward. He would not disgrace the Miami nation. He would die with firmness and courage, as becomes a true warrior!

Anthony's heart scarcely beat as he found himself now in a staring match with the Indian who showed such pride in his stance. He relaxed his shoulders and lowered his rifle, easing it toward the leather gunsling at the side of his horse, hoping this was a way to show that he was no threat. He hoped the Indian wouldn't take this opportunity to reach for and use his weapons. If anything, he should be ready to thank Anthony for saving his life. He had always thought that if he showed kindness to an Indian, it would be rewarded, in kind. Perhaps now was the time to make friends, not enemies, with this Indian; and, he hoped, later, with his people.

Moving slowly, Anthony dismounted his horse, never taking his eyes off the Indian. His every footstep cautious, he continued to watch the Indian. He hadn't been this close to an Indian before and perhaps wouldn't be again.

Anthony cocked an eyebrow. The way this Indian was studying him, it was as though the Indian wasn't here in this neck of the woods just by chance. It was as though the Indian *knew* him.

Anthony stopped in mid-step, his eyes growing wide. Could this be the same Indian who had been fired upon by Pamela? If so, should that make Anthony more cautious, or more friendly? Hadn't the Indian been watching his sister? Yet hadn't the Indian fled when Pamela's bullet had missed him?

Anthony's feelings were mixed. But he had come this close to the Indian. He couldn't see a way he could turn back. . . .

Making sure not to let his hand wander to the sheathed knife at his waist so that he would not pose a threat to the Indian, Anthony walked around the lifeless bear, then stood directly before the Indian. Their eyes locked.

His heart pounding, Anthony didn't offer a hand of friendship, since their ways of extending it were surely different. But he would seize this opportunity to show his interest in being friends. And wasn't it perfect? The bear had appeared from nowhere, as though by magic. It seemed that the bear was there to serve a purpose, to bring these two men of different skin colors together. Anthony would use it to his full advantage. He had always been a quick thinker, in whatever predicament he had found himself in. It was no different now, even though he had heard tales of the savagery of Indians against the white man. This Indian would surely not kill him after he'd saved his life!

"The bear is yours," he said, speaking slowly, distinctly, hoping the Indian could understand the white man's language. He gestured with a sweep of the hand toward the fallen bear. "I killed it to save your life. It is now a gift of friendship from me to you."

Strong Bear studied the white man before speaking. Now seeing him so closely, he had much in his facial features that resembled Pamela. They had the same sort of nose and cheekbones, and their jawlines were exact. But their hair and eyes were different. This man's eyes were strangely golden, and his hair was the color of a sunset.

"You killed the bear that was a silent threat to Strong Bear. You are a good man," Strong Bear said, seeing the surprise in the white man's eyes because of Strong Bear's ability to speak the white man's language so well. But wouldn't Strong Bear be as surprised if the white man suddenly began speaking in the Miami language?! "You did not let *Na-ha-ti-hot do-pol-ia na-peak*, a good warrior die. You are now Strong Bear's *ne-kaw-no*. You are Strong Bear's *friend*."

He looked down at the bear, then back up into Anthony's eyes. "Strong Bear accepts your gift of friendship."

Strong Bear had a keen ability to think quickly when cornered. At this moment it was no different. And he would use this skill well. He would use this friendship that the white man offered to his own advantage when the right time revealed itself to him. The bear had surely been sent from the Great Spirit for the white man to find and kill to save Strong Bear's life. The Great Spirit sometimes worked in strange ways, twisting fate to benefit Strong Bear!

Removing a small buckskin pouch from the side of his breechclout, Strong Bear loosened its drawstrings and opened it. Slipping a finger inside, he withdrew two things: a withered turkey's foot and a nice-sized gold nugget. He offered them both to Anthony.

"My friend, Strong Bear offers *you* gifts for appreciation of your kindness," he said, his eyes warmly gleaming. He gestured with his hand. "Take. Keep. But show no one else. These gifts between us must be secretly shared. Do you understand?"

Anthony's mouth dropped open when he saw both objects. One seemed ridiculous, the other . . . awesome! There was such a difference in both gifts it was hard to rationalize why they would be given. A turkey's foot . . . and, by damn, the largest gold nugget Anthony had ever laid his eyes on!

"You want . . . me . . . to have . . . these . . . ?"

"They are now yours. Take."

"Thank you . . ." Anthony said, bewildered as to why no explanation was made for the gold; wanting to ask, yet feeling dangers in doing so. Gold had been the cause of many deaths between men. Anthony would just have to thank God for at least this bit of luck that came his way this day. It hurt like hell to have to give up the bear meat to the Indian. Thus far, Anthony still hadn't had any luck finding game this morning. But the offering of the bear was a small price to pay for making friends with an Indian who one day might have decided the Boyd family were intruders. And Pamela! Anthony still had the feeling this Indian was the one who had been watching her, perhaps even *hungering* for her!

But Anthony was sure now that if this was that same Indian, neither he nor Pamela had anything to fear from him. There was mutual trust between Anthony and the Indian now. Yet it was beyond believing that they had reached any sort of understanding between them!

"You go on your way, white man," Strong Bear said, nodding toward Anthony's horse, not liking how time was passing when he knew that he should be traveling back to the cave. If Pamela should arrive and he would not be there . . . ? "Strong Bear go *his*."

"My name is Anthony," Anthony said, squaring his shoulders. "Please, if you see me again, call me Anthony."

With that one more offering of friendship, Anthony went to his horse and swung himself up into the saddle. He took the reins and began to ride off, but Strong Bear had something else to say. Anthony looked. He listened.

"May the Great Spirit always be in your heart as he is now," Strong Bear said, gesturing with movements of his hands, as though also using sign language. "So may he always be with you on the long trail of life ahead."

Anthony's eyes widened as he nodded, then wheeled his horse around and galloped away.

Strong Bear watched Anthony until he was only a speck on the horizon, then he picked up the bear and carried it to an enormous oak tree. After tying it up in the tree, high off the ground, to keep it from being devoured by predators, he then swung himself onto his strawberry roan and began riding hard away from the campsite. He had already tasted the sweetness of Pamela's lips . . . had felt the satin of her flesh. Today! She would be his today! And soon after, the land on which she and her family had homesteaded would once more be Strong Bear's!

Smiling smugly, he held his chin high, his smoky black eyes flashing.

Swinging her basket at her side in one hand, Pamela lifted the hem of her dress with the other and began running slowly alongside the creek. The sun slanted toward her through the overhang of trees above her, marking the time of day as mid-morning and way later than she would have hoped for her planned rendezvous with Strong Bear. He may even have given up on her, believing she was not going to come after all.

Would he stay a while longer? Or would he return to his village where everyone would see his wound and question him about who had inflicted it? Would he tell them? Or would he brush them aside and ignore the questions? He surely would not want them to know that he had not killed the person who had shot him. He would look possibly less the powerful leader in their eyes!

Her mind's feverish workings were exhausting to Pamela, so she focused her attention on the positive side of life. Her father was no worse this morning. Surely that was a good sign, a sign that perhaps in time he might even begin improving! She didn't even feel all that guilty for leaving him this morning, to pursue her own wondrous pleasures of life!

Smiling, Pamela thought of Robert's reaction to her

wanting to leave the cabin again this morning. He had at first argued, telling her all the reasons she must not be so carefree in these wilds of Kentucky. But when she had reminded him of the fresh greens and the plentiful mushrooms, he had agreed to let her go. Pamela had thought that he would. She knew quite well that his love of food came only second to reading and she had promised to fry him many mushrooms for dinner!

The neighing of a horse just ahead made Pamela's heart begin its usual wild thumping at the prospect of seeing Strong Bear again. He had stayed, had waited for her. Again her thoughts began to race, wondering if his wound was better this morning? Did he have much pain through the night? Had he gotten cold sleeping in that damp, drafty cave . . . ?

Spying the lovely roan through a break in the trees ahead, Pamela moved in its direction. She was in awe of herself, of how her blood was flowing heatedly through her veins as she drew closer and closer to the man who had intrigued her since that first time they had exchanged glances—and so much more between them. Could she truly be feeling so much for a complete stranger . . . for an *Indian*? Was this how being in love felt?

Oh, surely it was. Nothing else could feel as beautiful as these feelings stirring within her when she looked at Strong Bear. All through the night she had dreamed of the rapture of his kiss . . . the bliss of his touch . . . !

And now suddenly he was there, in real life, stepping from the shadows of the cave, his dark eyes lit with passion as he watched her approach.

Pamela's knees weakened and her stomach felt warmly, strangely queasy when she looked upon his handsomeness, his magnificently squared shoulders, the copper sheen of his powerful chest, and his lean hips. He wore the usual breechclout, but today he had his hair groomed and hanging long to his shoulders with several small feathers—turkey feathers, it appeared—placed at the coil of his hair at the back.

His face, with its high cheekbones, bold nose, strong chin, and thick, sensuous lips, made Pamela look up at him with wonder, with longing. She felt no shame then, wishing to be kissed by him again. She was no longer a child. She was a woman, with womanly needs. And only now did she truly wish to have these needs fulfilled. No other man before Strong Bear had made her even come close to being willing to lose her virginity because of this drive—this hunger—that was now torturing her insides. She did love him.

Oh, but how could it ever work? Their sort of love was forbidden! He was Indian. She was . . . white.

Casting all cares and woes aside, Pamela went to Strong Bear and stood before him, feeling awkward since no words had yet been spoken between them this day. The one question that had been troubling her all night was answered within this closer proximity of him. His wound was all but well! There was only a faint puckering of skin where the gunshot had grazed his flesh.

Smiling with relief, Pamela reached her hand to his temple. "My medicine is not needed after all," she said softly. "Most surely not the bandages. My word, Strong Bear. How did you manage to heal so quickly?"

Strong Bear's insides rippled sensually as her delicately soft fingers touched his brow. The mere feel of her flesh against his emblazed him with needs. His gaze swept over her, a love so keen for her building within him that it frightened him. Should a man love a woman so much? Could it in the end destroy him as a man? But, no. He had waited a lifetime to love this deeply. He would not turn his back on such love!

His eyes took in her absolute loveliness. Her long, drifting hair fell across her shoulders and down her back in a silken, dark luster. Her dress was the color of purple iris that grew wild along the river.

Strong Bear could tell that she was feeling many things for him by the heaving of her lovely breasts where they pressed against the inside of her low-swept bodice. The valley of her breasts beckoned him to touch them with his mouth. Her delicately long neck made him ache to taste the sweetness of her there!

Reaching a hand to hers, to ease it from his temple, Strong Bear smiled down at Pamela. "The Great Spirit blesses me and makes me well," he said huskily. He held her hand within his. His eyes grew dusky, feeling how her hand trembled. "Strong Bear glad you come."

"I told you that I would," Pamela said, swallowing hard to suppress this growing sensuousness she was feeling for him. She must not appear whorish! She would not want him to think that she behaved this way with every man who intrigued her.

Slipping her hand from his, yet sorely hating to, she lifted her basket up before her. "I've brought something besides medicine for you," she said, pushing the checkered napkin aside. She had taken much pain in folding the blanket tightly so as to not be noticeable beneath the napkin. She had hidden the bandage, horehound, and ointment beneath the blanket. "Well, some would say what I am going to offer you is also medicine. But I compare it to *candy*, instead. I like the different taste of horehound."

"Horehound . . . ?" Strong Bear said, an eyebrow lifting inquisitively. He watched eagerly as she withdrew something that looked like the maple sugar made into squares of candy at sugaring season. When she handed this to him, he studied it, turning it from side to side. It was the color of his skin. Copper. It was hard and oblong, yet very small.

"Go ahead," Pamela said, laughing softly, loving his innocence. "But I must warn you. Though it's sweet, there is something else quite different to the taste that some abhor. I'm anxious to see what you think. I do so love horehound, myself."

Strong Bear gingerly placed the horehound drop into his mouth, enjoying this light moment with Pamela, but he was not going to let it remain the same between them for long. He remembered the haste in which she had left him yesterday. It would be no less today, for she still had family concerned about her. Though he had already formed a special bond with her one brother, Strong Bear could not chance successfully eluding her family if they came looking for Pamela. That was not in his plan. He would approach *them* when he felt the time was right.

It was imperative that he first carry Pamela to heights with him today that she would never forget. He must make her want of him be so great, she would not hesitate to join him at his village when he felt the time was right to make this request of her. She must want to be his wife of first importance; his wife now awaiting his arrival back to his village would be second!

Circling his tongue about the horehound drop, its taste sweet, yet tangy on its tip, he nodded and smiled down at Pamela. "Strange," he said, chuckling low. "But Strong Bear *likes*."

Pamela was awash with so many feelings at this moment she could hardly contain herself. She returned his smile and placed her basket on the ground. "I'm glad you like it," she said, clasping her hands nervously behind her.

Her smile faded. Her face became a mask of serious reflections. "I am so glad that you are well." She looked past him, into the mouth of the cave. "I trust that you kept warm beside a fire through the night?" she tested, having worried so about his being cold, yet at the same time, knowing how foolish she was. Indians were people of the land. They knew all the ways of survival. Even when the world was swallowed beneath a veil of snow they had learned the art of keeping warm and healthy.

Strong Bear swallowed the last of the horehound drop, tensing at her question about being warm. Would she notice there had been no fire? Yet why should he worry about whether or not there had been or that he had gone elsewhere to spend the night? Did she not see that his wound was almost healed? She would expect him to be strong enough to travel!

Yet, something deep inside him told him not to labor

over this point, nor yet to disclose to her that he had befriended her brother!

Taking her arm, he guided her away from the cave and to a place beneath a towering oak where the grass was a cushion to sit upon. "How is your father?" he asked, artfully drawing her into believing that he truly cared. "Did you find him well upon your awakening this morning?"

Amazed at his caring this much for a man he did not even know, and a *white* man at that, Pamela's insides melted with loving him even more. "He is no worse," she said, easing down on the ground beside him. "I'm encouraged at least by his not being worse today. Just perhaps he may get well."

Strong Bear looked away from her, into the distance, his heart hammering inside him, for the waiting was becoming sheer agony.

He turned his eyes to her suddenly, seeing a sort of eager anticipation in hers. "Do you not feel this thing that has grown between us?" he said huskily, placing his fingers to her shoulders, turning her directly to face him. "My night was troubled with remembrances of your kiss. Was not your night also a restless one, Pamela?"

The way he said her name, so deep, so vibrant, made a tremble course through Pamela. She nodded silently, afraid to speak, knowing that her voice would reveal too much to him of how she was feeling by his mere presence.

"Let Strong Bear kiss you again," he said, drawing her closer.

Pamela shut her eyes, having waited oh, so long for a man who could send her to such heights of wonder. Desire welled and surfaced when he kissed her with a fierce, possessive heat.

Even when his hands moved lower and cupped her breasts through her dress, she did not refuse him. She was beyond coherent thought. She wanted him now, more than . . . life itself.

Five

❧❧

I love my Love, and my Love loves me!
—Coleridge

Pamela drew a ragged breath as Strong Bear's lips lowered and kissed the hollow of her throat. His hands slowly lifted the skirt of her dress higher . . . higher. Could she let this continue? Was she going to allow herself to be disrobed . . . to be actually naked with a man?

As her dress moved higher and her flesh was touched by the soft caresses of the morning breeze, she scarcely breathed, wanting to fight this need building inside her, wanting to keep her respect intact. No man had ever seen her nude before. But she had never before wanted to be with a man in such a way. Strong Bear had brought her to life. Totally! Her every nerve ending cried out for his lips, for his touch! She could not deny any part of her this that she had been awakened to.

Yes, as Strong Bear eased away from her and looked down at her from his haunches with his dark, stormy eyes, she did understand what the next moments held for her. And she was willing. Oh, Lord, she was willing. But a part of her was afraid, a part of her was anxious. She had been taught that proper ladies did not share such moments with a man until words of a preacher had fused them.

But how was this possible in these wilds of Kentucky . . . ? She may never even *see* a preacher again.

She would not think any more about it. What she was sharing with the Indian, the man she loved, had to be right, for nothing that caused her to feel so deliciously lethargic could be wrong! It would be so easy to give herself to . . . to take *from* him. She already felt like a part of him, as though their hearts were already woven together, fused as one between them.

That it had happened so quickly, so profoundly, was not important. That it had happened at all was wondrous in Pamela's eyes. She had never dreamed that finding a man to love could be like this, so complete in her feelings for the man. That his skin was red and hers was white had not mattered from their first eye contact. And it would never, ever matter. It seemed that something mysterious had drawn them together, to meet in such a way, as though there was a purpose behind the meeting. But she would not question it! The mysteries of life were many!

"*Me-tam-sah pac-kah*," Strong Bear said, drawing the dress up across her shoulders. He eased her down fully onto the grass with one hand, his other busily continuing to disrobe her. His eyes raked over her silken nudity as he tossed the dress and undergarments aside, overwhelmed by the treasures of her liquid curves. In his eyes she looked so beautiful it was as though she were petals of a delicate flower, waiting to be plucked.

"*Pac-kah*," he repeated huskily, the palms of his hands against her ankles, gently, slowly moving his fingers upward, wanting to touch her all over before fully possessing her in the way a man possesses a woman. In his heart and mind he would memorize her body to carry the thought of her with him while they were apart. She would be with him both day and night. She would be with him *always*.

A sensual thrill coursed through Pamela's veins. Her breath harsh, she pressed her body fully into the bed of grass upon which she lay, writhing softly as her passion became aroused to a higher pitch, each level of desire astounding her in its endless spiraling of delight.

She placed a hand to Strong Bear's smooth cheek and smiled sweetly up at him. She was again in wonder of his finely chiseled features, the beautiful copper color of his skin, and his eyes growing darker with his own unleashed passions.

"What did you say to me in your language?" she murmured. Trust was no longer in doubt between them. Even that he had led her into sensual moments with him did not cause Pamela to mistrust him. He did not seem the sort to use love as a weapon! "Though I did not understand, it sounded lovely."

"In the tongue of the Miami, Strong Bear calls you beautiful," he said, his hands now smoothing over her thighs, purposely letting his thumbs graze against her pulsing bud of womanhood. "In all ways you are *pac-kah*, so very, *very* beautiful."

Pamela squirmed uneasily as she felt the touch of his thumb on the part of her that seemed to have strangely come to life. Until today this part of her anatomy had seemed to be separate from the rest of her body. It had had no purpose until today. Now it seemed to be awakening from a dormant sleep, possibly even like a butterfly emerging from its protective cocoon.

This bud of pleasure seemed even to be fluttering, like butterfly's wings as they open for the first time to reach out for the sun's warm caress. She ached for Strong Bear's fingers to fully possess this newborn section of her body but then reveled in his touch as he moved his hands to cup her breasts.

Pamela leaned herself into his hands, now wondering how *this* part of her body could receive such pleasure from

the mere touch of a man's hands. Never had her breasts
responded to her own touch. They had also been like
something separate from herself, lifeless.

Until now. Her breasts were sweetly aching, her nipples
sensitive and swelling within Strong Bear's thumb and
forefinger as he slightly squeezed them. Pleasure spread
through Pamela's body. When she heard a quiet moan
break through the silence of the forest where she was
discovering the secrets of her body, she soon realized that
it was herself making the sound.

And then her moans were quieted when Strong Bear
leaned his lips to hers and kissed her with strength, with a
possessive heat. His fingers reached behind her and dug
into the soft flesh of her buttocks, lifting her so that she
was pressed into the hardness of his body. She could feel
his rising manhood, which still lay protected behind its
breechclout. Strong Bear was so fiercely grinding it into
her it was surely molding its outline against her abdomen.

Twining her arms about his neck, Pamela responded by
moving with him sensually, his fingers loosening, allowing it. As his tongue pressed between her lips and searched
within the honeydew recesses of her mouth, Pamela felt as
though she were melting, becoming one with him. She had
never expected this intense passion his kiss, his hands, his
man's strength had evoked. The euphoria that filled her
entire being was threatening to rob her of all her senses.

But let it, she thought wonderingly to herself. Let . . .
it. . . .

And then Strong Bear pulled away from her. Kneeling
at her side, he placed his thumbs to the waist of his
breechclout and, while watching her with his feverish eyes,
surely for her reaction, he began drawing it down, over his
hips.

Having by accident seen her brothers unclothed in the
small spaces of their latest home, Pamela knew how a
man's makeup differed from her own. But seeing brothers
was not the same as seeing a man to whom her heart had
been given. She could feel the heat of embarrassment

claim her cheeks as his manhood was revealed to her in its ready hardness.

Her eyes burning with a sudden apprehension of being with him in a such a way, Pamela began inching backward on the ground, away from him. She glanced downward at her own nudity, shame suddenly engulfing her. What was she doing? How could she?

Grabbing her dress she hid her nudity behind it and turned her eyes away from Strong Bear. "I . . . can't," she said, her voice strained with emotions never before felt by her. Tears pooled in the corners of her eyes, threatening to spill, but she blinked them away. She so wanted to fulfill this hungry ache that now ate away at her insides. And only by giving of herself totally could she expect to have such fulfillment. Though she had never experienced these feelings before, it was instinct that made her know what must be done to make her body return to its normal, less excited state.

But seeing how large he was, and realizing just what being with him fully could mean, had brought her back to reality and to what she must and must not do.

"You turn away?" Strong Bear said, laying his breechclout aside. He loosened the turkey feathers from his hair and placed them on the ground behind him. He slipped his moccasins from his feet. He had come this far, had drawn her into loving him this far, neither he nor she could be allowed to turn back, as though the time together had not happened. He must make love to her to win her totally. And win her he must. So much depended on it!

"Why do you turn away?" he said, now placing a finger to her chin, forcing her eyes around to meet the questioning in his. "Do you not feel the special bond that is shared between us? Do you not want to experience total pleasure? Let Strong Bear teach you many ways of pleasure. I wish to do it now."

Pamela tremored even though the sun was warm on her flesh as it spiraled like satin ribbons through the overhead branches onto her. But she knew that she was tremoring from something much different than from being only cold. Her body was still responding to the desire she was denying herself. The part of her at the juncture of her thighs that his touch had brought to life ached, throbbed unmercifully.

"I cannot just . . . just . . . be with you in this way without feeling some . . . apprehension," she said softly, becoming awash again with this liquid sensation speeding through her veins as his eyes commanded so much of her. "My father and brothers would call me shameful. Even in my own eyes I am shameful!"

Strong Bear cradled her face between his hands. He bent a soft kiss to her lips. "Strong Bear should be the only one you wish to please," he said, looking into her eyes the color of the sky. "Strong Bear make you happy in many ways that no one else can. Pamela make Strong Bear happy in ways none other has had ability to do! And Strong Bear has had many women!"

His words of other women stung Pamela's heart; for the first time ever in her life she knew the meaning of the word *jealous*! Should she deny him, he would go and take from another . . . then another . . . and another. He would forget her. Totally! And she could not bear the thought of never being with him again.

She nodded. She wiped a stray tear from her cheek. "Yes, oh, yes . . ." she whispered. "Love me, Strong Bear. Make love to—*with*—me."

He twined his fingers through the lustrous satin of her hair. "You will never want to love another," he said, easing his body fully atop hers.

Spreading her legs with a knee, Strong Bear softly probed with his hardness where she was now willingly flowering herself open to him. His lips claimed her mouth, his hands traveled across her body, touching her breasts, the sensuous bud of pleasure where he was slowly making access with his throbbing hardness.

Then he made the plunge. He kissed her hard to drown her wince of pain. And then he felt her relaxing against him again, giving him silent permission to begin his slow, easy thrusts inside her. He could feel the tightness, the warmth of her virgin canal, and he relished in the thought of now knowing for sure that he was the first man to have ever been with her.

And . . . he would be the last. Never would he allow another man to get so much as even close to her. She would reign at his side as his first wife of importance until they both were gray and wrinkled. They would have many sons . . . they would have many grandsons!

Feeling the slow thrusting of his pelvis and the sharp momentary pain now dying away and turning into something sensually sweet, Pamela opened herself wider. Her hips responded in her own rhythmic movements. She clung and rocked with him, coming even more alive than before, now knowing that life had *not* been complete, until now . . . until Strong Bear. His hands running up and down her flesh set little fires along her body, blending into one massive flame as he rediscovered her breasts and began kneading and fondling them.

He allowed his lips to pull back a fraction. Within his eyes Pamela could see how drugged they were with building desire.

"*Tap-a-lot*," he said huskily. "Is not love such a beautiful word when spoken aloud?"

"Being in love is beautiful," Pamela said, her voice foreign to her in its strange huskiness. "What we are experiencing *is* love, is it not?"

"How could you think it could be called anything else?" he said, again finding her lips with his own, silencing her questions, those which she should already know the answers to!

Pamela was experiencing an endlessly spiraling sweep of pleasure spreading throughout her. Her insides were bubbling with this newfound happiness. His kiss was all consuming; his arms were enfolding her within his solid strength.

Strong Bear savored the sweet warm press of her body

against his and the way she was responding to his every nuance of lovemaking. He kissed her hungrily, feeling the sought release dangerously near. He buried his face in the valley of her breasts just as the tremors overtook him. He thrust harder; he groaned. And when he felt her body responding in kind, knowing that he had led her into the full feelings of a woman, he smiled and welcomed the soft cry of her release against his cheek as his lips grazed her ear.

"Oh, my . . ." Pamela sighed, still quaking from these newborn wonderful, magical feelings. And Strong Bear was the one who had given her this gift! He had taught her, she had let him. And now she was a woman. A . . . total . . . woman.

Strong Bear crept from atop her and leaned on an elbow at her side, smoothing a stray lock of her hair from her damp brow. "You enjoyed?" he asked, an eyebrow cocked.

Pamela's eyes lowered. She felt a blush rise to her cheeks. She smiled and looked slowly over at him. "Oh, so very much," she whispered, reaching to trace the sensual outline of his kiss-swollen lips. "Thank you, Strong Bear. Thank you."

Strong Bear chuckled, taking her hand, kissing its soft palm. "You do not thank one who shares the same pleasure as you," he said, his eyes twinkling. "You are glad you returned to Strong Bear this day?"

"Nothing could have kept me away," she murmured. Then her eyes grew wide with remembrance of just who might be wondering about her at this moment. Robert! He had allowed her to leave without much argument, but he would not expect her to be gone long. What if he came looking for her? If he found her in such a way with a man—an Indian at that—she would not only be shamed for life in his eyes, he would want to kill Strong Bear!

Panic rising inside her, Pamela scurried to her feet. She grabbed her clothes and began dressing. "Strong Bear, I don't know what I was thinking by taking so much time away from the cabin," she said, her eyes wild with worry.

"My brother, Robert, may come looking for me. He mustn't find us together. I must find a way to reveal my love for you to my family in my own way, at the right time. It can't happen in *this* way."

Strong Bear's mind momentarily swept to her other brother. Even he could come upon them at any moment now. That was not in Strong Bear's design. Strong Bear wanted to be in control of all his destinies, not controlled by destiny, itself!

He moved quickly to his feet and pulled his breechclout on. So far everything was going as planned. Nothing could be allowed to go awry!

"Were you allowed to leave your dwelling this morning without many questions?" he said, now repositioning his turkey feathers in a loop at the back of his head.

"I told Robert that I was coming into the forest to fill my basket with mushrooms and pick *greens* for our evening meal," Pamela said, dressed and now combing her fingers through her tangled hair. "And I must return home with them or Robert will suspect I've been up to something." She moved to Strong Bear and looked up into his eyes, seeing how they had so suddenly become moody. "Please understand?"

Strong Bear clasped his fingers to her shoulders. His jaw was tight. "I must make an appearance in my village," he said thickly. "I have been gone too long, also, from my people. I did not plan to come this far, to see the land of my vision this time while on my travels from my people. But it has been many moons since I have cast my eyes upon this land of wondrous beauty. I had to see it again, to dream of the day I would lead my people here." His brow creased into a troubled frown. "It is good that I decided to come. Had I not, I would not have seen that a dwelling shadowed my land." His eyes wavered. "Strong Bear would not have discovered *you* so soon, to find love so sweet in your arms."

He drew her close. His fingers reached up to entwine in her hair as his mouth found hers and began kissing her, sensuously, hot and demanding. He crushed her to him so hard, she gasped. But finding herself again enveloped within his strong arms, ecstasy crept back in with bone-weakening intensity. Their kisses were promises spoken without words that they would see one another again. Neither would be whole without the other!

Strong Bear drew his lips only a breath away from hers. "Strong Bear will return soon," he whispered, his hands framing her face. "Soon you will follow Strong Bear to his village. You will become a part of my people. You will become my wife."

Pamela's face warmed with a blush, her lips parted with a tremoring smile. "But . . . *how* . . . ?" she murmured. "My family—"

Sealing her lips with a forefinger, Strong Bear hushed her. "It will happen," he growled. "You will see."

He took her hands and smiled down at her. "But now Strong Bear will help you fill your basket with mushrooms and what you called *greens*," he said. "Two can work much faster than one. You can return to your dwelling sooner."

"That would be so nice," Pamela said, laughing softly. "I would so enjoy doing this with you."

He swung away from her and squinted his eyes, probing the deeper shadows of the forest. "You know where these can be found?" he questioned, his eyebrows forking.

"Yes. I saw both yesterday on my way here, to find you," Pamela said, bustling over to pick up her basket. She frowned when she saw the bulky blanket pooled in the basket. She had brought it for Strong Bear to use while he was recuperating. He was now almost well. He did not need it. And if she left it in the basket she would have no room for the mushrooms or greens. And if she returned with it draped over her arm, Robert would be quick to know that she had been up to something besides getting food for the dinner table.

A mischievous smile curved her lips. She gave Strong Bear a half glance, then looked at his strawberry roan still grazing peacefully at the cave's entrance. On its back was the saddle of blankets. There was surely room for one more!

Taking the blanket from the basket, Pamela marched over to the roan and swung it over his back. "Strong Bear, this is my second gift to you this day," she murmured, smiling over at him. "My first was my *love*."

Strong Bear went to her and drew her into his arms, looking devotedly into her eyes. "My woman, when you are my wife, you will receive gifts from Strong Bear that will set your face aglow with gladness," he said thickly. "You will see. Soon."

Again he swung away from her. "Take me to the mushrooms," he said, swelling his chest out proudly, having never been as content as now. Everything was working out as planned. Now nothing would stand in his way of possessing not only the land of his vision, but also *her*.

Giggling, feeling like a child again with a light, trouble-free heart, Pamela ran with the basket through the woods. When she spied the great clumps of mushrooms on a mound of ground just ahead where the sun was drenching them with its warmth, Pamela grabbed Strong Bear's hand and half dragged him along beside her.

But the sound of an approaching horse quickly stole Pamela's heartbeat away. She came to an abrupt halt. The palm of her hand became sweaty against Strong Bear's firm grip.

"Who . . . ?" she said in a shocked whisper. "Oh, Strong Bear, what if it's Robert?"

Strong Bear jerked his hand free. He looked across his shoulder in the direction of the cave, his foolhardy ways having made him forget the importance of having his weapons with him at all times.

His eyes were drawn around again as the horse grew closer. He looked at Pamela with a momentary, cautious stare. Then he turned to run back to the cave for his weapons, but stopped when a man's shout vibrated from tree to tree on either side of him.

Strong Bear did not have to turn to see who had discovered him with Pamela. He recognized the voice. It was not the brother Pamela had worried openly about. It was her other brother, Anthony, the one who had saved Strong Bear's life earlier in the day.

But would the white man now be sorry for what he had done? Wouldn't he wish him dead because he was too savage to love a woman of their kind . . . ? And when that woman was his *sister*, how even then would the white man react?

Strong Bear now expected that he would openly have to challenge the white man for Pamela. But Strong Bear would lose either way. She would not be able to love him if he killed her brother; her feelings for family were too deep. Strong Bear hoped what they had experienced together only moments ago would make her feelings for him soar.

Pamela's insides splashed cold and the color drained from her face when Anthony's gelding came to a shuddering halt close beside her. "Lord, Anthony," she gasped, placing a hand to her mouth. "Oh, Lord . . ."

Anthony's eyes were firelit. He looked from Pamela, to Strong Bear. Cold dread rushed through him. His sister and the Indian . . . ? Together . . . ? What did it mean? Had the Indian even been with Pamela before this morning? Had the Indian silently mocked Anthony while they had been talking, exchanging friendships, all the while knowing who he was? There *had* been a recognition of sorts in the Indian's eyes. Anthony could recall wondering about it at the time.

The wonder . . . the knowing . . . ate away at Anthony's gut. His own sister? How could she be so foolish to make this sort of friendship? Had she become so bored that she would make friends with the first person who came along? And was it only friends' . . .?

Anthony curled a hand into a tight fist at his side. If the Indian had so much as laid a hand on her . . . !

"Pamela, what the hell's goin' on here?" Anthony finally was able to squeeze through his clenched teeth. "What are you doing with this Indian?"

Pamela shuffled her feet nervously. Her knuckles were white where both hands clutched the handle of her basket. "I'm getting ready to pick mushrooms and greens," she stammered. "I'm picking them for dinner."

"Yes. That's what Robert told me when I arrived home and found you gone," Anthony growled, his free hand finding a home on his sheathed rifle. "Well, we don't need no damn greens and mushrooms. I shot a big deer. Now you just get yourself on home. Do you hear? I don't think I dare ask any more questions about you and this Indian and why he's here with you apparently willin' to help you with your chores of pickin'. I see too much in your eyes I don't want to see."

"Anthony, please . . ." Pamela said, casting her eyes downward.

"And you, Strong Bear," Anthony shouted. "When I made friends with you this mornin', that didn't include my sister in the deal. You stay away from her. Do you hear?"

Pamela's eyes shot up. She turned questioning eyes to Strong Bear, then Anthony. "What do you mean?" she asked, confused. "You mean you and Strong Bear have met?"

"We sure as hell did," Anthony said, squaring his shoulders. "Under circumstances quite unique, I'd say." He nodded with his head in the direction from where he had just traveled. "But it wasn't anywhere close. It was yonder. About a mile through the forest, I'd say."

Strong Bear took a step closer, knowing that many questions were running through Pamela's mind. She had thought that he had spent the night in the cave. She would wonder why he hadn't told her differently. She would most definitely wonder why he hadn't told her about having made the acquaintance of her brother. To Strong Bear it was important to fit the pieces together slowly to make his plan work, and her knowing that he had met her brother was not in that plan until later.

Now he could tell that doubt was flooding her heart, where love had once held sway. And he could not convince her otherwise while in her brother's presence. There were too many dangers in that.

"Strong Bear, because we did vow friendship between us today I'll not question or say more about why you have chosen to come and make yourself known to my sister," Anthony said tersely. "But don't let me catch you in this neck of the woods again, or, by damn, I'll shoot you."

Fire and ice blended in Strong Bear's eyes. He tightened his hands into fists at his sides. He glared in silence at Anthony, then spoke with no visible emotion. "White man, never threaten Strong Bear," he said. "Never threaten a powerful Miami *chief,* or soon *you* will be dead. *Not* Strong Bear!"

Pamela glanced from one to the other, paling even more. Both were making threats! Oh, what could she do? She had never felt so helpless! And, oh, Strong Bear! Did she even know him at all?

Unable to understand any of this, and knowing that she mustn't plead her case with Strong Bear in front of Anthony, Pamela shook her head fitfully and ran from them both. Tears blurred her vision, so that she found herself fighting tangled briars and fallen limbs at her feet.

But she was scarcely conscious of these barriers. Her heart was bleeding. She had thought Strong Bear had been honest with her. But he hadn't. Why . . . ?

"Pamela!" Anthony said, his gelding catching up with her. "Get on. I'll take you home. That way I'll know you'll get there. Damn it, Pamela. Don't you know the dangers of letting an Indian fool you into talkin' with him?"

Letting Anthony help her up on the saddle before him, Pamela circled an arm about his waist with one hand and held her basket with the other. Placing her cheek to his

chest, she rested it there while he rode on with her through
the forest. Perhaps too many lessons had been learned
today. Trust? Would she ever know the true meaning of
the word? Would Strong Bear? Had he used her *and*
Anthony? Had he done so in an effort to eventually get
them from the land that he declared to be his?

But if he wanted the land so badly, why would he
bother to get it by means of making friends with Anthony,
and a lover of her? Indians usually took what they wanted
by killing, didn't they?

A faint ray of hope lit her heart. Surely Strong Bear was
behaving this way only because of her. He must love her.
He surely couldn't pretend the feelings that he had shown
with her. They were too beautiful to fake!

Her thick lashes closing over her eyes, Pamela stifled a
sob against her brother' s buckskin shirt. She loved Strong
Bear so deeply. But it surely was as everyone had always
said. It *was* a forbidden love.

A shiver raced across her flesh when in her mind's eye
she could see Strong Bear as he voiced his threat to
Anthony. Was it a true threat, or one spoken in haste?

Suddenly Pamela was . . . afraid.

Six

✺

Wait and know the coming of a little love.
— Sandburg

Pamela was awakened with a start from her troubled sleep. She gasped when she saw the shadow of someone standing close beside her bed. "Who . . . ?" she said, squinting her eyes, trying to see more clearly in the darkness of her loft bedroom. She drew the patchwork quilt closer beneath her chin.

Then she flinched when Anthony leaned down and yanked her quilt away and shoved clothes into her arms.

"Get up," he ordered flatly. "Get dressed. And be quick about it. You're travelin' with me to the British fort."

"What . . . ?" Pamela said, leaning up on an elbow. She was not only shocked by Anthony's gruffness, but also by what he had just said. "What's happening, Anthony? Why have you decided to go to the fort so suddenly? Why must I go with you? I don't understand any of this."

"Papa's worse this mornin'," Anthony grumbled. "We've no choice but to go to the British to see if they might have some sort of medication to lend us for Papa. His brow's hot as fire this mornin'. He's dehydratin' at a fast pace."

"Oh, no," Pamela cried softly, scurrying from the bed in her floor-length cotton nightgown, the clothes Anthony had forced upon her draped over her arm. She followed Anthony to the ladder that led from the loft. "Anthony, is Papa going . . . to . . . die?"

"I'm beginnin' to fear that he may," Anthony said, taking the first step downward. The fire's glow from the hearth outlined his broad shoulders and rusty-colored hair, which was drawn back into a pigtail at the back. "But we're goin' to do our damnedest to see that he don't."

Pamela dropped to her knees as Anthony kept descending the stairs. "But, Anthony, why have you decided that I must accompany you to the fort?" she asked, in awe of the suggestion. A sadness engulfed her when her thoughts fleetingly strayed to Strong Bear. Though Anthony had refused to discuss the fact that she had been with Strong Bear, would not even reveal to her what he had meant when he had said that Strong Bear and he had met under unique circumstances, she knew that he would never allow Strong Bear to come near her again. She had found the man that she was destined to love even when she had been only a tiny speck in her mother's womb, and she had lost him in the blink of an eye.

But Strong Bear's threats to Anthony had plagued her night-long dreams. Had she been too hasty to give her heart and soul to this Indian who had savage thoughts against her own brother? Would he carry out his threats?

Anthony glowered up at Pamela as he stopped on the fourth rung of the ladder. Even in the dim lighting of the cabin she could see his dark scowl.

"You're goin' with me because of that damn Indian," he snapped. "I can't leave you here with only Robert to protect you. Strong Bear wouldn't dare try forcin' you away from *me* after what I done for him. By damn, Pamela, why'd you have to make friends with him? Don't you know he had more things on his mind than friendship as far as you were concerned? Even when he made friends with me so easily it was for a damn purpose. It was because he had seen you and wanted you.''

Pamela felt her face flame with a blush, recalling the sensuous moments in Strong Bear's embrace. If her brother knew the full truth of his sister and the Indian, oh, what then?

"Anthony, what did you do for Strong Bear?" she tested, seeing an opportunity to finally get the answers she was seeking. "How did you meet him? How?"

"What'd I do?" Anthony said dryly. "I saved his life, that's what I did."

Pamela was taken aback by his answer. "You . . . saved . . . Strong Bear's life?" she said in an almost whisper. "Lord, Anthony, *how*?"

"I killed a bear just as it was about to attack him," Anthony said, chuckling sarcastically. "I should've let the damn bear *eat* him. That'd give me one less worry on my mind. As it is—"

He stopped and flung a hand in the air. "Get dressed, Pamela," he growled. "Time's a'wastin'."

Pamela swallowed hard. "Yes, sir," she said, glancing down at the clothes. Her eyes widened and she looked questioningly back at Anthony as he stepped from the last ladder rung to the floor. "Anthony, why must I wear *these* clothes? They're so . . . so . . . unfeminine."

Anthony's eyes were dark pits as he looked up at her. "When we had those buckskin breeches and shirt made in Williamsburg they were for you to wear on the journey to Kentucky *if* it became necessary for you to look like a boy to protect you from woman-hungry Indians or stray men wandering footloose along the trail. Well, it seems now is the time you must wear them. You must look like a boy accompanying me to the British fort. It won't fool that damn Indian, Strong Bear, but it'll fool any other man who might come along, Indian, American, *or* British.''

Disgruntled at his choice of clothes and reasoning, Pamela went to her bed and placed the fringed buckskin breeches and shirt on it while drawing her nightgown over her head. A deep, hacking cough breaking through the silence of the morning made her cringe.

Then she rushed into the rest of her buckskin attire, no longer caring how she would be changed from a woman into a boy. Her mind was consumed with worries of her father. What if the decision to go to the fort had been made too late? Was her father beyond help? Would the British even be civil enough to listen to a plea for a dying father? Wouldn't they even possibly place her and Anthony in shackles?

Taking great pains to bind her hair into a tight coil atop her head so she could hide it beneath a hat, fear now replaced all other emotions swimming around inside Pamela's consciousness. This wasn't exactly the sort of excitement she had been hungering for. Suddenly the four walls of the drab cabin looked good to her!

Moving down the ladder, Pamela looked solemnly around her, seeing everything familiar to her that meant *family*. Would this be the last time she would be seeing it? Would she ever see Robert and her father again?

Robert met her at the foot of the ladder. He drew her into his arms and hugged her painfully.

Riding astride a gentle blond mare, a fine horse that had cost her father seventy dollars, Pamela puffed and wheezed. She and Anthony had ridden long and hard. Though she looked almost one hundred percent a boy, at least from a distance, she was glad that her buckskins didn't reek of body odor as did Anthony's. The toilet water that she had splashed onto her body after bathing the previous night still clung to her skin, petal soft in its sweetness. But her lips tasted of dust, and her eyes burned from the incessant sting of the bright rays of the sun.

Her mare snorting and shaking its magnificent mane, Pamela leaned over and gave her a reassuring pat, yet cringing when her flesh made contact with the lather of sweat that spread along its body in a sleek, pearly shine.

"Anthony, just how much farther?" Pamela sighed, wiping the mare's sweat from her hands onto her buckskin breeches. "You know that I'm not used to riding so far on horseback. And, Lord, you're pushing so *hard*. Can't you let up for at least a moment?" She brushed a stray strand of hair back beneath her coonskin hat, grimacing at how her hair would look when it was released from the hat's tight, hot confines.

"We should be there soon," Anthony tried to reassure, yet knowing how Pamela must be feeling. He even felt the drawing of his thigh muscles and the numbness of his buttocks from riding so long.

But the dangers in moving slower were twofold. First they had their father to consider. Time was against him. Second, they had the fear of Indians. The Delaware were known to be fierce in these parts, working diligently for the British in their pursuit of settlers' scalps.

And there was always Strong Bear. Anthony had to wonder what *his* next move would be. There was no doubt that the Indian was interested in Pamela in ways that Anthony shuddered to think about!

"Can't we just stop and rest for a moment?" Pamela begged, every bone in her body aching. She had been wrong to forget to bring gloves to protect her hands! The mare's reins were cutting into her fingers like wild rose thorns that scrape and tear one's skin. The sweat was trickling down and along the valley of her breasts, itching her.

Anthony cast Pamela a harried look as he rode relentlessly onward, his gelding not showing signs of fatigue as it held its head high. "You'd be home where you'd be comfortable had you not been so foolish as to make the acquaintance of that damn Indian," he shouted, his rusty pony tail bobbing in the wind. "I thought you knew better, Pamela. What got into you anyways?"

"Anthony, this isn't the time for scolding," Pamela fussed, afraid that his questions could pull more from her than she knew was safe. He could never know that she and Strong Bear had done more than exchange conversation. Anthony would never understand. Did *she*, even?

Yet just the mere thought of Strong Bear sent a rapturous thrill coursing through her veins. No matter what would happen, or when, a part of her would always love him. She prayed that somehow everything could be rectified between Anthony and Strong Bear and that she could eventually confess her true feelings for Strong Bear not only to Anthony, but to her entire family. She was ready to give up her existence as she had always known it just to be with him. No other man could ever fill the empty spaces that had once been in her heart the way Strong Bear did. No one! Somehow she had to make things work out for them. She was only half-alive without him!

"No, perhaps this isn't the time for a scolding," Anthony said at last. "Perhaps it never will be. I don't think I even want to talk about it. You've learned your lesson, anyhow, haven't you?"

Pamela saw no choice but to nod, to let him at least believe for now that she was going to forget Strong Bear. But later . . . ? She would tell him later how it truly must be!

Finally their travels were slowed when they moved their horses into tall marsh grasses. The soil was a loose, yellow sand and was so soft their horses could hardly draw their hooves from it as they gave way to great sucking noises. Pamela dodged giant horseflies buzzing around her head. She swatted and screamed as one settled on her cheek and stung her.

Solid land was heartily welcomed and with it brought the first signs of the British fort, barely visible ahead through the heavy growth of timber.

"I'd say just in time," Anthony said as he gave Pamela

a grin, seeing how she still fought one last pestering horsefly. The rest were left behind in the marsh.

"Do you see it, also?" Pamela said, her heart skipping a beat when she saw the fort. She sighed with relief when the horsefly darted away from her, in the opposite direction. "Are we actully just about there, Anthony?"

"It won't be long now," he shouted, spurring his gelding onward beneath tall oaks and elms, and through swamp alder and wild roses. "But I'm not so sure we should be feeling all that anxious. We don't know what our reception will be. You do know that, don't you, Pamela?"

"Yes. I know the dangers as well as you," Pamela said, sitting tall in her saddle, trying to look as courageous as Anthony; yet deep within, the pit of her stomach was queasy. She would never forget the horrid tales of what the British did to settlers. Why should their fate be any different? Yet, she and Anthony didn't have any choice but to seek help from them. Though the humid air seemed to crackle with a sense of impending danger the closer they drew to the fort, everything must be chanced for her father!

When they came to a clearing in closer promixity to the fort, Anthony reined his gelding to a halt, nodding to Pamela for her to do the same. Pamela was glad to comply. She inhaled a nervous breath and, along with Anthony, studied the fort. Built on a bluff some distance from the shoreline of the Ohio River, its walls were at least six feet high. Blockhouses were positioned at each of its four corners, equipped with musket-proof doors and shutters. The fort was cleared for at least a thousand feet all the way around, so that no one could sneak up on it under cover.

Pamela squirmed uncomfortably in her saddle, her gaze now looking farther than the fort. Several soldiers were standing guard along the river, where various small craft were moored. And then Pamela looked toward the massive gates of the fort. They were open, and sentries stood guard, fully equipped with firearms.

"Anthony, I'm afraid," Pamela blurted, her whole insides trembling. "You know American settlers are hated by the British. They are hated even more than *Indians*."

"Yeah, I know," Anthony said, wiping beads of perspiration from his brow. He gave Pamela a quick once-over. "Now you be sure to keep that hat on your head and stand behind me when I talk to the one in charge. There ain't no need in gettin' their interest piqued over you bein' a woman. Do you understand?"

"But, Anthony, surely they can tell by my face alone that I am a woman," she fussed.

"Keep your head ducked," Anthony scolded. "Pamela, just use common sense."

"All right," she muttered, following Anthony's lead as he thrust his heels into the flanks of his gelding, galloping determinedly toward the fort. The fringes on Pamela's leggings and shirt whipped wildly in the air, and the wind stung her face as she pushed her horse at a fast clip, not wanting to stray too far from Anthony.

But when horsemen left the fort and began riding suddenly toward her and Anthony, Pamela felt renewed doubts about their sanity and their plan to seek medicine for their father from the British. But there was no turning back *now*. Her hair bristled at the nape of her neck when she saw a line of soldiers departing the gates of the fort on foot, their rifles leveled at her and her brother.

Pamela reined her horse to a stop alongside Anthony's when they were flanked by two British soldiers on horseback. Sitting stiffly in the saddle, she exchanged a quick glance with her brother, then gazed coldly at one of the British soldiers who was returning her studious stare, his powdered white wig catching the shine of the sun in it, his blood-red coat spotless.

Her face becoming hot with a blush, Pamela soon remembered Anthony's warning to keep her head ducked. It seemed that it was already too late, for the soldier most assuredly had recognized that she was not a man.

"State your business," the soldier ordered, now directing his attention squarely on Anthony, his pale blue eyes slowly scrutinizing him. "Why are you here? Where have you traveled from?"

Anthony edged his gelding closer to the soldier, trying to block the soldier's vision of Pamela. He had seen the recognition in the soldier's eyes and knew that Pamela's identity was no longer a secret. He took great pains to explain his plight carefully, scarcely breathing while watching the two soldiers exchange quick glances, and then smug smiles.

"Come along," he was then commanded by the same soldier who had already addressed him. "Colonel Bradley will grant you and your . . . uh . . . companion an audience. It isn't every day settlers come to call. He'll find this—" He gestured with a hand toward Pamela. "He'll find the costume of this one settler quite amusing."

Anthony's insides knotted with the soldier's last remarks about Pamela's attire. Either way he had looked at it he wouldn't have won where she was concerned. If not the worry over the Indian wanting her, there was now the British!

But he was glad at least that he and Pamela hadn't yet been taken prisoner.

With a wildly thumping heart, Pamela rode alongside her brother between the two soldiers. She paled when they reached the fort but tried not to feel the continued threat of the rifles as she made her way along the long row of soldiers standing on each side of the gate. As she entered the courtyard, she had to continue focusing on thoughts of what had driven her and Anthony there. The welfare of their father! Her only hope—*Anthony's* only hope—was if the British colonel could sympathize with a son and daughter who were risking all for their father! And he *would* know that she was a female, for if the soldier had so readily recognized her, so would the colonel!

After dismounting before a grim, gray structure that showed signs of dampness by its warped log siding, Pamela and Anthony were ushered into the dimly lighted cabin. A candle flickered on a desk on the far side of the room, its dancing light reflecting onto a face of hawklike features framed by a powdered wig. Eyes as gray as stone looked up at them from a ledger, showing within them a strange sort of amusement one minute, a cold hatred the next.

"Well? What have we here?" Colonel Bradley said, laying his quill aside. "Two stray settlers?" He looked away long enough to sprinkle the page of his ledger with sand to dry the ink, then funneled the sand back into a small jar.

Pamela's insides tightened, having seen too much in the eyes of this man, and hearing too much mockery in his voice, ever to expect any kindness from him. The English colonel even looked misplaced in the drab setting. He was in full uniform, clean and polished down to his boot tops. He was dressed even more handsomely than that. His scarlet coat was richly laced with gold trim and shining brass buttons; his white shirt was rich with ruffles at the cuffs of his sleeves, and neck.

Anthony edged in front of Pamela, having seen the colonel's eyes linger on Pamela longer than himself. "We've come to seek medical aid for our father," he said, nervously clasping his hands together behind him. "He lies perhaps even now near death. If you could lend a hand . . . lend us some medical supplies . . . ?"

Colonel Bradley leaned forward, his nose twitching at the vile smell of perspiration on Anthony's garments pervading the small spaces of the cabin. He craned his neck to look around Anthony, smiling wickedly as he picked up the sweet scent of toilet water, having already recognized this person to be a woman pretending to be a boy. Well, he would play along with the scheme. He would pretend to believe she was a boy. Later he would take her as what, in truth, she was: a lovely wench just ripe for seducing!

Colonel Bradley's eyes narrowed as he closed his ledger and settled back more comfortably in his chair, placing his fingertips together before him.

"It's obvious that your allegiance is not to England,"

he said blandly, scowling. "You *are* damn American settlers, are you not? Why would you even think you could get *any* sort of assistance from me? If I had my way about it your scalps would be hanging on my wall right now. How is it that the Indians missed you on their rounds?"

Pamela and Anthony exchanged quick glances. When Anthony saw how pale Pamela had become, anger caused his face to flush the color of the colonel's coat. Placing the palms of his hands flat on the wide desktop, he leaned down into the colonel's face and began a slow, lazy banter with him while Pamela looked on, mortified.

But then Pamela glared down at the colonel, just now recognizing his name. She should have recognized it earlier! His reputation was even known back in Williamsburg. Colonel Bradley, the man in charge of this small group of British militia, was well known not only for his dealings with the Indians, but also for the incessant drilling of his soldiers and his whippings and shooting of deserters. Most of his soldiers feared him even more than the Indians.

Colonel Bradley was a man who would stop at nothing to further his career or to increase his wealth. If it were possible to gain the credit for another man's work, he would do it. He was smart and would never do anything to endanger his own person. He was ruthless to the point of encouraging the Indians to fight the Americans instead of wasting war on each other, supplying them with British knives, paying them a bounty for every American scalp that was brought back to him.

Colonel Bradley had realized that a defeat of the Indians by Americans would endanger the British forts still held illegally in American territory, and in such an event the Indians would turn on the British. The British had been obligated to supply ammunition and information to the Indians to stem the tide of American settlement.

Pamela looked slowly past Colonel Bradley's shoulder. Her insides grew cold when she recognized the fine hair of a child and the gray hair of surely a grandmother hanging on the wall from pegs with many other scalps.

A humiliated sort of rage tore through her. Sitting before her was a British fop in a white wig . . . the real savage, even more so than the Indians.

Her gaze shifted. Beside this display of scalps was a map, yellowed and curling at its edges. It represented a half million square miles of land that England had wrestled away from French control, but now legally belonged to America!

Pamela knew the guilt that Anthony must now be feeling for not having joined the Kentucky militia to rid this land of such filth as the British. An armed militia was increasingly needed to chase the remaining British back to England, *and* for protection from the Indians.

But Anthony had heard that the army life was not all fighting. Bridge and road building had been a part of the daily lives of the soldiers. Anthony had felt that surveying was just as important. So he had chosen to follow in his father's footsteps, thinking they could do as much for their country by finding land suitable for developing.

The rising pitch to her brother's voice drew Pamela from her reverie. She took a step backward, startled by Anthony's antagonistic tone as he still spoke squarely into the colonel's face.

"I didn't come here to discuss anything about Indians *or* the duties you assign them," Anthony said dryly. "I've come to ask for help. Either you give it . . . or you don't. I won't beg."

Colonel Bradley leaned his face into Anthony's, so close they exchanged the warmth of each other's breath. "You found your way here," he growled. "Now find your way back. I won't lend British aid to *any* land-greedy Yankees." He waved a hand loosely in the air. "Now get along with the two of you. I've paperwork to complete."

"I . . . hope . . . you burn in hell," Anthony growled back, his eyes flashing, yet understanding the consequences too well of saying anything so malicious to the colonel.

But he suspected that for some god-awful reasons his and Pamela's lives were going to be spared for now, or the colonel would have ordered them shackled and taken away. That the colonel had most assuredly recognized Pamela to be a woman and was letting her go so easily was even more puzzling to Anthony. He didn't like it. Not one bit! Surely the colonel had a trick up his sleeve as far as Pamela was concerned.

Anthony decided, however, that it would be best not to worry Pamela over this. If they *were* allowed to return to the cabin, he would worry silently about what might happen in the next few days! He would keep watch for any intruders of the night. No one would be allowed to abduct Pamela. No one!

"Burn in hell?" Colonel Bradley said, chuckling low. "Perhaps we'll burn together." He scooted his chair back and rose quickly from it. He motioned with a hand toward the waiting soldier. "Let them leave the fort unharmed. They're no threat to us. There's only two of them. Seems the only strong point about this one is his ability to speak. As I see it, that is no threat at all."

Anthony grabbed Pamela's hand and half dragged her alongside him as he stomped away, but he flinched when Colonel Bradley's voice boomed from behind them again.

"When you get back to your cabin the best medicine for your father is to get him on horseback and take him back where you came from," Colonel Bradley threatened. "That's the only cure I can offer you. Just very good *advice*."

The urge to wrap his fingers around Colonel Bradley's throat was so intense that Anthony had to clench his fists tightly to his sides to keep from actually doing it. He took a deep, quaking breath and rushed out with Pamela, helping her onto her mare. Then he mounted his own bay gelding.

Nodding for Pamela to follow, he wheeled his mount around and galloped from the courtyard, out toward the forest. Their father was the same as dead, and perhaps even themselves. Anthony knew that Colonel Bradley wasn't going to let him *or* Pamela get away all that easily.

Pamela sidled her horse up next to Anthony's, sighing

with relief as the forest cover was reached. "Anthony, perhaps we were wrong about the British," she shouted, momentarily forgetting the scalps that she had seen on the pegs in the colonel's office. "We were allowed to leave unharmed! And you *know* they recognized me to be a woman. Though we weren't able to get medical assistance for Papa, at least we weren't taken captive. Perhaps they've had a change of heart about settlers but just not enough to offer medical assistance."

Anthony moved his head in what seemed slow motion to Pamela. Should he warn her to expect anything at any moment from the British? Should he tell her that the British were just playing a game with them?

But, no. As before, he felt it was best not to alarm her unduly.

"Yes, perhaps you're right, Pamela," he said, his insides cold with fear, more for her life, than for his.

Colonel Bradley sat back down behind his desk and opened his ledger. Not looking up when he heard footsteps enter the room, he spoke smoothly, without emotion, to the soldier who was now standing alert, awaiting specific orders.

"Lucas, follow the Americans. See where they make their residence. Then report back to me."

"Yes, sir," Lucas said, standing to attention, stunned that the Americans had been allowed to leave, wondering *why*?

Lucas Boatright's face was youthful; his hair, free of a powdered wig, instead lay tied in a pigtail down his back in its true golden color. He was not dressed as the others at the fort. He wore buckskins, having become more of an errand boy for the colonel, than a soldier.

Lucas's demeanor was stiff and cautious, fearing this colonel whom some even called mad. Whippings were in order for those who did not follow his orders exactly. But Lucas had even more than that to fear. He did not wish to leave the fort to travel far into the forest. Ofttimes those

who left did not return. Only the Delaware Indians who
were in alliance with Colonel Bradley seemed to come and
go without harm done to them.

Yet the settlers had arrived unharmed, had they not?

Still, Lucas did not wish to travel from the fort alone,
to do his duties as ordered. Dare he ask for others to join
him . . . ?

"Sir, whom do you prefer I take with me?" he blurted,
hoping beyond hope that the colonel would not see him as
a coward for asking. Cowards were shot, not whipped!

Colonel Bradley raised his eyes slowly upward. He
glared at Lucas, his narrow lips pursed. And then he
spoke. "You go alone," he snapped. "Too many horses
following the Americans could be detected by them. I
don't want them to know they're being followed." He
flicked his wrist as he waved toward the door. "Now get
along with you. The Americans have already got a head
start on you. We can't let them get much farther. They'll
be too soon lost in the thickness of the forest for you to
find."

Lucas swallowed hard, his face paling with the thought
of what lay ahead of him. By evening his scalp could hang
from either of two tribes of Indians' scalp poles, the
Delaware or the Miami. Both tribes were known to make
residence in this part of Kentucky. But Lucas hoped that if
he came face-to-face with any Indians, it would be the
Delaware. It was the Delaware who brought scalps to
Colonel Bradley . . . *settlers'* scalps.

Yet perhaps it wouldn't be all that bad to meet up with a
Miami Indian. Those in this area were not known to be
ruthless or greedy. As far as Lucas knew, the Miami
Indians kept to themselves, surely trying to live the same
sort of life of peace among their people that they had
known before the arrival of the white man.

"Yes, sir," Lucas said, no enthusiasm at all in his
voice. "Whatever you say, sir."

"And, Lucas," Colonel Bradley said suddenly from
behind him. "See just how many more make residence

with these Americans. There was a mention of an ailing father. But no one else. See just how many I must do away with to have the lady all to myself.''

Lucas's eyes widened. "Lady?" he gasped.

"Didn't you recognize that one of the two Americans was a lady?" Colonel Bradley chuckled. "Young man, she's going to be *mine*. But it must be done in a way that she will not know that I am the one responsible for her being totally alone in the world. She must come to me because she thinks that I will care for her. Now if she knew that I had the rest of her family slain, she would kill me before I would be allowed to touch her. Isn't that right, Lucas?"

A numbness seized Lucas. He now knew why the colonel had let the Americans leave, unharmed. The Americans were unknowingly riding into a trap by returning to their cabin, alive. Colonel Bradley was tired of the long, lonely nights of the wilderness. Instead of wanting another scalp of a female American settler to decorate his wall, he wanted *her*, to humiliate, personally. He wanted her, for *ravaging*. And it was apparent that he was going to do anything he could, to have her.

"Yes, sir," Lucas said, his voice flat and solemn. "I'll see how many make up the household. Good day, sir."

Lucas hurried from the cabin. He circled around behind it, hung his head, and let the bitter bile pour from deeply inside him, retching. He wanted nothing more than to run and never return to this dreaded fort. But he knew the fate of . . . deserters.

Seven

❧ ❧

I want you with your arms and lips to love me
Throughout the wonder watches of the night.
— Gillom

The bark cabin was hung with war clubs, bows, and arrows. In the center of the earthen floor a fire burned in a shallow pit, a corresponding smoke-escape hole in the roof above it. On each side of the room, bunks covered with furs were used as either beds or seats. The cabin had been built with poles planted upright in the ground and laced together with hickory strips supporting large pieces of elm bark, pressed flat and fastened to the poles by thongs of bark. A six-foot-high narrow doorway faced the east and, when necessary, was closed by a piece of bark placed beside it and fastened by a brace.

The savory smell of opossum roasting over the fire filled the air. Strong Bear sat before the fire on a pallet of furs, watching his wife, Snow Owl, at work. Preparing his evening meal of opossum and blackberries, she possessed a picturesque beauty with her black hair pulled back in the Miami clubbed hairstyle, which accentuated her high cheek-bones and large, dark eyes.

Dangling from her pierced ears were several pairs of gold earrings, the jewelry a mark of family wealth and distinction. Fringed leggings covered her slim legs, and she wore a buckskin dress adorned with large circular ornaments of silver.

Although she was beautiful and a dutiful wife, Strong Bear's heart felt nothing special for her. Their marriage was one of convenience, nothing more, nothing less. He had married her because he was the great chief of this band of Miami Indians and no chief should be without a woman to gratify his manly needs. She was with him also to satisfy his plan to have many sons in his lifetime.

But now there was Pamela. He wanted many sons born of *her* womb. He wanted her to fill his lonesome nights. And she would, in time. An obstacle had only temporarily been placed in their way: a brother with a forked tongue. First the white man vowed friendship, and then he so easily made threats to Strong Bear!

Strong Bear was trying to fit the pieces together inside his mind, what his next move should be, and when. . . .

Snow Owl glanced over at Strong Bear, wondering about his subdued silence. When he studied her in such a way she always wondered if it was because he had guessed that she'd agreed to marry him because she'd seen that it was a way to have position in the village.

Or was he thinking about how she had wanted to marry him because he was a great Miami Indian chief, the one who had the power to acquire many nuggets of gold, which held within them some sort of magic? Because of their importance to the Great Spirit, Snow Owl knew they were surely worth more than any amount of hides offered for trading, if only Strong Bear would use them.

But he continued using them only for family ornamentation and as an offering to the Great Spirit as his father had before him, and his father before him. It was tradition, one that she dare not question.

Placing the prepared wooden platter of food at Strong Bear's feet, Snow Owl went back to her own pallet of furs and resumed making leggings, the character of this work requiring a great quantity of colored ribbon.

Working the ribbon into a pair of leggings, Snow Owl again eyed Strong Bear questioningly. After she had given him a prepared drink of the ground *ouissoucatcki* root placed in warm water to replenish the strength drained from him due to his loss of blood from the head wound, he had been quieter than usual after returning from a journey to the secret land where the valuable gold nuggets were found. This journey had taken even longer this time. She wondered why.

She stirred uneasily, seeing how Strong Bear still studied her in silence. Yet was he truly seeing her? There was something else in the way he was looking at her. Had he, on his long journey, cast eyes upon a new woman? Was not Snow Owl enough to satisfy his nightly needs? If she did not keep favor in his eyes, she could lose the pleasures of gold earrings in her ears! She could be made second wife, one of much less importance!

Setting her jaw firmly, her eyes suddenly afire with determination, Snow Owl placed her sewing articles aside and went to kneel before Strong Bear. She began drawing her dress over her head, purposely baring her magnificent breasts to him. She understood a man's needs and many nights had passed since Strong Bear had fulfilled his.

Thoughts still too full of Pamela, Strong Bear placed firm hands to Snow Owl's wrists. "*Ne-we-wah*, my wife, now is not the time," he said hoarsely. "Do you not see that food and rest is what your husband needs? Leave your dress in place. Lovemaking will come when your *ke-mawth* requests it."

Snow Owl's dress fluttered back down across her bared breasts. She suppressed the urge to shout at Strong Bear, to make him come to his senses and understand that what she had to offer was even better than rest or food. She could receive all of his seeds into her womb, quenching the desires that surely were gnawing at his insides. Now, even more than before, she feared that a woman was the cause for his disinterest in her. Nothing had ever caused him to forget lusts of the body!

"*Doges ska-noh-nai*," she said, unable to hide the venom in her voice. She settled back down beside the fire and resumed her sewing, avoiding the elusiveness in his eyes. "Perhaps Snow Owl can warm your body later."

Strong Bear began eating the roasted opposum meat with his fingers, yet tasting nothing. His eyes were fixed on the fire, seeing an occasional dancing maiden within its tongues of flames. But it was not Snow Owl. This maiden had skin as white as fresh snows in winter, eyes as blue as summer skies, and hair as soft as cattail down.

As he ate, he fantasized, seeing Pamela swirling, dancing to the time of a drum's rhythmic beats. The skirt of her dress billowed out away from her, revealing tiny tapered ankles, and higher still, the sensual curves of her thighs.

Then he was remembering Pamela's brother and his angry threats. In Strong Bear's mind's eye he was seeing the hate etched across the white man's face framed by hair the color of a flaming sunset. A slow hate was burning inside Strong Bear's heart for Anthony. Yet the white man had saved Strong Bear's life! Oh, how torn he was over what to do finally to have Pamela *and* the land of his vision.

He set his jaw hard, his eyes on fire with determination. He would have both, no matter what he had to do to get them!

Wiping grease from his mouth with the back of his hand, Strong Bear stormed to his feet, emitting a low growl. He grabbed his buckskin pouch of gold nuggets gathered a few sunrises ago. His great-grandfather had also had his special visions! One had led him to the land where gold nuggets swam like miniature sunbeams in crystal clear water. Since that time, only the reigning chief of this village of Miami was allowed to know where. Strong Bear's father had shown him the special waters when he had become old and ailing, as one day Strong Bear would show his own son.

Walking determinedly toward the door, Strong Bear clutched hard to the buckskin pouch. He would not use any of the gold nuggets this time for personal gain. He would offer them all to the Great Spirit. Perhaps the Great Spirit would favor him by guiding him into knowing what must be done about Pamela and her spiteful, fork-tongued brother. The more he thought of her, the more his heart pained him. He must find a way to ease this pain, and soon.

Feeling Snow Owl's eyes on him, Strong Bear stopped and turned to face her. He could see in her eyes that she was looking into his soul. She could possibly even picture the woman in his heart, so clearly was he carrying her around with him!

"In your eyes there is a questioning," Strong Bear grumbled. "While I make offering to the Great Spirit you continue with your chores and cleanse your mind of wonder of your husband!"

"But you are so quiet," Snow Owl said, stilling her fingers of her sewing. "Why are you, Strong Bear? Are you not glad to be among your people again?"

"It is not for woman to question . . . only *do*," Strong Bear snapped, glaring down at Snow Owl. "Do as your husband commands. *Now*, *Ne-we-wah*."

Squaring his shoulders, Strong Bear stepped from his cabin, where the waters of the Green River flowed and gurgled softly past at the riverbank. A gentle breeze stirred the tree branches overhead while a red-winged blackbird sang in the far distance.

The area around the Miami village was alive with ash, elm, maple, oak, and birch trees. It was now awash with color from the dogwood and flowering crabapple. Violets, purple thistles, and black-eyed susans dotted the ground with their own lovely colors of spring.

Strong Bear began walking through his village of industrious people. Young girls were running about picking violets, praising the Great Spirit for his goodness in returning the warm weather. Wide fields in every direction were being planted with crops, the vista that lined the river one of field rather than forest.

There were a number of bark lean-tos, a few circular-bent-sticks-and-reed-mat-covered wigwams, and some log cabins. It was a place of peace and happiness. Strong Bear had discovered long ago how to survive. After seeing the many losses of his father due to constant warring when he had been chief, Strong Bear had learned the hard lesson of survival.

He had grown tired of burned villages and women and children crying for food when he had witnessed such things as a child. He had strived to make peace with the neighboring Miami tribes, even the Delaware, so that the women and children of his village would not live in fear. He had ignored the presence of British foreigners. His father had aligned himself with such forces but had chosen the French for such an alliance. But now the French were gone and Strong Bear was glad. He was a man of peace, not war.

In the center of the village Strong Bear arrived at the great medicine lodge, the place where the Miami Indians worshiped the Great Spirit. It was larger than any other dwelling in the village, its ten-foot walls built of split logs, with a door at either end.

With humility Strong Bear entered the sacred lodge. Center poles supported a gabled tree-bark roof that displayed three smoke holes, beneath which three fires were kept kindled at all times. Several large, fancily painted earthenware jars sat at the far end of the room.

Strong Bear made his way to these jars. His eyes still humbly lowered, he opened his drawstring pouch. One by one he shook gold nuggets onto the palm of his hand, then dropped them into the earthenware jar closest to him. The Great Spirit, the Ruler of the Universe, would be happy with the sacrifice and not only forgive Strong Bear for his weaknesses, but also bless Strong Bear's people. They would have the ability to grow much food and catch plenty of game so they would not be hungry. This was why the most valuable gifts must be sacrificed to the Great Spirit. He was all powerful and mighty and must be pleased so he would in turn show favor to these children of the forests.

Dropping the last gold nugget into the jar, Strong Bear backed from the dwelling. He would now go to his people and inform them of the recent offering. They would file into the medicine lodge and look into the jar. The gold nuggets inside the jar would reflect into their eyes and show them what was being done to thank the Great Spirit for his kindness toward them.

And now that his offering had been given to the Great Spirit and heartily accepted, Strong Bear must make his plans to bring Pamela back to his village. She was more valuable in Strong Bear's eyes than any amount of gold nuggets found swimming in water. Hopefully the Great Spirit would also approve of her, for had he not in his wisdom just touched Strong Bear's mind and heart with the answer as to how she would be his?

Tomorrow. He would go to claim Pamela as his, tomorrow!

Frazzled to the point of feeling faint, Lucas Boatright limped into Colonel Bradley's cabin. He was lucky to have survived the journey alone. But now he longed only for a bed to spread his weary body upon. Would he ever be the same again? The fear of Indians had urged him through the forest without stopping until he was safe again within the confines of the fort.

Yet now that he was there, the dread of what he had to report to Colonel Bradley made his insides roll. If anything should happen to the beautiful, innocent woman he would find it hard to live with the guilt. But if he didn't tell Colonel Bradley about her, he wouldn't live at *all*.

Soft candlelight danced from across the room where

Colonel Bradley stood attired only in his breeches, his face lathered with soap. Not seeing Lucas standing in the shadows, he removed a razor from a tooled leather box shaped like a book. Six other razors rested in the leather box, each numbered, one for each day of the week. If the box was turned toward the magnetic pole and the razors lay unused for a week, the blades would regain their sharpness.

Taking the one razor by its silver-and-tortoiseshell handle, Colonel Bradley began smoothing the lather from his face, leaning close to a cracked mirror, which hung from the wall behind his massive desk. Everything was quiet in the room except for a clock ticking in a steady rhythm on another wall. The room smelled pleasantly of expensive shaving cream and an opened bottle of Madeira.

Lucas moved from the shadows, closer to the desk. "Sir?" he said, his voice weak from exhaustion. "Colonel Bradley, I've returned, to report my findings."

Startled, Colonel Bradley scraped his razor blade too close to his face and broke the flesh. Spinning around, pressing a finger to the draining wound, he glared over at Lucas. "So you're finally back," he said, now popping the tip of his finger into his mouth, sucking blood from it. He placed the razor back in the box and wiped his face clean with a towel. "And what *do* you have to report? Where have the settlers squatted?"

Lucas combed his fingers through his unbraided hair, his eyes wavering nervously.

"Well? Cat got your tongue, or what?" Colonel Bradley demanded, slipping on a sparkling white shirt. "What did you find? Or did you lose them? Or have *you* been lost? It'd be more like something I could expect from you."

Lucas was tempted to use this as a way out of a situation that left a bitter taste on his tongue. But again he was reminded of the colonel's ruthless ways. Once the truth was known, Lucas would quickly face the firing squad.

"I trailed them all the way to their cabin," Lucas said hurriedly. "I know where they reside." He saw a glint enter the colonel's eyes and a tiny smile lift his narrow lips. "And, sir, only one other person makes residence there."

Now combing his wig, which rested on a "blockhead," Colonel Bradley lifted an inquisitive eyebrow. "The old man? The one who is ailing?" he said, chuckling low.

"No. He's dead," Lucas said. "It's another brother. I saw him run from the cabin, shoutin' the news of the father's passing to the two I was following."

Colonel Bradley kneaded his chin. "So there are only two left to dispose of, eh?" he said, smiling smugly. "And where did you say they made their residence?"

"A full day's ride north, on land the Miami Indians normally claim as theirs," Lucas quickly answered. "What do you plan to do about it?"

"Ladies in these parts are hard to come by, don't you think so, Lucas?" Colonel Bradley said, fitting the wig onto his head.

The low snicker accompanying the colonel's words sent goose bumps across Lucas's flesh. "Yes, I guess you could say that," he said, clearing his throat nervously.

Colonel Bradley eased down into the chair behind his desk. He began to drum his fingers on the arms of his chair. "But to get to her I must get rid of two brothers," he said contemplatively. "What would you say is the age of the other brother?"

"I'd say he's younger than even the lady," Lucas said, his spine stiffening. "You intend . . . to . . . kill her brothers?"

Colonel Bradley chuckled low. "No. I only intend to kill *one* of them," he said. He rose from his chair and hurried to the door. He lifted a hand and shouted at a Delaware Indian who was waiting outside to have an audience with him.

Lucas stood somberly by as he heard how the brothers were to be dealt with.

"Flying Deer, I've got a job for you," Colonel Bradley said, his eyes gleaming as he grasped the muscled shoulders of the young Delaware brave. "You will be paid well. I'll give you many hatchets with new, brightly painted red blades, if you'll do me a favor."

"Flying Deer likes British tools," the Indian said, his dark eyes eager. "What do you want me to do for you?"

"You're to go to a white man's dwelling and steal a young man to do with as you please once he is in your possession," Colonel Bradley said without feeling. "Take him as a slave, or take him to skin him alive at the stake. It doesn't matter to me. All that I care about is that you take him away from the cabin that Lucas is going to point out to you."

Lucas grew cold inside. His knees became rubbery weak. "Sir, I have only just returned," he said hoarsely. "I need rest."

Colonel Bradley flung a hand in the air, his wrist loose. "Get your needed rest; then you will show both me and Flying Deer where the cabin is," he said nonchalantly. "Flying Deer will take the young brother. I will follow the older brother into the forest when he leaves to hunt for food; then I, personally, will kill him." He chuckled low. "Only, when he is found he will look as though he were killed by an Indian, to draw suspicion away from *me*."

"And . . . the . . . lady?" Lucas dared to ask, his face pale of color.

"I will give her time to realize her losses, feel totally alone in the world, and then I will go to her, to offer her my services. This way she will come willingly to my bed," Colonel Bradley said, pouring Madeira into a crystal glass for himself. "It's perfect. Just . . . perfect."

Eight

A perfect woman, nobly planned,
To warm, to comfort, and command.
— Wordsworth

Pamela stood at the table, rolling out cookie dough. Out of the corner of her eye she watched Anthony arm himself to go and take a look around outside the cabin, and even farther. He had made no mention of fearing the English . . . only Strong Bear. He had said more than once that it didn't seem right for the Indian not to return to try and see Pamela again.

A tremoring ache troubled Pamela's heart every time she thought of Strong Bear. *She* didn't believe anyone would ever see him again. Anthony had been too hostile to him. But if he did decide to return, would it be because he missed *her*, or because he wanted to show Anthony that he would not be treated so callously by a white man!

She and Strong Bear had shared so much in such a short time. How could he forget those beautiful moments?

She would never forget them. Oh, how she longed to be with him again!

But common sense told her that she must adjust to life without him. It wasn't meant to be. It should never have *been*! Yet she would never let shame shadow thoughts of those blissful moments in Strong Bear's arms. She would treasure the memories, forever.

Dressed in his full buckskin attire, his rusty hair drawn back and secured into a pony tail at the back, Anthony slipped his hand into a pocket and withdrew two objects. The gold nugget picked up the light of the fire and made it shine. The withered turkey foot lay like a dead leaf in his palm.

Glancing over at Pamela, he sneaked the gold nugget back into his pocket. There was no need to show her that the Indian somehow possessed riches beyond any man's wildest dreams. It was apparent that she was fascinated enough with the Indian!

Going to the fireplace, Anthony reexamined and wondered again about the turkey foot, then pitched it into the fire and watched as flames consumed it. What a useless piece of trash to offer a man out of friendship! Yet Anthony would always wonder *why* it seemed so valuable to the Indian. It was as though it was as valuable as the gold nugget in Strong Bear's eyes.

Gold. Anthony hoped one day to go in search of the source of the gold!

"Anthony, you seem preoccupied this morning," Pamela said, cutting the cookie dough into the shape of gingerbread men. "Are you deciding not to go this morning? Do you feel we are safe enough now without you having to keep guard? Surely you've given up on the idea that Strong Bear might come to cause harm to you."

Anthony glowered as he turned to look at Pamela. Didn't she realize how lovely she was and that she was the sort men would fight over? This morning her lovely breasts curved above the low, round neckline of her gray, homespun dress with a ruffle at its hem. Her hair tumbled down her back; sunlight bathed her face in a soft, reflective glow from the open door; her delicate cheekbones bloomed with color.

It wasn't only Strong Bear that he feared might come for her. He had seen the look of lust in the British colonel's eyes when he had recognized that she was a woman in a man's garb. There had to have been a good reason why the British colonel let him and Pamela leave the fort. It had to be because of Pamela. The colonel surely planned to come for her. But when?

"I'm just thinkin' on our future this mornin' more than usual," Anthony said, still not sharing his worry of the British with Pamela *or* Robert. It was enough that *he* was losing sleep over it. No need in them all having the worry. "You know how Papa wanted this land. He wanted us to stay." Robert moved to his side, placing his eyeglasses on the bridge of his nose. Anthony swung an arm around his shoulder. "Robert, do you agree that we should stay?"

"Now that we're here, yes, I'd say let's stay," Robert said, his last words fading when in his mind's eye he was seeing the fresh mound of dirt not far from the cabin. "We can't leave Papa, you know."

"Pamela?" Anthony said thickly.

Pamela's eyes wavered. She wished to say that she only wanted to stay because of Strong Bear! But those thoughts must never be voiced aloud. Only her papa could have eventually understood her love of an Indian. Never was there a more compassionate man than her papa. "Yes, we should stay," she said dryly. "It's what Papa would want. This land was his dream. It is also *ours*."

Anthony grabbed his flintlock rifle and walked to the door. "Then, by damn, we'll *stay*," he said determinedly. He gave Robert a stern stare. "You get out there this mornin' and get goin' on that fence. There's nothin' to fear. I'll be out there somewhere keepin' watch."

"You can depend on me, Anthony," Robert said, combing his fingers nervously through his hair. "I'll get right to it."

Anthony nodded and hurried outside to his bay gelding. Swinging himself up into the saddle, he galloped away, taking a lingering backward glance over his shoulder at the cabin. This time it seemed unnatural sitting there in the cleared land of the forest, somehow . . . alien.

Pamela spread the skirt of her dress as she eased down onto a rush-bottomed chair and positioned herself at the spinning wheel close beside the fireplace. She was going to take full advantage of the free hour at hand to busy herself spinning wool, while her morning's baking had begun in the hot coals of the fire. She had rolled out Robert's favorite gingerbread cookies. She had prepared many flat round loaves of bread. A mincemeat pie was baking for Anthony. It had also been her father's favorite. But now he was gone. The swell of ground outside the cabin was a constant reminder of how she missed him.

After smelling the tantalizing aroma wafting from the kitchen to the outdoors where he was laboring over the fence, Robert had stopped long enough to return to the cabin to taste a sample of hot bread. He stepped up to the table and broke off a chunk and spread a slab of butter across it. "Do you think Anthony is ever going to relax and start living a normal life again?" he asked, taking a large bite of the buttered bread. "So far we've seen no signs of trouble. Surely both the British and the Indians are going to leave us be."

"I hope Anthony is careful," Pamela fretted, frowning up at Robert. "Each time he leaves I worry." She glanced toward the open door, where Robert was leaning, absorbing the fresh, warm air of morning. "I worry so about *you* working on the fence alone, Robert."

She busied herself with her spinning, her fingers lightly controlling the long flaxen fibers as they ran off the skein, onto the wheel. "I feel uneasy this morning, Robert," she fussed. Her blue eyes were shaded by a thick fringe of lashes as she looked up at him. "Please be careful? Take the rifle and powder horn with you. I feel as though we're not totally alone this morning. I think I'd feel better about you leaving the cabin, to work outside in the open, if you have a firearm real handy.''

Robert wiped his mouth free of butter with the sleeve of his shirt. ''Oh, horse feathers!'' he scolded. ''You worry too much.'' He grabbed his long flintlock rifle from beside the door and draped his powder horn across his shoulder. ''But if it'd make you feel better I'll take the rifle. You're right. If that damn Indian, Strong Bear, comes anywhere near this place I'll blow his head clean off'n him.''

Pamela paled, Robert's words cutting into her heart as though knives pierced her. When she had mentioned feeling as though she were being watched, and fearing this, she hadn't meant that she feared Strong Bear. She would have to learn to measure her words more carefully. She could never fear Strong Bear. It was the other Indians in this part of Kentucky that she knew to fear. And the British!

She could never believe that Strong Bear would harm anyone she loved, though the threatening tone he used with Anthony haunted her more oft than not. Would he want her badly enough to kill for her? Did he want this land on which the Boyd cabin stood badly enough to kill for it? Pamela had been weighing these questions in her mind while alone in her bed at night, when only night sounds pervaded the walls of the cabin.

Robert went to Pamela and bent a kiss to her cheek. ''Now you just be sure not to burn my gingerbread men.'' He laughed. ''I'll be in later to take a taste of one while it's good and hot.''

Pamela reached a hand to touch Robert on a cheek, looking up at him with moody eyes. ''Little brother, take care of yourself,'' she said, then laughed softly. ''But build a fence Anthony'd be proud of, though.''

''Don't you know? I'm a master carpenter,'' Robert said from across his shoulder as he moved back to the door. He stopped and looked outside, inhaling deeply as he breathed in the wondrous, fresh air. Sunlight was showing into the clearing but the forest muted it, making shadows deep into the space. Weeds grew lushly around the plants sown among the tree stumps in the clearing, yet Robert knew that seeds grew eagerly in the virgin soil. Yawning, he moved on outside, content.

Pamela's fingers lightly controlled the long flaxen fibers, listening to Robert earnestly at work again outside the cabin. With every sound of the hammer she breathed more easily. As long as she heard the hammer she knew that Robert was all right.

The sound of the great hammer pounding the wedges echoed farther than the cabin, far into the distance. They were set every few feet, to split the long hickory log into rails. Robert had told Pamela that one trunk would make enough rails for maybe thirty feet of fence.

Pamela's fingers tensed, and she looked toward the door, her breathing shallow: now she was not hearing the hammer. Everything was mutely quiet. The crow that she had only moments ago heard cawing from someplace close by was no longer making its racket. It was as though time was standing still as Pamela waited to hear the hammer resume its incessant pounding. But still, no sound.

"Perhaps Robert has stopped for a drink," Pamela whispered to herself, knowing that Robert kept a wooden bucket of water and a tin cup handy for refreshing himself on his long days of labor.

But her heartbeats threatened to drown her when the silence lasted for way too long. Fear of what may have happened pressed onto her heart, making her knees weaken as she rose from the chair and began inching her way toward the open door. She grabbed a rifle, loaded and primed it, then slipped from the cabin.

She searched the clearing ahead with her eyes and found the hickory log that had been in the process of being split into rails. Her stomach lurched and she felt a sick feeling grab her as she saw the large hammer on the ground where Robert should be standing. But no Robert.

Forgetting caution, more afraid for Robert than for herself, Pamela began to run blindly to the spot where her younger brother should have been. But when she got there her worst fears were confirmed, for all she found was Robert's eyeglasses on the ground, the lenses splintered, the gold frames bent. Her brother had been abducted, and most surely by . . . Indians.

Pamela's screams echoed through the forest as she fell to her knees and buried her face in her hands.

Colonel Bradley, with a bloody scalp hanging from the saddle of his horse, heard the screams and smiled. He laughed as he looked over at Anthony, who was draped lifeless across the back of his horse, his head free of its scalp, oozing blood. Everything was working as planned. The woman's screams meant that her younger brother had been abducted. Soon she would have reason to scream again, for when the horse carrying her older brother moved into the clearing close to the cabin, she would know that even worse had happened to him.

"I'll let her get frightened enough and then I'll return for her," Colonel Bradley chuckled to himself. "Soon, my pretty lady, you won't have reason to be lonesome again. You'll have *me*."

Now close enough to the clearing to set Anthony's horse's reins free, Colonel Bradley let them ripple from between his fingers. Then he leaned and gave Anthony's horse a slap on the rear, urging it into a gallop in the direction of the cabin.

Watching, to be sure the horse carried Anthony to the exact spot as planned, Colonel Bradley nodded, then wheeled his white stallion around and moved into the protective darkness of the forest. He had hungered to see the lovely miss again, knowing damn well that she was worth any sort of gamble taken. It would have been too risky to move closer to the clearing. Had she seen him just prior to her older brother's arrival on horseback, she would know that an Indian hadn't scalped her brother. She would have guessed quickly that it had been the English colonel!

Slipping his hand into the right pocket of his breeches, he brought out a gold nugget. Placing it before his eyes, he studied it. Now where would this settler get a gold nugget? Had he brought it with him to Kentucky, or had he found it *in* Kentucky?

"First I get me the lady," Colonel Bradley whispered. "And then I'll search for more *gold*."

Pamela's fright soon gave way to a sense of loneliness and isolation. She crept slowly to her feet, wiping scalding tears from her eyes. With her spine stiff, her heart cold, she began scanning the forest around her. Could the one who had abducted Robert be watching even now, ready to rush in, to get *her*?

"Oh, Anthony," she quietly cried. "Please hurry home. I'm . . . so . . . frightened."

The sound of hoofbeats approaching sent a faint glow of hope into Pamela's heart. She placed a hand to her throat, waiting for the horse to appear in the clearing. Anthony! He had most surely heard her scream and was returning, to see *why*. He would go in search of Robert. He would find him!

Her heart beat in unison with the horse's hooves against the ground. But, where was it?

And then finally she saw it in the far distance. It was traveling in the deep shadows, where the clearing reached out from the forest in muted grays. She cocked her head, seeing something strange . . . something amiss. Though she knew that the shadows were distorting her view, she still felt that she should be able to make out a figure sitting in the saddle.

Wiping her eyes, clearing them through the blur of tears, she peered more intensely at the horse. The color quickly drained from her face as she was able to see that it ferried Anthony's lifeless body.

Grief-stricken, terror leaping through her like bolts of lightning awakened her senses as she registered what had happened to her older brother; her eyes riveted to his bleeding hairless head, Pamela at first had no ability to scream.

But when Anthony's body began slipping from the loosened ropes that had been anchoring him to the horse's back and fell with a hollow thud on the ground at Pamela's feet with his sightless, golden-brown eyes looking up at her, screams finally rose from deep inside her.

Dropping the rifle to the ground she clasped her hands over her eyes and began screaming. Over and over again she screamed. . . .

Strong Bear rode straight-backed on his saddle of blankets, proud to have a reason to show why he was returning to this cleared section of forest, studded with a cabin where trees had once grown. To secure Pamela's love and the ownership of this land without shedding blood, Strong Bear was bringing Pamela's ailing father his own medicines with which to make him well. It was an offering of friendship.

Many pouches of medicinal herbs were anchored about Strong Bear's strawberry roan's neck. He would offer the magic of the Miami village shaman to the sick one, forcing himself to forget the hatred that had flashed in Anthony's eyes when he had discovered Strong Bear and Pamela together!

To Strong Bear, Pamela and the sacred land were more important than letting himself get caught up in the same seething hatred. When he spoke words of friendship to *anyone*, even a white man, it was forever!

Attired in his usual breechclout and moccasins and his face painted yellow to honor the spirits who would safeguard his journey today, Strong Bear rode steadily onward. His heart gladdened as he recognized the scenery, a signal that he was getting closer to Pamela all the time.

A broad smile lighted his face as his horse carried him through the forest. Pamela, his love, would most assuredly welcome him with a song in her heart to mirror the one in his own! If she had missed him as much as he had missed her, she would light up like the sunshine when she saw him at the door studded with friendship offerings. Hopefully her two brothers would welcome him, too.

Suddenly his thoughts of self were lessened. His heart skipped a beat when through the forest just ahead screams echoed toward him. His muscles corded, his eyes became two points of fire; his legs spurred his horse's flanks, recognizing the screams to be that which would only come from a woman. And the only woman within these borders was Pamela! And she would only be screaming if she had found herself in some sort of trouble!

Leaning low over the flying mane of his spirited horse, Strong Bear thundered on through the forest, weaving his way around the trees until he finally reached the clearing. Reining his horse to a stop only a few feet away from where he was quickly witness to a death scene, he looked from Pamela to Anthony, whose scalp was now missing, and then again to Pamela. Who was responsible for the white man's death? The Delaware? Was a Delaware Indian now carrying his prize, the white man's scalp, back to the British fort to receive his bounty? But, no. Surely not. The Delaware Indian would also have taken the woman's scalp.

Hearing the horse suddenly arriving and then stopping so close to where she stood, Pamela jerked her hands from her eyes and looked toward Strong Bear. Something clicked in her consciousness, recalling how Strong Bear had spoken so vengefully to Anthony and how Anthony had threatened Strong Bear. And now Strong Bear arrived just after Anthony's own grisly arrival!

"No . . ." she cried softly to herself, her heart breaking at the thought of what must certainly have happened. "Strong Bear, how . . . how *could* you? Why?"

She took a cautious step backward, faint with anguish. Strong Bear had most surely kidnapped Robert first, then killed Anthony later, and had now come for her.

Glancing quickly toward the rifle, which lay only a few footsteps away, her insides ached as she debated whether or not she should use it. Surely Strong Bear was not at all as she had first thought. He was a cold-blooded killer. He had used her for his own evil purposes and now he had come to *claim* her. Had he, in truth, wanted her all along just for a slave? He had made sure that no one was standing in the way of either her or the land that he had claimed from the first was his!

Strong Bear dismounted his horse. He studied Pamela with intensity, his pulse racing. Even in her grief she was ravishingly beautiful. Her dress billowed prettily about her as the wind blew against her, the ruffles of her dress seeming to foam around her delicate ankles.

But it was the fear and the hate in the depths of her eyes that daggered silent words he did not want to hear. Her look was accusing! She must think that he was the one who had committed this heinous crime. Strong Bear could not let her continue believing such a wrong any longer!

Taking wide steps toward Pamela, he watched as she grew more ashen in color and even weaved as though she might faint. Hurrying to her, he clasped her shoulders and stared down into her limpid blue eyes. As she looked guardedly up at him a daring glint entered there. She was proving to Strong Bear that she was still as strong-willed as before. He could even feel it in the way her shoulders stiffened beneath his fingers. Her hatred for him was giving her the strength momentarily robbed by her grief.

"First you steal my younger brother away and then you kill and scalp my older brother?!" Pamela found the strength to shriek, though every nerve inside her was tingling with denial. Would the man she loved do this brutality? Rage quickly replaced love!

"Why didn't you kill me that day you were watching me in the forest?" she screamed, tossing her hair back from her eyes. "I'm the same as dead now with both my brothers gone from my life! First my father dies and then my brothers are taken from me? It isn't fair! It isn't fair!"

She doubled her fingers into tight fists and began pummeling them against Strong Bear's chest, though it sorely pained her to do so. She didn't want to hit him! She

wanted to be swallowed up in his arms, to be comforted!
But this could never be. He was no longer the man she had
known when she had given herself to him so willingly. He
was a savage. A . . . red-skinned savage! Even now he
wore a fearful yellow paint around his eyes that only
savages would wear!

When Pamela's arms weakened and her fists became too
sore, she let them drop to her sides. Even then did Strong
Bear tolerate her instead of act threatening. When he
released his hold of her and began gesturing with his hand
as he talked, Pamela blinked a renewed onslaught of tears
from her eyelashes.

"You have so little faith in the man you have declared
to love?" Strong Bear said, his eyebrows rising questioningly. His gaze shifted to Anthony. "You blame Strong
Bear for death of brother? You speak of other brother who
was abducted? You said your father is dead? You are now
alone?"

"Isn't that what you want?" Pamela cried, doubling her
hands into tight fists at her sides. "Well, I've something to
say to you, Strong Bear. You've done this all for nothing.
I'll never be your slave! I'll find a way to escape. You'll
see!"

She stood up on tiptoe and spoke into his face. "Where
have you taken Robert?" she hissed. "And don't act as
though you don't know what I'm saying. You abducted
him. I know it! Where is he, Strong Bear? Where is he?"

A sparkle entered Strong Bear's eyes, enjoying the re-
kindled spirit in this woman! But he had much to prove to
her to make her believe him. "Strong Bear not responsible
for any harm that has come to either of your brothers," he
said thickly.

Pamela sighed. "Please don't play me for a fool by
pretending innocence," she spat. "Surely before you and I
met face-to-face you studied my family's movements for
days before choosing how you would deal with each one
of us, separately. Well, my whole family is now gone.
Why not kill me also?"

Tears welled up in her eyes as she looked down at Anthony. "Poor Anthony," she cried. "My precious brother."

Then fire entered her eyes again as she brushed tears from their corners. "Where is Robert? Take me to him," she flatly ordered.

"Strong Bear knows not of Robert's whereabouts," he said, folding his arms across his chest. "You not listen to truths now? You will *later*."

"Strong Bear, no matter what you say, you are wasting your words," she said, now solemnly ready to accept her fate. "My main concern now is for my brother Robert. Please . . . take me to him."

"There is no Robert," Strong Bear grumbled, tiring of bantering with her. And whether she liked it or not, he was going to assume responsibility of her. He would not leave her here to be taken by the Delaware. It was apparent that not only had they killed her one brother, but also had abducted the other.

But she was not ready to believe anything Strong Bear had to say. He would take her to his village and prove to her that he meant only good *for* her. She would eventually believe him and would become his first wife of importance, Snow Owl *second*.

Though tragically achieved, this white woman with eyes the color of the rivers and sky was free to love. If Strong Bear could lead her into loving him again, it would be a special, devoted love! Somehow he would erase the hate from her heart. He would treat her as one does a Miami princess!

"Come. Strong Bear will take you *na-min-o-gish*, to safety of Miami village beside the Green River," he said, gently taking her arm. "*Doges*. You will be no safer than when with Strong Bear's people."

Pamela stumbled over the hem of her skirt as he began leading her to his horse. Tears again erupted. "You said there was no Robert," she softly cried. "That must mean that you killed him. You killed him and—"

Strong Bear turned on a heel and faced her. He looked down into her eyes, his own flashing. "Strong Bear not kill brother called Robert," he said flatly. "Not *see* Robert."

Then he again resumed half dragging her to his horse. But when she shrieked and jerked away from him, he turned and stared after her as she ran away from him to drop on her knees beside Anthony.

Reaching her side, Strong Bear took her by an arm and urged her back to her feet. "You must leave him. You go now with Strong Bear," he said, not so much in a command, as in a pleading manner.

"I must first give Anthony a proper burial," Pamela said, sniffling. "To leave him like this is . . . is . . . barbarian. His body will be . . . be . . . mauled by forest animals. Please, Strong Bear. He must be properly buried. Then I will go peacefully with you."

Eager to get this over with and to get her away from this place of death, and also understanding the need of proper burial rites of a loved one, Strong Bear complied with her wishes. He even accepted a shovel as she handed it to him. And after Anthony was buried beside the fresh grave of their father, and Pamela had spoken soft words over the grave, Strong Bear asked for a white cloth. Secured to a pole, it served as a flag. Strong Bear raised it above the grave, Miami-style, so the Great Spirit could find the grave of his future wife's departed brother.

Pamela was momentarily in awe of Strong Bear's understanding nature. But she felt as though he was doing all of this to trick her, so that she would warm up to him. For now she would go with him. But she would search for Robert in his village and if she did not find him, she would escape and seek help for herself and Robert at the British fort. Though she knew that the British colonel in charge of this particular fort was a heartless bastard, she had no choice but to go to him.

With her head held high, trying to show strength and courage, Pamela walked beside Strong Bear toward his beautiful strawberry roan. When black smoke began bil-

lowing from the cabin door and she recognized the smell
of burned cookies, her heart began a slow aching. Robert
had looked forward to his Gingerbread men. But now they
were gone, as was he.

Thinking enough time had passed for Pamela to bury her
brother and to discover that she was totally alone in this
wilderness, Colonel Bradley rode toward the cabin, his
heart beating wildly with excitement. He felt that this was
the perfect time for him to arrive, for she would most
surely welcome any assistance he would offer her. She
would return to the fort with him and eventually become
his *wife*.

Riding the horse right up to the cabin, Colonel Bradley
dismounted. Adjusting the saber at his side, and feeling to
see if his wig was in place, he stepped up to the door,
wondering why it stood ajar. He was even now aware no
smoke coiled from the chimney as he approached. Surely
the lovely lady, though alone, would keep a fire blazing,
for she would want warm, not cold, meals.

A burned smell stung his nose as he entered the cabin.
His eyes searched the still darkness, the hair rising at the
nape of his neck when no flurry came to life.

"She's gone," he said in a strained whisper. He flung a
gloved hand into the air. "Damn it, she's gone!" he
shouted, unbelieving, as the truth rang in his ears.

Stomping angrily to the fireplace, he knelt and tested the
ashes. "Cold. Damn cold," he growled. His nose wrinkled at the smell of burned cookies and bread. He even saw
the remains of a burned pie in a pie tin.

"She left in a hurry," he said, rising back to his full
height. His face creased into a dark frown, recalling the
gold nugget that he had found in Anthony's breeches
pocket. Like a man gone mad, he began ransacking the
cabin, searching for more gold. When he found none he
determined that Anthony had most surely brought it with
him from Williamsburg.

Gathering all the weapons he could find in the cabin, he rushed back outside and mounted his horse. He rode away, cursing. Who had foiled his plans? He vowed to find out. It was surely a damn Indian . . . but which one?

Nine

✦⟞⟝✦

If ever any beauty I did see
Which I desired, and got, 'twas but a dream of thee.
                                        —Donne

Weary boned, yet having been too stubborn to succumb to her need to sleep on the long journey from her cabin with Strong Bear, Pamela felt no emotions whatsoever when she saw the smoky fires in the distance. Though she soon would be arriving at Strong Bear's village, it did not mean the same to her as it would have in other circumstances. Before the tragedies that had befallen her brothers, she had even dreamed of accompanying Strong Bear to his village, to become a part of his everyday life.

The thought of awakening in his arms every morning had flooded her with a sweet cozy feeling when she let her mind wander to such fantasies during her long days of chores.

But now it was oh, so different. She could even consider herself a captive. He most surely hadn't meant anything that he had said about her becoming his wife. All along he had looked to her as a future slave. He could have many unpleasant things planned for her, most of which made a coldness almost numb her with fright.

Yet up to now on this journey to his village Strong Bear had not acted so much like one who possessed her, but, instead, like her *protector*, as though he had assumed responsibility for her. No man could have been, or could be, as gentle as Strong Bear had been to her. Even now as he held her securely on his horse, very close to his body behind her, she felt only tenderness in his touch. If she could let herself, she could even believe that he was innocent of the crimes of which she was accusing him. When they had stopped and had shared parched corn from a pouch on this journey north, it had been almost the same as when they had shared such sweet moments those times before tragedy had struck and had left Pamela without a family.

But then she would recall just who he was and what he must have done to enable him to be free to take her as his own. Anthony was dead. Robert had disappeared! Surely Strong Bear was responsible for both ugly deeds. If the British or the Delaware were responsible, *she* wouldn't have been spared. With an icy heart, she could so vividly recall the women's scalps hanging on the pegs in Colonel Bradley's office. It would make no sense at all that she would be spared the same sort of cruel death! And why was Robert abducted, not killed and scalped? Why had Anthony been the one chosen to be killed in such a horrible way?

No. None other than Strong Bear could be responsible. And she would remember. With an ache in her heart, she would remember. Forever!

Yet, where was Anthony's scalp? Wouldn't Strong Bear have kept the scalp after having gone to the trouble of taking it?

This unanswered question was the only thing that gave Pamela a ray of hope, for just perhaps Strong Bear was innocent of her brothers' fates. Until she had proof, though, hate for him would be imbedded in her heart. And soon she would escape to try to find Robert. What could she do but go to the British fort for help? Surely the British colonel would see the need of her finding the last surviving member of her family. She needed family now, as never before in her life. She had never felt so alone, as now.

To keep herself awake, Pamela had busied herself by watching all about her as she had traveled on horseback with Strong Bear. To find her way back to the British fort, she had tried to memorize every turn in the forest that Strong Bear had taken. And while doing so, the land again awed her, the land her father had brought her to. Never had she seen such sumptuous land. The tales of huge buffalo herds feeding on great stands of cane, and deer at every salt lick, had been true.

The land was there for the taking, except many obstacles blocked the way of settlers brave or brazen enough to try to claim it. If the American settlers didn't have the Indians to fight off, then they had the British. And Pamela's father and brothers had known the dangers. Even *she* had known the dangers and been willing to risk it all for a piece of this Kentucky wilderness.

And it seemed that she had lost it all. Perhaps soon even *she* would be dead. If she escaped and couldn't find her way to the fort, what would her fate be? If the forest animals didn't claim her, there were many other ways to die when alone and lost!

But until her last breath was snuffed from her body she would focus on surviving. She was aware that many tribes of Indians were in the surrounding area. Pamela had studied Indians while in school and knew that the Indian population increased and decreased in the fall, depending on hunting or sugar-making seasons. When the Indians packed up to move, they took everything with them.

But this was spring, fast turning into summer, so Pamela knew many Indians would swarm over the area and the dangers numbered many. To get to the British fort, she would have to avoid all Indian villages, at all cost.

But she would succeed in her endeavors! In Williamsburg she had been a high-spirited tomboy, having been raised the only girl among brothers. She had loved to show off her strength and agility to Anthony and Robert. She had ridden the meanest horses bareback and had broken in horses Anthony and Robert had shied away from.

Pamela was well rounded and sure of herself. She knew that she was very feminine, called dainty by most, and that she had the strength necessary for survival. And she *would* survive. Perhaps she was the last surviving member of the Boyd family. But she would never give up hope of Robert still being alive. She would search until she found him. He would be her reason for surviving.

It was this strength, this courage, that kept Pamela sane, for if she let herself recall Anthony and how he had looked up at her with sightless eyes after falling from his horse to lie on the ground at her feet, she could quickly lose her grip on reality. Whenever that gruesome revelation of his murder would enter her mind, Pamela was somehow finding a way to magically sweep it away. Crying would come later. In the eyes of Strong Bear she must look brave. Never, never weak.

With a stiff reserve, Pamela entered the Indian village behind Strong Bear. Night was closing down softly on the peaceful village. Owls called out and an occasional dog barked. A drum was beating a steady rhythm in the far distance.

Pamela could feel eyes following her as Strong Bear guided his steed past the dwellings. Though Pamela kept her eyes fixed straight ahead, not wanting to give the Indians an opportunity to see the fear in her eyes, she had seen just before entering the village that it was an assortment of different types of dwellings. She had seen many bark lean-tos, wigwams, and log cabins.

This had come as a surprise to her, for she had thought only to find the conical types of dwellings, the tepee that she had always associated with Indians. As she was becoming aware, some even lived in better homes than she had seen in Kentucky. Didn't this make them less than savage?

For the moment, this gave Pamela another reason to have hope. She was recalling Anthony's feelings for Indians. Hadn't he said that he felt that as long as he behaved civilly toward the Indians, so would they, toward *him*?

A coldness surged through Pamela. Anthony had been wrong! He had saved an Indian's life, then to have his life taken by the same Indian. Surely the Indians didn't even know the meaning of "civil." Even the man that she had so foolishly let herself fall in love with had two sides to his nature. With Anthony's death Strong Bear had proved himself to be a cold-blooded, murderous savage. And soon he would surely show *her* his savage side. When he discovered that she was in no way going to cooperate with him, oh, what would he do to her?

Pamela was torn with conflicting feelings. She sorely hated him now, yet it was impossible for her to erase the memories of what they had shared together. The beauty of their union could never be duplicated with another man. He had been gentle, sweet, and understanding. There had been such warmth in his eyes. His touch had been so loving. He had treated her so tenderly!

Yet it had all been pretense! He had only been these many things to her to win her. But win her for what? She did not want anything but freedom from this Indian who had proved to be more savage than . . . man.

Soon she would surely know the answers to all of her troubled questions, for now he was transporting her to a dwelling separate from the others.

When Strong Bear reined his horse to a halt before a large, neat cabin, Pamela's pulse began to race. Would she soon know of her true fate? When she entered Strong Bear's cabin, what *were* his plans for her? Was she about to be ravaged, this time taken by force instead of joined with him *willingly*, as she had before? Would she have to bow down to him, be his slave, taken sexually at his beck and call?

Setting her lips into a stubborn, straight line, Pamela knew that she would steal his knife and plunge it deeply into his heart should he treat her inhumanely, as though she were a female dog being attacked by every sniffing male dog within reach. Then she would flee.

Avoiding eye contact with Strong Bear, Pamela stiffened as she realized his absence behind her on his saddle of blankets, knowing that he had dismounted from his lovely strawberry roan. She flinched when she felt his hands on her waist, lifting her from the horse. Still he was gentle. Still he treated her as something precious. She scarcely even felt the ground meet her feet as he set her onto it ever so gently. And as he placed a hand to her elbow and led her into the cabin, he still treated her as though she were a delicate flower.

But Pamela would not let herself be fooled by such kindness. As he had been from the very first, he was still playing a game with her. Wouldn't it be simpler for him if she would go easily into his bed because of his gentle ways? Surely he was wise beyond his years, used to scheming his way to the end. Well, this time, he would not succeed so easily. Pamela would fight for her dignity to the very end, if it came down to that.

The warmth from the interior cookfire touched Pamela's face in a soft caress, the night air having just begun to cool her on the last few miles of the journey. The savory smell of turkey breast cooking with onions in the pot over the fire stirred the hungry ache gnawing at her insides. The fire's glow lit the interior of the cabin, throwing in relief Strong Bear's warring paraphernalia and many beautiful animal pelts hanging from the walls.

But it was not the bows and arrows, war clubs, or furs that caught Pamela's eye. Her heart lurched when she discovered a beautiful Indian squaw sitting quietly beside the fire, sewing the intricate silk appliqué that Pamela had read the Miami were so skilled in making.

It was apparent that this beautiful maiden was Strong Bear's wife, for she would not be dutifully there, waiting for him, if she were not. Pamela couldn't shake the sudden seizure of jealousy that shook her. She now felt twice betrayed! She had given herself to Strong Bear willingly and he already had a wife!

At last Pamela truly understood her worth to Strong Bear. Since he already had a wife, she could be nothing more than a possession! Even the wife could order Pamela around, forcing her to do the daily chores!

Pamela was dying a slow death inside. She stifled a sob behind a hand, suddenly feeling degraded, so very . . . very used. How could she have ever seen Strong Bear as anything but an enemy? How could she have been so foolish?

Her eyes wavering, Pamela let her gaze wander over the Miami Indian squaw. Oh, wasn't she beautiful with her large, dark eyes? Wasn't she so petite and lovely in her buckskin dress and leggings?

Then Pamela's gaze found something else of interest to capture her attention. Gold earrings. The Indian squaw was wearing gold earrings! How could the Indians acquire anything of such wealth? No white traders would part with anything so precious in exchange for animal pelts. Surely these were taken, not given! Pamela was learning more and more about the man she had given her heart to, and none of it was pleasant! She had never known him at all.

Strong Bear guided her more deeply into the cabin and urged her to settle on a pad of milkweed down. But finally she was given a reason to smile smugly when she saw the look of anger in the Indian squaw's eyes as she looked from Pamela, back to Strong Bear. It was apparent that the squaw did not approve of another woman being brought into her cabin, and especially a *white* woman. Surely the Indian women hated white women even more than white *men*. Were not white women a threat in more ways than one? Strong Bear's plan just might go awry because of his wife not appreciating having another woman brought into their cabin!

"*Kow-e*," Strong Bear said to Snow Owl in greeting,

moving to position himself on his haunches before the fire between Pamela and Snow Owl.

Snow Owl slammed her sewing down on the mat beside her. She glared over at Strong Bear, yet he would not humor her by looking her way. He knew that he was wrong to bring a white woman into a dwelling of a Miami man and wife. Yet, he was the chief, and the chief did anything he pleased and she knew not to question him about his decision.

Snow Owl let her gaze scour Pamela's features. She studied her with venom in her heart and fire in her eyes. Yet a slow smug smile spread across her face when she saw how pale and ugly the white woman was. Even her eyes were pale as the sky. Surely Strong Bear saw nothing intriguing about her. He had surely captured her to enjoy one night, then discard the following day.

No. Snow Owl had nothing to fear from this white woman's presence. If Strong Bear took the white woman to bed he would find that even in this way the white woman would prove to be colorless. Surely anyone as pale and ugly could not stir anything either inside the powerful chief's heart or in his loins.

No. The white woman was no threat to Snow Owl. Snow Owl would just be patient with her husband for wanting to use such entertainment this one night. Tomorrow night he would again be Snow Owl's! Perhaps Strong Bear would even let Snow Owl have the white woman to use as a slave once he fed his lust for her flesh.

This made Snow Owl happy. She had always wanted a white slave. She would make this white woman carry all of the wood . . . build all of the fires . . . cook all of the food. Snow Owl could spend more time *sewing*!

"My *me-tam-sah*, leave Strong Bear alone with *wa-bah-shik-ki me-tam-sah*," Strong Bear said flatly, casting Snow Owl a sidewise glance. "You go outside dwelling. Sit. Wait."

Snow Owl's insides tightened, having heard Strong Bear compare the white woman to a bright, white stream. Was he seeing her differently than Snow Owl? Did he not see her as pale and *ugly*? Could he enjoy time alone with the white woman and actually decide to choose her as first wife over Snow Owl? Had this white woman been the one who had only recently caused Strong Bear's eyes to take on such a faraway cast?

Oh, the thought of being replaced by anyone was pure torture to Snow Owl's heart. But should that woman be white, Snow Owl would never be able to live with the shame!

Strong Bear turned his eyes directly to Snow Owl. A frown creased his brow as he glared at her. "My wife, did you not hear my command?" he grumbled. "Go. Sit outside. Strong Bear wants private audience with white woman."

Her heart pounding, echoing in her ears it was so severe, Snow Owl rose quickly to her feet. For a moment she let herself forget exactly who Strong Bear was and looked fearlessly into his eyes, then backed away from him when seeing how such disobedience caused his eyes to burn and his jaw to set firmly.

Bowing her head, Snow Owl crept from the cabin. Then when she was out of Strong Bear's sight she raised a doubled fist into the air and cursed not only him, but also the woman who was an intrusion in her life. Somehow Snow Owl would make the white woman pay. If not as a slave, something more shaming than even that.

Sitting down beside the cabin door, Snow Owl looked straight ahead, seeing nothing, yet feeling her standing in this village of Miami was threatened, as never before . . . a standing she prized much more than the marriage itself.

In the Indian Delaware village a great semicircle of gleaming copper faces looked up at Robert where he stood tied to a stake, naked. The hot day had an ominous, waiting sort of quality as he thought of death. The murderous redskins were surely waiting, taunting him, later to strip the hair from his head.

The sun was at its zenith, burning its way down from the pearl-blue sky. Robert could feel the weight of its heat on his bare chest and bound, outstretched arms and legs. He kept his face ducked as much as possible, but not enough so that he was not conscious of all that was happening around him.

Without the aid of his eyeglasses he could only see a blur of color and movement in front of him. But he knew that he was surrounded by many giggling, tormenting squaws. As a drum was beating from somewhere close by the squaws rhythmically chanted a tuneless song. And as they chanted, they danced. There was a continuous flash of gleaming copper faces, metal armbands, greased skin, feathers, and beaded necklaces before his weak, near-sighted eyes.

The squaws began to take turns moving closer to Robert, looking up at him with eyes flashing haughtily. With them now so close he could see that they wore knee-length skirts, beaded, fringed blouses, and headbands of wampum. Their cheeks, eyelids and ear rims had been carefully colored with bright red rouge.

Robert tensed as one of the squaws moved to stand before him, holding a sharpened mussel-shell tweezer. With hate and mockery in her dark eyes she began plucking the hair from his chest, watching him for his reaction.

When he did not flinch another squaw stepped forward with a sharp knife. Kneeling down before him she began to scrape his pubic hairs away, deliberately cutting into his flesh more deeply than the hair. Blood began to run in slow streams across his shrunken manhood.

Cold sweat beaded Robert's brow. He bit his lower lip to keep from crying out in pain as the squaws now took turns scraping and tweezing more hair from his body. His flesh felt as though it was on fire. He could now feel the blood trickling across his bare toes.

Yet he still did not cry out. The squaws were surely testing him for courage. To cry out might mean instant death.

Robert tried to focus his thoughts on other things. The first to come to mind were his brother and sister. The pain inside his heart now seemed more severe than that of his flesh, for surely his brother and sister's fate would be no less than his. Were they even still alive? Or had they been taken as slaves to another Indian village?

Robert had heard the grisly tales of captives taken from the Ohio riverboats. Some were kept as slaves. Others were burned at the stake or skinned virtually alive. If the abducted party was lucky, their relatives could get them back by sending money to the British who would buy them from the Indians and return them to their families.

But most of those abducted were never heard from again.

Robert's pulse raced as he waited for the knives playing along his body to begin removing his skin. Through his hazy vision he could see other stakes in the distance. Earlier in the day after his arrival, several braves had returned victorious from a raid on other white people. The Indian scalp whoops had been so numerous the very air had seemed to expand with the din. The plunder from the battle had weighted their horses down. Meat from slaughtered cattle now graced the cooking pots of every wigwam. The captives had been slowly burned at the stakes.

Robert would never forget the screams. They were forever imbedded in his memory. But soon, he surely would have no ability to remember. He would also be killed. Slowly, yet deliberately.

Trying to control his breathing, fearing that breathing heavily would show the squaws that he was in severe pain, Robert raised his chin to continue looking brave in the eyes of his tormentors.

Ten

Young lover, tossed 'twixt hope and fear,
Your whispered vow and yearning eyes.
—Hayne

Alone now with Strong Bear, Pamela scarcely breathed. Her gaze roamed about the room, seeing so many things that spoke of intimacy between Strong Bear and the Indian squaw. The blankets, the rich furs, most surely used when together at night. And now that he had ordered her from the cabin, did Strong Bear plan to make Pamela a substitute wife for this night? Would he force her? Her heart pined for the way it could have been! But now not only her brothers' misfortunes stood in the way, but also a wife.

She looked toward the door, wondering how the Indian squaw could leave, knowing just what might transpire between her husband and another woman. But Pamela had heard the command in Strong Bear's voice, had seen it in the coldness of his eyes as he had looked at his wife. All the while with Pamela, he had spoken much more kindly to her, as though respect was more in order for her, than for his own wife. Indian women more than likely were the true slaves, not the American settlers who were stolen for that purpose.

Pamela couldn't see herself ever bowing down to any man, not even if she loved him with all of her heart. She had hoped that when she became a part of Strong Bear's life their relationship would be one of total sharing.

Then a sadness crept into her eyes. She must forget comparing what was and what might have been. The only thing that was important to her now was finding a way to escape and to find Robert. In her eyes, Strong Bear no longer existed. She only wished that she could make her heart realize the same! Even now, in his presence, she understood the occasional crazy skipping beat of her heart. How could she *not* experience feelings for what they had shared in the privacy of the forest? That time it had been beautiful beyond description. Hopefully the memory would lessen eventually, as well as the longing deep within her! He was not worth a moment of the misery she was now feeling!

Straightening the skirt of her dress about her on the soft milkweed-down mat, lifting her chin with determination, Pamela looked toward Strong Bear. He was still sitting quietly on his haunches, staring into the flames of the fire.

"So what are your intentions for me now?" she said dryly. "Now that you possess me, do you intend to . . . to . . . ravage me? If so, Strong Bear, you will have to kill me first."

Strong Bear turned his eyes slowly to Pamela, troubled anew by her doubts of him and her haunting image of loveliness. Though her hair was now tangled from the long ride on the horse, it did not detract from the beauty of her vulnerable face, of her sublime, long neck, and her delicate cheekbones flaming with color.

His gaze shifted lower. His heart soared when seeing the soft swells of her breasts where they lay heaving in her low-swept bodice. She was like maple syrup, hard to resist. *He* was like a spirit who had come to life again in her presence, never having been so captivated by a woman before, as now. She was awesome, yet winsome, in her beauty.

And she *was* free now to be totally his.

But she must again want Strong Bear as much as he wanted her. One day she would know the full truths of who had taken her brothers from her. But for now Strong Bear would be wasting his words to try to make her believe him. In her state of mind she would not listen to reason.

Perhaps she even wanted to believe that he was guilty! It would make her rejection of him and his people that much easier. Hadn't he seen her reaction to his having a wife? It had seemed that seeing Snow Owl in his dwelling had caused Pamela more hurtful anger. Didn't the white man take two wives? Perhaps not!

But Pamela would learn that Strong Bear would have as many wives as he pleased. He was a powerful chief! He always got what he asked for, even *her*! He would give her time to get over her grief; then he would make her realize how things were to be, and with whom!

Destiny had brought them together, and Strong Bear would do nothing to change destiny.

"Ravaging is a harsh word to use while in Strong Bear's presence," he said thickly. "I believe that what we shared . . . what Strong Bear wishes to share again . . . would be more gently called love. But Strong Bear knows that you are speaking from hurt, not from how you truly feel. I will be patient. You will learn the truths and then you will wish that you could take back the ugly words you have spoken to the man who loves you."

Slowly shaking her head, Pamela sighed. He was still trying to trick her with gentle words. It was becoming tiresome. She looked toward the door, thinking again of escape. But that would have to come later. Surely Strong Bear would leave her alone while seeing to his duties outside the cabin. She would just bide her time, play along with him. At least she now felt safe with him. He had convinced her that he did not have ravaging in mind after all.

But, perhaps later, when he would catch her off guard?

"You confess to loving me. If what you say is the truth, why not let me go to search for my other brother?" she found herself saying, finding it impossible not to dwell on Robert's safety. "Why not let me go to the British fort? I would be much better off there than with . . . with . . . you. My place is not with Indians, but with my own kind."

Anger enflamed Strong Bear. How could she mention the British and ridicule him, an *Indian*. When they had been making love it had not seemed to matter that their skin coloring or cultures differed. Had her feelings changed so much that she even hated this about him?

"Your place is not with the British," he grumbled. "Your kind is not the British. You are not *like* the British. Your place is with *me*. When your mind becomes clear, you will know that what I say is true."

He rose to his full height, towering over Pamela as he walked to the back of the cabin. When he returned, Pamela strained her neck to see what he had in the wooden basin, discovering that it was filled with some sort of liquid.

"The British are evil," he said, now splashing a liquid solution of sweet fern onto his face, removing the yellow paint. "Many moons ago soldiers came to the Indian camp, placed Strong Bear's ancestors in a pen, and then the evil soldiers smashed my people's heads, one by one. Only a few Miami escaped, unharmed."

Pamela paled, raising her hands to her throat. "Why, that's . . . that's ghastly," she said in a murmur. "How could they?"

"The surviving Miami allied themselves with the French," he said, wiping his face clean with a soft buckskin cloth, now smelling of a woodsy perfume, the Indian "toilet water."

Strong Bear went and tossed the sweet fern liquid out the door, then returned and settled down again before the fire, this time fully on the milkweed-down mats with his legs crossed. He reached behind him and picked up a long-stemmed pipe festooned with many colorful feathers and tamped down a load of kinnikinnick, a mixture of dried leaves and tobacco, into its calumet bowl. He held the pipe before him in both hands and inhaled, then exhaled. The rich, pungent smoke wafted into the air.

Strong Bear looked over at Pamela. "It is best that Strong Bear now lead his people into making friends with American settlers rather than be scalp takers for the British," Strong Bear said dryly. "Strong Bear is chief. Strong Bear is *wise*."

Pamela gasped softly. "How can you say that after what has happened to my family?" she cried. "Strong Bear, when are you going to quit lying to me? When?" Just because he had confessed to not being British-enlisted did not mean he would refrain from taking a scalp if there was a reward in it. Wasn't she the reward . . . in his eyes?

Strong Bear's eyes wavered, her words weighing heavier on his heart. "Again your words accuse me," he said softly. "Again Strong Bear will ignore it." He nodded toward the kettle of steaming food. "You must be hungry. You *eat*."

There was no denying how hungry Pamela was, yet the thought of food made her almost ill. The memory of Anthony was too fresh in her mind. And there was the worry of Robert. How could she relax beside this warm, inviting fire and eat, while uncertain of Robert's fate . . . ?

Hot tears threatened to spill over her cheeks when she let herself dwell on recent events. She hung her head and sniffled. Oh, sweet and gentle Anthony. He had never harmed anyone in his life. He had even saved an Indian's life! And now he was dead, so young. His life had only just begun; he had seen such promise in this new land.

As Pamela now saw it, this land was hell . . . a place of

viciousness! Surely she could never see it as lovely again. Kentucky would surely be a reminder of what she had lost in life.

Wiping a stream of tears from her cheeks, not wanting Strong Bear to see her weakness, Pamela lifted her chin and firmly set her jaw. "No thank you," she said quietly. "Food will not fill the emptiness I am now experiencing. But perhaps if you would lead me to my brother Robert . . . ?"

Strong Bear's head turned slowly. There was no anger in his eyes this time, just a hurtful sort of expression. "Do you not hear Strong Bear when he tells you he knows not of younger brother?" he said hoarsely, holding his pipe down away from his lips. "He is not in this village of Miami. He was taken surely by the Delaware. They practice slavery quite well."

With a nod he looked toward the bunks. "If you do not wish to eat, then you may wish to rest," he said, his eyes reflecting a gentleness. "You are free to eat or rest. Strong Bear wishes to enjoy pipe. Nothing more."

Pamela felt torn. If she took his suggestion and went to the bunk, which looked so invitingly soft with its thick layer of furs, would he wait until she was asleep, to join her on its wide platform made for two?

But, perhaps, it would be best to test him and get it over with. She could pretend to be asleep; if he joined her, she could catch *him* off guard and knock him away from her. There were many weapons for her to choose from, should she get the chance. A sheathed knife lay quite close to the bunk she had already chosen with her eyes.

"Yes," she said, stretching her arms over her head, pretending a heavy, lazy yawn. "Perhaps it would be best if I get some rest."

She smiled her most winsome smile toward him. "Thank you for your kindness, Strong Bear."

As she rose to her feet, she was stopped in mid-step when he spoke from behind her. "Trust will return in time," he said, his voice uneven, filled with emotion. "Strong Bear knows the art of patience."

The skirt of Pamela' s dress rustled against her petticoat as she turned to face him. She was again struck by his handsomeness as her gaze settled on his wide, sensuous mouth.

She tried to fight the sensual feelings stirring inside her, forgetting for the moment that he had taken so much from her. He had a young man's hard, lean form. He was tall, his height framed by a well-muscled body. His handsome face spoke to her in seductive, forbidden ways.

But she could not control her heart, which seemed to be relaying messages to her brain that could not be blocked. She was still attracted to Strong Bear in ways she'd never felt before. She could see her feelings mirrored in the depths of his heavenly dark eyes, sparking her senses alive. Knowing how she still appealed to him frightened her.

Feeling a blush coloring her cheeks, the result of Strong Bear's almost hypnotic stare, Pamela abruptly turned her back to him and hurried to a bunk.

Her heart was pounding. She felt a strange sort of light-headedness sweep through her when she realized where her thoughts had taken her. She curled up on the softness of the furs while watching Strong Bear, then looked quickly away, lest he note that she was studying him . . . seeing again his strong face, his magnificently sculpted features.

"Oh, what am I doing?" she wondered to herself, her thick lashes closing over her eyes. "Oh, Anthony . . . Anthony . . ."

The warmth of the cabin and the softness of the furs beneath her eased Pamela into sleep. It felt too soothing to resist. And with sleep surely would come the blessing of forgetting what had happened to Anthony and Robert.

A peaceful lethargy crept through Pamela. Yet when she was fast asleep dreams took the place of reality and in them she found a renewed sadness, causing sobs to rise from deep within her.

Tossing on the bunk she cried out softly, the sound of

her voice piercing Strong Bear's heart. Looking toward Pamela, seeing her troubled state, Strong Bear knew what was required of him. He must go to her and comfort her. Though it would not be the comforting of a brother, but rather that of a man whose heart now belonged to her, Strong Bear would take the place of the white man this night, as does a brother comfort a sister.

The time for Strong Bear to treat Pamela as a desirable woman would come later. He would make her want him again as a woman wants a man. Passion would fill their lives, Strong Bear would make it so!

Tapping the tobacco from his pipe, then placing the pipe aside, Strong Bear went to the bunk and crept onto it, molding his body snugly into the shape of Pamela's from her backside. Desire swelled inside him and he knew that he would have to practice restraint now as never before in his life; no woman had ever felt so good against his body.

And as her sobs lessened and she responded to his body by wriggling more deeply against him, Strong Bear had to quell the raging hunger that seared his insides. He drew a ragged breath and encircled her tiny waist with his arm. His hand was tempted to touch her breasts through her dress, but he forced himself to rein in his urge and remain the protector he had vowed himself to be.

Pamela sighed in her sleep, enjoying the feel of the warm muscular body pressed into hers, making her feel less alone in the world. Exploring, she found the hand loosely draped over her waist. Clasping it, she continued relishing this closeness, this comforting closeness. . . .

Then memories drew her from sleep. Slowly she let her eyes move to the hand held within hers. Strong Bear had come and joined her on the bunk! Her feelings battled within her, staring breathlessly at the copper hand that had taught her so much about her body, sending thrilling spirals throughout her. The hand had awakened the woman in her! Oh, how she hungered to be caressed even now! She longed for his arms to embrace her, to be kissed by him! But such desires were wrong. She could never let him touch her in all those ways again. It just wasn't meant to be.

Sobbing, Pamela rose quickly to a sitting position, staring wildly down at Strong Bear's face, her own twisted in disbelief.

"You waited until I was asleep, then . . . then took advantage of me after all," Pamela cried, managing to crawl over him, to jump to the floor. "Please . . . leave me alone," she pleaded, backing away from him, her pulse racing.

Strong Bear was alarmed at her reaction, yet knew that he shouldn't be. For within her heart she was convinced that he had wronged her. She saw him as nothing more than a savage!

Pamela's body shook with sobs as she buried her face in her hands. "Perhaps I'd be better off dead," she cried. "I'm so alone. Oh, so alone . . ."

Strong Bear's heart ached, seeing her so distraught. He went to her and smoothed her hair between his fingers, then drew them quickly away when she flinched and looked up at him, her eyes fearful and tear filled.

"Strong Bear feels your pain," he said thickly. "Strong Bear has experienced many losses in life. First my *Ninge-ah,* mother, and then my *No-saw,* father. Cry, lovely one. Tears will wash away the pain." He reached for her, daring to touch her arm. "Tears wash away *mistrust.*"

Locking his fingers around her arm, he led her back to the bunk. "You sleep. Strong Bear leave you alone," he said, now guiding her down onto the bunk as she trembled and stared up at him. "Strong Bear leave dwelling. For the night, it is *yours.*"

Reaching for a blanket, Strong Bear unfolded it over Pamela. Then he walked in long strides from the cabin. When he was outside and the outdoor fire reflected on the face of Snow Owl as she sat obediently waiting for him, he gave her a blank stare, then strode away to sit and think beside the river.

He had met many challenges in his lifetime, but this white woman was the most challenging yet.

Eleven

> *Your arms held me fast; oh! your arms were so*
> *bold!—*
> > *Heart beat against heart in their*
> > *passionate fold.*
> > > —Hunt

Pamela tossed and turned in her sleep, finding herself lured more deeply into a spinning, black void. She moaned and clutched hard the blanket spread atop her. Cold sweat beaded her brow. And then through this darkness thundered a horseman. It moved steadily toward Pamela. The sun was suddenly bright in the sky, threatening to blind her. She shielded her eyes with her hands and watched the approaching horseman, now recognizing his handsome visage. It was Strong Bear. He had come to rescue her from her troubles and woes. He was going to comfort . . . was going to enwrap her in love. He was her beloved protector, the man she would always adore!

Then she began to inch backward. Strong Bear's face

was painted a gruesome black, grotesquely distorting as he raised his hand and brandished a hatchet dripping with blood. Anthony's pale face of death flashed before Pamela's eyes. Her gut twisted with agonizing memory of who had scalped him. Strong Bear. Oh, God, Strong Bear!

Pamela turned and began to run frantically in the opposite direction. But she could hear the hoofbeats drawing closer. She could smell the horse's lathered body, could even feel its breath hot on her neck. Her every nerve ending was on fire with fear! And when she felt fingers grab her hair and begin to jerk, her screams echoed wide and far. . . .

The cool night air had enveloped the earth. The moon lit the countryside with its pure, white radiance, illuminating the tense, kneeling figure of Strong Bear beside the water. He was fighting his feelings for Pamela. But it was hard! He had seen the desire in her eyes when she looked at him. She had struggled to hide it, but he had seen it! He had seen it!

Before Strong Bear had first cast his eyes upon the white woman that day while she had been looking at herself in the mirror of the water, his life had been much simpler. The survival of his people had been the main force behind his existence. Now there was another element in his life. And this—*she*—threatened to drive him into near mindlessness.

Picking up a pebble, tossing it into the water, Strong Bear watched the circle of ripples radiate the shine of the moon. He tossed another pebble, again watching the scattered moonbeams. The only noises disturbing this tranquil velvet night were the yapping of a she-fox and her pups from somewhere close by in their shelter, and the faraway shriek of a screech owl.

And then another sound split the silence of the night. A scream! A woman's scream!

Strong Bear bolted to his feet and turned his eyes in the direction of his dwelling, searching them for Snow Owl. Had she grown so jealous of the white woman that she stole back into the cabin like a cat in the night and harmed Pamela?

Such a thought sent a shiver of fear through Strong Bear. If his wife dared to touch the white woman, she would pay. He'd banish her from the tribe!

His eyes adjusting to the distant darkness, Strong Bear not only saw that Snow Owl had dutifully added more wood to the outdoor fire close beside their dwelling, but she sat dutifully *beside* it.

Yet Snow Owl's gaze was not upon the fire. She was looking over her shoulder at something else behind her.

Strong Bear's gaze shifted quickly to see what had captured Snow Owl's interest. It was Pamela. She was just now running from the cabin, shrieking, waving her arms wildly in the air.

Such a sight, and hearing Pamela's cries of fear, her utter sadness, made Strong Bear's heart lurch. If Pamela was so distraught over being with Strong Bear, would her feelings ever change?

Yet Strong Bear had to hope that she was crying over her losses . . . *not* because she mistakenly believed he had proved their bane.

Seeing Pamel continue running blindly toward the forest engulfed Strong Bear's heart with fear. Her screams followed after her. Many heads were at the village doorways, looking at this woman who seemed to have gone mad.

Cording his muscles, tightening his hands into fists, Strong Bear ran after Pamela. His moccasined feet carried him past his village, into the forest, across nature's mat of leaves and litter that protected the woodland soil from rain erosion.

His breath became raspy, his heart pounded. He lost sight of Pamela after she disappeared into the forest. But it was her screams and crying that led Strong Bear on, and drew him to her.

And when he found her, she was curled up into a ball on the ground, her screams and cries having faded to soft sobs.

Strong Bear stood over her, touched by her vulnerability; she looked more child than woman at this moment. The silken down of her long, drifting hair blinded his view of her shoulders and breasts as it lay like a protective shawl about her. Her feet were bare, her toes curling from the damp coldness of the night.

Her sadness and her hurt piercing him, and having assigned himself the role of her protector and loving her almost more than he could bear at this moment, he bent to his knees and reached out his hands. Pamela flinched.

"Pac-kah me-tam-sah," he said softly, now placing his hands gently to her shoulders to help her up. "Do not cry. Do not be afraid. You once said that you loved me. You even understood the meaning of love. You vowed never to love another. How could that have changed? Why have you so little faith in me? Why?"

Pamela looked blankly up at him, scarcely recalling these past moments at all. Then she looked frantically around her. Where was she? How had she gotten here? Her feet pained her from having been pierced with briars. Her body felt icy with the clutching fingers of the night wind stinging her flesh. Her eyes burned as though on fire from her fitful crying.

She directed her attention back to Strong Bear, her breath ragged, her thoughts engulfed by feelings she'd forgotten since dismissing him as her lover. But how had it happened? Why was she alone with him in this forest? She had been left alone in his dwelling!

"Where are we?" she murmured. "How did I get here?"

Strong Bear was shaken by her innocence, by her inability to remember. "You must have had a dream," he said thickly. "You ran into the forest. I followed."

Pamela blinked her eyes, memory slowly invading her senses. She was now recalling every moment of the nightmare. Her eyes became wild, remembering how in her dream Strong Bear had come after her with a hatchet dripping with blood.

Squirming, she tried to break free of his grasp. She had

not only had a nightmare while she was sleeping, her life had become one. Everything that she had held precious had been taken from her. Even her love for Strong Bear!

"Let me go," she cried, weakening as he refused to release her. "I hate you, Strong Bear. I hate you."

Strong Bear winced as though having been cut by a knife, her words were so tormenting. Yet he would not give up. He knew that in time she would understand how wrong she had been. "Your grief forms cruel words on your tongue," he said hoarsely. "But time will heal your hurt and teach you again how to love Strong Bear."

His sincerity, his gentle touch, his midnight-dark eyes fathomless in their hurt, brought a fresh onslaught of tears to Pamela's eyes. It was as though she would never be able to stop crying again! She so wanted to be free to love Strong Bear. She *did* love him. But how could she? Oh, sweet Anthony! Anthony!

Strong Bear understood the burden Pamela was carrying around inside her, reliving the scene of death over and over again in her mind's eye. Nothing but continued tenderness could help her at this moment in time. He removed his fingers from her shoulders and reached beneath her and drew her into his arms. His eyes widened and he scarcely dared to breathe when Pamela twined her arms about his neck and sobbed against his chest. Was it because she was accepting him as one who would comfort her? Or was she again so carried away in her grief that she did not know from whom she was seeking comfort?

But it did not matter to Strong Bear. That her arms were about his neck and that she *was* finding comfort against his chest were enough for Strong Bear to feed his hunger of her at this time. It gave him hope that, sooner or later, she would want more from him than mere comfort. If she could trust him this much, perhaps in time she would totally accept him as her protector . . . as more than even that . . . as her *man*!

Pride etched across his face, his eyes gleaming, Strong Bear began to run with Pamela back in the direction of the fire glow in the distance. Always the fires of his village were a beacon in the night.

Now within the boundaries of his village, Strong Bear ignored the puzzled expressions of those who still watched from their doorways, wondering about this chief who brought the white woman back into their lives. His people could question with their eyes all they wanted but never dare they question with their mouths. What he did, he did out of love. In time his people would know this without even being told. The white woman would rule at his side. Pamela would be his first wife of importance in his life. Together they would bring many beautiful *nen-que-sahs* into this world. Sons were as important as breathing, to keep the Miami prophecy fulfilled. And sons begat sons, did they not?

Moving on toward his cabin, Strong Bear saw that Snow Owl still sat obediently beside the outdoor fire. But within her scalding eyes he did not see the same obedience! If not for Pamela in his arms, Strong Bear would openly scold his wife, who had too much fire in her veins for one married to the powerful Miami chief!

Yet did he not admire the same sort of fire in the white woman? Had not that attracted him to her even more when she had so openly defied him not only with words, but also the flashing of her crystal-blue eyes? Had he not seen courage and strength in her behavior since it was a powerful Miami chieftain to whom she had so openly spoken?

But it was her weakness that spoke more to Strong Bear's heart now. His heart was melting into hers as she continued to cling to him, appearing to have fallen asleep against his powerful chest. She no longer sobbed. Her breathing was easy . . . gentle. Strong Bear had been given the power by the Great Spirit this night to help cast the sadness from the woman he loved. He silently thanked the Great Spirit not only for this, but for having given her to him, to keep. . . .

Undaunted by Snow Owl's obstinate stare, Strong Bear took Pamela back into his cabin. Padding across the floor, he carried her to his bunk, placed her onto it, then spread a blanket across her sleeping form. Strong Bear paused and let his eyes feast again upon her gentle, flawless features. Her thick eyelashes folded down over her eyes, dark against the paleness of her cheeks, her lips perfectly shaped, ready to be devoured by Strong Bear's mouth. A vision of loveliness, as her hair haloed about her head.

Strong Bear's gaze moved lower. Seeing the soft curves of her breasts against the low-swept bodice of her dress made a tinge of heat touch his loins. He was recalling his time of ecstasy with her. Never had breasts been so soft. It pained him not to be able to touch them again . . . to kiss them.

But for now, Pamela's peace of mind must be fed. Not Strong Bear's aroused hungers. And to keep her fears at bay, he must again stay by her side to comfort her if she awakened in the night.

Strong Bear removed his moccasins and crept onto the bunk beside her. In her sleep Pamela had turned on her side away from him, allowing Strong Bear the privilege of fitting his body against hers from the behind. His whole insides quivered at the touch of her body against his, her warmth transferring into him. And knowing that being so close was too much of a temptation, he forced himself to turn away from her, their backsides now only touching.

Strong Bear's heart thundered hard inside his chest, his loins aching from rejection. He stared into the flames of the fire curling around the logs in the fire space, trying to let this hypnotize him into thoughts other than his agonizing needs.

But then his eyes widened and he tensed. He looked downward, where he felt the warmth of a hand circle about his chest, clinging to him. And his heart frolicked like a flash of lightning when he felt her perfect shape fit into his backside. In her sleep she was reaching out to him. Her breath was even warm on his arm as she nestled against him.

Strong Bear could stand the temptation no longer. Never

had he so wanted a woman as now. And was she not seeking him out? Was it not true—her mouth so close to his flesh, warming his, her hands clutching to him—that she was signaling her desire to be kissed . . . ?

Moving like a spirit through the forest—soundlessly, effortlessly—Strong Bear eased around to face Pamela. He smoothed a lock of her hair from her brow, replacing it with a soft kiss. And then his mouth lowered. Quivering, his lips sought hers. The sweet softness of her lips made a headiness sweep through him.

With his tongue he fully tasted her lips, wonderingly, running it around the sensuous outline of her mouth. Never could a woman taste as sweet. It was the same as the rose petals he had chewed for refreshment while traveling through the woods. Her mouth had been born for kissing, for sharing with Strong Bear. The cry of passion within him was building, was being fed by his hands as he now searched her body through her dress, all the while enjoying her lips as they quivered beneath his.

Currents of warmth swept through him as his hands took in the roundness of her curves, her dress as vulnerable as a wall from the white man's forts against the Miamis. The warmth of her body reached out to him, melding his wandering hand and her flesh.

Trembling, he explored the valley of her breasts, daring to reach inside the bodice to fully cup one. His insides threatened to explode with need as he circled a thumb about the nipple where it grew hard against his flesh.

But fearing that he would awaken her, he moved his hands away from her breast and instead let them wander over her body through the dress, again memorizing the curve of her thighs, her exquisite waist, the whole of her slim, sinuous body.

Drawing his lips away, opening his eyes, Strong Bear gasped when finding her eyes wide open, looking into his. He tried to read the expression but could not, for again she lowered her thick lashes. But her hands spoke to him what neither words nor eyes could speak. She was pushing him away from her. Only in her sleep had she accepted him. Awake, she could not!

Frustrated, feeling the hunger of a man's needs gnawing away at his insides, desiring these needs satisfied, Strong Bear rose from the bunk and looked solemnly down at Pamela. He bent and drew the blanket back over her, then turned and walked with deliberation away from her. Time with her would come later. Once their bodies became fully acquainted again, she would never turn him from her bed. But for now, he would leave her to her mourning. He would get his desires—his needs—fed elsewhere!

Trembling, Pamela clutched her arms about her chest as she watched Strong Bear leave the cabin. She stared at the doorway even after he was gone, in wonder of these feelings he had once more aroused in her while kissing and touching her, when in truth she wanted so to hate him!

Though she had been drifting somewhere between exhausted sleep and being awake, she had felt him kiss her. She had even felt his hands exploring her body! She had allowed him the privilege, because Strong Bear had for a moment somehow caused all sadnesses to leave her, to be replaced by feelings so familiarly beautiful, warm, and delicious. She had found it hard to send him away!

Then she turned on her side, her back to the doorway and hopefully to him, torn with conflicting feelings.

Yet how could she hate someone who had full possession of her heart? She desperately wanted to believe that he was innocent of all that she accused him. And perhaps she *was* wrong about him. How could he possibly be guilty of such crimes when he was otherwise so kind, gentle, and understanding?

If he had killed to have full possession of her, wouldn't he have only moments ago taken her sexually to prove that she was now his? A moment longer with him and perhaps she would have even *let* him! If being in his arms could erase everything ugly from her mind, perhaps that was the best escape of all.

Weary, Pamela drew the blanket up just beneath her

chin and closed her eyes, letting the peace of sleep slowly claim her, even though she dreaded more nightmares.

But as she drifted, slowly drifted, a different dream hovered just below the threshold of her consciousness. A pleasant smile swept across her face as she let herself dream a dream more sweet than the sticks of candy her father had given her to soothe her childish tantrums.

She was standing with Strong Bear in his cabin. She was his *wife*. Her body was weightless, yet filled with wonder for the intense love she felt for Strong Bear.

Strong Bear touched her hair meditatively, smoothing it to hang lustrously down her back. Then he twined his fingers through it and slowly drew her mouth to his. "Say again that you are mine," he whispered seductively against her slightly parted mouth.

His hands lowered. He cupped her breasts, feeling through her dress how her nipples rose into a hardened peak against the palms of his hands. His loins burned, afire with need of her.

Wrapping her arms about Strong Bear's neck, she spoke softly, lovingly. "You are my husband. You are my only love," she whispered. "Never shall I love another."

"Did you miss me while I was gone on the hunt with my braves?" Strong Bear said huskily, teasing Pamela with soft kisses across her lips. "Will you miss me when I must leave again?"

"My heart did not beat while you were gone; my breath failed me," Pamela said, laughing softly. "Do you not see how you affect me, my husband?"

"I am here now," Strong Bear said, kissing her tiny, tapered neck, his hands busy disrobing her. "Let me feel your heart beat with much strength. Let me hear you become breathless from my touch . . . from my kisses."

"Oh, yes, my husband, oh, yes . . ." Pamela said, feeling heat rise to her cheeks in anticipation of what was about to transpire. She sucked in her breath when her breasts were bared and Strong Bear's tongue flicked over one nipple and then the other. Her pulse began to race when her dress fluttered downward and lay limply about her ankles and the heat of the firespace touched her flesh with a caress all its own.

Then as Strong Bear lowered her to the milkweed-down pallet, she ever so boldly let her hands wander to the bulge that had risen beneath the softness of his breechclout. Enjoying the feel of his largeness, she caressed him until he emitted a husky groan, then stood over her and quickly disrobed, exposing his distended sheath to her watchful eyes.

With outstretched arms, Pamela beckoned Strong Bear to come to her. When he lay above her, their thighs and stomachs touching, she shuddered sensuously as he caressed her womanhood with his hardness and only momentarily stroked her swollen bud.

And then he kissed her. Wildly. Passionately. He plunged himself inside her. She shuddered again, arched and cried out against his lips, responding to his plunges with a wildness and desperation never experienced before. Her hands sought out the sleekness of his back, the smoothness of his firm buttocks. Golden flames of desire leaped higher and higher within her.

And then Pamela softly cried out when everything inside her seemed to explode into a delicious, spreading heat. She clung to Strong Bear's rock-hard shoulders as he kept moving rhythmically within her. She could feel his body shudder in waves that matched her own. Together they had sought and found that which only lovers shared.

Then they lay clinging, their cheeks pressed together, their breath mingling.

"Does not my heart beat so soundly?" Pamela whispered, lacing her fingers through Strong Bear's sweat-dampened hair. "Do you not see how my breath has been stolen away? My love, I shall prove to you over and over again just how much I hunger—ache—for you. . . ."

Pamela's eyes flew open with a start. Her heart was beating so hard she could hardly breathe. She placed her hands to her throat, remembering the dream. It had seemed so real! So wonderfully . . . intensely . . . real!

"Strong Bear!" she cried. "Oh, Lord, Strong Bear, surely I'm wrong about you. You couldn't have killed Anthony! You couldn't have!"

Tears silvering her cheeks, Pamela jumped from the bunk and ran toward the door. She must go to Strong Bear. She must tell him that no one as sweet and gentle as he could have killed her one brother, and stolen the other! Anyone who loved her so sincerely couldn't have killed those whom she held so dear! Strong Bear was honest! He wouldn't lie to her!

She stepped outside, her eyes searching the darkness for Strong Bear. But when she saw his handsome profile illuminated by the outdoor fire, and saw what he was doing, everything within her that had moments ago trusted him faded to a nothingness.

Pamela lifted a hand to her mouth, stifling a soft, remorseful cry while she watched in muted silence as Strong Bear offered Snow Owl a hand, within his eyes a silent command that could only mean one thing: He wanted his wife tonight . . . to *be* his wife.

Pamela had momentarily forgotten that he knew deceit well. He had spoken of her being his wife when, in truth, he was already married.

Twelve

⊰∽∽⊱

The want of you is like no other thing.
                                    —Wright

Strong Bear moved to Snow Owl's side and looked down at her seated beside the outdoor fire. When she turned her eyes upward to meet his, she saw the command in them and accepted his outstretched hand which signaled it was time to perform her nightly duty.

Snow Owl's lips curved into a smug, sure smile as she accepted and rose to stand before him. He had left the white woman to be with Snow Owl. Most surely he had seen the white woman as not only pale and ugly, but also weak. Never had Strong Bear seen Snow Owl cry. Snow Owl was strong, never weak! And a chief needed such a woman at his side. Strong Bear needed his wife.

Their hands intertwined, Strong Bear led Snow Owl toward his other cabin at the far end of the village, one he had purposefully built for when he needed to be alone, away from this wife who was only with him as a necessity.

Not ever having special feelings for her he had needed time alone away from her.

They were now inside his smaller cabin, which not only offered a continuous blaze in the firespace but also a thick, comfortable pile of pine boughs covered by many plush blankets and bear furs. There was no need for the furnishings or show of weapons that usually enlivened the Miami dwelling, since this cabin had been built for reveling sometimes in aloneness, other times in the pleasurable companionship of a beautiful squaw.

Snow Owl knew of these other women but had never mentioned it to Strong Bear for fear that to speak it aloud would be confessing that she was not enough woman for him. Soon she would be quite shaken by the news that she would no longer be the first wife of importance in Strong Bear's life. But he would make up for this dishonor by showering her with many gold trinkets. This would again make the shine return to her eyes and heart.

Strong Bear knew she loved the gold trinkets more than life itself. They made her look important because no other Miami wife was adorned in such a fashion. Only the wife of this chief boasted of such possessions! And to Snow Owl, social position was of utmost concern.

Strong Bear led Snow Owl to the soft bed, seeing a guarded expression in her eyes as she studied her surroundings. He knew that she had always wanted to come to this cabin, to see his secret private life so she could know him better.

And now that she had soaked in its small and intimate dimensions, Strong Bear could understand if jealousy was invading her senses. If she would allow herself, she could even smell the stale odors of lovemaking, for of late Strong Bear had used this bed more for being with a woman, than for being alone.

His needs were never so easily quenched. It was like a fire inside him, forever burning. And this night had enflamed those fires even more.

Had Snow Owl not been sitting in a strategic spot where

she could witness his behavior, Strong Bear would have chosen a more spirited squaw with whom to share his rich bed of furs this night. He needed a woman whose skills were beyond Snow Owl's! He, in truth, needed Pamela. Only she could quell these burning flames that scorched his insides.

But he could take Snow Owl quickly, at least rid his throbbing member of its built-up seed.

"Your dwelling compares not to the dwelling I keep lovely for you," Snow Owl said in a pout. "How could you choose this over our dwelling so often, Strong Bear?"

His silence was the answer she had not wanted to hear. Now that she was inside this smaller dwelling her suspicions were confirmed. Though he had accepted her as his wife, she had not been enough.

But she knew of his virility and deep down inside she was glad that he did not use her as often as he needed to feed his hungers of the flesh. She bored so of coupling! She only participated to keep him as her husband! She would never want to live as less than the wife of a powerful Miami chief!

"Strong Bear does not bring you here to discuss differences in dwellings," Strong Bear said, his fingers already at the hem of her dress. He began lifting it over her body, his eyes appraising her when he saw how the fire's glow emphasized the soft curves of her body and shadowed the dark juncture of her thighs.

And then his thumbs grazed the soft flesh of her breasts as he raised the dress past them and over her head.

"My *Ke-mawth*, chief husband, is not Snow Owl *packah*?" Snow Owl tormented as she slithered next to Strong Bear after he had tossed her dress aside. She pressed her breasts against his chest as he skillfully removed her leggings.

Strong Bear ignored her reference to being beautiful. Though Snow Owl was beautiful in her own way, in his eyes there was only one truly beautiful woman. And she had turned him away to seek pleasure from another.

But soon Pamela would plead with him not to share her love with another! Though she had not spoken of jealousy aloud, her eyes had silently spoken the truth of this to Strong Bear. She was jealous of Snow Owl! That was good. She would turn to him sooner if she realized that he had Snow Owl to quench his hungers of the flesh!

Slowly Strong Bear lowered Snow Owl down to the bed of furs. His lips bore down upon hers, his fingers digging into the flesh of her wrists. As usual her kiss held within it no special taste, no special fire. But the feel of her breasts crushed against him made his mind wander to how it had felt to touch Pamela's breasts. He could even now feel how Pamela's nipples had hardened against his palms. And, ah, had not her lips been so rose-petal soft, even had the taste of a rose?

Letting his mind stay in the world of thoughts of him and the white woman, Strong Bear moved away from Snow Owl and removed his breechclout. And then he knelt down over her, his mouth beginning to explore a skin of smoothness, of utter softness. But it was not Snow Owl's skin that he was savoring. It was . . . Pamela's.

Even when his mouth lowered and he flicked a tongue to Snow Owl's bud of womanhood, he imagined he was with Pamela and that she was responding to this special way of making love, begging him to taste of her fully there.

But it was not Pamela. It was Snow Owl and she was not responding as Strong Bear would have wished. She was moaning, yet she showed no skills in moving her body to respond to his. He had grown used to just seeking his needed release from Snow Owl to fulfill his duties of a husband to *her*, and finding this other sort of pleasure elsewhere.

Tonight he had hoped that it might be different with her. He had hoped that she would become totally alive beneath his tongue. If she could become a skilled lover, perhaps he could even forget the white woman!

Yet it was the same as before. She was not totally pleasing to him. And she would never be.

Moving to position himself fully over her, wanting to finish the needed chore, Strong Bear quickly impaled Snow Owl with his swollen shaft. He closed his eyes and sought out her silky breasts. His heart thundered wildly, feeling the pleasure mounting, as he plummeted faster . . . faster.

And when he reached the pinnacle, he was only half-aware of whose name he had spoken as the pleasure consumed him in fiery splashes.

Snow Owl's eyes widened with horror. Never before had Strong Bear uttered another's name while with *her*. And it had not just been any name. It had been the name of a white woman . . . *the* white woman who even now slept on Strong Bear's and Snow Owl's bed! Though Strong Bear had abandoned the white woman to seek pleasure from Snow Owl's body, his thoughts—his hunger—had been with the white woman. He had most surely been with the white woman sexually before! Or how would he know to whisper her name? Tonight it was to be Snow Owl. Tomorrow night . . . the white woman again?

Snow Owl would not openly scold Strong Bear for his mistake. The less the white woman was brought into the conversation, surely the sooner she would be forgotten by Strong Bear.

Snow Owl curled her arms about Strong Bear's neck. She fit her body into his, enjoying the musky smell of her husband.

"Again you drew pleasure from your wife's body?" she purred, forcing the sweetness in her voice. "Am I not a perfect wife, Strong Bear?"

Snow Owl's words touched Strong Bear's heart with a warning. It was now that he must tell her what the future held for her, for the white woman, and for himself. He would not delay the telling. As he saw it, tomorrow would be the beginning of *all* his tomorrows. He had not only imagined Pamela responding to his kisses and caresses while she lay beside him on his bunk in his wigwam. She *had* responded.

Fear swept through Snow Owl when Strong Bear did not accept her again into his arms. He had not only refused her, he had looked down at her with contempt in the dark depths of his eyes.

"Strong Bear, did I displease you so much?" Snow Owl asked, realizing that she had again not responded as she knew he would have liked. It was not that he was not masterful at loving. It was *she* who lacked so much, whose body stiffened at the thought of lovemaking. She only did it for gainful purposes. It was her duty. And she was rewarded for such duty!

Even now the earrings at the lobes of her ears were a reminder. Oh, how their clinking warmth thrilled her. Oh, how they seduced her. She even gained some strange sort of passion by their possession, a passion which she shared with no one!

Strong Bear slipped his breechclout up the powerful expanse of his legs, covering his spent manhood. Without looking her way he handed Snow Owl's dress to her.

"Dress. Now is time for *talk*," he said thickly, leaning to place a log on the embers of the fire. In the dancing flames he saw a face, a lovely face that was radiant with a smile. Pamela's long, slender fingers were beckoning him to her. Her voice was soft and seductive, forgetting all those ugly doubts that had made her turn away from him as though he carried some sort of plague!

Pamela. Pamela . . . beautiful Pamela, who no longer shed tears of despair and longing.

Smoothing his fingers across his eyes, wiping them clear of these troublesome fantasies, Strong Bear focused his thoughts, now even his eyes, on Snow Owl, whose dress was now in place, whose face was delicately pretty. Yet her eyes showed her true feelings. Within them Strong Bear could see rage and fright fused into one emotion. She feared his words, and for good reason!

"The white woman," Strong Bear suddenly blurted.

"Pamela. She will be staying in the village of Miami. She will be staying in Strong Bear's dwelling with Strong Bear."

Snow Owl flinched as though she had been hit, yet she kept her composure. This was a time to show pride befitting a great Miami chief's wife.

"Strong Bear's dwelling is also Snow Owl's dwelling," she said in a monotone voice, a numbness creeping through her. "Snow Owl is forced to share everything with white woman?"

Strong Bear looked away from her, guilt creasing his powerful face. Though it was proper for a Miami chief to have two wives, he did not wish to inflict pain on one because of such a choice. Yet he had no choice. Pamela would be his wife.

"No, you will not share everything equally with white woman," Strong Bear said, now commanding Snow Owl's obedience as he gave her a stern look.

Snow Owl smiled triumphantly up at him. "That is good," she said smugly. "Only food and clothes. Not Strong Bear!"

Strong Bear placed a hand to Snow Owl's tiny shoulder. "No," he said dryly. "That is not the way it is to be."

Snow Owl felt color escape from her cheeks, replaced by a strange coldness. "My husband, what are you saying?"

"Snow Owl, you have been my only wife for one winter now," Strong Bear said, his voice still commanding and flat. "It is time for Strong Bear to have second wife. It is the way of the Miami, and I must do as my father did, and before him, his father."

He raised a fist to his breast. "I speak from the heart when saying that it is not my intention to bring hurt into your life," he said thickly. "You must understand the ways of chiefs. You must understand Strong Bear's needs."

"Snow Owl will still be first wife of importance in your life?" Snow Owl said, clasping her fingers together on her lap.

Strong Bear shook his head slowly, seeing the understanding of what he was not saying enter Snow Owl's eyes. He gripped her shoulders. "You have been first wife of importance for one winter now," he said thickly. "Now it is time for another wife to have this honor."

Snow Owl's insides coiled with hate. She glared at Strong Bear, her hands now reaching to touch her earrings. "Secondary wife still share bed with husband?" she said in a strain. "Secondary wife still receive gifts from husband?"

"Secondary wife share bed with husband, even gifts, but—"

"But—?"

"You will not share the same dwelling as Strong Bear and wife of first importance."

"No!" Snow Owl gasped, her hands flying to her throat. "You shame me . . . ?"

"There will be no shame in Snow Owl having her own dwelling separate from Strong Bear and white woman wife. You will have assistance—little ones will serve you," Strong Bear said thickly. "Strong Bear will divide time between two wives . . . two dwellings."

Snow Owl turned her eyes away from him for fear he would see the disobedience in their depths, for she sorely hated the knowing! She sorely hated the white woman! Until she had come into Strong Bear and Snow Owl's life everything had been perfect.

"Do you understand how it is to be, Snow Owl?" Strong Bear asked, placing a finger to her chin, turning her face so that their eyes would meet and lock.

"Yes, I understand," Snow Owl murmured, hate growing more strongly inside her heart.

"Come. We will return to our dwelling tonight," Strong Bear said, taking Snow Owl by the elbow. "Tomorrow I will see that a comfortable dwelling is erected for you."

Snow Owl followed along beside him, yet her thoughts were not on what he had said. She was thinking about the white woman. She would find a way to rid herself and

Strong Bear of this obstacle in their lives. Somehow . . . somehow . . .

Stepping outside, Strong Bear sighed, realizing that night had already passed him and Snow Owl by. Dawn was breaking, adding faint color to the muted grays and vertical lines of the forest. This was the tomorrow that he had spoken to Snow Owl about. This was the day of all new beginnings for him, for him and Pamela.

Thirteen

Forget thee? Bid the forest-birds
forget their sweetest tune?
                                    —Moultrie

Her stomach comfortably warm with sassafrass tea, turtle eggs and raspberries, Pamela watched Snow Owl cautiously as she prepared food to place inside the black iron kettle heating over the fire. It was Snow Owl's icy glances that made Pamela's insides recoil. It was evident that this Indian squaw hated her, and Pamela understood why. Strong Bear had chosen a white woman over his Indian wife to spend the full night in his cabin. And though Strong Bear hadn't spent the night with Pamela, the short time that he had been with her had been enough to give cause for Snow Owl to be jealous . . . even to hate Pamela.

But Pamela couldn't confess to anything less than the same sort of jealousy toward Snow Owl. Strong Bear had most surely made love to her the previous night. But

161

wouldn't he? She was his wife! For a while Pamela had forgotten this truth. She had even forgotten that she must hate Strong Bear for what he had done to her family, and also for deceiving her into believing she was the only woman in his life.

She had her proof of this latter deceit, and until he proved his innocence of the other, he would remain guilty in her eyes!

Still, Pamela's insides were unwillingly stirred into a strange sort of mushiness when she allowed herself to recall how Strong Bear's hands and lips had so aroused her again. It had been wrong of her to enjoy that time with him on his bunk in the guise of her being asleep. But it had been so easy to enjoy it, while at the back of her mind lay the part of her that was accusing him of so many ugly things. For a few moments with Strong Bear she had been able to forget Anthony and Robert.

Her senses had now returned, and she was aware of the realities of life. She must find a way to escape. She must try to locate Robert. Perhaps he was imprisoned in this very village.

"Snow Owl, are there white slaves in your village other than myself?" Pamela blurted, placing a wooden platter aside. She attempted to smooth the wrinkles from the skirt of her dress, frowning at the ripped ruffle at its hem. It only took her fingers touching her hair to know that it was tangled. She must look very ugly in the eyes of the Indian squaw.

Pamela hungered for a hairbrush and clean dress, even a cake of soap with which to clean herself. But all of these comforts would have to come later. Escape. Robert. She must keep these thoughts foremost in her mind, not her vanity!

Snow Owl glanced sourly at Pamela, then resumed cutting wild carrots into slices, dropping them into the water warming over the fire. "You no slave," she said solemnly. "White woman has been chosen by Chief Strong Bear to become *ne-we-wah*, wife. Snow Owl second wife of importance. White woman soon to be first wife of importance.''

Snow Owl clutched the handle of the knife tightly. She wanted to plunge it into the heart of the palefaced woman, yet that would not accomplish anything for Snow Owl but disgrace and banishment from the tribe.

''This Snow Owl's last day in this dwelling,'' she spat, her eyes sparks of fire. ''From this day forth this dwelling Strong Bear's and white woman's!'

Pamela began inching herself back from the fire, scooting on the thick mats beneath her. She saw the hate in the Indian squaw's eyes. She heard it in the way she spoke. And the knife was too handy.

But perhaps it would be best to let the squaw kill her. It might be the only answer to Pamela's predicament. The realization that she had been singled out to become the wife of an Indian who was a coldhearted murderer sent her heart into a tailspin of despair. Though Strong Bear had set her insides lame with desire, she could never let herself show him that she still had such feelings for him. How could she ever forget Anthony? Robert? Surely Strong Bear was responsible.

''You didn't answer me, Snow Owl,'' Pamela dared to say, yet sighing with relief when Snow Owl turned her attention back to cooking. ''Are there other slaves, white captives in this village?''

''There are none,'' Snow Owl said matter-of-factly. ''The Delaware practice this more than Miami.''

Snow Owl's eyes glinted as she smiled crookedly over at Pamela. ''It would delight Snow Owl to have *you* as slave,'' she said, laughing. ''Snow Owl would use you in many ways. And you would find none of those ways *pleasant*.''

An iciness swept through Pamela's veins. Even if she ever found out that Strong Bear was responsible neither for Robert's abduction, nor Anthony's death, Pamela had to escape this village. Her life would be short if Snow Owl had anything to say about it. Snow Owl probably knew ways to make Pamela die that could be blamed on other sources. Strong Bear would never suspect his wife, Snow Owl.

Yes, she must escape. And soon.

"Where is Strong Bear?" Pamela asked, looking slowly around her, deciding just which weapons she would take with her when she escaped. She also searched for Snow Owl's clothes. She must change her dress so she could blend in with the Miami as she made her way toward the horses fenced in at the far end of the village.

"He didn't come into the cabin this morning," Pamela added. She let her gaze meet and hold Snow Owl's, again feeling an iciness creep through her, making her flesh crawl with soft beads of cold sweat.

"Strong Bear in council with braves," Snow Owl said, rising to her feet, now turning to walk toward the doorway. "Snow Owl now go for more wood." She stopped and turned and smiled wickedly at Pamela. "Tomorrow white woman go for wood for Strong Bear's dwelling, white woman cook his meals, white woman perhaps soon become heavy with child. Strong Bear only brings you here because he wants many sons."

Cackling low, Snow Owl walked outside, leaving Pamela alone in a near-panic. Snow Owl's words were like arrows piercing her heart. Strong Bear wanted many sons! Had he truly wanted her for childbearing, or for loving? There *was* a difference. Wasn't Strong Bear ever sincere in any of his feelings? Was she just a thing to be used by him? Never! Never!

Now she felt desperate to leave. And, by damn, she *would*. And perhaps the only opportunity to escape had just been provided. While Snow Owl was in the forest gathering wood, Pamela could sneak from the cabin. Her only hope was to flee to the British fort and just pray that the British colonel would be civil enough to help her find

Robert. Only then could she go on with her life. Robert was now her only living relative.

She bit her lower lip, tears erupting from her eyes again. "*Is* Robert still alive . . . ?" she whispered.

Then she lowered her face into her hands and said a soft prayer, asking the Lord that Robert and she would one day be reunited. Somehow . . . reunited.

Her heart pounding so hard from fear of what lay just ahead of her made her light-headed. She blinked her eyes and clasped her fingers together tightly before her to steady them. Then she rushed to the bundles of clothes that lay beneath the bunk on which she had spent the restless night.

Her fingers still trembling, she tore one bundle of clothes apart and then another, sighing when she finally found some of Snow Owl's clothes. Jerking a dress and beaded moccasins from the bundle, Pamela lay them aside and hurriedly undressed. And when she had the soft doeskin dress pulled down over her curves and her feet fitted into the moccasins, she rushed to the firespace and knelt. Dipping her fingers into the cool ashes, she slowly applied the ash to her face as though it were a fine powder. She was careful not to add too much, for that would make it too obvious that she was not Indian, but one who had recklessly covered her face in an effort to *look* Indian.

She was grateful that her hair was dark; once braided it would make her appear more Indian.

With her hair wound in one long braid down her back and her eyes wide with anxiousness, Pamela studied the collection of weapons from which to choose. She couldn't carry a bow and arrow for it was not a proper weapon for a squaw. The axlike weapons on the side would also be too conspicuous. That left a sheathed knife, which she hurried to and secured to her thigh beneath the doeskin dress.

She moved stealthily toward the doorway. Lifting a water jug she took a nervous breath and stepped outside. Hoping to look like an obedient squaw doing her morning duty of going to the river for water, Pamela kept her face lowered, hoping not to draw undue attention her way.

Her knees were weak and her pulse was racing as other squaws passed by her on both sides. But Pamela found it easy enough to pretend to be one of them, for they were too caught up in duties to their husbands to bother with anyone else.

As she approached the fenced-in horses, Pamela mentally chose a red roan for her escape. A careless Indian had left its bridle in place; and this horse was the closest to the section of the fence where only loose logs were stretched across, used as a substitute for a gate. Pamela would only have to lift the logs out of their joints, grab the horse, and walk it hurriedly into the cover of the forest. Her only fear was Snow Owl. Snow Owl had gone for wood in the forest. Should Snow Owl see Pamela's escape . . .

Setting her lips into a grim line, Pamela began edging away from the path that led to the river, instead moving in the direction of the fence. Choosing not to look back to see if she was being watched, she set the water jug down and hurried to the horse. With cautious speed she grabbed the reins and walked the horse into the woods. Not yet having been discovered, she swung herself onto it bareback and galloped away at high speed.

Fearing discovery, Pamela lay low over the horse's mane, clinging to its sides. Her eyes looked guardedly about as she rode hard across the leaf-covered ground, winding her way beneath the massive growth of trees.

She reached a broad, gently rolling meadow where wildflowers dotted the land in a delicate patchwork of colors. Pamela welcomed the dazzling sunshine on her face. She squared her shoulders and straightened her back and held her head high. It was strange that in this bright sunshine overlooking a field of flowers around her, danger and death lurked nearby.

The serenity of this beautiful countryside beckoned to her from all directions. A fresh breeze sent clouds scudding over the lush bluegrass. A huge buffalo herd was thundering past low-lying hills in the distance; deer were grazing.

Pamela's breath was momentarily stolen when she saw another wonder of this magnificent land that she wanted to hate, not adore. She had never seen so many pigeons amassed together in her life. There were so many flying overhead in close proximity, a stick could be used to strike them from the sky to fill a cooking pot!

But food was the last thing on her mind. She lowered her gaze from the sky and determinedly looked straight ahead where the long, fine grass bowed in waves over the land, gusted by a slight wind. She clung to the horse, her body bouncing, hoping that she had chosen the correct route to the British fort.

She smiled joyously when she saw a sparkling of water just ahead. She was near the Ohio River! She would travel alongside the great body of water and let it lead her to Colonel Bradley, and hopefully an offering of assistance. . . .

Having traveled relentlessly onward, not stopping for water or food, Pamela grimaced as the darkness of night fell around her in a menacing shroud. She looked down into the waters of the Ohio, seeing how the newly risen moon reflected its silver beam onto its surface. It was as though many lanterns had been lit beneath the water as the glow spread over the lapping of the waves.

And then Pamela's nose picked up the scent of smoke. She tensed. With squinted eyes she peered curiously into the distance. Tightening the horse's reins she urged it into an easy canter and scanned the horizon.

And then her pulse quickened when she saw a dot of flames moving in what seemed midair just ahead through the break in the trees.

"What is that . . . ?" she whispered.

Pamela urged the roan closer to the mysterious flame and then a wide smile of relief spread across her face. She could make out the full outline of a fort beneath the brilliant rays of the moon just ahead in a clearing. What she had seen was a man carrying a torch, moving along an inside ledge of the uppermost part of the great wall, doing his guard duty for the night.

"I've done it!" she whispered harshly. "Oh, Anthony, you would be so proud of me! I've actually escaped the Indian village and found the British fort!"

But Anthony's words about the English colonel came back to haunt her. Even she knew the dangers. Colonel Bradley had refused them medical assistance for their father. He had even warned them, telling them to leave the area. So why would he treat her any differently *now*?

"Surely he'll take pity on a woman in distress," she whispered. Keeping this thought in mind, letting hope instead of despair be her guide, she thrust her heels into the flanks of the horse and rode determinedly onward.

The moon cast Pamela's shadow on the ground beside her and then suddenly another shadow was there as a man on horseback appeared from, it seemed, nowhere. Had the British soldiers such skills they knew how to ride soundlessly into the night? She looked guardedly at the man who was riding alongside her. He seemed to be more boy than man in his youthfulness, long braid of wheat-colored hair hanging down his back.

Her gaze swept quickly over him. He wore no uniform at all, but instead a fringed buckskin outfit. And as the moon illuminated his face more fully Pamela failed to feel fright as she would have expected when coming across a stranger in the night. A friendly warmth oozed from this man's pores as he looked gently back at her, scrutinizing her.

She smiled to herself, remembering the ash on her face. She *must* look a fright.

Lucas Boatright spurred his horse closer to Pamela, forking an eyebrow when he recognized her even though her face was covered with ash and her body clothed in Indian attire. By damn, she had escaped from whoever had abducted her before Colonel Bradley had gotten to her cabin. Here she was, live and in the flesh. And little did she know that she was riding right into the arms of Colonel Bradley, despite her obvious intention to solicit the British for help.

Looking guardedly about him, Lucas's first thoughts were to guide the beautiful lady away from the fort, to protect her in his own chosen way. Perhaps he could get her to an American settlement up the Ohio. That was her only hope for surviving Colonel Bradley's ravaging.

But when Lucas glanced up at the fort and saw a torch held by a soldier, he knew that he had no choice but to do his duty as a British soldier and take the woman to the Colonel.

"Ma'am, please follow me," Lucas said, his voice cracking with apprehension. "I'll take you to Colonel Bradley."

Pamela's mouth fell. She hadn't suspected it would be this simple . . . that she would be escorted to the colonel so quickly and without getting quizzed at gunpoint by the soldiers. Instead she was in the company of a gentleman, being treated as a lady. It was as though the young man knew her and understood her reasons for being there!

Though she did not understand, she was not one to argue. "Thank you, sir," Pamela murmured, flicking her reins, following alongside him through the wide gate of the fort as other soldiers swung the door open.

Feeling eyes peeled on her, seeing the glowing lamps bordering the wide expanse of stockade, Pamela directed her gaze straight ahead. She didn't avert her attention until she was squired to Colonel Bradley's cabin in the center of the courtyard. And then she watched in appreciation as the young man quickly dismounted and came to her side to offer assistance in climbing down from her borrowed horse.

"Again I thank you," Pamela said, smiling at Lucas as he placed his hands around her waist and helped her from the horse. She was taking a quick liking to this young man of gentle eyes, smile, and ways. If all of the British soldiers were this kind, she had nothing to fear!

"Ma'am." Lucas said, setting her easily on the ground.

"You wait right here. I'll go and check to see if Colonel Bradley is presentable. He returned to the fort only a short while ago." He would not tell the beautiful lady that the colonel had spent the entire day searching for her and had returned in an ugly mood, empty-handed.

Pamela nodded. She wrung her hands nervously as she waited in the shadows of the shabby cabin. But then she smiled up at Lucas as he appeared again and took her elbow.

"He'll see you now," Lucas said, guiding Pamela into the cabin. He glanced from Colonel Bradley to Pamela, then turned on a heel and hurried outside. When he let his mind conjure up what the next hour might hold for this lovely lady, he couldn't help himself. He rushed to the back of the cabin and hung his head and retched.

Pamela stood just inside the cabin beside the door. Her heart racing, she was embarrassed as she looked across the room to discover the British colonel was only half-clothed. He wore breeches. His chest was covered with hideously thick fronds of dark, curly hair. Without his powdered wig, his dark hair was slicked back from his narrow brow. His gray eyes appeared bottomless as he peered at her with a mocking smile.

Pamela was relieved when he turned away from her to cross to a crude liquor cabinet. This enabled her to steady her breathing and wipe the sweaty palms of her hands on the skirt of her doeskin dress.

"So we have us a fair maiden come in the night from out of nowhere?" Colonel Bradley said, pouring himself a glass of Madeira.

Turning to face Pamela, he twisted the tall-stemmed glass between his fingers and studied her face. It hadn't been necessary for Lucas to explain who had come to call. The lady's loveliness was marred by what looked like ash, but he readily recognized her. Though his plan to have her had at first gone awry, it was now falling into place for him. He had wanted to place her in the position of coming to him for help, and she had.

Kneading his chin contemplatively, he raised an eyebrow. His gaze was sweeping over Pamela. It was obvious that it *had* been an Indian who had abducted her. The proof was in the way she was dressed. But which Indian?

"Come over here in the light," Colonel Bradley said, gesturing with his free hand. He threw his head back and released a dry laugh, then let his eyes meet and hold hers. "So you're a clever one, are you? You colored your face to look like an Indian, to escape *from* the Indians. You are even dressed like one."

Pamela touched her hands to her face. She smiled awkwardly, having forgotten about the ash.

Colonel Bradley stepped closer to her and glared. "*Which* Indian?" he flatly ordered. "Tell me. *Now.*"

Blanching, a warning sounded in Pamela's head to withhold Strong Bear's name. Though Strong Bear was more than likely guilty of many things, she could not take it upon herself to send the British after him. Deep down inside her, where her desires had been born in Strong Bear's arms, she still dared to hope that he was innocent. Even though he had kept the existence of a wife secret, it did not make Pamela want to see him dead!

"Sir, if you could please forget my face, my attire, and the damn Indian who forced me to go with him, I would sorely appreciate it. I need your help," she said dryly, now feeling ill at ease as his gaze lowered and his eyes followed the heaving of her breasts. "You see, my older brother was savagely murdered and my younger brother is missing. Sir, could you please find it in your heart to help me find my younger brother?"

She swallowed hard when he moved so close she could feel his foul breath hot on her cheeks. "Sir, my brother Robert and I would then return to Williamsburg and never be a bother to you again," she quickly added.

Colonel Bradley began slowly to circle her while she stood breathlessly still. "Twice you have come to the fort for assistance," he tormented, smiling crookedly. "Twice you've worn a different disguise. Do you even own a proper gown?''

Pamela turned with a start and boldly faced him. ''So you *do* recognize me?'' she said shallowly, her spine stiffening.

''How could I *not*?'' Colonel Bradley said, touching a forefinger to her chin, turning her face one way and then another as he studied her. ''You could never hide your loveliness. Not in a man's breeches, or with ash spread across your face.''

Pamela knocked his hand away. ''Sir, *please*,'' she demanded. ''I did not come to be toyed with. My younger brother's life is in danger. You *must* help me.''

Colonel Bradley took a slow sip of wine from his glass, his eyes steel gray over its rim. Then he placed the glass on the desk. ''Your brother? The one who was with you before? He's your younger brother? He's the one missing?'' he asked, pretending to be interested, all the while knowing damn well what had happened to both brothers.

''No,'' Pamela said, casting her eyes downward. ''That brother is dead. An Indian killed him.'' Her eyes shot up, tears stinging at their corners, hurting inside with the remembrance of which Indian she was accusing of having done the ghastly deed to Anthony! ''My brother Anthony was my older brother. He is the one who is now dead. It's my younger brother, Robert, who is missing, but hopefully still alive. Sir, please help me find him. He is all that I have left.''

''You have come for assistance?'' Colonel Bradley said, reaching to smooth some of the ash from Pamela's face. ''Perhaps *tomorrow*?''

''Then you . . . will help . . . ?''

Pamela's words were cut short when she just happened to look past the colonel in an effort to shut out the lust rising in his eyes. She had planned to focus her thoughts on something more pleasant than what this colonel might have in mind for her, but she hadn't planned to see the . . . scalp, with the fresh, dried blood.

Her throat constricted with a sudden anguished pain. A dizziness spiraled through her when she recognized the hair. Its color. Its length. Oh, Lord. It was either Anthony's or *Robert's* scalp.

Numb from the discovery, she began to inch backward. "No," she was finally able to whisper. "Oh, Lord God, no—"

Many things were flooding her senses. She was aghast at seeing her brother's scalp, yet another part of her was relieved at seeing it *here*. Didn't that mean that Strong Bear was innocent? He had no connections with the British whatsoever! If he had scalped Anthony or Robert, he most surely wouldn't have given the scalp to Colonel Bradley. Strong Bear *was* innocent. Her insides were awash with such a relief! Yet seeing the scalp, being brought face-to-face again with stark reality, made sadness engulf any joy she had momentarily felt.

Colonel Bradley saw her wince. He glanced over his shoulder, looking in the direction of her vision. Damn! He had forgotten about her brother's scalp. She had seen it! Now she *knew*!

Turning, he glared at Pamela. His plans had changed again. But he would tame her into wanting him. He would make her forget. . . .

Sneering, he moved stiffly to Pamela and grabbed her wrists and yanked her against him. Fitting his body fully against hers, he crushed his mouth down, claiming her lips with a brutal kiss, ignoring how she struggled in his arms. His loins were on fire. Never had he wanted a woman so severely as *now*. And, by God, he would have her.

Prying her lips apart with his tongue, holding her pinioned against him with one hand, trailing the other over her back and buttocks, Colonel Bradley swept his tongue inside the honeydew sweetness of her mouth.

His tongue invading her mouth, his hands moving so familiarly over her body, made a keen revulsion overtake Pamela. It was more than she could bear! Without another thought she clamped her teeth down and felt the taste of salt in her mouth as blood spurted from his bitten tongue.

Colonel Bradley's eyes flew open, the pain searing into his brain like bolts of lightning. He jerked away from Pamela, yowling, tasting the blood, feeling it run in warm streams down the corners of his mouth.

His eyes narrowed as he glowered at Pamela, swallowing more and more blood as it seeped from his injured tongue. "You witch," he shouted. "You heathen *bitch*."

Pamela turned with a start as the gentle young man who had accompanied her to the fort raced into the cabin, his eyes wide. "Colonel Bradley, what—?"

Lucas's words were cut short when he saw the blood on the colonel's mouth and streaming down his bare chest. He glanced from Pamela to the colonel, his insides laughing. The lady had surely bitten the colonel's tongue! Ah, what courage she possessed. She dared to stand up against a man of such position in the British militia?

Colonel Bradley waved a hand fitfully in the air, his wrist loose. "Lucas, take her away," he stormed. "Tie her outside in the middle of the courtyard on the stake used for securing soldiers for whippings! She's proven to be as uncivilized as all the other American settlers I've come across. She's even worse than a savage Indian squaw."

Colonel Bradley glared down into Pamela's face. "I'm going to teach you obedience," he growled. "You're going to be tied out in the cold temperatures of the night and then in the sun all day tomorrow until you beg to be brought in so you can behave as a lady behaves."

He slapped her across the face. "If you don't behave yourself your scalp will join your older brother's on my wall," he chuckled darkly.

The color drained from Pamela's face as she took another quick look at the scalp. "Anthony . . ." she gulped, now knowing exactly which brother had met his death at the hand of this British officer. Everything within her hurt with the remorseful pain of knowing. But now, what of *Robert*?

Colonel Bradley gave Pamela a rough shove. "Take her away," he ordered, spitting a pool of blood at his feet. "And, Lucas, don't bring her back until she *begs*. Do you understand?"

Lucas nodded, his shoulders slumped, his eyes lowered. "Yes, sir," he gulped.

Colonel Bradley suddenly blocked their exit. He reached inside his breeches pocket and took the gold nugget from inside it. He held it before Pamela's eyes. "Recognize this?" he growled.

"No, should I?"

"It was in your brother's possession. Where'd he get it?"

Pamela's eyes wavered. "I don't know and if I did, I'd not tell you," she hissed, wondering, herself, where Anthony had gotten a gold nugget and why he hadn't shown it to her. He had shared most everything with her. No other brother or sister could have been as close!

"I didn't think I'd get answers from you," Colonel Bradley said, then nodded toward Lucas. "Go ahead. Take her away."

Lucas took Pamela's arm gently and led her from the cabin. The moonlight bright overhead illuminated the tears silvering Pamela's face. He turned her to look into her eyes. "It ain't what I want to do, miss. It ain't at all what I want to do."

Pamela smoothed tears from her cheek. "I shouldn't have expected anything better from that evil man," she half sobbed. "It seems that this has all been planned from the start."

She beseeched Lucas with her wavering eyes. "You're different," she murmured. "You're so kind. Could you please tell me if you know of the fate of my brother Robert?"

Lucas shook his head. "I'm not free to say," he mumbled, then guided her to the spot in the courtyard where a stake stood tall and menacing from the ground.

Looking bravely ahead, staring into space, Pamela let

Lucas tie her to the stake, knowing that escape from this hellhole was impossible. Then she let her mind wander to Strong Bear. Would he care enough to come, to rescue her? Or had her doubts of him dampened his feelings for her?

But, he already had a wife. He truly didn't even need Pamela!

Pamela tried to blank all thoughts from her mind. For the moment she was all that she had in life and she had never felt so isolated . . . so empty.

With only a blanket clutched about his nude body, Robert trembled from the chill of the night. His bare feet raw, he stumbled on through the night. That he had escaped from the Delaware Indian, Flying Deer, did not mean he was going to live to see another sunrise. The Indians had tortured him, half-starving him to a terribly weakened condition.

Humiliation over his treatment in the Indian village made a seething rage eat away at his gut. Day in and day out he had been led around nude by giggling Indian squaws with a leash secured around his neck. He had been forced to do women's chores. He had been forced to sleep with the Indians' pack of dogs!

Following a stream that cut its way through the dense forest, Robert hoped it forked into the creek that flowed peacefully by the Boyd cabin. He *had* to return home to see what had happened to Pamela and Anthony! Surely he hadn't been singled out to be treated so inhumanely. As vicious as the Indians had been to him, he knew better than to hope that his brother and sister would be spared the same humiliation.

His legs buckling, Robert fell to the ground. He crawled to the stream and sank a hand into its icy depths. Drawing a cupped hand of water to his parched lips, he drank greedily.

Then, clutching the blanket snugly about him, he curled up on his side on the ground and looked slowly about him.

Though the moon was bright, casting silver streamers through the foliage overhead, Robert only saw blurred shadows. Without his eyeglasses he was even more defenseless.

Fourteen

Your lips clung to mine till I prayed in my bliss
They might never unclasp from the rapturous kiss.
—Hunt

Streaks of orange colored the evening sky. From a tree's limb overlooking the fort, dark eyes traced the lowering sun until the western horizon began swallowing it. Strong Bear had not been patient. As each hour had passed he had watched the British soldiers torment Pamela as she stood bound to a stake by both her ankles and wrists. Only one soldier had treated her fairly, even gently. A young paleface with hair the color of wheat. Strong Bear had watched as this younger soldier had gently fed Pamela. And when he had tipped a cup of water to Pamela's lips even then had the young soldier been gentle.

A low growl emitted from deep inside Strong Bear when he realized just why Pamela had been fed and given water. The British colonel had most surely given the young soldier such orders, having the need to keep the beautiful

178

white woman at least strong enough to ravage when he felt the compulsion to do so! He had left her on the stake to *tame* her.

Strong Bear's lips formed a smug smile. Even with the soldiers she had shown courage and strength. She was surely like no other white woman. She had been born with the bravery of a Miami woman!

His gaze swept over her, seeing the doeskin dress, the intricately beaded moccasins, and her braided hair. She had chosen the dress of the Miami over her own to escape in. Though Strong Bear understood why, he was pleased to see her dressed in his tribe's familiar garb.

He frowned when he saw the ash on her face. Did she think coloring her face could make her appear a Miami? He did not approve of this that she had done, yet if she had not, her lovely face would have been burned by the sun. The sun's rays had not been able to penetrate the ash.

"Soon she will again be mine," he whispered to himself. "She will believe that Strong Bear *is* innocent of crimes accused. I will be patient no longer. I will explain everything fully to her. She will never want to escape from Strong Bear again!"

Watching the sky darkening, Strong Bear's pulse began to race. He had waited through the long day for darkness. When he had found Pamela gone from the Miami village, he had decided that he would search alone. He had foreseen trouble in numbers, should he take his warriors. Strong Bear wanted still to keep peace for his people. Warring with the British soldiers would surely only bring death to many of his braves, women, and children. Enough blood had been spilled in the past.

As he had traveled through the forest in search of Pamela, Strong Bear had tried to think as she might have when planning her escape. Each time he had come to the same conclusion. Of course she would go to people of her own skin coloring for help. That would lead her to the British fort, not knowing that the British at this fort were the enemies of all white settlers!

He targeted his search on the British fort. Once there he had climbed a tree close to the fort and had quickly seen Pamela tied to a stake. It had torn at his insides to see her suffering at the hands of the British, yet he could not rescue her by daylight. He was only one man, surrounded by dozens of soldiers.

He had begun the long wait, already planning how he would release Pamela. He had chosen what would be the easiest for her. Though fed by the British, she still might have been too weak to climb over the high wall. Strong Bear would dig a tunnel beneath the wall. His woman could crawl better than she could climb!

It was now dark, the moon a great circle of white against a black velveteen sky. Stars sparkled, twinkling like fireflies rising from the deep folds of grass for their early evening flights of romance.

Strong Bear moved his hands, testing his weapons. A great quiver of arrows was strapped to his back; his powerful bow was slung across his shoulder. A knife was sheathed at one hip; a hatchet for digging, and possibly scalping, was at the other.

Strong Bear wore only a breechclout and moccasins, his cluster of turkey feathers at the loop of his hair at the back, and he had chosen to paint his face quite appropriately this night. To frighten evil spirits and enemies and to please his own sense of the fitness of things, Strong Bear had painted his face both black and red on opposite sides, his eyes circled with red to heighten the savage effect. He was a fierce warrior this night! He was going to rescue his woman! His strawberry roan was reined close by, for the swift escape!

With the darkness acting as a protective shield, Strong Bear slid down from the tree. As he moved stealthily onward, he watched the movement of the torch on top of the fort wall. And when it was farthest away from him opposite the side where he had planned to dig, he ran with the speed gifted to all Miami braves across the clearing and up the bluff on which sat the fort. The blockhouse there cast a looming shadow across Strong Bear's own as he moved to stand flush against the wall, taking time to catch his breath.

And when his lungs were again filled and his heart was beating more evenly, Strong Bear removed the quiver of arrows and his bow. After laying them on the ground close beside him, he determinedly lifted the hatchet from the waist of his breechclout, fell to his knees, and began to dig. . . .

Pamela dozed on the stake, her head bobbing. When her body twitched, she was fully alert again. Her wrists and ankles pained her dreadfully, burning from the ropes digging into her flesh. Her head throbbed. Though it was only late spring the sun had been hotter than usual this day, beaming down on her as though she had been the only person in the world soaking in the fiery rays.

But she was thankful for at least one thing. Lucas, the young soldier, had fed her and given her drinks of water throughout the long day. If not for his kindness and the ash on her face, which had mercifully spared her skin from burning, she would not dare to think of how she would be faring.

Feeling the damp, cold fingers of night beginning to seep in, penetrating her buckskin dress as though she wore nothing at all, Pamela dreaded spending another night on the stake. But she would not give in to her body's aches and pains, or the demands of the British colonel. She would rather die first.

Tears threatened to spill from her eyes, but she stubbornly blinked them away. She could not help but think of Strong Bear and how his treatment of her had so differed from the British colonel's. It wasn't hard to know which of these two was the true savage! Colonel Bradley was hardly *human*!

Feeling the need to sleep again overwhelm her, Pamela lowered her eyes. Her head bobbed, but then a noise from somewhere close by drew her fully awake again. It was a movement behind her. Muffled footsteps as quiet as a panther's padded toward her. Fear grabbed her insides, wondering *who* . . . ? If it was the colonel, coming to get her to appease his lusty whims, he would not be sneaking up on her. He would boldly come, and command accompanying soldiers to release her!

So . . . who?

Pamela paled as she felt hands at her wrists working with the knots of the rope. With a jerk she turned her head and her insides fluttered when she saw Strong Bear wrestling with ropes until they fell away.

A wondrous joy surged through Pamela. Deep down she had known that he would come for her. And, oh, how glad that he had, and not only because she was being rescued, but also to give her the chance to apologize to him, tell him that she had been wrong to accuse him of murdering her brothers. She now knew that Strong Bear had most surely just happened along and foiled the British colonel's plans of having her to himself once he had taken care of her brothers!

Wriggling and stretching her freed fingers, Pamela was suddenly caught up in remembrances of the other reasons why she could not totally trust Strong Bear. Snow Owl's words of how he wanted so many sons were imbedded into Pamela's heart like a leaf fossilized in stone. Could he have come for her even now to take her back to his village, to use her only for childbearing?

Stormy feelings engulfed her. As she looked down at Strong Bear while he deftly untied the knot at her ankles, she wanted to reach out to him, hug him, say that she was glad to see him. But should she be? If he wanted her only for using . . .

But suddenly a thought crossed her mind. Surely he would not choose her for just *that*. Would he so doggedly pursue a white woman with whom to start a Miami family . . . ? Perhaps he pursued her for different reasons. Could he desire her, for desire's sake alone?

Now able to set her feet wholly on the ground, feeling

the blood rushing past her ankles, strengthening her ability to walk, Pamela turned and faced Strong Bear as he towered over her. The moon's beams reflected onto his face of many colors, making her gasp. But the moon caught something else beneath its shine. She was looking into eyes so intense with feeling, it could not be caused by a man who only had thoughts of many sons. In his eyes he was speaking silent words of love to her! A love that was real, not illusion.

"Come. We must hurry," Strong Bear said, taking her gently by a hand, to direct her away from the center of the courtyard. His insides were warm, for in Pamela's eyes he had seen gladness that it was he rescuing her. Something had happened to help her finally make peace inside her heart about Strong Bear!

"How are we to escape?" Pamela asked, breathless as she moved steadily beside him. "Surely we will be caught. And I doubt if I have the strength to climb the wall, Strong Bear. It is so *high*."

Sweeping an arm about her waist to hurry her on, Strong Bear kept watch on all sides as they crossed the yard. The torch set at the highest point on the wall barely flickered.

"No climbing is required," he mumbled, pointing toward the fresh mound of dirt that lay in two heaps flush with the wall. "My *me-tam-sah*, woman, we will crawl to safety."

Pamela's eyes widened. She gave Strong Bear an inquisitive look. "Crawl . . . ?" she questioned. And then she saw the dark hole of the tunnel. She didn't hesitate when Strong Bear ushered her down into it.

"Move quickly," he said, casting glances across his shoulder. "Strong Bear will follow."

Her heart pounding with excitement, Pamela grunted and groaned until she was finally on the other side of the wall. She rose to her knees and held her hands to her throat, awaiting Strong Bear's arrival. And when he finally appeared beside her, positioning his quiver of arrows again at his back, and slinging his bow across his shoulder, she felt they might escape.

But her gaze caught the vast land ahead as it sloped languidly to the forest. Could she run as quickly as Strong Bear? Her knees were still weak from her long imprisonment on the stake.

Strong Bear's movements were rapid. His eyes lingered for only a moment on Pamela's loveliness and then he drew her into his arms. "Strong Bear is known for his swiftness," he whispered. "Strong Bear carry you to full safety."

Though standing in the shadows of the fort wall, Pamela's breath quickened in passion as their gazes locked. In Strong Bear's eyes she saw much that spoke of love. And when his lips lowered to hers, grazing sweetly, as if testing her for approval, it was not at all hard for her to twine her arms about his neck and return the kiss with a raging hunger never known to her before.

It was then that he kissed her with a fierce, possessive heat that left her senses reeling as he pulled away and swept her up into his arms. Then he began running. The fortress loomed like a ghost behind them.

Pamela rested her cheek against Strong Bear's powerful chest, now fully trusting. Deep inside her heart she knew that he was not responsible for Robert's disappearance. Together they would find Robert. They would!

She tried not to let the memory that Snow Owl was Strong Bear's wife ruin this moment of sharing with Strong Bear. For now, he was *hers*. She was *his*.

Lucas Boatright stepped out from the shadows, smiling toward the empty post in the ground where Pamela had been tied. He had watched the Indian take her away. He had seen her go willingly with him. Somehow Lucas knew that she was better off with the Indian, than with the vile Colonel Bradley.

But Lucas's fate was now in doubt. When Colonel Bradley found that Pamela had been stolen away in the middle of the night, he would find someone to blame. And Lucas would more than likely be the scapegoat chosen for such punishment.

Lucas's weak stomach troubled him once again. He ran behind the cabin and hung his head, feeling the bitterness already rising inside his throat. Why had he ever believed that he had what it took to become a soldier? He had only wanted to travel, to see the world. Never had he thought he would be a witness to such hate, such greed, such *evil*. . . .

Still clutching the blanket about him to hide his nudity, Robert stumbled, finding it hard to place one foot ahead of the other. But he could hardly hold in the need to shout with excitement, for the blurry tree stumps he was now seeing were proof that he was near his cabin. In his mind's eye he could recall exactly when he and Anthony had shared time cutting these particular trees. They had laughed and teased each other as they chopped and sawed, using the logs later to spice up the odor of the cabin by throwing them on the fire.

He tried to peer ahead to see the cabin, but all he perceived was color and shadow, blending into an aggravating blur. If he could only see Pamela or Anthony in the yard beside the cabin, then he would know that only he had been chosen for the abduction. He did know at least that they hadn't been brought to the Delaware village!

"I . . . must . . . see for myself . . . if they are . . . all right. . . ." Robert panted, now forcing his legs to move at a faster pace. He ran, he stumbled, he breathed in ragged gasps. But finally he was there. The cabin. Only a few more footsteps away . . .

When he reached the cabin he moved cautiously to the door and eased it open. A cold horror filled him when he found the house not only cold and dark, but also *empty*.

Robert moved numbly into the cabin, looking guardedly around him. His bare feet discovered broken glass on the floor; his squinted eyes detected the disarray of the cabin.

Someone had come and rummaged through everything, as though searching for jewels.

His gaze stopped at the fireplace, where he saw the charred remains of food that had burned due to neglect from the cook, and the only cook in this cabin had been his *sister*. When he had last left her she had been baking gingerbread men!

Desperation welling inside, Robert lurched about the cabin, throwing blankets from the bed, knocking items from the shelves and table that weren't already dislodged and on the floor. Tears scalded the corners of his eyes, for he knew now that his sister and brother had met a dreadful fate.

Shaking away his grief, he bent to a knee and probed beneath his bed, drawing from it a small box where he stored his spare eyeglasses. His face a mask of determination, he lifted the lid, reached for his gold-framed spectacles, and settled them on the bridge of his nose.

Blinking his eyes, he looked slowly around the cabin, now able to focus on its emptiness. A sort of knifelike pain stabbed him as he conjectured on their fate. But he would find out. Now with his eyeglasses enabling him to see, he would go to any lengths to find answers.

He took one last lingering look about the cabin. His heart tugged when he glanced at the bed on which his father had weakened and died. And then he looked upward, at the loft, where Pamela had slept. A faint smell of the cologne she had brought with her from Williamsburg wafted down from the rafters, touching him, as though it were she. It took all of his willpower not to burst into tears, for he doubted now if he would ever see her again.

He spied, then picked up, the book from the floor from which he had read passages of *Robin Hood* to his ailing father. He opened the book and ran his fingers across the printed page, for the first time realizing what little importance lay in the pages of a book. If he could only relive the past, the hours he had spent reading, he would spend them with family!

Shoving the book aside, tormented by memories, Robert shook the blanket away from his shoulders. He found and quickly drew on a pair of his breeches and slipped into a shirt. But before he could put on his shoes a dark shadow fell across the door.

He turned slowly and froze inside when he saw Flying Deer standing there, leering at him. "You—" Robert gasped. Then he felt the fool he was. All along the damn Indian had been following him, toying with him. Robert had never truly escaped at all!

Another Indian stepped within view behind Flying Deer, carrying a lighted torch. Robert took a quick step backward, wondering if they intended to burn the cabin with him inside it.

But he soon had the answer. Flying Deer went to him and grabbed his arm and forced him outside, a long-bladed knife at his throat. Robert stood by and watched as the cabin went up in flames, carrying with it all memories—all hopes—of the Boyd family.

He grimaced when Flying Deer took his eyeglasses away and looked at them, puzzled, then dropped them to the ground and crushed them with the heel of his moccasin.

"You now return to village with Flying Deer," Flying Deer said in fluent English. "White man, the squaws have missed you."

Robert lowered his eyes and moved in jerks with Flying Deer to the Indian's horse. He was not at all surprised when a leash was fitted about his neck and he was led behind the horse on foot, again an animal instead of a man.

Sitting on a thick pallet of blankets, mesmerized by the black ovals of Strong Bear's eyes, Pamela relaxed as he smoothed a wet, soft buckskin cloth across her face, removing the ash. The campfire blazing next to a meandering stream sent a welcome warmth seeping into her pores. They had stopped to rest before traveling on to Strong Bear's village.

The sun was high in the sky, the air warm and caressing. The smell of the waving bluegrass was fresh and clean, even invigorating. It was easy to let herself for a moment forget everything but that she was with Strong Bear, whose lean bronzed face was so handsome it nearly took Pamela's breath away. Even with the strange sort of paint still covering his face, he was breathtaking.

As he continued gently to bathe her, she let her gaze sweep over his sleekly muscled chest to his face, marred by puckered skin where her gunshot had grazed his flesh that day of their first meeting. She lifted her hand and traced a finger across the marks, feeling his body tremor sensuously beneath her featherlight touch.

Her gaze moved slowly to his eyes. Ever so slightly, she tilted her head. "If I had taken time to aim, your wound would have been fatal," she murmured. "Strong Bear, what if—?"

He placed a finger against her lips. "One does not live life on 'ifs,' " he said thickly. "One lives on *facts*. You are here. I am here. We are alive and well. Be happy about this, my woman. Be happy."

"I am, but—" Pamela said. Then, laughing softly when she caught herself, she corrected, "I could be totally happy if I could understand things that to me now are only puzzling."

"You have questions?"

"I have thankfully found answers to much that made me almost hate you," Pamela said, lowering her eyes. "I now know that the British colonel caused all of my misfortunes." Then she looked up at him. "But, Strong Bear, I do need to know why . . . why you even bothered to come and save me. Aren't you angry at me for having left you as I did? Why would you want me? You *have* a wife." She cleared her throat nervously. "Or is it as Snow Owl said? You want me only for childbearing?"

Strong Bear's head jerked back, and then his eyes began dancing as he smiled down at her. "Strong Bear does want many children." He chuckled. "And Snow Owl has not yet given me a child. But that is not my purpose for wanting *you*."

"It's . . . not?" Pamela asked softly. "Then *why*? I had even thought it was because you wanted the land my family had settled on. But if that had been the reason, surely you would not have gone to all the trouble of winning me for that purpose. You would have *taken*. Isn't that so, Strong Bear?"

Strong Bear's insides rolled, knowing so very well that a part of him had used his feelings for her to his advantage. But the other part of him had wanted her only for herself. But he would never let her know that he had planned to win her and then the *land*.

But did he want it now? It was land known by too many people! And the graves of two white men now desecrated it. It could never be totally his and his people's. It was no longer sacred.

"Strong Bear's love for you is strong," he said thickly, partially evading her question. "Do you not know this? You are my *woman*."

"But, Strong Bear, you already have a wife," Pamela said, her eyes wavering, almost choking on the words. "That does not free me to be your woman. You are married to Snow Owl."

Strong Bear laughed softly, tracing the outline of her face with the soft touch of his finger. "Never think of her as important in my eyes," he said. "Our marriage has been one of convenience. Nothing more. When you and I become man and wife, never will it be just one of suitableness! We will share everything from the heart!"

Hearing him say that the marriage was not one of a true bond of the heart made Pamela's heart sing, yet it still did not free her to become Strong Bear's wife.

"But, Strong Bear, don't you see that though I am happy that you don't have special feelings for Snow Owl, she is still your *wife*," she said softly. "I can't marry you if you already have a wife."

Strong Bear framed her face between his hands and

smiled down at her. "In the world of the Miami two wives are accepted when the man who wishes it is a man of distinction . . . a *chief*," he said. "You will be first wife of importance, Snow Owl second."

A slow blush rose to Pamela's cheeks. She smiled awkwardly up at him, not knowing what to say. Everything was happening too fast, changing too quickly. She had lost so much. Her only gain was Strong Bear. And he could never be totally hers, for there would always be another woman standing in the way. She could hardly bear to think of sharing Strong Bear. But if what he said was true, she would have no other choice. And shouldn't she be happy that even a portion of him would be hers? Only yesterday she had believed him guilty of so many things! Today she knew that he was innocent! She was free now of all reasons not to give herself to him. Except for Snow Owl . . .

"It is now my woman's turn to bathe paint away from proud chief's face," Strong Bear said, his eyes gleaming. "My woman, do it now."

Though there was a comand in the way he spoke to her, she did not mind. It was the way he always labeled her as his "woman" that stirred Pamela's insides. Recalling his kiss of possession outside the walls of the British fort made her realize again just how much he meant to her. The only thing that could make her happiness almost complete was to find Robert and know that he was all right. There was nothing at all she could ever do about Anthony.

This was a new starting point in her life, and she must accept the fact that she may never step foot into a white community again. She *was* possessed by Strong Bear. Fully. Her heart belonged to him. And she had admired how he had shown respect for her by not forcing himself on her when she had treated him so distantly in his cabin. He had proven to her even then what a gentleman he was . . . something that the white community would never believe about an Indian. But she knew. That was all that was important.

Accepting the buckskin cloth from Strong Bear, Pamela wetted it, then wrung the excess water from it. Ever so lightly she placed the cloth to Strong Bear's face. Her fingers trembled as she began smoothing the red circles from around one of his hauntingly dark eyes.

"Why did you paint your face so colorfully?" she murmured, not wanting to share only small talk with him, but instead a kiss to compare with the last one he had given her.

Pamela's nearness—her touch—was evoking an intense passion in Strong Bear that could hardly be controlled. The smoldering memories of how her body had felt to him, and of the kisses they had shared, made him find it very hard to practice the art of restraint. He had been forced to wait because of her sadness and her mistrust of him. But now at least the mistrust had been cast aside. It was time to love her again, to help transport her sadnesses from her mind.

"Painting in all manners is a means of magic to the Miami," he said, an unbidden huskiness thick in his voice. "Miami warriors want always to be powerful, but if not, at least take on the appearance of one who is fierce. There are many reasons one paints the face. And each color has different meaning."

"Why did you choose red and black paint for rescuing me?" Pamela asked, now working at removing the black paint. Only a few more strokes and his face would be smoothly clean, the copper of his skin already gleaming from the fresh washing.

"Fierce warriors paint face both black and red," Strong Bear said, watching as she dropped the cloth back into the water, taking this to mean that his face was now as clean as hers.

Unable to hold back his need of her any longer, and—seeing the strong pulsebeat at the hollow of her throat—knowing that she wanted him just as much, Strong Bear reached for her wrists and drew her close to him, feeling the press of her breasts through the doeskin dress against his chest.

''Tell Strong Bear you wish to be kissed,'' he said huskily. His lips brushed teasingly against her mouth. His tongue lightly traced the outline of her lips. ''Desire me, my woman. Desire me.''

Pamela's lips quivered as she nodded her response. ''I do desire you,'' she whispered then. ''Oh, I do. I do.''

''My woman,'' Strong Bear said, then fastened his lips over hers as he lowered her onto the blankets beside the fire. His fingers trembled as he sought out the satin touch of her thighs beneath the skirt of the dress. When she parted her legs and let his fingers move even higher, he knew that she was ready again to accept him in every way that a woman sensually accepts a man.

He had waited so long, ah, so painfully long. . . .

Fifteen

❧❧

I love my Love, And my Love loves me!
—Coleridge

Strong Bear drew Pamela to her feet before him, moments away from fully possessing her again. He had waited this long, a few moments longer would only enhance the pleasure!

His fingers deftly unbraided her hair; Strong Bear devoured Pamela's hauntingly lovely visage, which, as she looked adoringly at him, reminded him again of a quiet meadow. Within her translucent eyes he no longer saw mystery, only innocence.

Pamela's loosened hair cascaded over her shoulders. Strong Bear touched it thoughtfully, smoothing it between his fingers as he wondered at its lustrous length.

Then he drew her pliant body against his so that he could feel her every contour through the softness of her buckskin dress. Her ripe, curving breasts pressed into his chest, firing his inner being and pulsing his blood furiously.

"There is now no one but Strong Bear to care for you," he said thickly. "Do you not understand this?"

A soft pain rose into Pamela's eyes. She drew away from Strong Bear, biting her lower lip. The remembrance of Robert caused bitter anguish to flood her senses. The fears of what had happened to her younger brother were deeply imbedded in her heart.

"My words cause you pain?" Strong Bear asked, cupping Pamela's chin in his hand, forcing her eyes to meet his. "Why do they? Have not I proven myself—my love—to you in many ways? Do you not love me as much?"

Pamela searched his face with her eyes, a warmth inside her beginning to kindle, making her realize again he dampened the ugly memories. Time with him was beautiful! Beautiful! While riding a cloud of rapture she would at least for a while be at peace with herself . . . with the world.

With a strangled sob, Pamela flung herself into Strong Bear's arms. "Strong Bear, I do love you so," she cried. "I do want you. Please . . . love me. Love me now."

Every inch of Pamela tingled when Strong Bear's mouth seared into hers, his hands moving to her breasts to caress them through the thin buckskin material. Her nipples rose into twin peaks as he savored their feel.

Pamela's lips parted hungrily as he explored the honey sweetness of her depths, while his skillful fingers roamed to the hem of her dress, which he peeled back across her silken flesh.

Sensual chills shivered through Pamela. She stepped away from Strong Bear and let him continue undressing her. When she was nude, she, in turn, reached for the waistband of his breechclout and began lowering it over his lean hips, her eyes afire with passion as she gazed into his.

A soft smile played at Strong Bear's lips. Stepping out of his breechclout, he took her hand and guided it to his hardness. A blush rose hotly on Pamela's cheeks as her fingers circled his velveteen shaft. And as he guided her hand's movements, she discovered that this part of him that she was touching felt strangely alive, pulsing like an extension of her heart now thudding hard inside her chest.

"There are many ways of giving and receiving pleasure between two in love," Strong Bear said huskily, his eyes now hazed over with rising ecstasy. "Let me teach you. You give pleasure, then receive."

Only vaguely aware of being out in the open, with the heavens and the forest animals witness to the erotic love scene being enacted on this vast wilderness stage, Pamela followed Strong Bear's bidding as he gripped her shoulders and urged her to her knees before him.

"Love me, my woman," Strong Bear said hoarsely, leading her mouth to his distended manhood. "In all ways shall we share lovemaking. Soon you will be my wife. Each morning—each night—will bring new pleasures into our lives."

At first hesitant to perform this unfamiliar act, never having known of any ways to make love until with Strong Bear, Pamela acquiesced then, wanting him to unlock all of the mysteries of life for her. What he asked of her even made a strange sort of euphoria sweep through her, for it *did* seem most wicked!

Her tongue flicked at first until she became used to the new waves of pleasure loving him in this way caused her. And then it was beautifully easy to let herself give him what he seemed so dearly to want, for his moans of gratification were proof that what she did was *right*.

She continued for a moment longer until, with his hands on her shoulders, he guided her to a soft mat of grass. It bent beneath her weight as she lay back, Strong Bear looking down at her, his dark eyes gleaming.

"Now Strong Bear pleasures *you*," he said, leaning down over her. His lips explored her fiery flesh, first kissing the nipples of her breasts into a renewed hardness. Then his lips traveled lower, teaching Pamela that she had many secret places of pleasure along her body.

When his tongue approached the forbidden triangle at

her thighs, she looked down at him with shame. But when he spread her legs and kissed her pulsing love and then flicked his tongue where his lips had been, Pamela shimmered wth rapture and closed her eyes to enjoy this exquisite moment. Soft moans escaped from between her lips. She tossed her head and bit her lower lip as the pleasure mounted. And just as she achieved the ultimate joy, she felt the wondrous caress of his tongue replaced by his manly hardness as he eased into her.

Strong Bear's arms swept Pamela fully against him. She clung to him, reveling in the pulsating hardness that impaled her. Her lips quivered beneath his in a kiss that was surprisingly gentle. She was becoming weakened by her passion. His fingers, now caressing her breasts lightly, thumbs circling her hardened nipples, made her tremble with delight.

He was so skilled at lovemaking; surely he had given many women much pleasure. A jealous ache encircled Pamela's heart when she remembered she was not the first woman to lie with him. And she would not be the last. There was always Snow Owl!

But Pamela was determined to give of herself in all ways so he would desire no other woman. She wanted him to hunger for her, only her! If it was the custom of the Miami to have more than one wife, she would have to accept it. But Strong Bear would love only *one* wife. He would truly love only *her*.

Strong Bear thrust eagerly inside Pamela. As his hips rocked and his strokes became smooth and even, a lethargic feeling of floating was unleashed inside him. He smoothed his hands over Pamela's breasts. He probed his tongue gently between her teeth and again savored her sweetness.

His hands swept lower and clasped her buttocks to mold her slender body to his. As she locked her ankles about him, raising her hips, he brushed his lips against her neck and whispered her name.

The pulsing peak of Pamela's passion was cresting. She

rained kisses across Strong Bear's corded shoulders; she ran her hands over the sleekness of his back, savoring him, loving him. Her insides were on fire, with a blaze that was spreading . . . spreading. Their bodies rocked and tremored. Together they reached the ultimate blending shared between two people in love.

Then they lay quiet, clinging together. Strong Bear's hands explored the perfect curves of Pamela's silken flesh, in undying awe of her, his woman. They were two lovers, united as one. And they had all of the future before them to savor.

"Thank you, Strong Bear," Pamela said, suddenly breaking through their shared silence.

"A woman does not thank a man for making love," Strong Bear chuckled, giving her a lighthearted smile.

Pamela leaned up on an elbow, her free hand lightly touching the scar at his temple, the scar that she had inflicted. "I thank you for so many things," she said, her eyes misting as she looked into his steady gaze. She leaned over and pressed her lips gently to the scar. "I thank you for not being the one who . . . who killed my brother Anthony. I thank you for having chosen me to love."

Humbled by her sweetness, by her sincerity, Strong Bear swept her atop him, into his arms. His lips spread kisses across the gentle lines of her face. His hands trembled as they reveled in the creaminess of her flesh.

"So much that you thank me for comes easy for Strong Bear," he said, combing his fingers through her hair, then urging her lips to his. "So . . . so . . . easy."

Pamela's head was swimming with delight, yet there was one nagging worry that was preventing her from totally enjoying these moments with Strong Bear. Robert! Very soon, even this night, she must plead with Strong Bear to help her find her brother. Robert *had* to be alive. It was unfair that only she of all her family should find such paradise in this Kentucky wilderness.

Of course, for her the true paradise was not the land, but, instead, Strong Bear.

*   *   *

Lucas Boatright paced the courtyard. He had watched the sun rise slowly from behind the trees, counting off time until Colonel Bradley would awaken from his long night of sleep.

Looking skyward, Lucas stopped to knead his brow. The sun was at its highest point in the heavens and still Colonel Bradley had not come out of his cabin to check on Pamela. But the colonel had spent many long hours on horseback the past several days hunting for her; he had searched hard and long and then she had come and had willingly gone to *him*.

Strange how life had its ironic twists. Now she was gone again. The worst could be expected of Colonel Bradley when he discovered that Lucas had let her slip away into the night. Lucas's only faint hope to survive the wrathful encounter with the colonel was to say that he had needed to get some sleep and while he had slept she had gotten away somehow. Surely the colonel understood the need to sleep. Colonel Bradley was known for his long sieges of rest!

Suddenly the air exploded around Lucas when Colonel Bradley's voice resounded through the courtyard with a fitful shout of anger.

"By God, where is she?" Colonel Bradley ranted, stomping toward Lucas wearing only his breeches. He was barefoot and his hair struck up in all directions. It was evident that the colonel had only just awakened and had come to check up on his prize.

Lucas felt the color draining from his face and the strength leaving his knees when Colonel Bradley went to the stake and stooped to pick up the ropes which had bound Pamela.

Colonel Bradley rose to his full height and went to stand before Lucas. With a low growl he held the ropes in front of Lucas's face. "How could you allow this to happen?" he snarled. "You were supposed to keep watch. How could she escape if you were watching? You lazy bastard, you fell asleep, didn't you?''

"It just happened," Lucas said, lowering his eyes. "I couldn't help it. A body can only be pushed so hard and then it . . . needs rest.''

Colonel Bradley slapped Lucas, leaving the red imprint of his hand on Lucas's face. "You worthless imbecile," he growled. Then he spun around and studied the vacant stake. "How? How could she do it?"

A soldier ran up to the colonel, breathless. His face was almost the color of his blood-red uniform. "Sir, I just discovered a tunnel beneath the wall," he said, his dark eyes anxious. "That's how she escaped."

"A tunnel, eh?" Colonel Bradley said, looking toward the high fence in the distance. He kneaded his chin. "And who would have dug the tunnel but an Indian?"

"That's exactly my assumption, sir," the soldier said, nodding. He clasped his hands together behind him, looking over at Lucas, seeing the hand print on his cheek and the fear in his eyes. He prayed that he would not be the one assigned to use the whip on Lucas. Lucas was one of the most popular soldiers at the fort. If the choice were to be made, it would be the colonel who would be the recipient of a whip, even worse. . . .

"It doesn't take much thought to know which Indian, now that I made my earlier rounds, checking to see who could have taken her from her cabin," Colonel Bradley said dryly. "There are only two villages left to check."

He turned to Lucas. "You're the one who let her get away, so you're the one who's going to lure her back," he growled. "While I go in one direction in the forest, you'll go in another."

Lucas swallowed hard. "What do you mean?" he asked tremulously, afraid to hear the answer.

Colonel Bradley stepped even closer to Lucas and spoke into his face. "While I take several men with me to go search for the damn Indian who stole the woman away, you'll go to the Delaware village and tell Flying Deer you want the woman's younger brother, Robert, to bring back to the fort as bait. By God, if I don't find her, she'll return for her brother once rumor informs her he's here.''

Lucas paled. ''Sir, the Delaware village?'' he said hoarsely. ''I have to go to the Delaware village alone?''

''It's either that or take a turn on the stake,'' Colonel Bradley hissed. ''I could order your back bared for a good lashing and then lock you away in the stockade. Rats would have fun with you in there.''

Laughing wickedly, Colonel Bradley strode away. Lucas trembled, knowing that he had no choice but to go to the Delaware village. Anything was better than a brutal whipping. He could already feel the cold slice of the whip against his bare flesh!

Inside he felt like a little boy, wishing to begin life all over again, to be given a second chance to choose his destiny. . . .

Sixteen

❧❧

I need the starshine of your heavenly eyes,
After the day's great sun.

—Towne

At the Miami village, Snow Owl had watched soberly as Strong Bear had dismounted his strawberry roan, then carried the white wench into his dwelling, as though Snow Owl did not exist. Pamela had felt the heat of the squaw's eyes. She had even heard Snow Owl's harsh, angry breathing. Hate was surely not a word strong enough to describe the beautiful Indian woman's feelings for Pamela, and this stirred Pamela's fear again.

But before long she forgot Snow Owl, as she surrendered to Strong Bear's rapturous lips sensually fastened over her taut-tipped breast. Until he had drawn her into his arms she had been tense, struck by Snow Owl's anger and the knowledge that soon Strong Bear would leave her, to go in search of Robert. Would she find her brother? And if so, *alive?*

But now, for this moment, she let herself savor this

warm cocooned world where no worries lurked, no human follies beset her mind. Her body was again fusing with Strong Bear's, becoming one. Their destinies were intertwined, surely mapped out long before she had taken her first breath of life! Cuddled in his arms, it was so easy for Pamela to accept her preordained fate to be with this man. Strong Bear made everything sweet . . . oh, so acceptable.

"My *me-tam-sah*, woman," Strong Bear said huskily as he encircled her in his well-muscled arms, and drew her curvacious nakedness against him as he positioned himself above her.

The fire in the firespace was pleasant as waves of warmth radiated over Strong Bear's bare buttocks. The sound of children at their early morning play outside the cabin was muted by the piece of bark fastened over the doorway.

Inside the cabin their breath mingled, their eyes mirrored their love, and Pamela and Strong Bear shared another stolen moment of ecstasy.

"I now understand how you say the word *woman* in Miami," Pamela said, twining her arms about Strong Bear's neck. "How in Miami do I say *handsome*, my love, for you are very handsome."

Strong Bear's eyes danced with amusement. He did not reply to her question, only gave her something else that he knew she hungered for more than the lesson of words this morning. His lips lowered to her mouth in a kiss of fire, his tongue a sheath of flame as it speared between her lips and into the honeydew recesses of her mouth.

When her tongue flicked against his, answering him in kind, he spread her silken thighs and eased his manhood inside her and began his slow, easy strokes, wanting her to hunger for what they were once again sharing. That first time he had seen her he had known they would always be together in such a way. He would have moved both heaven and earth to have her. He still would.

If anyone should ever dare to threaten her again, they would pay . . . dearly pay.

Pamela arched her body upward as he anchored her fiercely against him. Her head felt as giddy as that first time he had buried himself deeply inside her. She welcomed these renewed exquisite sensations spiraling through her body. She drank in his nearness, and loved him with a passion so keen it frightened her.

When his hands swept across her hips in a soft caress, her insides melted. A soft cry of joy came from somewhere deep inside her as his lips lingered on hers.

And then his lips moved to the slender curve of her throat, warm and delightful. His hands molded her breasts as she clung to him, pressing a kiss onto the corded muscle of his shoulder.

When he lifted his head, he looked down at her with burning, dark eyes. She touched her hands to his face and rediscovered its handsome contours.

"How can this be real?" she said in a shaky whisper. "Strong Bear, you are what fantasies are made from. How could I be so lucky to have been chosen by you to be your woman?"

Then her eyes grew moody as she cast them downward. "Yet I am not your only woman," she said, quite aware of his slowed strokes inside her. "You have a wife. Snow Owl. I again feel ashamed." She would not admit to her keen jealousy of Snow Owl.

"Do not speak of Snow Owl when in Strong Bear's arms," he said in a low rumble. He lifted Pamela's chin, forcing her eyes upward to meet the command in his. "Time spent with Strong Bear is time spent in thoughts only *of* Strong Bear. And never feel shame. It is an ugly word when two are in love."

Pamela swallowed hard, seeing the hurt—the anger—in his eyes, hearing it in his voice. That he was giving her a direct order did not matter. What mattered was that he loved her, totally. And she loved him as much.

Throwing herself fully back into his arms, she wept softly against his chest. "I'm sorry," she whispered.

Strong Bear eased her face away from him and fixed her with a look. "You cry?" he said softly. "Why do you?"

Pamela wiped a tear from her cheek with the back of her hand. "Because of you," she said, half choking on another sob that threatened to surface. "Because you love me and care for me. Strong Bear, if not for you—"

He hushed her with a hand over her mouth. "No harm will ever come to you again," he said thickly. "You are safe with me . . . with my *people*."

His lips met hers with a tender quivering; his arms swept around her and pressed her breasts hard into his chest. "We make love," he whispered against her lips. "Now. We make love for *always*."

His lips took her mouth by storm as he renewed his rhythmic movements inside her. With a moan of ecstasy she returned his kiss, clinging wildly to his muscled shoulders.

A tremor deep within her smoothed out into a delicious tingling heat, then burst forth into something beautiful inside her mind as she learned again how it felt to be a total woman.

Strong Bear inhaled the sweetness of Pamela's skin as he pressed his cheek against hers, his own release now matching hers. They clung, they savored.

And then, too soon, it was over. They separated, their eyes making words unnecessary.

But it was Strong Bear who quickly broke the spell. He had given orders to his warriors the previous night to be ready at sunup for the hunt. This was a different sort of hunt, for they had never gone in search of a white man before.

But none of his warriors had spoken against Strong Bear's decision to spend valuable time in such a way. He was their leader, their *chief*. He was wise in all things, even in his choice of wives! Pamela would be accepted as the Miami had learned to accept all things in life, good or bad.

Strong Bear gently covered Pamela's shoulders with a

blanket and then offered her a buckskin skirt and blouse. "You dress soon. Be comfortable . . . be *patient* while I go and search for your brother you call Robert," he said thickly. "You have food and warmth to last you until my return."

Pamela gladly accepted the clothes. "Thank you," she said, clutching the skirt and blouse to her chest as she sat beside the fire. "And thank you, Strong Bear, for agreeing to search for my brother. He simply must be found." She lowered her eyes, not wanting him to see the shine of tears in their corners. When she had first met Strong Bear she had been too stubborn to let him see her cry. Now it seemed that she cried in his presence more often than not. "I've already lost one brother. I pray to God that my only other brother will be spared."

Strong Bear drew on his breechclout and slipped his feet into moccasins. Positioning turkey feathers in the coiled hair at the back of his head, he saw the questioning in Pamela's eyes and wondered why. He was not at all surprised when she spoke of her wonder to him.

"You wear turkey feathers in your hair," Pamela murmured, brushing a lock of her own hair back from her brow. "Why? Are the turkey valuable to you in some magical way, Strong Bear?"

Strong Bear hurried about the cabin, readying his weapons and setting two leather bags and a wooden saucer on the mats beside Pamela. She watched wide-eyed with interest as he moved to his haunches beside her and mixed some sort of grease and red paint drawn from the leather bags.

"All Miami Indians originated from some form of lower animal," Strong Bear said matter-of-factly, stirring the substance in the saucer. "My group of Miami came from the turkey. The foot of the turkey is our tribal sign. The turkey foot is a good-luck charm. When my braves hunt and bring home turkey, the bird is eaten, but the feet are saved."

He refrained from adding that if her older brother had taken the gift of the turkey foot seriously, it could have protected him against his assailant, the evil British colonel. But most surely he had discarded it as only foolish!

Strong Bear had to wonder how Anthony had treated the gold nugget. He had seemed quite impressed by its shine, but he may have paid heed only to its dollar worth. Where was the gold nugget now? If other white men had found it, it would not be good for the Miami Indians! It could lead the white men to the sacred land where the gold nuggets shone like moonbeams in the water. That must never be allowed to happen! He had been wrong to give such a valuable gift to Anthony. Strong Bear would never be so foolish again!

Pamela noticed that Strong Bear had finished stirring the paint and grease and was now rubbing some sort of other grease onto his face. "I know nothing of your customs," she said, leaning closer to Strong Bear, watching him intently. Since he had wiped the grease on his face it shone brightly. Now he was applying red paint on his face. "Your face was painted before. You are doing so again? What did you mix with the paint?"

Strong Bear smiled at Pamela. "It is good that you wish to learn about my people's customs," he said, smoothing the paint around his eyes. "They will also learn from *you*, my woman. It is good. Yes, it is good."

He looked into the fire's flames, as though meditating as he began to speak in a soft monotone. "The face is painted in honor of spirits," he said thickly. "Paint is sacred so it is kept carefully in special bags. When needed it is put in paint saucer and mixed with grease. Strong Bear rubbed tallow lard onto face so that when the paint is applied it lies smoothly and in well-defined lines. Grease makes the paint not so irritating to the skin."

"Did you not tell me before that the color of red represented power and success and war?" Pamela murmured. "Which of these is your reason for choosing this color today? Do you expect to fight for Robert's release?"

A shiver raced across her flesh at the thought. Not only would Robert's life be in jeopardy, but also her beloved

Strong Bear's. And she would be the cause, for she was sending Strong Bear into a lion's den in search of her brother.

If anything happened to Strong Bear, what, then, of *herself*? She already knew that Snow Owl hated her. Who else shared the squaw's hostile feelings?

Having finished layering the paint, Strong Bear returned his bags and saucer to their storage shelves close to his sleeping bunk. "Strong Bear wishes for success and power," he said, giving Pamela a glance over his shoulder. "If warring is required to achieve both of these things, that is the way it will be."

Pamela tensed as he chose a bow, which he slung across a shoulder; a quiver of arrows, which he placed at his back; and then a sheathed knife, which he attached at his waist. When he came to her with heavy eyelids, she knew that it was time to bid him a farewell. It should have been a happy one since he was going to search for Robert, but it was actually sad, for a fear that she would never see him alive again engulfed her.

Dropping the blanket and clothes to the floor, she ran to him and threw herself into his arms. His chest was firm against her breasts, the thighs of his legs tight as her legs leaned into them.

"Please . . . please be careful," she murmured, enfolding him in her arms in a tight embrace.

She looked up into his eyes, seeing so much in their depths, that her heart pounded with joy. The love he felt for her was there, visible in the way he looked lovingly at her.

She felt as though she might melt into him and forever be a part of him as he fought wars, hunted for game, worshiped his spirits.

When his lips crushed hers, she released a soft, painful cry, fearing so for him that she could hardly breathe.

And then he pulled away, and strode toward the doorway. Before she could even say another word Pamela was standing alone in the cabin, her heart pounding, her knees weak. How long would she have to wait to know the answers to all her worries? When this day was over would she have her brother returned to her? Or would she have lost both Robert and Strong Bear?

Knowing that she must busy herself to make the time pass more quickly, Pamela pulled on the Indian clothes and began puttering about the cabin, straightening first one thing and then another. Her heart plummeted when she heard the sound of the horses' hooves thundering out of the village, carrying Strong Bear and his braves away from her.

Pamela's true waiting had just begun. . . .

Many miles away from Strong Bear's village loud shrieks and babies' cries tore through the air, almost deafening as death and destruction was left behind. The billowing smoke from burning cabins in this Miami Indian village reached far into the distance, trailing along behind Colonel Bradley and his soldiers.

"Now that we know for sure Pamela wasn't in that village, let us now make a call on Chief Strong Bear," Colonel Bradley said, laughing. Then his laugh faded when he saw a spattering of blood splashed onto the gathered cuffs at his wrists, as though mocking the red of his uniform.

A faithful soldier edged his horse up close to Colonel Bradley's proud white stallion. "You suspected she had been taken to Strong Bear's village. Why did you burn *this* Miami Indian village?" he asked guardedly, never wanting obviously to question the colonel's decisions.

Colonel Bradley harrumphed, lifting his nose high as smoke assailed it with the stench of death. His white wig was askew, from the fierce fight, and his glossy black boots were covered with ash. "It's always best to leave examples behind." He laughed fiendishly. "And since this village just happened to be in our path on our journey to Chief Strong Bear's village, it was an easy choice for setting an example."

Colonel Bradley flicked his horse's reins and thundered away from the soldier, anxious to see if he was right that Pamela was with Chief Strong Bear. But if not, her brother would soon lure her back to the fort! Lucas had most surely already locked Robert away, putting him on a strict regimen of bread and water as ordered.

A gleam entered the colonel's steel-gray eyes. Perhaps once Pamela was found and returned to the fort, understanding that her place was with him, he could be more lenient on her brother. It was imperative that she be made to see the gentle side of the man who would bed her!

"But if she doesn't cooperate, she'll see her brother die a slow, grueling death," he whispered, glowering.

He rode onward, his thoughts filled with another victory just ahead. It had been a long time since he had savored the spilling of Indian blood. After he saw to Pamela's safety, he would leave no one alive in Strong Bear's village. No one!

Seventeen

So fold thyself, my dearest, thou, and slip
Into my bosom and be lost in me.
                                    —Tennyson

Drowsy from her long day of waiting, Pamela stretched her arms over her head and yawned. The warmth of the fire drew her down beside it, luring her into a lethargic spell as she stared into the flames licking the fireplace logs. The effect was of sleek, orange velvet as the fire caressed the wood in long, even strokes.

Pamela's eyelids grew heavier, heavier. Her head bobbed and then she gave in to the need to sleep. She stretched out on a thick cushion of furs, snuggling herself into them. If she did allow herself to drift off into sleep, she could, for at least a little while, quit wondering about Strong Bear and whether or not he was going to succeed in finding Robert.

Sleep. It would be her escape.

*   *   *

210

Snow Owl crept stealthily up to the door of Strong Bear's dwelling, clinging tightly to the handle of a knife. Within her heart she carried much hate, for she was no longer a part of this dwelling. Though Strong Bear had assigned her to another, one they would share together, it was not the same. When he had chosen another woman to take Snow Owl's place in his main dwelling, it had not only caused hate to stir inside Snow Owl's heart, but also shame. Her standing in the village had been lessened in the eyes of her people! Wearing gold trinkets and trumpeting her good fortune about didn't make a difference. She must regain all that she had lost. She must!

Snow Owl had decided there was only one way to recover her rightful status with her husband and her people. She must make this white woman ugly in Strong Bear's eyes. She must *disgrace* the white woman. Snow Owl would disfigure the white woman by cutting her hair. No woman was beautiful without lustrously long hair. When the white woman's hair was removed, Strong Bear would look away from her with disgust. Pamela would be forever ugly in his eyes!

Hoping that the white woman would be asleep by now, Snow Owl eased the bark covering away from the doorway. Her dark eyes were two points of hate as she peered into the dwelling. She smiled crookedly when she saw Pamela sound asleep beside the fire. It would be so easy for Snow Owl to succeed in her scheme this early evening!

When Strong Bear returned he would banish the white woman from his dwelling. He would be grateful to Snow Owl for showing him just how ugly the white woman could be! No children born of anyone so ugly could ever be raised in the Miami village. They would disgrace the Miami people. Surely Chief Strong Bear would see and understand this. He surely would not want a son from this ugly white woman, a son who would one day reign as *chief*.

Her moccasined feet soundless on the mats spread across the floor, Snow Owl moved slowly to the sleeping form beside the fire. Her fingers were trembling as she gripped the knife, the pit of her stomach feeling strangely weak. Though courage had prodded her to this cabin this evening, she could not help but fear being caught before the deed was done. Should Strong Bear return and catch her in the act, Snow Owl would no doubt be banished from the village. Her only hope was to sheer the hair quickly. . . .

Fearing that her anxious breathing might awaken the white woman, Snow Owl stopped long enough to calm herself by sheer force of will. Then, when in position, she knelt down behind Pamela, who was curled delicately on the pallet of furs.

Steadying one hand with the other, Snow Owl inched the knife toward Pamela's hair. But just as she was about to set the blade in position, sudden bursts of gunshot from outside the cabin caused her to jerk backward.

Pamela was jolted quickly from her deep sleep by the gunfire. She bolted upright to a sitting position, then winced with alarm when she found herself looking directly into Snow Owl's eyes.

"You! Why are you here?" Pamela gasped. Then she paled when she saw the knife in Snow Owl's right hand. "Lord! Did you come to . . . kill me?"

But Snow Owl had no chance to reply. She was too stunned by the noises erupting from outside even to think clearly. She exchanged looks with Pamela, terror casting them as allies, not enemies.

"What's happening?" Pamela asked, looking toward the door, hearing the staccato crack of deadly musket fire, the neighing of horses, the shouts of men, and the horrible screams of children and women.

"My God," Pamela said, rising quickly to her feet. "Snow Owl, the village is under attack!" She looked wildly about her. "What shall we do? Strong Bear is gone, and most of the braves went with him!"

Snow Owl's knees trembled as she stared wild-eyed at the doorway. No one had attacked the village since Strong Bear had become chief. Most knew that he sought peace for his people. No one had cause to attack the village. Why would they?

Her mind muddled, Snow Owl knew not what to do. Never before had she feared being killed in such a way. Strong Bear had always promised to protect her, to protect his *people*.

But this evening he was gone. How could he protect them now?

Pamela rushed to Strong Bear's cache of weapons and chose a knife. Then she inched to the door, to peer into the chaos outside. Her insides grew numbly cold when, by the light of the outdoor fires, she recognized the British uniforms worn by the attackers.

Then she recognized Colonel Bradley.

Guilt radiated through her like wildfire as she realized why these innocent people were being attacked. It was because of her; Colonel Bradley had come for her!

A sickness engulfed her as she witnessed a scene of death and mutilation at the hands of the British. The soldiers were firing point blank into the fleeing Indians. The braves who had stayed behind were becoming a mass of bloody bodies, killed as they groped for the mounted attackers to pull them to the ground.

Everywhere Pamela looked she saw blood. And when she heard the colonel's orders, she knew that if she did not flee now, she would never again escape.

"Search each cabin until you find the white woman, then begin burning and be sure not to leave anything of value!" Colonel Bradley shouted, waving his sword in the air.

"What about captives?" a soldier shouted.

"Don't bother with any except for the white woman," Colonel Bradley shouted back. "Kill all of those who don't escape into the woods."

"He's a fiend," Pamela softly cried, looking desperately around her, outside the cabin.

Then her gaze landed on Snow Owl. Even though Snow Owl had been ready to kill her, Pamela couldn't leave the women behind to be slain. And it was obvious that Snow Owl was frozen in place, unable to activate muscles that would aid her escape. Pamela rushed to her and grabbed her by an arm.

"Come on!" Pamela said in a dry whisper. "We've got to get out of here. One by one the cabins are being searched and then burned. We must escape. Now! I saw others escaping into the forest. So shall we!"

Snow Owl dropped her knife and began stumbling alongside Pamela, in awe of this white woman who had thought she was about to murder her, yet who was kind enough to see to her safety! Snow Owl did not want to owe the white woman a debt!

But now that Snow Owl was outside, seeing the death and destruction wrought around her, she knew that it would have been a fatal decision to stay behind.

Half dragging Snow Owl, Pamela aimed for the back of Strong Bear's cabin, then made a mad dash toward the protective covering of the forest. In her mind's eye she was recalling the last thing she had seen before running from the village. A soldier had shot an Indian brave. Pamela had seen him fall and writhe for a moment before becoming still. Then she had seen the British soldier dismount his horse and peel off the Indian's scalp. It had happened in the blink of an eye.

A bitter taste in her throat made Pamela aware that she was very close to retching. She took several deep swallows until the bitterness had smoothed away to blandness, then twined her fingers around one of Snow Owl's hands and began again to drag her through the growing darkness of evening. There was no opportunity to get a horse. The soldiers had rounded up what they could and were already leading them away from the village on the opposite end from where Pamela and Snow Owl were making their escape.

"I'm . . . so . . . tired," Snow Owl complained, her side aching from the hard running. "Please. I must stop. I must rest."

"No!" Pamela said, wheezing, her lungs feeling as though they were being pierced by knives. "We must run until we find some sort of shelter. Colonel Bradley will come searching once he finds me gone."

"You . . . ?" Snow Owl said, panting hard. She forced her feet to lift, one after the other, encumbered by her fringed skirt as it twisted about her buckskin leggings. White woman, why would he come looking for you?"

"You do not know?"

"Know what?"

"Colonel Bradley had imprisoned me in his fort. Strong Bear rescued me. This has angered Colonel Bradley! He has come to your village to get me and to kill your people, as payment to Strong Bear for what he did for me."

Snow Owl stopped cold. She jerked her hand from Pamela's, her eyes squinting with renewed hate. "It is because of you that this happens to my people?" she hissed. "White woman, you are *evil, evil*. Strong Bear has been blinded by your fair skin and eyes so much that he does not see the evil you represent for our people."

Pamela paled. She flinched as though Snow Owl's words had been bullets fired into her flesh. But she could not let now be the time for them to argue their differences. Time was against them. The soldiers had horses; Pamela and Snow Owl did not.

Yet she felt that she had to give Snow Owl some sort of explanation, for Snow Owl seemed determined not to move another inch from this spot with Pamela.

"Snow Owl, what has happened here is *not* my fault," Pamela murmured. "You see, Snow Owl, the British killed my brother Anthony," Pamela continued, casting a nervous glance across her shoulder, perking her ears in the direction from which they had fled. "My younger brother, Robert, is now missing, and I believe the British are responsible even for that. I did not maliciously draw the colonel to your village. I am innocent of all that you accuse me of. *He*—Colonel Bradley—is the evil one. Not

I. And do you not remember? I did not come to your village of my own initiative. Strong Bear brought me.''

"He brought you to our village for all the wrong reasons," Snow Owl said, wishing she had not left her knife back at the cabin. If she had it now, she would have plunged it into the white woman's heart. Snow Owl had been right not to want to owe the white woman any sort of debt!

"Nothing can change anything that has happened," Pamela said softly. "And for whatever reasons Strong Bear has done what he has done, it is not for you to question. Do you forget so easily who he is? He is your chief, the authority of all of your people, even *you*, Snow Owl."

Snow Owl's temper flared even more. She could not stand to have the white woman remind her of anything about Strong Bear and who he was. It seemed to Snow Owl that the white woman was behaving more Indian than white!

Forgetting why they had fled the village, too blinded by anger and jealous rage to think clearly, Snow Owl suddenly pounced upon Pamela. Taken completely off guard by this sudden attack, Pamela dropped her knife. She lost her balance and fell to the ground, with Snow Owl straddling her to hold her down.

"You speak too much of my man as though he is yours!" Snow Owl hissed, pulling at Pamela's hair, making Pamela cry out with pain. "You cannot share tribal status or earrings of sparkling gold coloring with Snow Owl! You will be dead!"

No longer stunned by the fall, Pamela grabbed Snow Owl's wrists and stopped her assault. Then, grunting and groaning, she forced Snow Owl from atop her. When Snow Owl fell to the ground on her back, Pamela sprang up and held Snow Owl's wrists to the ground.

"While we are fighting like this the British are searching for us," Pamela hissed. She shook her hair back from her eyes and away from her shoulders. "I see that you have decided the only way to be rid of me is to kill me.

Well, Snow Owl, maybe later. Right now, if we are both going to make it out of this alive, we must find a place to *hide*. Do you understand? You are letting jealousy stand in the way of survival.''

The snorting of a horse and hoofbeats drawing close from somewhere behind them made Snow Owl's face twist into a mask of fear. "They come!" she harshly whispered. "The men with the sticks that speak with fire are near!"

Pamela could tell by the look in Snow Owl's eyes that she was ready once again to cooperate. Releasing Snow Owl's wrists, she scampered to her feet and motioned the other to follow suit. "Hurry," she whispered, grabbing her knife up from the ground. "Surely we can find someplace to hide. Don't you know the land? Can't you think of someplace safe for us?"

Snow Owl jerked her head around, looking in all directions. Then her eyes lit up with remembrance. "Not far ahead there are outcroppings of rocks which make a break in the forest floor," she said, looking past Pamela, into the distance. "We will hide beneath them."

She began to run, speaking across her shoulder to Pamela. "Come. It is not far," she whispered harshly. "We share hiding place. But *never* Strong Bear!"

Pamela sighed heavily. It seemed that Snow Owl was never going to give up taunting her. But it had become clear to Pamela that Snow Owl was more worried about her standing in the community than about her relationship with Strong Bear. She didn't seem as mesmerized by Strong Bear, the man. And how could any woman not care for Strong Bear in that way . . . ? The only reason could be that the woman was frigid, not wanting what a man had to offer in bed, at night.

Now Pamela was seeing Snow Owl in a much clearer light. She did not feel so ashamed for having fallen in love with a man who already had one wife. He needed a second wife for what his first wife would not give him. She pitied Snow Owl.

It would be hard for Pamela to accept, that she would be

married to a man who had more than one wife. But to be
with Strong Bear? She would do anything!

"But will Snow Owl and I even survive to share this
handsome brave?" Pamela wondered to herself, running
behind Snow Owl. Now knowing how much Colonel Bradley wanted her, she knew to expect him to order his
soldiers to hunt every inch of the forest until she was
found. Hopefully Strong Bear would not be so distressed
by the fate of his village that he would forget her. If
he should even blame her, what then?

Filled with a hopelessness she had never felt before,
Pamela ran blindly onward.

The only way that Robert could tell that day was changing to night was the faintness of the light that streamed
across his feet through the gap at the locked door. In his
small prison, embedded deep inside the British fort, he sat
shivering and hungry. And then his stinging fingers took
precedence over everything else. They were a reminder of
what he must do.

Bending to his knees, he once again began digging in
the dirt flooring, having only managed thus far to dig out
a space the size of a hen's egg. The dirt was packed too
solidly for anything but a sharp-toothed tool.

The pain in his torn and bleeding fingertips too severe,
Robert again stopped his grueling task. Squatting, he rested
his arms on his knees, letting his hands dangle free without
touching anything. He hung his head, tears near. Now he
knew that it would be impossible to dig himself free. And
if he even did, he would not be allowed to leave the fort
alive.

First he was treated as a dog in the Indian village. And
now he was entrapped in the British fort! Either place
surely meant eventual death. But what of Anthony? Of
Pamela? Would he know their fate before he died? And
why had he been dragged to the British fort? What was the
connection between the British and the Delaware Indians?

The only positive thing that had happened thus far was

that Lucas, the British soldier who had escorted Robert to the fort, had given him clothes to wear. At least he wasn't a *naked* prisoner! But that was all that Lucas had extended. He had not shared conversation on the hard journey from the Indian village. It had been as though he was afraid to. But afraid of what? Of whom?

Robert ran his tongue across his parched lips and groaned as his stomach emitted a pitiful, empty growl. Since his confinement at the fort he had only been rationed bread and water. He had no idea how long he could survive. He already felt gaunt. Surely he looked worse than that!

A noise at his side caused Robert to draw his legs more closely to him, trembling. He squinted his weak eyes, following the sound. His spine stiffened when he spied a rat scampering through the hole in the wall. Having no desire to corner the rat, and kill it, then have to live with its death stench, Robert edged his back closer against the wall and watched it scurry cautiously about the small room, sniffing and dragging its long tail along behind it.

And then the rat scampered back through the hole, leaving Robert alone in the dark, sighing with relief that the rat didn't like the prison cell any more than he. Sharing with a rat was not Robert's idea of ideal companionship. And rat stew did not whet his appetite the least bit!

Chuckling low, glad to find something amusing about this new day of imprisonment, Robert stretched his long legs out before him. Then his eyes grew large as he watched the rat return, this time with a mouth full of dried grass. Aghast, Robert watched as the rat built a nest just opposite from where he sat. Then, when the nest was finished, he watched the rat leave and return again, carrying one tiny baby and then another until the nest was filled with several squirming bodies.

Robert was glad when the mother rat settled into the nest with the babies, seeming to ignore him. Afraid to move, Robert continued to watch. . . .

*   *   *

His fine-boned frame gleaming almost golden in the early evening light, his luxuriant black hair sleeked back with bear grease, Strong Bear rode his spirited strawberry roan, his thoughts more on Pamela than the rescue of her brother. If he should find her brother, might that not interfere with Strong Bear's plans for a future with Pamela? Would the brother stand in the way of such a future? Couldn't her brother insist that Pamela return with him to a community of white people?

Such a thought grated Strong Bear's nerves, yet he had promised his woman that he would find her brother, and promises made were promises kept! Strong Bear would deal with problems of a brother when the brother became a problem. Perhaps this brother was no longer even alive to become a source of vexation!

A secret smile crossed his lips but was too soon lost when Strong Bear's childhood training made him scent the undeniable odor of smoke in the air. He tensed, for the smell was not that of a mere campfire. It carried within its vapors the stench of death!

Wheeling his horse suddenly around, Strong Bear peered into the distance, seeking the source of the fire. When he saw the great billows of smoke coloring the evening sky black through the trees, his instincts were correct. Only burning villages made such dense, black smoke. And burning villages meant many deaths!

His heart thundering, fearing now for his woman's safety—his *people's* safety—knowing that perhaps not enough braves had been left behind to protect them totally, Strong Bear shouted to the braves who were accompanying him on this search to follow him. Though he knew that the smoke ahead could not be his village, for he had traveled too far, he knew he must go to the aid of those struck by tragedy this day. Then he would ride hard to his own village, hoping that it had been spared the wrath of the tormentor of Miami Indian tribes. Was it the British? Many moons had passed since the British had touched their lives with hatred. Why would they now?

Strong Bear's insides ran cold with the answer to his own question. There could only be one answer. Death was being wrought upon the Miami by the British colonel because of the white woman! Surely the British colonel planned to search and kill until he found her!

Strong Bear had been wrong not to anticipate such vengeful actions. Would his beautiful people pay for his hunger to own Pamela? Was Strong Bear to pay by losing her again?

Holding his head high, not letting guilt freeze him to inaction, since to do so would be futile at this time, Strong Bear led his braves into a village of total destruction and chaos.

His heart ached as he saw women wail over their slain spouses and children. Strong Bear could not help but wonder if it was now the same in his own village. Was he already too late?

But even with this fear eating away at him, Strong Bear had to think first of these people, before his own. No dwelling had been spared. There were only charred, smoking piles of ash left where once happy homes had been built.

Farther still he could see slain horses, the British having given the Miami who had survived this massacre no means to escape for help.

"The British colonel will pay," Strong Bear vowed between gritted teeth.

Not dismounting, he shouted out orders to his braves. "Half stay behind, half ride with Strong Bear!" he ordered. "Bury the dead. Then share your horses with the living and carry them to our village. They are now a part of our community of Miami!"

Barely able to withstand the sorrow in the eyes of those who were looking up at him from where they huddled, Strong Bear led his horse away from the disaster. Its hooves were a sullen thunder as he sped through the forest, the braves assigned to accompany him dutifully following behind.

Strong Bear was a strong, silent figure moving swiftly through virgin timber. But within his heart he carried a painful ache, a throbbing fear of what he would find upon his return home.

Pamela! Pamela! What of her?

Wraiths of mist drifted like silvery ghosts across the river at the first break of dawn. Colonel Bradley reined in his horse at the riverbank, wiping morning dampness from his brow. Grumbling to himself, he squinted his eyes as he looked down one long avenue of the river and then the other, trying to choose which direction he should continue traveling on. When he had found that Pamela had successfully fled the Miami Indian village he had become violently enraged, then found his determination enflamed. Her elusiveness made her even more special in his eyes. Damn. He had never met a woman quite like her before. And she, in the end, would be *his*.

A soldier eased his steed up next to Colonel Bradley's. "Sir, do you insist in still searching for the lady again this morning?" he dared to say, hoping he did not sound impertinent. There were too many reminders of how the colonel dealt with impertinence.

"Eh?" Colonel Bradley said, turning his head around in a jerk, to view the soldier straight on. "What is that you ask, lad, so early in the morning?"

The soldier, whose hair was the color of a raven, so black it appeared to be blue, circled the reins of his horse nervously around his fingers. "Sir, we found enough gold in that Indian village to last a lifetime," he said thickly. "Why can't that be enough? Isn't that more important than a lady?" He looked guardedly about him, cording his shoulder muscles as his eyes fearfully probed for surviving Miami Indians. "Sir, don't you think we should return to the protective cover of the fort? Each hoofbeat takes us farther away from it. If we continue, it will require another full night in the forest. Our men need rest."

Colonel Bradley's gray eyes sparked with fire as he

glared at the soldier. "Do you dare question my decisions? My authority?" he growled, clamping a hand on the handle of his saber at his side. "If so, are you prepared to suffer the consequences?"

The soldier spurred his horse away from the colonel's. "No, sir," he said, gulping hard. "I didn't mean to imply—"

"Then say no more about the lady *or* Strong Bear's gold," Colonel Bradley said, straightening his powdered wig. "You see, I intend to own both before another dawn breaks." He paused and lifted his lips into a smug smile. "And there is no comparison between the lady and the gold. In my eyes, she is much, much more valuable."

"Yes, sir," the soldier said, nodding anxiously. "Whatever you say, sir." He spurred his mount. Galloping hard, he returned to the rest of the soldiers, who sat on horseback behind the colonel, awaiting further orders.

Colonel Bradley paced his horse back and forth, kneading his chin. And then he motioned with a hand to the left. He had finally chosen a direction to ride. Pamela would not move in the direction of his fort. Neither would he.

His hawklike features becoming more pronounced as the morning sun began to dance through the rising foggy mist, Colonel Bradley continued riding along the riverbank, his eyes two points of fire as he watched for any breaks in the waving heads of cane stalks. He would find Pamela today, and if not today, *tomorrow*. He would not surrender. He had a lesson or two to teach her . . . lessons that she would never forget.

Eighteen

৯৯৯৯

I come to thee
On a steed shod with fire!
                    —Anonymous

Having hidden the full night behind thick lilac bushes and
beneath an overhang of rocks, Pamela was not only cold
and hungry, she was also thirsty. She eyed the river from
where she huddled beside Snow Owl, wondering if she
might dare venture there to get a much-needed drink. So
far there had been no sign of soldiers. Had they perhaps
gone in the opposite direction? she wondered anxiously.

Pamela hoped soon to feel safe enough to return to the
village, to see if Strong Bear had come back. But the
thought of revisiting the horrid scene of death and sadness
made her cringe. Never had she thought anyone could be
so heartless as the British! They not only butchered innocent settlers who threatened them, but innocent Indians, as
well.

Once Strong Bear discovered the massacre of his people, the British would surely regret their decision to storm through the Miami Indian village, leaving death and destruction behind.

Running her fingers across her dried, parched lips, Pamela could no longer stand the temptation of the water that was so near for the taking. She could also pick some blackberries that she was at this very moment spying bordering the riverbank. She needed strength for the tumultuous times ahead. Without it, she could not hope for survival!

Her dark eyes wide, Snow Owl watched Pamela's expression change as she reflected on their situation. First she saw doubt in the white woman's eyes, and then she saw traces of hope. Both emotions frightened Snow Owl. She would never forget the sight of her Miami people running from the soldiers, some bleeding, all screaming and yelling for mercy. It would be stored inside Snow Owl's memory for as long as she lived.

This new side of life was confusing to Snow Owl. Before now, everything had come easy for her. Strong Bear had made life simple. Now she was being forced to accept many changes that she could hardly understand! She had even spent a full night alone with the white woman, huddled against her for warmth!

Regardless, she could never like the white woman. To Snow Owl, Pamela represented everything that had gone sour in her life. And one day soon Snow Owl would put an end to it, one way or another. When Snow Owl got the chance, she would not stop at merely cutting Pamela's hair; she would also cut out her heart!

But until then Snow Owl must play a waiting game. For now she would disguise herself as a friend. Later, the truth of how she truly felt would be revealed. Then it would be too late for the white woman—she would be *dead*!

Pamela felt eyes searing her and turned to smile at Snow Owl, glad to find her more settled down and accepting of their straits. Surprisingly to Pamela, things had developed quite nicely between herself and Snow Owl, whereas only yesterday there had been a keen dislike shared between them. Snow Owl had even tried to kill her!

The long night of being huddled together in the darkness, listening to the occasional scream of a panther and the howling of wolves, had brought them closer. Pamela liked this new atmosphere between them. Yet when they returned to what could be called a normal way of life, where Strong Bear was to be shared, what then?

But this was now and survival was key to both their futures. . . .

"Snow Owl, let's go to the river and get a drink of water," Pamela softly encouraged. "I even see some blackberries close by. They should sustain us until we feel it's safe enough to return to the village to see if Strong Bear has returned."

Snow Owl inched back away from Pamela, fright clouding her eyes at the thought of being discovered by the soldiers. She shook her head fearfully. "No. Snow Owl not leave just yet," she whispered. "Not for *anything*. The soldiers might arrive with their great sticks of fire! Snow Owl die quickly! Did you not see how they kill my people? They kill again. Over and over again. Snow Owl afraid."

Seeing how talking about the soldiers resurrected both their anguish, Pamela simply nodded. "You don't have to go," she reassured, shocked that Snow Owl would continue showing her vulnerability. Before the British attack, Snow Owl had shown only a stubborn, strong side. "I'll go alone. I'll bring back enough blackberries not only to quench your hunger, but also your thirst. Just you stay here where you feel safe."

Snow Owl shook her head. "Yes. Snow Owl stay," she murmured. She looked past Pamela, toward the river, then became wild-eyed as she gazed at Pamela. "Listen for horses. Return quickly if you hear approaching horses!"

Laughing lightly despite their predicament, tossing her hair back from her face, Pamela nodded. "All right," she said, rising and stretching. "If I hear horses I'll return quickly."

Then Pamela stooped and laid her hand against Snow Owl's smooth, copper cheek. "But thank you for caring what happens to me," she said quietly, her voice cracking with emotion. "Yesterday you had much different feelings toward me. I appreciate your change."

Snow Owl had to force herself not to shudder beneath Pamela's hand. She lowered her eyes, hiding their devilish glint, knowing that she had fooled Pamela into believing she was a true, caring friend. "Circumstances change many things," she said, then smiled smugly when Pamela drew her hand away and walked out into the open.

Snow Owl rose to her knees and watched anxiously, hoping the soldiers would come and find Pamela. *They* could do for Snow Owl what she *must* do very soon. Surely they would butcher the white woman! Snow Owl would then escape and return victoriously alive back to her husband!

The sunlight streamed down through the quivering foliage overhead, touching Pamela's face with welcome warmth. She listened, cherishing the exuberant morning calls of the songbirds in the trees lining the riverbank. And when she heard the cry of a panther, for some reason she was no longer afraid. In the brightness of this fresh, new morning, all dangers, all sadnesses seemed distant.

Barefoot, attired in a fringed Indian blouse and skirt, Pamela could pretend that everything was right in the world for her and the man she loved. It was a blessing to see a new day in this wilderness. And she chided herself to feel thankful. She would drink. She would eat. Then she would worry anew about what the rest of the day would offer her!

Moving to the riverbank, Pamela knelt down onto a turf sprinkled with dandelion gold. Leaning over the water, cupping her hands down into it, she took a sip, enjoying the coolness as the water slid down her parched throat. After several other sips she sat back and momentarily enjoyed the water life swirling only a few feet away from her. Then she rose to start her task of picking blackberries. The sun's rays caught the gleam of silvery scales as fish gamboled in the water. Now and then a fish would break the surface with a sudden flip and a circle of ripples would radiate outward.

Pamela bent to run her fingers through the ripples but stopped cold, her heart lurching when she heard the thunder of hoofbeats suddenly close by. She froze from fear, unable to run back to her hiding place. When she saw a reflection other than her own in the water, terror gripped her: She was seeing the hawklike features of Colonel Bradley. And when she felt his strong hands on her shoulders, she knew that he was not an illusion at all, but very, very real.

"My soldiers never let me down, do they?" Colonel Bradley chuckled, pressing his fingers into Pamela's shoulders visorlike causing her to wince. "We've searched relentlessly through the night and early morning and by God, we *found* you."

Pamela screamed when Colonel Bradley entwined his fingers through her hair and yanked her roughly to her feet.

"No one gets away from me, didn't you know that?" Colonel Bradley hissed as he leaned down into Pamela's quickly paling face. "And there's no Indian close by to rescue you this time, is there? Where *is* your Indian friend? Deserted you *and* his people, didn't he? Well, he hasn't got much to come back to, does he?"

"How did you know I was in Strong Bear's village?" Pamela found the courage to ask, though her knees were weak and her heart was pounding.

"Not every Indian in Strong Bear's village died so quickly of their wounds," Colonel Bradley said with mock laughter. "I have ways of getting answers even from the *dying*."

Pamela shuddered. "I'm sure you do," she said shallowly. Then she squared her shoulders and glared up at the colonel. "Strong Bear will kill you when he returns and finds his people butchered." She glanced over her shoulder, worrying about Snow Owl. But she didn't see her and, thank the Lord, the soldiers hadn't thought to check whether anyone had escaped with her. Either they didn't care, or they had other plans.

"Let him come," Colonel Bradley said, a smile giving his face a pinched look. "My soldiers will just get the opportunity to finish what we started. We may as well kill the rest of the mangy Indians, don't you think?"

Colonel Bradley's face took on a look of distaste as he looked Pamela over, from head to toe. "Have you been with the Indian sexually?" he asked hoarsely. "If so, I'm not so sure you are worth all of this trouble. I'll have to think about whether I even want to bother with you any further."

Seeing this as perhaps an out, Pamela tilted her chin haughtily and looked squarely at Colonel Bradley. "Yes, I've been with him in such a way," she spat. "Now don't you think you'd best unhand me before you get soiled by the mere touch of me?"

Pamela jumped as Colonel Bradley dropped his hands quickly away from her, wiping them on his bright red breeches as though she were filth. "You little hellcat," he growled, then smiled wickedly. "But don't think your little scheme is going to work. You *are* going back to the fort with me. I've much to teach you. Several baths should make you touchable enough for what I intend to do with you."

Laughing fitfully, Colonel Bradley grabbed Pamela by the wrist and began half dragging her to his horse. "We'll ride until late afternoon, then make camp," he said blandly. "Then we'll arrive back at the fort tomorrow. Tomorrow is the first day of the rest of your new life, beautiful, feisty lady."

Grasping Pamela about the waist, Colonel Bradley lifted her onto his horse. Then he swung into the saddle behind her and wheeled his horse around and rode away.

When Snow Owl saw the sudden appearance of the colonel beside the river, trailed by soldiers on horseback, she had hugged the ground with her body. But now that she heard the horses riding away she felt that it was safe enough to rise to her feet, to see about Pamela. When she looked about her and didn't see Pamela, a warmth spread through her.. It was over! Never again would she see the white woman! Nor would Strong Bear!

Her smile faded as she considered the fate of her people. And what of Strong Bear?

Snow Owl stumbled out into the sunshine and began her fearful journey through the forest, not sure of her future, or of Strong Bear's. The Great Spirit was surely hiding his face behind dark thunderclouds, or he would not have let this tragedy befall the great Miami people!

All of his worst fears were confirmed as Strong Bear drew close enough to his village to see the drifting smoke rise from its ruins. The ache inside him threatened to tear him apart. He sank his heels deeply into the flanks of his horse and galloped hard until he finally rode into his village.

Seeing the pillage and plunder—seeing the death scene—made him vow to make his vengeance sweet. As a man and a warrior he would never fight in a wrong cause. But this cause he would fight for was right. Until those who did this to his people paid dearly, he would forget the peaceful side to his nature. They would pay! They would pay!

"*Na-ho-ti-hot do-pol-ia na-peak*," he said, dismounting his horse, seeing many of his braves fallen in pools of blood. "Many good warriors die!" He saw children and women scattered lifeless along the ground. He clenched his fists to his sides. "Many women and children die!"

His gaze sought and found what had once been his own dwelling, seeing nothing but a slow column of drifting smoke, rising from its grave of ash. "Pamela!" he cried, almost choking on the words. "Snow Owl."

"Snow Owl comes to you with heavy heart," Strong Bear heard from somewhere close behind him. Turning on a heel he saw Snow Owl walking in a slow stumble toward him, her buckskin skirt full of rips and tears.

Her hair, usually radiant in its perfect braids, now hung long and limp across her bent shoulders. Her face was ghostly in color, weary and pinched with sadness.

Behind Snow Owl others came who had successfully fled the village, their faces drawn, their eyes empty. Though Strong Bear shared their emptiness he was at least thankful that some of his people had been spared. He was looking upon a mixture of survivors: women, children, wounded braves.

But still . . . no Pamela.

It would be a struggle, but one day their band of Miami would again be strong. Those survivors of the other raided Miami village would join with the survivors of Strong Bear's! They would go to a land free of white man's interference! Strong Bear knew of a place. Thus far it had been denied to his people, known only to Strong Bear and his father, and his father before him.

Strong Bear had already decided to relinquish the land of his vision; it was now known by too many people who were not a part of the Miami tribes of Kentucky. Strong Bear would take his people, instead, to the land of the sacred gold nuggets. The spirits of his father and his grandfather would surely understand that this was the only escape for their proud people! The land would no longer be known only by the chief of this band of Miami Indians. It would be shared with them all!

Strong Bear let his gaze move slowly about him, to capture the sight of his approaching people. The children who were now clinging to the skirts of their mothers had learned the struggles of survival the hard way. It was perhaps a lesson of lessons inside their hearts. They would remember. They would ready themselves for the future and for what a white man might again bring into their lives.

Survival. It was the key to the future existence of his people . . . of *all* Miami Indians!

"Snow Owl—" Strong Bear said, rushing to catch her just as she began to fall listlessly to the ground. Drawing her into his arms, he held her close to his chest, where she limply lay her cheek.

"British soldiers with sticks of fire do this to our people, Strong Bear," Snow Owl said, her voice weak. "Snow Owl escaped but has returned. Snow Owl so glad you are here now, Strong Bear. You are strength to our people. You will lead us away from this place of death."

Strong Bear's heart was a storm set free inside him, thundering . . . thundering . . . thundering. It *was* the British. The evil colonel *had* come for Pamela and had not stopped at just stealing her away from Strong Bear. He had also taken the lives of many of Strong Bear's people. The colonel had left a path of destruction behind him, surely as some sort of warning.

But Strong Bear would never heed the warnings of such a cruel, heartless man. Soon the colonel would wish that he had used better judgment in his plan.

"Snow Owl, is Pamela now with the British colonel?" Strong Bear asked stiffly, yet already knowing the answer. "Did you witness her being taken away?"

"White woman escape with Snow Owl," Snow Owl said, leaning her face away from Strong Bear's chest to look up into his fiery eyes. She would not tell Strong Bear that Pamela was now with the British colonel, knowing that Strong Bear would go for her if she did. Strong Bear was again Snow Owl's! "White woman escape from Snow Owl."

Strong Bear clasped Snow Owl's shoulders. "What do you mean she escaped from Snow Owl?" he said hoarsely, his voice becoming louder with each word. "Where *is* she? Why did you two separate from the other? Didn't you know the dangers?"

Strong Bear studied Snow Owl's expression. He stepped

away from her, his fingers coiled into tight fists at his sides. "You lie," he said icily. "Why do you?"

Snow Owl took a shaky step backward. Her eyes wavered beneath his accusing stare. "White woman now with the evil British soldiers! They take her away," she blurted. "They did not see me or I would not have survived. They would have killed me as they have so many other women of our village. They only wanted the white woman. Why, Strong Bear? Is she worth this much to even her own kind, the white soldiers who carry sticks of fire?"

Strong Bear's brow creased in a dark frown. "Pamela has shown her worth to you, has she not?" he grumbled. "She is special . . . the sort that has caused wars surely between men and nations from the beginning of time!"

Jealousy of Pamela overwhelmed Snow Owl. Hate was too gentle a word to describe her true feelings for the white woman. "We must speak of our people. Not of the white woman," Snow Owl said stiffly, feeling the press of bodies against her as the survivors began to congregate on all sides of her and Strong Bear. "What are we to do now, Strong Bear? We will leave this place, won't we? You will lead us to a place of peace?"

Strong Bear looked over the heads of his people, on past where his lodge had once stood, to a grave of ash where an even more important lodge had stood. In his distraught state he had not even absorbed the prime loss of all to his people. The medicine lodge had been desecrated . . . burned! The jars, which had held the sacrifices to the Great Spirit! They had surely been stolen and were now in the possession of the soldiers!

A growl, as though coming from a giant bear, surfaced from somewhere deep inside Strong Bear. Looking to the heavens, he uttered a loud, mournful cry. *"Ai-ee, ai-eee!"*

"Great Spirit, Ruler of the Universe, why?" he cried, raising his hands to the sky. "How did you allow this to happen?"

Then he humbly lowered his eyes, meditating quietly to himself for a few moments. Finally he lifted his chin and looked at his braves, who had dismounted their steeds and were awaiting his instructions.

"My braves, we must find and kill those responsible," he shouted, his fists doubled at his sides. "Then a place of peace will be shown to you all. Your children . . . *my* children . . . will be spared any more of these abuses and humiliations!"

He waved a fist into the air. "Prepare yourselves for the fight," he ordered. "Today you will fight as warriors. We will kill."

Loud shouts and war whoops resounded in the air as a frenzy of excitement rippled from brave to brave. But all was silence when Strong Bear made a further announcement.

"Some will stay behind and bury the dead and watch over the living," Strong Bear said, looking from man to man. "We will draw lots to decide who will stay . . . and who will go. And, my braves, nothing must stand in the way of finding my white woman! She is soon to be my wife!"

The braves silently nodded, but soon war songs filled the air.

Nineteen

❧❦❧

I love thee, I love but thee,
With a love that shall not die.
　　　　　　　—Taylor

The campfire was flickering low. Pamela was lying on the hard, cold ground close to the fire, working at the ropes binding her wrists. Hearing the even snores from the soldiers who lay on bedrolls on all sides of her, she knew this was probably her only chance to escape. Up until a short time ago Colonel Bradley had been there, entertaining himself by sorting through the gold pieces stolen from Strong Bear's village before returning them to the saddle-bags on the horses, for delivery to the British fort.

Pamela had been rendered speechless at the sight of the gold, never having believed that Strong Bear's people could have amassed such wealth. She had been in awe of Snow Owl's gold earrings, had even wondered where they had come from. But now? There was so much to wonder about than mere earrings. Somehow Strong Bear had access to massive amounts of gold. And even if the British had stolen some away from him, Pamela didn't doubt that there was much more where Strong Bear had taken this from.

But now was not the time to wonder about gold. Pamela had to focus on escaping. Colonel Bradley had left with a few of his soldiers whom he had assigned to deliver the gold safely to the fort. He had warned her that he would be gone for only a short time; he was only going to ride with his soldiers a short way. He would be gone long enough to guide his men in the right direction. And when he returned, Pamela knew to expect possibly the worst from him.

Squirming, twisting her wrists one way and then another, Pamela winced as the rope cut painfully into her flesh. But she smiled to herself when she felt the rope finally loosening. And then, with one more yank, the knot flipped open and her hands were free.

Her pulse racing, Pamela rubbed her burning flesh, looking cautiously about her. The soldiers were in a deep sleep. She peered past them into the dark cavern of the forest. Would Strong Bear even now be somewhere close by, coming for her? Surely if not for her, at least to avenge his people. The sight of the bodies of his people would surely set off a rage so explosive, it would not be soothed until he killed those responsible.

But she couldn't wait for Strong Bear's arrival. She had to escape from the British this time on her own. Colonel Bradley could return at any moment now. She could not bear the thought of him hovering near her, much less touching or kissing her.

Such thoughts sent Pamela scampering to her feet. Bent low, she moved stealthily around one sleeping soldier and then another, afraid that at any moment now she might feel a man's hand clasp her ankle to stop her. She fixed her eyes on the dark forest ahead, leaving the warmth of the fire behind her . . . and also the dangers the soldiers imposed.

Once free and clear of the dangers, in the dark cover of

the trees, Pamela broke into a run. At this point in the forest she could not see the sky through the thick foliage overhead, so she did not know in which direction she was running. It was enough to know that she was free. She could not allow herself to be captured again.

Winded, Pamela stumbled, her bare feet on fire from thorns piercing their tender flesh. She inhaled the fresh breath of night, mercifully filling her lungs with badly needed air. She groped through the darkness and found a tree on which to lean and rest herself. Lowering her face in her hands, she rested, though the campfire light was still visible behind her. Ahead was just more darkness, but freedom, at least.

The forest was quiet except for the singing of crickets.

His face painted black, the color denoting death, Strong Bear blended well into the darkness of night as he dismounted his strawberry roan. Along with his braves, who had also dismounted their steeds, he edged closer to the soft flickering of a campfire just ahead.

His eyes enflamed with hatred, Strong Bear clasped the handle of the knife sheathed at his waist. At the same time he felt the handle of his hatchet pressed into his flesh at his waistband on the opposite side to where his knife was secured.

Across his left shoulder a great ash bow was slung, and at his back a massive quiver of arrows, some points tipped with poison. Strong Bear had come to kill. He would make sure no soldier was left alive to tell his grandchildren about the soldiers' attacks on the Miami Indians!

Now at the edge of the forest where trees thinned toward the embankment of the Ohio River, Strong Bear saw the sleeping soldiers circling the campfire. Carefully he scanned the land, looking for soldiers who might be serving as guards for those taking time to rest.

But he saw none. The soldiers had grown careless, not having been given the insight to understand that the Miami

Indians could be pushed only so far before they would react with a vengeance never previously known to man!

His heart racing with the need to slay the men responsible for the massacre of his people, Strong Bear had to restrain himself. He first had to find Pamela among those who were sleeping. Once he had her safely away from the scene, which would soon be soaked with blood, he could order his men to attack, show no mercy, as none had been shown to the Miami!

Letting his eyes measure the size of the bedrolls and blankets about the fire, sorting through them to find one smaller than the rest, which would mean that it held his imprisoned woman, Strong Bear's spine stiffened. She was nowhere in sight. Only soldiers filled the spaces about the fire!

Clenching his teeth, his eyes a mixture of ice and fire, Strong Bear spoke in a soft whisper to his men, instructing them to stay behind. He had a chore that must be done. And he would do it alone.

Dark eyes following him, Strong Bear crept to a sleeping soldier. With the speed of lightning he clasped a hand of steel across the soldier's mouth. Smiling devilishly, Strong Bear looked down at the awakened soldier's widened, terror-filled eyes. Still holding his hand firmly over the struggling soldier's mouth, with his other hand Strong Bear dragged him into the darkness of the forest where his braves dutifully awaited his return.

With his braves looking silently on, Strong Bear knelt down and spoke in a heated whisper into the soldier's face. "The white woman—*my* woman," he growled. "She is not among those of you who are resting. Where is she?"

Strong Bear released his hand from the soldier's mouth, now placing it at his throat, a silent warning not to cry out. One pinch of the soldier's jugular vein by Strong Bear's powerful fingers and the soldier would be silenced forever!

"She's there . . . beside the fire," the soldier gasped, his eyes wild. "Look. You'll see." He pleaded with Strong

Bear in a quivering voice. "Please. Let me go. I've told you what you wanted to know."

His hand still firm on the soldier's throat, Strong Bear looked past him, searching again for Pamela. His insides knotted angrily as he glared down at the soldier. He half lifted him from the ground, his visorlike stronghold on his neck continuing. "You lie!" he hissed. "She not there. Where is she?"

The soldier craned his neck and looked across Strong Bear's shoulder, to the spot where Pamela had been rooted. His heart skipped a beat when he saw it vacant. He squinted his eyes, seeing the ropes cast away. Damn it. She had managed to escape!

"She's gone," the soldier said tonelessly, looking up at Strong Bear with dread. "She was there. But now she's gone. Look. You'll see ropes that were used to tie her wrists. She escaped. She can't be too far away in the forest. Only moments ago she was there. You believe me, don't you?"

Strong Bear glowered down at the soldier, then nodded to one of his onlooking braves. "Finish him," he ordered. "He must not be allowed to warn the others."

Releasing his hold on the soldier's throat, Strong Bear did not watch his brave plunge the knife into the soldier's chest. He didn't even wince when he heard the gurgle of death sound from the soldier's mouth. This was one less soldier that would be killed in the massacre to follow.

Motioning with his hands, Strong Bear gathered his braves about him. "My woman has fled into the forest," he said gruffly. "She must be found before harm comes to her." He gestured with a wide sweep of a hand. "Spread out. Look until she is found. *Then* we will return and finish what we started here."

Feeling rested enough, Pamela resumed her running. Then, when a hand clasped over her mouth and another grabbed her arm, she became faint with fright. She struggled against the hold of steel as she focused her eyes on the assailant. He stepped around, before her.

Wide eyes looked desperately up at Strong Bear above his clasping hand and then he could see the fright in them smother and be replaced by joy.

"Strong Bear!" Pamela whispered as he eased his hand from her mouth, moon beams streaming faintly through the foliage overhead, illuminating Strong Bear's face.

Pamela recoiled somewhat when she saw the black color of his face. She glanced quickly about her, seeing the fierceness of Strong Bear's braves. Their faces were as black as his, and their knives and hatchets were drawn, ready to kill.

She was not frightened. She was glad, knowing they had come not only to rescue her, but to avenge the deaths of their people. She would even fight alongside them, if allowed!

Strong Bear gently framed her face between his hands, looking intensely down into her eyes. He had come close to losing her again. But this would be the last time. "You are all right?" he asked thickly. "The evil soldiers did not harm you?"

"No. I am not harmed. I am fine," Pamela said, in awe of his being there. "How did you know I was with the soldiers?"

"Snow Owl."

Pamela's eyes widened. "Snow Owl? She is safe?" she whispered, recalling where she had left Snow Owl, alone.

"She safe. She tell of your abduction."

"Perhaps she *is* truly my friend now," Pamela said, wanting to believe it, yet finding it hard thus to ennoble Snow Owl. But for now, all she wanted truly to believe was that Strong Bear was there with her! Joy filled her every nerve; her heart beat with radiant love for this man she would always love. Again he had come to rescue her. She hoped one day to repay him for all that he continued to do for her. If ever they could settle down into some sort of normal life, she would repay him by totally devoting her time and her love to him. Surely that would be reward enough for him. It would be, for her!

Fearing the passage of time could cost him more braves'
lives, Strong Bear stepped back away from Pamela and
peered into the distance, where death awaited the sleeping
soldiers.

Then he looked down at Pamela, his eyes leaden with
hate. "You are safe but the soldiers are not," he growled.
He lifted a doubled fist into the air. "Death comes soon to
them all! Many scalps will be taken to show my people the
proud trophies of war!"

Strong Bear circled his hands around Pamela's waist and
lifted her upon his nervously pawing horse. He led the
horse to tether it with the others some distance from the
sleeping soldiers, so their neighing wouldn't awaken their
intended victims.

He took Pamela's hand and clasped it tightly between
his and looked up at her. "You will await my return. I see
much written in your eyes! Do not even ask to accompany
me. You will be much safer here," he said thickly. "Then
we will travel far away from this place of restless land."

Pamela looked adoringly down at Strong Bear. "Again I
have cause to thank you," she said, amazed at how he
had read her mind, knowing that she wanted to accompany him into the midst of the soldiers, to help rid the
earth of their vile stench. Yet she understood his wish that
she stay behind. "And, Strong Bear, please be careful."

Then something pinched Pamela's insides. So much
had gotten in the way of her thinking logically that she had
momentarily forgotten why Strong Bear had been away
from his village when the massacre of his people had
occurred. He had gone in search of her brother!

A look of desperation arose in her eyes. "Oh, Strong
Bear, what of my brother?" she cried in an anguished
whisper. "Did you—?"

Strong Bear's eyes clouded over with memory as he
spoke. "The smoke from burning Miami village drew me
away from the search for your brother," he said hoarsely,
a painful regret stirring at the pit of his stomach. Deep
inside he felt guilty for having chosen to search for this

white man when he should have been with his people to protect them.

But he knew that he still would search for his woman's brother, for her soul would not rest until she knew of his welfare. And to be a good wife, she must be free of all torments!

"Search for brother will come later. Now is the time to kill the British colonel and his men. Now is the time to reclaim our *gold*!" he added, releasing Pamela's hand to wave his hatchet in the air. "My braves, come! Follow me! The time is ripe for killing! The time is ripe for *scalping*."

Pamela jumped when Strong Bear moved so quickly away from her. She'd had no chance to question him about the gold and how he possessed such wealth, or explain to him that he would not find the gold among the sleeping British and that Colonel Bradley was not among those who were sleeping. Strong Bear was already approaching the sleeping soldiers with his braves accompanying him.

Turning her face away and closing her eyes, Pamela was amazed at how silently death came to the camp of British soldiers this night. Not one outcry was heard. It was as though the soldiers had never, ever existed, their deaths were so swift in their sleep.

When Strong Bear and his braves returned victorious in their venture, Pamela could not bring herself to look upon the blood-soaked scalps, yet she felt nothing for those who had lost them.

"But what of the gold?" a brave questioned Strong Bear as the chief was tying his trophies of war at the neck of his waiting steed. "What of the evil British colonel? He was not among those we killed! He has escaped our wrath. Do we now go in search of him? Surely he has carried the gold away with him."

Strong Bear looked up at Pamela, seeing how she refused to return his gaze. Something within him told him it was because of the bloody scalps. Then she slowly turned to gaze down at him and he was glad. He wanted her to accept this part of the Miami custom, also! If death was required, so were scalps!

"Colonel Bradley did leave with the gold," she said flatly, averting her eyes from the direction of the scalps. "He . . . he left with some of his soldiers who were carrying the gold to the British fort. But he said that he would return. He only traveled partway with his soldiers."

Strong Bear looked into the distance, contemplating what should be done. It was important to get the survivors of his village to safety. And Pamela. She must never be placed in the eye of danger again.

His decision was made. He would return later to kill the British colonel. He would once again own the sacred gold! But for now, his people—his—*woman*—came first.

"Let us return to our people," he said, swinging himself up onto his strawberry roan behind Pamela. "We have a long journey ahead of us. Then, my warriors, we will return later to finish what we have started. We will go to the British fort! We will kill *all* the soldiers this time! None will be spared! None!"

Looping his strong arm about Pamela's waist, anchoring her against him, Strong Bear took the time to reach around to kiss her softly on the cheek. "My woman, do not let my trophies of war separate your feelings from me," he murmured. "It was necessary. You must understand all ways of the Miami, to become Miami, yourself."

Pamela turned her eyes to meet his questioning gaze. "Nothing ever again could change my feelings for you," she said softly. "I love you, Strong Bear. Totally. Forever and ever. And, Strong Bear, I welcome the scalps as war trophies. It is . . . only . . . the blood that has turned my eyes away from them."

Strong Bear chuckled low. "My woman, where there is a scalp, there must be blood," he said, thrusting his heels into the flanks of his steed, urging it into a quick trot away from this newest massacre.

He shouted orders to his braves to steal the soldiers'

horses, then emitted a loud shriek of victory as he rode away. Pamela's hair flew as she clung to him from behind. Her cheeks were on fire with the sting of the wind. Her heart was filled with many emotions.

Colonel Bradley was ashen as he stepped into the midst of the bloody remains of his soldiers. He had arrived just at the moment the Indians were silently killing his soldiers! Hidden behind a tree, he had watched, stone cold with fear. Only he and the soldiers with the gold safely hidden in saddlebags on their way to the fort survived the Miami Indians' vengeance.

Glancing toward the spot where he had left Pamela for the night, a chill coursed through his veins. She was gone. Again he had lost her to the damn Indian! But her brother would draw her back to him. When she received word that Robert was being held prisoner at the fort, she would come for him.

Colonel Bradley paled again. Perhaps he had not planned so well after all. If Pamela went to the fort for her brother, would not her Indian friends accompany her there? God forbid, he must return to the fort with the warning!

He swung around toward the spot where the horses had been left to graze. Had the Indians—?

His feet mired into the blood-soaked earth as Colonel Bradley began running. He looked desperately around him for the horses, spotting not a tail of them roaming around. Even his own mount was gone. He was alone, to travel by foot. Perhaps death would have been better to come swift and sure, as it had to his soldiers. It was far to the fort, too far to walk. If fatigue didn't claim him, wolves or panthers could!

And there were always the Miami Indians who knew he hadn't been among those killed. Would they return for him even before Pamela heard of her brother's abduction?

Sobbing, Colonel Bradley turned and viewed his slain soldiers once again; then he walked away, his head hanging low. He had lost everything this night: he had lost his honor by letting his soldiers be so unmercifully slain; he had lost the lovely Pamela; and he sure as hell had lost the gold. When he didn't arrive at the fort as planned, the gold would be everyone's but *his*.

The usual faint light drifted through the space at the door, settling in a white spray across the busy mass in the rat's nest. The babies were larger, their dark, beady eyes having grown used to Robert's presence in the small cubicle of the room. But their mother's milk was their only true concern. Their paws worked against their mother's abdomen, as their tiny mouths suckled on her breasts.

Robert stretched his arms, though they were growing weaker and weaker by the day. He had been sharing his bread with the mother rat to appease her appetite so she would leave him alone. She had even begun to behave like a pet. Robert enjoyed watching her and the babies each day. Time passed more quickly, more enjoyably.

The door creaked open. Robert tensed.

"Robert?" a voice called hesitantly.

Robert looked toward the door, squinting his eyes as the morning light poured in, shadowing a tall, lithe figure standing in the doorway.

"Huh? What do you want besides bringing me my rations of bread and water?" Robert asked, not used to Lucas actually taking the time to talk. He had always seemed too afraid. Not of Robert, but surely of his commanding officer, Colonel Bradley!

The aroma of cooked rabbit wafted across the room and up Robert's nose, causing his stomach to rebel with a loud, slow growl. What was this? Was he going to be tortured now by the aroma, only to be denied the actual food?

"Robert, I've got good news," Lucas Boatright said as he lumbered on into the room.

When Lucas stooped down in front of Robert with a tray of rabbit meat and buttered bread and strips of cooked carrots, Robert was afraid to hope that this had been brought for him to eat. He didn't want to let himself hope about anything anymore. He had already given up on Pamela or Anthony being alive.

"What're you doin', Lucas?" Robert moaned, turning his eyes away, closing them. He covered his nose with his hands, not wanting to smell the enticing aromas.

"Didn't you hear me?" Lucas said, leaning the tray of food closer. "I said I have good news."

"No news is good," Robert grumbled.

"Not even news about Colonel Bradley possibly bein' dead? At least lost in the woods, alone?" Lucas quipped.

Robert's heart jolted with the news. His head jerked around, his eyes wide. "What . . . did you . . . say?" he gulped.

"Here," Lucas encouraged, shoving the tray against Robert's stomach. "Eat. There ain't no harm in it now. The damned colonel won't ever know the difference."

"You truly think he's dead?"

"The same as. Word has reached the fort of the massacre of many of our soldiers. Flying Deer brought us news. Only a few soldiers arrived safely back at the fort and those were the ones sent ahead by Colonel Bradley, himself. He returned to join the others who were then killed by Indians."

"God. Does that mean that I may be released?"

"I don't see why not," Lucas said, feeling almost human again.

Robert eyed the food. His fingers lurched and grabbed a broiled rabbit leg. His teeth tore into it, almost choking as he swallowed a big bite. Thus occupied, he didn't hear Lucas's loud gasp, but he saw Lucas draw a gun from his holster.

In danger of dropping his tray of food to the ground, Robert grabbed Lucas's hand and stopped him just before he aimed to shoot the rats.

"Don't!" Robert shouted, coughing as he sucked a piece of meat down his throat.

"Robert, have you gone daft?" Lucas shouted. "Damn

it, look at those rats! A whole nest of 'em. Why don't you want me to shoot 'em?"

Robert set his tray of food aside. He took the bread from the tray and began rolling pieces of it into little balls. His eyes twinkled as he began rolling them toward the mother rat, the balls stopping just where her mouth could reach, a point he'd practiced to perfection. Over and over again he rolled pieces of bread to her, enjoying watching her reach and satisfy her appetite.

"Robert . . . ?" Lucas said, kneading his chin as he watched.

"They won't hurt a soul," Robert said, laughing awkwardly. "Why shoot 'em?"

"You've been feedin' 'em all along, Robert?"

"Yep."

"Damn."

Lucas turned and walked slowly back to the door. He stepped from the room but spoke softly as he began closing the door between him and Robert. "Robert, I'll be back later today to tell you if there's any more news about the colonel," he said. "When we know there's no chance for him to show up here we'll let you out."

"I understand," Robert said softly, now pitching a pinch of meat to the mother rat. "Don't worry about it. It ain't all that bad in here, you know. I've got my friends."

Lucas closed and bolted the door. He walked away, nodding his head. Robert was deranged . . . surely deranged. Lucas couldn't help but wonder if he would have also gone berserk if he had been locked away like that.

A deep shudder engulfed him as he hurried at a faster clip across the courtyard, where sanity might be found. He had thought to tell Robert about Pamela being alive and well and protected by the Indian who apparently loved her, now that the colonel was no longer a threat to Lucas's being totally honest with Robert. But he had changed his mind when he had seen Robert's mental state. Robert would probably not remember who Pamela was. In his twisted mind he probably was not even aware of once having had any relatives.

Twenty

꒰ ꒱

Things can never go badly wrong
If the heart be true and the love be strong.
                              —MacDonald

The cold water stung Pamela as though it were a million bees impaling her body with their vicious stingers. She could hardly stand the intense pain of the icy fingers of the river. But she needed a bath. Strong Bear had ordered all of his people to take one, even himself. First the men and boys had gone into the river to cleanse themselves of the stench of death. And then the women and young girls, Pamela being no exception.

The moon cast its beams into the river, a rippling shine of white as the women splashed on all sides of her. And then she followed them out of the water to the riverbank, surely an ice statue, she was so intensely cold!

Shivering, she grabbed her blanket up from the ground and wrapped it fiercely about her. Her teeth wouldn't quit chattering, nor would her knees stop knocking together.

Pamela looked over at Snow Owl and was in awe of how she stood so composed, freely drying herself, showing no signs of being at all cold. It was obvious to Pamela that Snow Owl and the other women were used to bathing in cold temperatures. It was a ritual that she would have to learn to accept. Though the Miami Indians lived in a proper dwelling of sorts, no bathtubs were used, and no water was heated over the stove *for* the baths.

To prove herself as strong as the Miami women, Pamela willed herself to quit showing signs of being so cold. She began rubbing herself briskly with the blanket. Then she snuggled it about her shoulders, making sure to cover herself fully, as she marched along with the women back to the campfire. The rest of the tribe, except for Chief Strong Bear, awaited them.

Pamela cast a sidewise glance toward Snow Owl, seeing how she obediently went to her lean-to built for her beside one of exact proportions built for the chief of the tribe. Snow Owl and Pamela had been given instructions before their baths as to where each would sleep the night. Pamela with Strong Bear, Snow Owl alone.

Snow Owl had accepted the order without even so much as a grimace, making Pamela feel a twinge of guilt for having taken Snow Owl's place in Strong Bear's life. Yet Pamela understood now that, though Snow Owl preferred still to be the first wife of importance in Strong Bear's eyes, she did not desire to perform the nightly duties of a wife. She preferred to sleep alone, to have her body untouched by a man . . . *any* man. This made Strong Bear's choice of women much easier for Pamela's conscience to deal with. Though she wasn't Strong Bear's wife, she was already the most important woman in his life! Soon she would become the first wife of importance in his life, Snow Owl second.

Pamela realized that this was simply another Miami custom that differed with those of the white man. Two wives were accepted. Pamela had this to get used to as well as the cold baths. And she could, just as Snow Owl already had, only if she didn't ever know when Strong Bear would be in Snow Owl's arms, making love to her. The thought of that was almost unbearable.

And if Snow Owl bore Strong Bear a child? What then?

Pamela's heart seemed to rip apart at the thought of another woman's child calling Strong Bear "father." Was that something she would be able to accept?

Oh, Lord, she doubted it!

Glad at least for the blankets draped over Strong Bear's lean-to for full privacy, Pamela lifted the corner of one and stepped inside the temporary dwelling that was already warm from a fire. The ground was covered with thick layers of furs and blankets. A rabbit was roasting on a spit, sending waves of its savory aroma toward Pamela.

Curling her toes into the warmth of a cozy fur beneath her feet, Pamela stood for a moment looking down at the man she loved. Strong Bear hadn't yet noticed her entry. Instead, he was staring into the flames licking at the rocks that surrounded them, his eyes mirroring the glow of the fire, hauntingly golden. And in their depths Pamela could see an unspoken remorse. She knew that he was thinking of his losses.

The same sort of expression had accompanied Strong Bear on the full day's journey from the ruins of his village. Though he had given a hearty speech of the new land of promise that would be reached when the sun rose halfway in the sky tomorrow, Pamela had known that his voice held within it no sort of pride of such a venture. Too much had been taken from him. The Miami Indian burial ground had too many fresh graves . . . too many new white, waving flags.

Realizing that Strong Bear needed her now more than ever before, Pamela moved farther into the makeshift dwelling and settled down beside him. Immediately she felt warmed, not only by the fire, but by Strong Bear's powerful presence. It seemed an eternity since they had been alone. But it had in truth been only a short time. It was just that so much that was unpleasant had happened to create a barrier between them. Pamela had to wonder if this was what life with Strong Bear would always be like. Complication after complication? Couldn't life ever be good to them? Must there always be something that interfered?

Pamela lowered her eyes, again thinking of Snow Owl. Snow Owl . . . Snow Owl and Strong Bear's children. A sudden chill engulfed her at the recurrent thoughts, which brought so much doubt into her life.

"You shake. You are cold," Strong Bear said, having looked over at Pamela just in time to see her body quake fiercely. With an arm around her waist, he drew her next to him, holding her tightly. "You are not used to bathing at night in the river coldness. But, my woman, even accepting this will come in time."

His possessive hold, his touch through the thickness of the Indian blanket, momentarily chased all of Pamela's doubts and wonder away. Strong Bear had claimed her as his. He had chosen to be her protector. She would not deny him any part of her. She was his, fairly fought for and won.

She would relish in his claim, letting the future and what it held take care of itself. She would not think of children, or of Snow Owl sensually encircled in Strong Bear's arms. Had he not chosen her instead of Snow Owl this night to comfort him in his time of grief and losses? Surely he would always choose her above Snow Owl. She must make sure that he did.

And she would let nothing spoil any time spent with Strong Bear. Even tomorrow they could again be forced apart, possibly never to be together again.

That was what this wilderness stood for: uncertainty in everything, especially life.

"I didn't mind the cold bath," Pamela lied, smiling sheepishly up at him. "It was invigorating."

Seeing the pain linger in his eyes, she reached a hand to his smooth copper cheek and lightly caressed it. "Oh, Strong Bear, it is so obvious how you hurt inside," she murmured, feeling his pain transfer to her as his smoky eyes pierced her very soul. "I'm so sorry for what has happened to you and your people."

She cast her eyes downward, moving her hand to drop it lightly on her lap. "I feel . . . so responsible. If not for me—"

Strong Bear grabbed her by the shoulders and turned her to face him. "Never blame yourself for British soldiers' madness," he said hoarsely, drawing her eyes upward with his strong feelings evident in his voice. "My woman, only they are responsible for their actions. You are innocent of any crime. Do you understand?"

Pamela nodded silently, so glad that he didn't blame her, for he so easily could. The British colonel *had* mutilated his people because of her. This was a harsh reality that she would always have to live with. But she would never speak of it again. It was best left unspoken.

"Tomorrow we will reach land thus far untouched by the white man," Strong Bear said, reaching to smooth Pamela's dark hair away from her shoulders. "It will be a new beginning. But even then some of our past must be dealt with."

Pamela's eyes widened. "You're speaking of Colonel Bradley?" she asked, a strain evident in her voice. "You are speaking of my brother Robert?"

"Yes. I will find your brother for you. And then I must find and destroy the English colonel," Strong Bear said harshly. "He will not live to bring shame and death to my people again. He will not live to touch *you* again."

With eyes dark and charged with emotion, Strong Bear began easing the blanket away from Pamela's shoulders. "You are Strong Bear's," he said huskily. "Only . . . Strong Bear's."

Pamela was mesmerized by the touch of his fingers as he continued to lower the blanket from about her. But then she shifted her gaze away from his lean, bronzed face, her eyes drinking in his magnificent physique as he sat with only a blanket draped across his lap. The scar left by her gunshot was faint, but a reminder of that part of her life she must leave behind. Anthony. Sweet Anthony. Her father. And, perhaps eventually, Robert . . . ?

Forcing her thoughts back to Strong Bear, Pamela silently admired the expanse of his sleekly muscled chest, his flat stomach and slim hips, and his well-muscled thighs peeking out from beneath the blanket cover. No other man could be as perfect, as handsome. No other man could be as gently kind as he had been to her. No other man could send such chills of desire spiraling through her!

Strong Bear peeled the blanket away from Pamela's curvacious nakedness. His night-black eyes feasted on her slim, sinuous body, the tantalizing cleavage of her full breasts, and her long, tapering calves and silken thighs. Her drifting dark hair tumbled down the straight lines of her back. Her blue eyes held within them desire that no words could frame. He understood such desire. It was a raging fire inside him, a fire only she could extinguish.

"There is a place not of this earth that knows no sorrow . . . no heartache," Strong Bear said huskily, enfolding Pamela's breasts within the warmth of his hands. "Go with me there, now, my *me-tam-sah*, my beautiful, beautiful woman. Go where the boundaries of love are measured by the beats of the heart!"

Pamela's breath was momentarily stolen away when Strong Bear leaned down and drew one of her nipples into his mouth, nipping it sensually with his teeth.

"We have traveled there before, Strong Bear," she gasped. "Yes. Take me again. Reveal to me the pleasures that one finds on that peak of sheer paradise."

His eyes smoldering with passion, Strong Bear snaked his arms about Pamela and eased her down on the soft cushion of furs and blankets beneath her. She closed her eyes, reeling with drunken pleasure, as Strong Bear began a slow worship of her body with his lips. He fluttered them first across her brow, then on each cheek, bypassing her lips to claim the hollow of her throat with an ardent kiss.

And then he continued his path downward, kissing first

one breast and then another; her tummy tremored as his tongue and lips claimed her even there. When he moved lower, his breath hot and enticing along the insides of her thighs, a tingle now familiar to her rose from the tips of her toes to the top of her head. A deep sigh of ecstasy quivered on her lips when Strong Bear teasingly explored her love bud.

"Strong Bear . . ." she whispered. "Love me. Now. Please . . . make love to me."

Running his hands across the dark hair at her beckoning triangle, skillfully caressing her womanhood, Strong Bear positioned himself over her. After a soft nudge of his knee, Pamela opened herself to him, trembling with rapture as he sheathed his hardness inside her.

His lips quivering, Strong Bear sought and found Pamela's mouth. His tongue traced its outline, tasting the pure sweetness of her, then moved inside as his lips seared into hers with intensity, kissing her savagely.

Pamela twined her arms about his neck, her legs about his back, and lifted her hips to meet his sweet thrusts inside her, answering him with a heat and excitement that matched his own. Her hands moved to his sinewed shoulders where she clung to him, savoring the long, hard kiss, the strokes within her. Delicious shivers of desire rode up her spine. It was a time of magic . . . a time of euphoria.

Then the euphoria spilled over, filling her entire being with a soothing yet burning flame. She knew that Strong Bear was experiencing the same, for his body shuddered hard, then lay quiet as he enfolded her within his arms, panting against her silken shoulder.

"*Pac-kah*," Strong Bear whispered. "What we share is always beautiful."

"My love for you is beautiful," Pamela said, laughing softly, kissing Strong Bear on the cheek. "I do love you so much, Strong Bear. Oh, so much."

"Will your love remain strong through many trials of learning my people's customs?" Strong Bear said, leaning up away from her, penetrating her to the core, it seemed, with the darkness of his eyes. "You will not think about white people's ways, longing for them after finding that our ways are so very different from yours? Is Strong Bear fair to ask you to stay and become as a Miami . . . live *as* a Miami?"

Stunned almost speechless by such a question, Pamela leaned up on an elbow and looked incredulously at him. "How can you ask such a thing?" she gasped. "Haven't I proved that you are more important to me . . . than . . . than life itself?"

Moodily, Strong Bear rose to his haunches and stared into the fire. "You are with Strong Bear and his people not by your own choosing," he grumbled. "I know that. You know that. It is because of the loss of your family that you are with Strong Bear."

He turned his eyes slowly to Pamela, his lids heavy. "If you had a chance to return to your kind of people, would you go?" he asked thickly. "If you were given a chance to return to your life as you have always known it, would you go, Pamela?"

Pamela's mouth dropped open. She stared up at him and then threw herself into his arms, almost toppling him into the fire. "Strong Bear, why are you doing this?" she nearly sobbed. "Why *now*? We just made love so sweetly. Please don't spoil the moment with foolish questions."

"Foolish?" he asked, combing his fingers through her silken hair, unable to stop the tremoring that was plaguing his insides. If she were ever to choose another way of life other than this he offered her, would he be able to let her go? Or would he force her to stay, become his captive, if necessary?

"Yes. Foolish," Pamela said, raining kisses across his corded shoulders. "I love you so much. I thought I had proved it to you. Please say that I have. Please? Our future will be wonderful together!"

His hands traveling lower, he gingerly explored her breasts and ran his hands down her backbone. Strong Bear relished the comfort of being with the woman he loved. He nodded. "Yes. I believe you have," he said hoarsely. He kissed her softly, then eased her away from him, drawing a blanket up about her shoulders. "But now we must sleep. Tomorrow is another long, tiring day. Many dwellings must be established in our new village."

Cocooned in the blanket, Strong Bear eased her down onto the furs and blankets beside him for the night of sleep. Pamela took one of his hands and squeezed it. "Tell me about this place we are traveling to," she urged. "Tell me more of your people, where other bands of Miami reside. I want to know everything I can of your people. In my heart I want to feel as though I *am* Miami!"

Proud of her words, of her desires, Strong Bear drew her closer to his side and clung to her hand. "This flight is taking my people—*our* people, Pamela—to a part of the country that is private, just off the Wabash River, on the banks of the gently moving Mississinewa River," he began almost dreamily. "It hasn't been settled by any other Indians because they chose to live nearer the traders at Kekionga, the main headquarters for all Miami tribes. And since this is such secluded land where I take my people, the soldiers have never invaded it, and at this point in time aren't even aware of it. For now it will be only for my people. It will be Strong Bear's stronghold!"

"But you have spoken so often of the land where my family settled," Pamela said, watching him guardedly. "You . . . you have changed your mind? You no longer want that land?"

Strong Bear's eyes narrowed as he frowned. "That land has witnessed such sadness . . . it is old before its time," he growled. "It has lost its luster in my eyes!"

Pamela wanted to question him further, but he began talking again of the land to where he was guiding his people. She sat and devotedly listened.

"This land to where I now lead my people has belonged to Strong Bear for many moons as it belonged to my father and his father before him," he said, no longer able to keep the secret of this sacred land from his people . . . his woman. "You see, in the waters that snake along the land the gold that is used to honor the Great Spirit is plentiful. This land of the gold has been known only to the chiefs of our band of Miami, until now. Now I will share it openly with all of my people. It is required. Only in this place of seclusion will my people be safe!"

Pamela lifted an eyebrow, looking inquisitively at Strong Bear. She now knew where he got the gold that the colonel had stolen. She was astonished that Strong Bear had power over such massive amounts of gold! Didn't he know that it was what men had fought and killed for? If not, she was not going to inform him. His innocence was charming!

Instead she turned over on her stomach and propped her chin up with her hands. Though fascinated by his mastery over such wealth, it was *he* who intrigued her the most! "You made mention of a place called Kekionga," she said softly. "You said that many Miami make residence there. Why have you chosen not to?"

A frown creased Strong Bear's handsomely sculpted features. He turned to stretch out on his stomach, propped his elbows up before him, then clasped his hands together. "In Kekionga there are many villages, and many tribes in the surrounding area," he said thickly. "The Delaware and Shawnee live nearby. They, along with the Miami, have traded furs with the British and French at Kekionga. Here the British have for many moons bought scalps from Indians and furs from all points in the Northwest Territory. As Strong Bear saw this, it was dangerous for his people to mingle in such a way with these assorted people. Peace has been my goal since my father's death. Peace can be better achieved when living isolated from those who stir up troubles between different factions of Indians and whites!"

"And until now, this *was* achieved," Pamela said, sighing heavily. She couldn't help but think that she was bad for Strong Bear and his people. She didn't want to believe it but she knew that they would be better off if she were pried loose from their lives. Surely he believed this also!

"All things in life happen for a purpose," Strong Bear said, drawing her to him. They leaned their heads together and silently watched the fire burning low, ashes gray at the edges.

Colonel Bradley stumbled in the darkness along the banks of the Ohio River. The lapping of the waves threatened to lull him into sleep even though he was walking. Never had he been so tired . . . so weary. But if he stopped and gave in to the need to sleep, he might never wake up. Asleep, locked in an unconscious cocoon, he could be scalped. He could be eaten alive by a bear!

No. He must move relentlessly onward if there was a chance of finding his way back to the fort. He had lost track of time. Just how long *had* he been walking? He had stopped only long enough to pick blackberries to quench the hungry, pitiful ache at the pit of his stomach.

Having shed his wig long ago, he found his dark hair plastered to his head and the stench of perspiration assaulting his senses. But now he was shivering with the cold chill of night. He longed for the warmth of a fire, the taste of wine. . . .

Something in the water ahead drew Colonel Bradley's attention. His heart skipped a beat. Surely he was hallucinating! But, no! He was seeing an abandoned pirogue, a hollowed log boat, floating free along the riverbank. Had it worked free from an Indian's campsite? Or had it been abandoned because it had sprung a leak?

His hawklike features pinched with anticipation, Colonel Bradley began to run, stumbling over fallen limbs and crooked tree roots growing from the ground like grotesque fingers groping in the night.

And then he finally came to the spot where he could step ankle deep into the water and reach the pirogue. His heart pounding, echoing in his ears, he drew it to the bank and let his eyes search for any damage at the bottom of the boat. Finding none, he laughed and climbed in. Luck was most surely with him this night for paddles rested on the pirogue's floor.

"Thank the Lord," he whispered harshly, looking into the dark, star-bespeckled sky. He had never been a praying man but tonight, yes, he had cause to pray!

"I shall make it now," he said, chuckling low as he took long, even strokes through the turgid water to the center of the river. "Now just let my soldiers try to take full possession of the gold!"

A vicious look of hatred flashed into his cool, gray eyes. "And one day I'll run across Strong Bear again, *and* that white wench," he growled. "One day . . ."

Twenty-One

Flowers within her eyes more white
Than midnight . . .
                                        —O'Brien

Outside the freshly built cabin, one that had been built quickly, yet carefully, by Strong Bear's people, low, gentle hills rolled onward, gleaming lush and green among the tall chestnuts. The banks of the meadow were sweet and tall, the grass heavy with clusters of violets. Beside the massive outdoor communal fire of the newly established Miami village, an elderly Indian was singing in a droning fashion, timing his mournful tune by beating on his drum.

Inside the cabin, Pamela lay snuggled on plush bear furs in Strong Bear's arms beside the fire in the pit on the earthen floor. Together they listened to the sad song of the Indian beyond the walls where Pamela was again finding momentary solace in her lover's arms.

The continuing sound of the elderly Indian's droning voice could not help but send a shiver of dread across

Pamela's flesh. Her body became tense as she pictured what the coming days could bring to the man she sorely loved. He was going to avenge the deaths of his people, the destruction of their village, the loss of their gold.

"And also the death of Anthony," Pamela brooded, knowing that she would somehow find a way to travel with Strong Bear to witness the comeuppance of Colonel Bradley.

When she had spoken of her desires to Strong Bear, he had forbidden it. He feared for her life. But knowing that she would accompany him, if even secretly, she had acquiesced. She had stretched her game with him even further by saying that, yes, she would stay behind, but only if he promised to bring proof back to her that Colonel Bradley was dead.

When Strong Bear promised her the colonel's scalp for proof, she had momentarily reeled in nausea, then found her senses clearing as she remembered another scalp . . . Anthony's.

"An eye for an eye . . . a scalp for a scalp," she whispered, yet unable to quell a shudder at the renewed thought of actually having Strong Bear present the scalp to her upon his return.

"But I will accept the scalp proudly," she vowed in a whisper, then blushed when she found Strong Bear's eyes upon her as he aroused himself from a brief rest before departing on the quest to locate Robert.

Pamela smiled at Strong Bear, embarrassed that he had found her talking and fussing to herself. Attired in a loosely fitted doeskin dress, she turned to face him, smoothing a thumb over the seductive curve of his full lips. "You heard me, didn't you?" she murmured, laughing softly. "You heard me talking to myself like a crazy person."

Strong Bear clutched her wrists and drew her against his powerful, bare physique. He pressed her breasts into his chest, relishing the feel of them, of how he could feel even through her dress their taut nipples hardened with her need of him.

"My woman has much on her mind?" he asked thickly. "You worry too much. Always!"

"I've much to worry about," she pouted, yet unable to deny that she was being catapulted again into a frenzy of rapturous feelings as his hands crept to her breasts, kneading them through the thin material of her Indian dress.

She closed her eyes and sighed, holding her head back so that her hair tumbled over her curvacious, silky back. "But, Strong Bear, when you touch me as you are touching me now, all of my worries are stolen clean from inside me. You have such powerful, wondrous hands!"

"Time allows that we make love. Then I must return to my braves," he said huskily. "Soon my longing for revenge must be my substitute for *you*. Vengeance is a lust quite similar to that which at this moment troubles me. Its reward is almost as satisfying as your lips . . . your touch."

"I wish you didn't have to go to the British fort at all," Pamela said, a crease on her brow. "I wish events hadn't made that necessary. Life seems to be such a continuing struggle."

"Survival has been a struggle since the beginning of time," Strong Bear said, his deft fingers lifting her dress, easing it over her head. "Survival comes to those who fight and *win* it. As love comes to those who win."

His fiery eyes touched her all over, setting her aflame with burning desire. His hands awoke within her unimagined splendor. "Today you ride for other reasons than are usual for you," Pamela said softly, looking up at him, idolizing him and everything that he stood for. "You go to search for a white man. My *brother*. I shall always be grateful. I will always be here for you. Always."

Knowing that time was short, Strong Bear tugged at his breechclout and removed it. Then, without preliminaries, he thrust his velvet sheath inside Pamela's love canal, finding it welcomingly warm and wet.

Pamela's throat arched back into a languid sigh as he buried his lips along its delicate column. His fingers sought the silken feel of her buttocks and pressed into them, lifting her higher, guiding her in her movements against him. A soft purr arose from somewhere deep inside Pamela. Her body was turning into a deliciously warm liquid, spreading . . . spreading. . . .

Strong Bear's lips flamed desire along her flesh as he kissed his way upward from her throat, claiming the sweetness of her lips in an incendiary kiss. It was a kiss of total demand, of savagery, the drumbeat outside the cabin reminding him of his feverish passion for the battle that would soon be fought once this chore of finding the white man was behind him. Once his woman's tormented fears of her brother were quelled, Strong Bear could fight the British soldiers with a free spirit! When his woman was happy, he would feed all his hungers! The need of battle with the white man who had humiliated him by defeat, and the need of this woman! In the end he would reign victorious over all his needs!

Burying himself even more deeply inside Pamela, Strong Bear reverently breathed her name against her lips, hearing her breath quicken with yearning. Pamela clung to him, savoring her spiraling senses, the wondrous joy of the sought-for climax that engulfed her. She arched her hips, welcoming his harder thrusts, realizing that he was also absorbed in pleasure's quiverings.

But too soon it was over, and Strong Bear had again clothed himself in his brief breechclout. Leaning down over Pamela, he gave her a smoldering kiss. "I will search this time until your brother is found," he swore solemnly. "Trust that I will return him to you soon." He gave her another fleeting kiss before leaving her alone with her thoughts.

Drawing a blanket snugly about her shoulders, Pamela stared into the fire. Though she had just been to heaven and back, she was once again thrown into the abyss of the real world and what it had handed her. The loss of her parents, the murder of Anthony, and the uncertainty of Robert. Upon Strong Bear's victorious return would she finally at least know of Robert's *fate*? Pamela could never rest peacefully until then!

Focusing on more pleasant thoughts, she let her mind wander to the bounty of this land, to the gold that was so plentiful! As she had gazed in astonishment into the waters of the Mississinewa River, the gold nuggets had resembled miniature sparks of sunshine peeking up at her through the translucence of the water from where they lay in their bed of gravel, indeed a sight to behold.

Robert rubbed his eyes frantically as the light flooded in from the open door. He backed closer to the wall.

"Come on, Robert," Lucas said, holding a hand out to him. "It's safe to come out. The colonel is surely dead. No one's seen hide nor hair of him for two days now." He lowered his eyes and swallowed hard. "I'm sorry I didn't come as promised yesterday. I was afraid to let you go free *that* soon." His eyes lifted in wonder. "You see, it's hard for me to believe the bastard can be dead."

Robert's whole body shook from weakness and fright. He still cowered against the wall. "I don't even know why I was imprisoned," he cried. "I didn't do anyone harm." He glanced toward the huddled rats. "And what's to become of them if I leave now?"

Lucas followed the path of Robert's eyes and cringed when he spotted the boy's source of concern. How could anyone . . . ?

A great explosion of gunfire resounded outside, started from somewhere inside the fort and causing a strained silence to yawn between Robert and Lucas.

"Colonel Bradley!" a sentry shouted from his high lookout post after firing the alert to the soldiers in the fort. "He's arriving by river. He's alone in a pirogue. He's *alive*. He's *well*."

A melee burst out inside the fort walls, faces pale from fearing discovery at having lapsed in their duties, or at having stolen several bottles of Colonel Bradley's finest wines in premature celebration.

Seeing the fort, knowing that he was safely back home, Colonel Bradley found the strength returned to his legs as he prepared to disembark. After leaving the pirogue he stomped quickly to the fort and entered its wide gates, growing steadily enraged as he realized what had happened.

"What have we here?" he shouted, raising a fist in the air, undaunted by how his disheveled appearance struck the gawking soldiers. His eyes went immediately to Lucas Boatright, who was standing at the open stockade door, looking like a child just caught in the act of stealing candy. Did he realize that if he had brought Pamela's brother to the fort as ordered that he would now join the settler in the stockade? Colonel Bradley was tired of the weak-stomach bastard. He wanted him out of his life.

Colonel Bradley then looked around and saw a man grasping the neck of one of his finest bottles of wine, reserved only for himself on his loneliest of nights. It seemed that he had more than one chore to tend to on his return!

Determinedly, Colonel Bradley strode past Lucas and stepped inside the stockade. He smiled crookedly when he saw Robert collapsed on the floor, pale and thin. Yes, it would work. Pamela would soon arrive, begging for her brother's release! This time she would not be allowed to leave!

Turning on a heel, Colonel Bradley glowered at Lucas, then, without another thought, he grabbed him by an arm and shoved him inside the bleak cell. "Rot alongside him," he said flatly. "I've had enough of your bumblings!"

"But, Colonel Bradley—" Lucas stammered. He jumped with a start as the colonel slammed and bolted the door behind him. "Why . . . ? I did everything you asked me to do even when I didn't want to!" he shouted. He pounded on the door until his fists ached, then stood and stared blindly at it, the pit of his stomach churning with fear and hate.

Colonel Bradley went to a soldier and motioned toward his pistol. "Ready your gun for firing and give it to me," he ordered coldly, staring at the soldier who was still clutching the bottle of wine. "I've got some examples to set!"

Still numb, yet wondering what Colonel Bradley was shouting about, Lucas leaned his ear against the closed door. When he heard the gunfire, his stomach lurched and his knees buckled from beneath him. Trembling, he crawled to where Robert sat against the wall opposite the rats scurrying to the far corners. Colonel Bradley hadn't shot *him*, but wouldn't he have chosen that . . . over *this*?

Colonel Bradley looked down at the lifeless form of the soldier. "You drank my wine?" he scolded. "I've been out alone, fighting for my life, lost most of my regiment to the Indians, even the woman I had planned to bed, and the rest of my soldiers are celebrating these losses?"

He tossed the pistol aside and looked scathingly from man to man, each shrinking from the scalding gaze. "Now the rest of you listen well," he shouted. "As soon as we are outfitted with new recruits, you'd better be ready to fight those damn Indians until they are all wiped clean off the face of the earth. And I aim to get that damn lady back. Do you hear?"

He paused, then added, "Take me to my gold. None had better be missing. For each nugget that's gone, another man dies!"

Her body smelling as fresh as the river in which she had just bathed, Pamela knelt looking into the mirror of the water while Snow Owl knelt behind her, braiding her hair. Snow Owl had already placed bright red rouge on Pamela's cheeks, even on her earlobes. Gold earrings hung from Pamela's ears, blending beautifully with her lovely Indian blouse and skirt, which were adorned with loops of gold and pastel-colored beads.

On Pamela's feet she wore fringed, beaded moccasins. And once her hair was fully braided, she knew that she would take on the full appearance of an Indian, except for the color of her skin.

Beneath the splash of the sun, her skin shone petal white, surely a defiance in itself of that which the Miami Indians would have wanted in a wife for their great ruler, Chief Strong Bear.

But thus far, no one but Snow Owl had shown any undue resentment to Pamela. Now even Snow Owl seemed to have a keen liking for her. Pamela found it hard to believe that Snow Owl could truly want her for a friend when she, at first, had seen Pamela as a curse.

Pamela wanted to trust Snow Owl, even tried to accept the fact that they would be sharing a husband. But—oh! —such a fact was so hard. The test of her strength and courage to please the man she loved had become such a shattering issue!

"Your hair is now pretty," Snow Owl said, leaning over the water beside Pamela to see Pamela's reflection. She cringed at the sight of the gold earrings that Pamela now so openly flaunted. Only Snow Owl should wear the trinket of gold in her ears! Not the white woman!

But Snow Owl had presented this gift to Pamela to add to her pretense of friendship. Snow Owl would steal them away in the night and let Pamela believe that someone else had gone off with them! They were Snow Owl's. Snow Owl's alone!

"You pretty. At first Snow Owl thought you ugly. Even laughed at your ugliness. Only Miami women should be pretty. Not white woman with eyes the color of the sky and skin the color of the delicate petals of flowers that grow white along the forest floor," Snow Owl said in a forced, silken purr.

Pamela's eyebrows arched at Snow Owl's confession. She turned and looked at her, finding a semblance of a smile on her lips. "Why, thank you," she murmured, though it became harder and harder truly to believe her. There was an edge to Snow Owl's words, as though it had been hard for her to say them! Pamela even felt awkward being with Snow Owl. But when she had accepted the fact that she loved Strong Bear enough to live with him under any circumstances, she had known that it would never be easy!

The sound of horses approaching from somewhere close by drew Pamela's head around sharply. An alarm seemed to go off deep inside her. Although several braves had been left behind to guard the village from intruders, none had traveled to their guard posts on horseback. They were standing at all four corners of the village, having traveled there by foot.

So who could this be on horseback now, pushing the horses hard, their hooves sounding like distant claps of thunder as they pounded the ground beneath them?

Pamela turned fully toward the deafening sound, gasping when she recognized the lead rider. It was Strong Bear. She rose shakily to her feet, her eyes wide, her every nerve ending raw with fear. Strong Bear would be returning to the village in such a rush for surely only one reason. Something unforeseen had happened while he and his braves were searching for Robert. Had they found him? Was he . . . dead?

Strong Bear spied Pamela and Snow Owl beside the river. Their skins contrasting so against the other distinguished them from the rest of the women who were at the riverbank, using the mirror of the water for primping. His heart soared with pride when he saw how his two wives had become so devoted to the other. In the beginning it had been just the opposite between them. It could still so easily be different, with bitterness and hatred existing between them. Snow Owl was known for her ill-tempered, spiteful tongue.

Something had calmed her. She did not seem at all the same woman that Strong Bear had always known. Somehow she had lost her fiery spirit. Strong Bear was skeptical of this new mood. Could it even be a game of sorts, to fool him and his white woman? Would they in the end find that Snow Owl was anything but accepting of her new position in life?

Only time would tell. Now there were more important

things plaguing Strong Bear's mind. Pamela's brother. Would knowing that Robert was alive change things in Pamela's mind and heart? Would Robert try to persuade her to return to the white man's world with him?

Bringing his spirited strawberry roan to a shimmering halt at Pamela's side, Strong Bear gazed down at her, his face devoid of any emotion. Though he had fulfilled his vow to uncover the truth about her brother, he did not relish this moment.

But Strong Bear realized that this was what Pamela had wanted all along: to know that her brother was alive. And once released from the British fort, he would be ready to return to an American settlement. He would most surely request that his sister accompany him there! After having been so mistreated by one faction of Indians, Robert could not have good feelings about any others.

Strong Bear's jaw tightened. He was not prepared to give up this woman that he loved with all of his heart. The only way that he would part with her would be if she made the decision, herself, to leave. He would not hold her against her will. He would not make her a captive, though she was already a hostage of his heart!

Her heart racing, Pamela feared the news that Strong Bear ferried to her. He was not smiling! Surely the news was not good! Oh, did she truly even want to hear?

Dismounting, Strong Bear looked down upon Pamela with moody eyes. Seeing him still so intense, believing the worst, Pamela wavered, a light-headedness engulfing her, making her feel like a feather, as if she would blow away with the wind. Though she had wondered if her brother had survived, certain knowledge he was dead overwhelmed her. Oh, *could* she bear it?

An arm of steel encircled Pamela's waist. She found midnight-dark eyes looking down at her, commanding her to control her reeling senses. Her dizziness quickly passed when she saw Strong Bear's devotion and iron will.

"He is alive," Strong Bear said thickly, absorbing how lovely she looked, so Miami in appearance. Even her hair was braided, her face rouged! And she wore earrings worn by only the privileged, such as Snow Owl! Could Snow Owl truly be so generous as to lend a pair of hers? It was unlike her!

Strong Bear was seeing too much now that was un-like Snow Owl. Could he trust Snow Owl alone with Pamela while he traveled to the British fort? But did he have a choice?

"Your brother is imprisoned at the British fort," he added. He nodded toward his horse where a scalp hung soaked in blood "My scouts searched and found Flying Deer, who was rumored to have abducted your brother. I forced the truth from Flying Deer. He said the British colonel has your brother at the fort to lure you there."

A smug smile curved his lips. "I killed Flying Deer to silence him. The British will not be alerted of our attack! We leave soon. Your brother will be set free. The British colonel will *die*!"

Pamela blinked her eyes nervously, absorbing his every word. Her brother was alive! The Indian who had abducted him was dead! A sob of happiness erupted from her. Her eyes brightened with joyous tears. "My brother is *alive*," she exclaimed, wiping her nose with the back of her hand. "He is truly . . . alive."

"There is no time for talk now," Strong Bear said stiffly. "Warring has been delayed because of your need to find your brother. We must now prepare for war. My braves have grown restless in their waiting."

The wind was warm on Pamela's face; contentment flooded her senses. She now had not only Strong Bear to love, she also had her younger brother! Was life finally going to be fair to her? Could she even allow herself the wondrous feelings flooding through her? Hadn't she learned that one minute she could be happy, the next *sad* . . . ?

"Strong Bear," she said, anxiously following him as he walked away from her. "Let me go with you. I, too, have grown very restless in my waiting," she asked. "I, too, wish to see the British colonel dead. And I wish to see my brother. He surely isn't well. He has had a most terrible experience!''

Strong Bear stopped so abruptly Pamela ran into him. She smiled awkwardly up at him as he glowered down at her. "You ask much of the man you love," he said dryly. "You ask to do what is not normal for a future wife of a great chief." His lips formed a gentle smile. His hand caressed her cheek. "But so much about you is different from what one expects of a woman. This is one of the many reasons my love for you is so strong."

"Are you saying that I—?" Pamela stammered.

"Yes," Strong Bear nodded. "You can ride with Strong Bear as far as the gate of the fort. *Then* you must stay behind while death and destruction come to those within the high walls. Strong Bear will send your brother to you." He would not tell her that he was letting her go because he no longer trusted leaving her alone with Snow Owl.

Pamela threw herself into Strong Bear's arms and fiercely hugged him. "Thank you," she cried. "Oh, thank you."

Snow Owl stood watching and listening. She coiled her hands into tight fists behind her. Though she had not asked to travel to the British fort with Strong Bear, his braves, and the white woman, she would go anyway. And when Strong Bear left the white woman outside the high walls of the fort, Snow Owl would plunge the knife into Pamela's heart. The deed would be blamed on someone else. No one would ever know that she was anywhere close by, for she would quickly return to the Miami village. At last she would again reign supreme of all women in her village! Even if Strong Bear chose another Miami woman later to become his second wife, Snow Owl would make sure the same fate befell her. Snow Owl would never share with anyone again!

Twenty-Two

*There will be no stars this night
But those of memory.*
                    —Anonymous

Sitting cross-legged, Indian fashion, beside the great out-door communal fire, Pamela felt steeped in another world. Could it be true that she would soon join an Indian prewar party, garbed and anointed as a Miami warrior who was programmed to spill white man's blood?

Strong Bear's deft fingers had already rubbed her face with deer tallow so that as he now applied the black war paint across her face and around her eyes the alarming pattern would set in unblurred.

Was Strong Bear truly going to allow her to accompany him to the British fort? He had agreed much too quickly when she had asked for his permission. Why? She had already planned secretly to follow him. But now? She was going *openly*. She did not—*would* not—fret about his impulsive manner. She would count her blessings and see what befell them. Soon she would be with Robert. The thought warmed and soothed her frayed nerves. Soon, she vowed, she would have every reason to voice her complete happiness to the world.

Pamela kept her spine stiff and her shoulders squared at the last application of paint. She smiled up at Strong Bear, whose face shone in an intimidating red-and-black design. He was representing one who was ready to kill and who possessed unusual power to wreak havoc on any enemy— important ingredients in the upcoming raid on the vile British soldiers.

Pamela had agreed to the black paint on her face so that she would not stand out from the others who rode on matching missions through the forest. Her hair hung in one long braid down her back. She wore fringed leggings and shirt as did Strong Bear and all his warriors this day. Turkey feathers emblazoned her hair at the back, and a shriveled turkey foot graced her neck, a good luck charm matching the one hanging from Strong Bear's neck by a leather string.

The sun crept low behind the distant, gentle swells of meadow, casting a color of flame along the land and onto the log cabins of this newly established Miami village.

In the village core Pamela rose to her feet to stand beside Strong Bear. A bright fire burned, illuminating the faces of the Miami warriors as they gathered for battle. Their faces were also painted in red and black. Each carried a tomahawk, a bow slung across his shoulders, and a quiver of arrows at his back. Moving forward they formed a great circle about the fire and Chief Strong Bear, whose white woman stood proudly at his side.

Clutching their tomahawks determinedly, the Miami warriors listened intently to the words of their leader. Their hearts thundered, their blood pulsed fiercely, scorch- ingly, through their veins as they listened to a speech about warring . . . about vengeance!

They were mesmerized now by the ancient rituals, anx- ious to spill the blood of those who had so unmercifully

slain their people. Their scalp poles would soon display
the spoils of war. There had been no cause for warring
since Strong Bear had become chief. Until now!

Ah, for so long they had thirsted for war as one craves
water on a hot summer's day!

"You have heard me say often that as a man and a
warrior I would never fight in a wrong cause!" Strong
Bear shouted after explaining in detail the plans of attack.
"But this cause is right. The British soldiers must die. We
must return to our village with spoils of war from the
dead! We must show our people that the deed was done!
We must return the gold that was stolen to the Great
Spirit!"

Shaking a doubled fist into the air, Strong Bear framed
words to fire his warriors' spirits. "*Shan-ge-la-wah-lo-
not!*" he shouted. "*Mah-coo-lot! Mah-coo-lot!*"

In unison the warriors pointed their tomahawks toward
the Mississinewa River and gave a hideous yell. Then they
watched anxiously as Chief Strong Bear tamped down a
load of kinnikinnick into his pipe festooned with brightly
colored feathers. A young brave carrying a tray of hot
coals broke through the crowd of warriors. He held the
tray close to Strong Bear for the chief to lean his pipe into
the coals to light it. The lad then fled from the circle
again as Strong Bear passed the pipe on to the warrior next
to him.

Each warrior who wanted to go to war took a draft or
two on the war pipe, enlisting himself for duty. And after
the pipe had gone around the full circle and a sufficient
number of Indians signaled their intentions, a war dance
and round of songs began.

Strong Bear had earlier officiated over the cutting of a
pole and had ordered a young brave to paint it red, the sign
of war. A hole had been dug in the ground near the
outdoor communal fire and the painted pole had been
dropped into it, then the soil pushed in around the pole so
it would stand alone. It was now time to dance the war
dance around this red pole.

Each warrior emblazoned with his warlike gear and painted in his warlike colors would show his enemies that he was angry and ready to fight and kill. Each took turns performing about the pole, while all the others were engaged in calling aloud, "*He-uh, he-uh!*"

They constantly chanted this while each warrior danced up to the red pole and struck his tomahawk into it to mimic what they had promised by smoking the war pipe. With each tomahawk blow to the pole, renewed shouts of joy resounded through the air.

Pamela had edged away from the celebrants and was now standing at the outer edge of the frenzy, enthralled by Strong Bear as he officiated over the prewar ceremony. She glanced over her shoulder when she felt eyes boring down upon her. Her insides went cold when she saw Snow Owl standing among the observers, venomously glaring at her.

Pamela had become so involved in the war preparations, flattered to have been accepted by the anxious warriors, that until now she had not considered the idea that she was the only woman to be so honored. Although she knew Snow Owl wasn't the sort who would want to partake in such a venture, she realized the squaw would not want Pamela to, either, since her presence signaled to their people that Pamela was Strong Bear's most favored woman.

A chill shimmered along Pamela's flesh as she saw Snow Owl touch a sheathed knife at her waist. Now Pamela understood why Strong Bear was allowing her to travel with him. He did not trust leaving her with Snow Owl! As Pamela had begun to realize, Strong Bear also saw that Snow Owl had only been pretending to be a friend to her. Snow Owl most surely still planned to kill her! The gift of gold earrings from Snow Owl had been only a deceitful ploy.

Feeling uncomfortable under Snow Owl's scalding stare, Pamela jerked her eyes away, troubled by a racing heart and a feeling of dread. Though she would be spared Snow

Owl's wrath this time by accompanying Strong Bear on the journey to the British fort, what about later? Each day and night Pamela would have to watch and listen for Snow Owl to sneak up on her and thrust the knife into her flesh. What could have been a life of sheer rapture with Strong Bear could, instead, be one of sheer torture. With death possible at any moment, nothing in life could be sweet. Not even Strong Bear's lips!

Pamela's thoughts of Snow Owl were distracted when two wailing dogs were dragged to the inner circle of the chanting warriors. Ice filled her veins when, accompanied by a steady, rhythmic drumbeat, the dogs were slain and laid limply at Strong Bear's feet.

Clapping her hands over her mouth to stifle a gasp, Pamela watched weak-kneed in horror as Strong Bear sliced into the dogs and removed the hearts and livers from each. After cutting these into strips, Strong Bear dangled them from the red ceremonial pole.

The warriors formed a circle about the pole and began dancing and chanting. One by one a warrior broke from the circle to shout with a deafening yell his boasts of victory over the many animals he had slain for food and had brought home to his family. He vowed to be as skillful when facing the evil soldiers and promised many scalps upon his return!

To Pamela's disgust she witnessed each warrior taking turns biting and swallowing a piece of the meat from the pole, dancing to the rhythm of the Miami dog dance as the other warriors whirled, singing. It was another custom she would have to learn to accept, yet she couldn't help but wonder if she ever could.

This part of the war ceremony drew to a close. Pamela wondered if she could ever block its gory details from her mind. Yet when she looked at Strong Bear as he began to hold his last conference with the leaders of his battle wings, Pamela forgot everything but the chief and her awe of him. He was such a man of strength, of prowess, having surely been born a leader.

"Once we arrive close to the British fort no fires will be allowed in our camp," he shouted. "It will be a surprise ambush. The British usually expect Indians to attack at dawn. We will wait until later in the morning. We will kill them from all sides. Now we will sing the song of war to Manito to ask for his help in ridding our lands of the British scourge!"

Goose pimples rose upon Pamela's arms, and tears silvered the corners of her eyes as she listened to Strong Bear sing to his people.

"Oh, poor me who is going out to fight the enemy and know not whether I shall return again, to enjoy the embrace of my loved ones! Oh, poor creature whose life is not in his own hands, who has no power over his own body, but tries to do his duty for the welfare of his nation! O, though Great Spirit above, take pity on my loved ones! Grant that I may be successful in this attempt, that I may slay my enemy and bring home the trophies of war to my dear family and friends that we may rejoice together. Oh, take pity on me."

A stilled silence in the village followed the war song. The warriors disbanded and went to embrace their loved ones, voicing a sad farewell.

Pamela welcomed Strong Bear at her side though he was not saying a goodbye. He snaked an arm about her waist and walked her to her waiting horse, a gentle gray mare. There, they looked into one another's eyes for a moment, soundlessly speaking promises of devotion.

Then Strong Bear drew Pamela into his embrace and gave her a lingering, gentle kiss, after which he eased her away from him to hold her at arm's length. His eyes were two dark pits as he peered at her, sensing her vulnerability. Even with her face painted she was lovely in her womanly innocence.

Yet she would not be spared the traumas of war, even though she had already experienced enough of such madness to last her a lifetime. But she would be safer with him than without!

"My *me-tam-sah*, ride with me with faith," he said, his voice low and husky. "By the time the sun rises twice in the sky I shall present you the British colonel's scalp. You will be joined with your brother again. All of this I promise you. My love, the future holds only good things for us. All that is bad will be put behind us. We will have only good things to share between us after the warring with the British is over."

Wriggling free from his grasp, Pamela drew back to stare into Strong Bear's eyes. "I love you," she whispered. "Oh, how I love you." Then, with a strangled cry, she threw herself into his arms.

She wanted to beg him to be careful but she knew that to do so would be to display doubt in him. At this moment, as in all her other trials and tribulations, she had to show courage she did not feel. Inside, she was a quivering mass of anxieties. If she should lose him, what then?

Her only comfort was that she was going to be with him, no matter what the outcome of the fight. If he should die, somehow she would make sure that she would die alongside him. She could not envision a future without him!

Strong Bear engulfed Pamela's lips in a fierce, possessive kiss, then released her and lifted her onto her saddle of blankets on the horse. He gave her another lingering, adoring look, then whirled around and shouted commands to his warriors, who promptly mounted their restive steeds.

Mounting his own anxious strawberry roan, Strong Bear gave the order for his warriors to leave. Pamela rode proudly alongside him. But her eyes were drawn to a movement behind a tree not far away. She flinched when she saw Snow Owl on a horse, scornfully watching. . . .

Lucas Boatright cringed where he sat huddled in the darkness listening to the colonel's shouts and occasional gunfire outside in the courtyard. It seemed that the colonel had gone mad and was killing soldiers at random. Because so many had been slain by the Indian attack, not many remained at the fort in the first place and new recruits could not arrive quickly enough to make up for the colonel's whims. It made no sense whatsoever to kill the remaining soldiers at the fort, even though they *had* looted the place when the colonel did not return on cue.

A strained silence outside the stockade door made Lucas sigh with relief. When no more gunshots erupted, he felt the colonel had finally reached some sort of satiety and would refrain from slaying any more men. For at least a while longer Lucas thought that some peace might descend on the embattled fortress.

His hands groped in the darkness for Robert. "What're you doin'?" he asked, drawing his hand back when he failed to find him. He was in constant fear of the ravenous rats. "Let's talk. Wouldn't you like to talk some more about your sister? I ain't never seen such a lovely lady as your sister. Ain't you glad that I told you she's safe?"

Robert's silence made Lucas's stomach churn with queasiness, yet he had grown used to the lack of response. Robert was in another world, one that could not know of a sister, or of any past. The colonel was not the only crazy fool at this fort.

Pushing to his knees, Lucas crawled toward the sound of Robert's breathing. "Robert, damn it," he sulked. "What *are* you doing?"

He recoiled when he finally found Robert, a baby rat in one hand, stroking it with the other.

"Damn . . ." Lucas said, shuddering all over. He scooted back to the wall and placed his back hard against it. He hung his head in his hands. Would this madness never end . . . ?

Twenty-Three

꾱ꞏꞏꞏꞏꞏ

My cheek is cold and white, alas!
My heart beats loud and fast.
                              —Shelley

All through the long night of waiting, the fort appeared a black, almost indefinable silhouette set against a night sky filled with stars. Pamela waited, impatiently, wondering about the fate of her brother inside the sinister walls. With the coming of broad daylight the true hideous shape of the fort was revealed, beam by pocked beam, until the hour of caution had passed for all concerned.

The fort was now under a skeleton guard, the gate open as soldiers filed in and out, moving to the riverbank where small crafts were moored to exchange goods. The sun rose higher in the sky as midmorning arrived. Pamela lay beside Strong Bear in the swaying bluegrass that rimmed the forest and thinned away as the land sloped to the protective walls of the fort.

Strong Bear rose to his haunches. He raised his tomahawk with one hand and gave silent commands to his warriors with the other by employing sign language. Pamela watched, fear pulsing inside her heart as she realized Strong Bear was signaling his men to ready for attack. She watched as some of Strong Bear's warriors ran stealthily through the tall timber of the forest toward the river. They had been assigned to kill the soldiers who were away from the protective walls of the fort.

Pamela then welcomed Strong Bear's arm circling about her waist, drawing her against him. "You will be safe here, away from the actual fighting," he promised. "Soon it will all be over and I will return to you."

Pamela felt as though a knot were choking her at the base of her throat, as she gazed into Strong Bear's eyes. Words could not even pass her lips. She could only nod, yet deep down she wanted to fight with him, side by side. But she knew that she was lucky to have been able to venture this far; she would not ask him for more than that. The task set before him was fraught with danger. She could not become another burden for him to shoulder.

Throwing her arms about Strong Bear's neck, Pamela clung fiercely to him, a choked sob erupting from her lips as he released her. He joined the wave of warriors who ventured into the open. As the soldiers were alerted to the attack, they began firing from their sentry posts at the top of the wall. The warriors retaliated with their bows, sending volleys of arrows sailing through the air, and continued to swarm over the open ground.

Pamela dropped to her knees, anxiously watching Strong Bear's movements, afraid that at any moment he would fall under the hail of gunshot. But he was too quick on his feet . . . too agile. And soon he disappeared through the wide gate of the fort and Pamela could only guess at what next happened. She clutched her hands into tight fists, her fingernails digging painfully into her palms. Her throat was dry; her heart pounded wildly as she listened to the scalpers' cries of triumph and the clap of incessant gunfire.

Unable to stand the waiting any longer, Pamela rose

cautiously to her feet. What if Strong Bear was wounded and needed her? What if Robert was caught in the crossfire of the battle and was shot? Both the men in her life needed her now.

Her eyes surveyed the fort walls for soldiers who might fire upon her as she would make a mad dash across the wide clearing. The only ones that she saw were those who were draped lifeless over the top of the wall, arrows protruding hideously from their chests or backs. There were others sprawled on the riverbank, lying in a pool of their own blood.

Pamela shivered violently. She turned her eyes away, gagging. She had to remind herself repeatedly that this loss of life was necessary. The British were evil; they deserved to die. They were responsible not only for Anthony's death, but also for Robert's abduction! The British had planned it all. And now they were going to pay. When they had slain Strong Bear's people in their efforts to rid the land of this one more family of settlers, they had made a fatal error in judgment!

The odor of gunpowder wafted through the air and stung Pamela's nostrils, filling her with dread. Strong Bear! Robert! What could be happening to them if so much gunfire was exploding in the air?

Setting her jaw determinedly, no longer able merely to stand by and wait, Pamela ran across the cleared stretch of land. Her spirit quailed as she came directly in the line of deadly musket fire near the open gate.

As gunshot whizzed by her head, she fell to the ground and clutched at the grass, gasping with fear. Yet her eyes were fixed straight ahead, seeing the horror of the fight within the fort's walls. Everywhere there was confusion as howling Indians jumped into the battlefield, scalping the wounded soldiers. She could hardly stand to watch as a soldier was hacked alive with a war hatchet. She jerked her eyes away when she saw an Indian pack mud and sand into the mouth and eyes of one of the soldiers.

"You want land! Take this!" the angered Indian shouted in his vengeance. "You never take *or* kill again!"

Pamela's spirit rebelled, making her wonder if she could truly accept the Indians' way of life. Though she had never looked on Strong Bear as a savage, the way he and his warriors killed could be described as nothing less. Yet, hadn't the British been as savage in their slaughter of the Miami Indians? Were all men the same, no matter the color of their skin? Was killing something that came so easy to them all . . . ?

Pamela studied the grounds inside the fort, astonished by how many of Strong Bear's warriors were dying of wounds. Panic seized her when she looked anxiously through the battle scene and could not spot Strong Bear. Was he among those who had been shot? She must go and see. . . .

Pamela started to rise, to rush ahead, but another gunshot whizzed past her head and made her collapse in a heap. When she heard a soft cry of pain close behind, she craned her neck and started. Snow Owl lay mortally wounded only a footstep away.

Grieving at first, Pamela then spotted the knife still in Snow Owl's fist. She had apparently followed the war party from the Miami village and had awaited her chance to murder Pamela! It would have been easy enough to let Strong Bear think the deed had been done by a soldier. Snow Owl could then return to the village and her people unbesmirched by the white woman's blood!

Snow Owl clutched now at the bleeding chest wound, her eyes clouded over with pain. Tears rolled down her cheeks, and her ragged breathing tormented Pamela's ears. Even though Snow Owl had planned to kill her, Pamela could not sit by and watch her die. It would not be Christian. She could at least drag Snow Owl to safety and let her die in peace!

Glancing ahead, checking to see if it was safe at least to jump to her feet and aid Snow Owl, Pamela's insides flooded with a warmth when she spotted Strong Bear in the fort's courtyard, shouting orders to his remaining warriors. The battle appeared about won, the Indians victorious. Pamela couldn't help but wonder about the fate of Colonel Bradley! She would have preferred to have delivered his death, at her own hands, but she knew that was impossible. He was probably already dead. She prayed that Robert was well.

Now knowing that Strong Bear had survived the terrible ordeal, Pamela crawled to Snow Owl and whispered to her face.

"Snow Owl, I'm going to drag you over to the protective cover of the trees," she whispered. "You . . . you will be more comfortable there."

Snow Owl looked through her tears to a face full of compassion. She puzzled over this white woman whose heart did not seem to know the meaning of the word *hate*. Perhaps the white woman *did* deserve to be Strong Bear's first wife of importance. And she would be. Snow Owl knew very well that she was dying.

Wincing in pain, Snow Owl forced herself not to cry out as Pamela placed her hands beneath her arms and began dragging her across the clearing. Each movement of her body felt as though a dozen knives were piercing her flesh where the wound continued to spout blood. Then she sighed with relief when Pamela set her on a soft sponge of bluegrass. She knelt over Snow Owl, softly smiling down as she fought to make her comfortable. Snow Owl looked away, ashamed.

Pamela glanced at the fort, then again at Snow Owl. Pity for the dying squaw engulfed her. She tore a remnant of Snow Owl's buckskin skirt, and amassed it atop her wound; then she caressed Snow Owl's brow with her hand, trying to understand the reasoning behind everything that had unfolded. Troubled by many things, she found Snow Owl's behavior most puzzling.

"Snow Owl," she murmured, urging Snow Owl's face around so their eyes could lock. "Why would you want so desperately to kill me? Do you truly hate me so much? You had only pretended to be a friend?"

Snow Owl licked her parched lips and blinked her heavily lashed eyes. "You took . . . my . . . place in my husband's life," she whispered harshly. "You soon would be his *wife*. Snow Owl could not let that happen."

"But, Snow Owl, you don't even love him," Pamela said, almost pleading. "Why would you be so possessive of a man you don't love? And did you not always know that he would take another wife? Though I do not yet quite understand this custom of your people, *you* have been schooled in your culture. Do you hate me so much you deny me the right to happiness with Strong Bear because I am a white woman?"

Snow Owl lifted a trembling hand, then dropped it again to her bleeding chest. She coughed, spitting up blood and choking. Then she looked over at Pamela with dark, cold eyes. "It is not just because you are a white woman," she wheezed. "And, yes, it is a custom for the Miami chief to have two wives, but Snow Owl would never have let Strong Bear take another wife besides Snow Owl, no matter the color of the skin."

Pamela was taken aback by this confession. She had always assumed it was her color that had offended Snow Owl. Did her confession mean that she would have killed any woman chosen by Strong Bear? Even an Indian?

"But you don't *love* him," Pamela insisted.

"No. Snow Owl does not have the ability to love a *man*," she said in a hoarse whisper, panting for breath. "Only what material offerings he gives me. *That* is what has made Snow . . . Owl . . . happy. . . ."

"But, Snow Owl, Strong Bear would still have given you—" Pamela began, but stopped when she saw Snow Owl's eyes widen with fear as she clutched her chest feverishly, then cry out in pain just prior to turning stone silent.

"No—" Pamela cried, realizing Snow Owl had just taken her last breath of life. She stared down at the woman for a moment, stunned. With trembling fingers she reached and closed the lids of Snow Owl's sightless eyes. Then she hung her head in her hands and began to weep softly. She wasn't crying so much for Snow Owl, as for the inequalities in life, its senselessness. The pieces just never seemed to fit. Would they ever—? Would life ever be right again?

A strong arm suddenly at Pamela's waist drew her up from the ground. She turned her head and sighed with relief when she looked up into the warm dark eyes of Strong Bear. "My love," Pamela whispered, creeping into his arms and holding him tightly. "You came through the horrible ordeal alive! I feared so for you."

Strong Bear's embrace was at first gentle; then Pamela felt his body tense against hers and she understood why. He had spotted Snow Owl.

Easing from his arms, Pamela saw the hate for Snow Owl etched across Strong Bear's features. She knew that it was unnecessary to explain what had happened. He already knew why Snow Owl was there, for she had traveled without his knowledge, without his permission, and she would have done so for only one reason. To kill Pamela!

In Strong Bear's eyes he was not seeing a dead wife. It was as though he were staring at an inanimate object. It was plain to see that if Snow Owl hadn't died from her wound, she would have been banished from the tribe, left to wander aimlessly through the countryside without a people. Only in death was she finding true solace.

A remembrance so keen in her mind that it pained her shook Pamela from her reverie. Her brother! Strong Bear should know now of Robert's fate.

She touched Strong Bear faintly on the arm to stir him from his thoughts as he stared down at Snow Owl. "Strong Bear, my brother—"

Pamela's words were cut short when she heard footsteps approach from behind. Swinging around, she blanched when she saw Robert being led to her by one of Strong Bear's warriors.

"Robert . . . ?" Pamela gasped, unable to believe her

eyes. It was Robert, yet it *wasn't*. He was looking at her, a vacant glint in his eyes.

"Oh, Lord, what has happened?" Pamela cried, her gaze taking in Robert's bedraggled condition. His clothes were disheveled and stained. He was gaunt, his sunken cheeks covered with rust-colored whiskers. His walk was unsteady, as though he might collapse at any moment.

Filled with conflicting emotions, Pamela ran to Robert and hugged him as sobs escaped her lips. But he did not respond in any way to her. His arms hung limply at his sides.

Feeling numb from fear of what had happened to her brother, Pamela stepped back, flinching when she spotted drool pooling in the corners of his mouth, down his chin, then dripping onto the front of his buckskin shirt. She covered her mouth with a hand, holding back a cry of shock, for it was quite plain to see that her brother had lost his mind.

Then anger surged into a fiery ball inside her. Only one person was responsible for this new tragedy in her life. Colonel Bradley!

Turning on a heel, Pamela faced Strong Bear. "The colonel," she said venomously. "What happened to him? Is he dead?"

Without a word, Strong Bear circled Pamela's waist with a muscled arm and began to usher her to the open gate of the fort. She nearly stumbled when she looked back across her shoulder, concerned for Robert's welfare. When she saw that he was being sheltered beneath a tree, she knew that he was safe for now. But what of later? He needed specialized doctoring to draw him out of this strange shell into which he had retreated. But how? Where?

Her attention was drawn back as they approached the towering, menacing fort wall. As she walked up to the wide gate, a sick feeling overcame her. Dozens of bodies lay twisted on all sides of her.

Twenty-Four

And, on its full, deep breast serene,
Like quiet isles my duties lie.
                                    —Lowell

Strong Bear set an example as he strode past the amassed bodies spread across the courtyard, almost serene in his bearing. Pamela gulped and reached deep within herself to draw on whatever strength she might find there to retain her composure as she trailed behind. It was hard. She had never witnessed such mutilation . . . such death!

Swallowing hard, she tried to fix her eyes straight ahead, but found the task overwhelming. The courtyard reeked of blood where heads had been scalped and limbs lay missing. Only a few Indians had met their death this day, but all but two British soldiers had died. And Strong Bear was taking Pamela to these two survivors.

The sun spilled golden beams over the figures of two men tied to two separate stakes, one wearing a brilliant red uniform, the other a simple buckskin shirt and leggings.

One had dark hair plastered down to his head with perspiration, the other golden hair flecking yellow in the sun.

Pamela stepped up to the two men, recognizing both. She looked from soft blue eyes filled with fear, to gray, cold eyes filled with loathing. She had warm feelings for the one . . . a searing hatred for the other. Lucas Boatright was misplaced on this torture stake beside the evil colonel. Pamela recalled how kind he had been to her on more than one occasion. It seemed that he was a victim of his own poor judgment by having chosen to fight for the English under the command of Colonel Bradley.

"You asked about the colonel," Strong Bear said, motioning with a hand toward the leering British officer. "His life has been spared for much better things. Before he dies he will be begging for mercy."

Pamela stepped closer to the colonel. She glared at him, then slapped his face and spat at his feet. "You deserve everything that happens to you," she hissed. "My poor brothers. You are responsible for both their fates! I shall watch you die, and laugh over every lingering torment!"

Colonel Bradley's eyes flashed angrily back at her, but he didn't speak. But Lucas Boatright struggled to frame his thoughts, feeling that this woman he had treated kindly might be his last chance for life.

"Ma'am," Lucas said, his voice drawn. "Ma'am, please help me. I didn't do nothin' to deserve dyin' like this. I wasn't truly like the rest of the British soldiers. I was even imprisoned with your brother because of my differences. I tried to help your brother. He's in such a terrible state."

Lucas looked nervously over at Strong Bear, then again at Pamela. "Don't let the Indian kill me. You and he both owe me a debt. That night he rescued you from the courtyard? I saw you. I could have reported what you were doin', but I didn't. I let you go free! Let me go free in exchange for my kindness."

"You . . . saw . . . me escape and you didn't report it?" Pamela asked, recalling the scene. He *had* always seemed out of place among the others. Surely he was here by mistake!

"You deserved better treatment than what the colonel had planned for you," Lucas said somberly. He wriggled his fingers, straining the ropes at his wrists. "Let me go free. Then I can take you and your brother by boat up the Ohio to Louisville. Your brother needs medical assistance badly. I'll help you find a doctor. Please, ma'am. Please?"

His words sliced through Pamela. She liked his suggestions about what must be done for Robert. It was imperative that he be taken to an American settlement for medical assistance, she mused. She had seen what had happened to her father because there had been no available means other than horse travel. Now there was a quicker *and* safer alternative available. Though some riverboats were not making it past renegade Indians, the suggested route offered safer passage over such a distance than by land.

Pamela turned and looked up at Strong Bear. If Robert traveled to Louisville, she must travel with him. She could never rest easily until she knew that he had arrived safely and was properly attended to by someone schooled in the appropriate field of medicine.

But Strong Bear! He surely would never understand her need to accompany her brother on such a journey. And she must, she must. She had lost one brother. She could not lose another, neither to mental illness, *nor* to neglect.

"Strong Bear, much that he says is true," she said, nestling her hand onto Strong Bear's crossed arm. He seemed to relax under her silky touch. "He is not like the colonel. He *did* treat me kindly. And did you not hear that he let us go free when he saw you helping me escape? Will you release him, Strong Bear? He truly doesn't deserve to die."

Strong Bear glowered down at Pamela, having carefully measured each and every word spoken by the man with hair the color of golden wheat. The man had made a suggestion that Strong Bear did not approve of. Strong Bear had feared what finding Pamela's brother might prompt.

He had thought the brother would be the one to demand that she return to the white man's world that could be reached by traveling up the broad, flowing waters of the Ohio. But now the suggestion was coming from another! And she was even defending this man who threatened Strong Bear's future with his woman!

Strong Bear was torn between choices. If he refused to release the golden-haired man, Pamela would not understand, possibly even turn her back on Strong Bear. Yet, if he released the man, would she accept his invitation and leave on the river craft? If she left, would she return?

But Strong Bear understood much of life, of its many complexities, and had known from the beginning that the time might come when this white woman would depart. And if she did? He would not stand in her way. He would give her the chance to see if she could truly be happy without him. He felt he would never feel good about himself if he forced her to stay.

Without further ado Strong Bear went to Lucas and released him, then turned and watched Pamela's eyes well with happiness. Was this man even more a threat than what Strong Bear had earlier thought? Could Pamela see something in him as a man, that other men did not know to look for?

Pamela looked from Strong Bear to Lucas. She clasped her hands tightly behind her, not knowing how to tell Strong Bear of her decision, one that had to be made. He would say that she was choosing her brother over him, and that was not the truth of it. Her brother was helpless; Strong Bear was not. It didn't take much to see who needed her the most! But without even telling Strong Bear, she knew that he would not understand.

While Lucas stood rubbing his raw wrists, he waited anxiously to calculate his next move. He glanced over at Colonel Bradley, seeing the intense hate in the depths of his gray eyes. If there was ever any chance that the colonel could be set free, Lucas knew that his life would not be worth a plug nickel. Escape to Louisville would not be far enough. And what of Louisville? Would he be regarded as a foreign traitor and turned away? Or would Pamela book passage on the boat and help him pass as an American? Would she even help him in this pretense . . . ?

But surely she would. She had already, only moments ago, acted in his behalf. If he could only convince her that she must travel with him. Then Lucas would remind her again that she owed him a debt, for he would be the one delivering her and her brother to civilization.

The only drawback was her feelings for the Indian, Strong Bear. It was obvious it was not a brotherly sort of fixation.

Pamela shuffled her feet in the dirt, dreading revealing her wishes to Strong Bear. Today he was being such a quiet, withdrawn figure of a man, it was as though he were someone she didn't know. But didn't he have cause? He had just fought a major battle with an enemy. He had lost several of his men. He had even lost a wife. What might he say when Pamela revealed to him that he was about to lose her, if for only a brief time span.

"Strong Bear," she blurted, finally getting the nerve to speak, the image of a mentally frail Robert filling her mind. Even if she lost the man she loved in the process, she would see that her brother became well again! "I would like to take this man's suggestion. I believe it is best for me to see that my brother is taken safely to Louisville for medical treatment. I must accompany him there. I must see that he is cared for properly."

When Strong Bear did not speak, but stood stiffly, staring down at her with no emotion whatsoever in his dark, penetrating eyes, Pamela feared what she had not thought of before. He did not seem to care at all about what she had suggested! It was as though he wanted her to leave.

"Strong Bear, say something."

"There is nothing to say. You want to go. *Go*," he said, gesturing toward the open gate. "Go now."

Pamela's insides grew numb. "Strong Bear, you do not

ask me to stay?'' she murmered, paling. ''You will let me go that easily? Do you not care?'' She had refrained from telling him she would return once Robert recovered his health. Now she was afraid to tell him. She was afraid that he did not even care!

Strong Bear folded his arms across his massive chest and looked down at her under heavy-lidded eyes, then walked boldly away, leaving her staring in disbelief after him. A sob nearly surfaced but she swallowed it down. She would not show her feelings of loss to anyone. Strong Bear had grown tired of her, or perhaps he had seen too many of his warriors lost in her behalf, and because he blamed her, she was tarnished in his eyes. Had he ever loved her? Had she been wrong about him?

Pain tore at her heart, yet she forced herself to think of Robert. Only Robert. She was her brother's only hope. . . .

''Come, Lucas,'' Pamela said, grabbing Lucas by an arm. ''You have offered my brother and I a ride by boat to Louisville? We accept.''

Again a sick feeling welled inside her as she moved past the massacre. She clasped a hand over her nose, trying to keep the smell from invading her senses. And once through the gate, she broke into a run toward the fringe of trees. Her brother needed her now. But could she truly live with the knowledge that Strong Bear no longer loved her? He *was* her existence. Her heart was his, she was a hostage of his heart, forever . . . and ever. How could he so easily turn his back on what they had shared? Was love to a man so easily cast aside? Had he ever truly loved her at all?

Moving away from Lucas, Pamela ran to Robert and knelt down before him. She framed his face between her hands, studying his eyes, seeing how vacant they were. And she knew that he did not really see her, for he would be the first to mock the black paint on her face. It must be removed. Soon. She wanted nothing to remind her of Strong Bear.

She looked down at her buckskin attire. Soon she would

be wearing cotton fineries again. But how? Who could provide her a place to live once she arrived in Louisville?

Fear of all her tomorrows surged through her like widfire, yet she clasped Robert's hand and led him to the river. Once there and postioned comfortably in a small boat with Lucas at the helm, she refused to look back, to search for Strong Bear on the shores. If he could forget their love so easily, so could she!

As Lucas sliced the paddles into the water, directing the boat away from the shoreline, terrible, soul-shattering screams rent the air. Pamela turned her head with a start and paled at their ferocity. They were a man's screams. In her haste to ferry Robert to civilization she had forgotten Colonel Bradley, and the fact she had wanted to witness his execution.

Smiling to herself, Pamela was satisfied enough. His screams proved that Strong Bear was not being at all merciful.

Then her smiled faded. Strong Bear. She had never truly known him, at all. . . .

Her face sparkling, the war paint now only a bad memory, Pamela held Robert's head in her lap, trying not to feel the fatigue that was enveloping her. A full day and night had passed as they traveled up the Ohio, stopping only long enough to prepare fish over a fire. Pamela had fought sleep, feeling the need to watch and care for Robert at all times. Lucas had ventured onward. Both had exchanged much idle conversation, in the end negotiating expectations for each other. She was to pretend that he was American. He was to help her find proper lodging and medical assistance for Robert.

Neither begrudged the other this aid, for a true friendship had formed between them. Pamela felt as though she had gained another brother, yet she feared that he considered her more than that. Though she may have lost Strong Bear forever, she could not imagine ever feeling anything for anyone else akin to the passion he ignited in her.

Somehow she would make Lucas understand that she could never love him. She most surely was destined to be alone, a spinster.

A great roar sounding from somewhere ahead of the boat drew Pamela from her silent thoughts. She squinted her eyes and looked through the pearly shine of the afternoon sun and gasped as she caught sight of an awesome creation of God. It was a great waterfall. The water tumbled over the limestone outcrop from a great height. She knew that she was close to Louisville, for what she was gazing upon was the Falls of the Ohio. Below the falls, sitting on the limestone table above the water, was the town of Louisville.

From this distance Pamela could see that the falls had three different channels. One channel consisted of many steps of smooth and pointed rock; another shot down like a mill dam, another still was a very rapid, frothing stream, full of stones.

Bordering the falls on both sides of the shore were beautiful Lombardy poplar trees. The land on the south side of the river had a more southern atmosphere than on the north side for the grass grew lusher and magnolia trees bloomed. The Ohio River seemed to be the line between the northern and southern climates.

Pamela urged Robert from his deep sleep as Lucas rowed the boat closer to shore where she soon discovered the Louisville Fort to be nothing more than piles of dirt against the walls of the cabins, surrounded by a log fence. Soldiers were uniformed, wearing form-fitting pants, white buttoned vests, and coats that hung down to the knees in back. Long rows of shiny buttons decorated the front and shoulder while large bushy hats, complete with feather, completed the outfit.

As Pamela helped Robert from the moored boat, she felt welcomed by the soldiers and knew that she had not been wrong to bring Robert to Louisville. But deep down where her desires lived, she sighed at the thought of Strong Bear.

Twenty-Five

❧ ❧

I love her with a love as still
As a broad river's peaceful might.
—Lowell

Several weeks had passed. The great bell clanged the morning hour of eight from the slender tower of the church steeple and then quivered to silence. Dressed in a pale yellow muslin frock with little puffed sleeves, high neck and waist, accented by a knitted shawl draped about her shoulders, Pamela glided down the long, dark corridor. On either side, behind closed doors, were the nuns' quarters. She and Robert had been taken in by Father Joseph, a Catholic priest of high prominence in the thriving community of Louisville. Lucas Boatright had been accepted into the community and was now an apprentice for the local baker, having earlier in his life learned much of the craft from his father, who had been a master baker in England.

Autumn now hung crisp in the air. Pamela was anxious to get on with her day, eager to take her stroll to the Falls of the Ohio to stand her usual vigil: watching the Indians glide in by canoe to the trading post to exchange their furs for supplies. Deep within her heart she hoped that Strong Bear would be among them, come to claim her.

But, alas, he had most surely forgotten her as one who has died!

More and more Pamela had hungered to go to him. She had learned to endure many things in her life, but not the absence of Strong Bear. She had gone about her daily chores with forced enthusiasm. She felt only half-alive.

Though Lucas Boatright had tried to court her, she had tried to direct his attentions and affections on Priscilla Taylor, the daughter of the baker; it would not have been fair of Pamela to let Lucas believe there could ever be anything between them. Though she did watch for Strong Bear most every day, Robert was the only true force behind her existence now. Only Robert! He cared for her; Strong Bear did not!

The door squeaked as Pamela opened it. She peered into the room assigned to Robert. A warmth seized her when she saw Robert sitting up in his great Tudor oak four-postered bed hung with crewelwork curtains, reading. His face was cleanly shaven. His cheeks were healthily filled out, pink and glowing. Neatly groomed, his rusty red hair just barely reached his squared shoulders. He wore a cotton robe, and his bare feet were propped up on a tall stack of blankets. With a sparkling new pair of eyeglasses perched atop his nose, his eyes eagerly absorbed the pages of a book lighted by candlelight from a bedside table.

"Robert?" Pamela whispered, tiptoeing into the room, not wanting to disturb the nuns in the room adjoining Robert's. She closed the door and smiled as Robert lowered the book and looked at her with full recognition.

"Sis," Robert said in a half-scolding tone, seeing the shawl, knowing where she was headed. "You'll never give up, will you? You're up early to go stand watch again, aren't you? How could you want the Indian to come? My brains still seem scrambled because of what the damn Indians did to me.''

He scooted the sleeve of his sleeping gown back, revealing marks on his wrists where he had been tied and tortured. A shudder overcame him; sometimes he found himself thinking it might have been best had he not regained all of his faculties. In flashes, the tormenting moments could come back to him and make his whole body become drenched in cold, nervous perspiration. It had been good to escape for a while by losing his ability to think. But now, he was trying to drown all remembrances by catching up on reading. Thank God he had found reading a pleasant escape early on in life.

He pushed his sleeve back down to hide the ugly markings, then smiled at Pamela as she moved to the window and slid the heavy velveteen curtains open. He frowned when he saw where her eyes were directed. More oft than not she watched the river. Should the Indian ever come for her, would she truly return to the Indian village with him? Would she forget that she had a brother all that quickly?

''As I told you before, the Indians who abducted and tortured you are not the same as those I lived with,'' Pamela said, throwing open the window so Robert could savor the fragrance of the autumn air.

Lifting the hem of her dress, she went to Robert's bedside and leaned over to kiss his cheek; then she stood back and looked at him, everything within her bursting with happiness. He was almost completely well again, after much counseling from a physician and Father Joseph.

It was a miracle, it seemed. There were now only moments when he was tormented by flashbacks. He'd cup his eyes until the painful images passed. Soon they even would be erased, for he grew more and more interested in life.

''Oh, Robert, you don't know what it does to my heart to see you so well,'' Pamela sighed, twining her fingers together before her. ''I had so worried that—''

Robert lifted an eyebrow and chuckled low. ''You had

worried that I would be loony the rest of my life?'' he asked. He lay the book aside and rose from the bed, the full night robe scraping his bare ankles. He drew Pamela into his arms and hugged her. "Sis, I'm all right. But you? God, how I worry about you and your foolish notion about that Indian. He's not going to come for you. Can't you forget him? Don't go to the falls today. Get involved in the preparations for the autumn dance at the courthouse. Lucas'd make one damn good husband. He'll soon have enough money saved to build you a house.''

"Priscilla is in love with Lucas," Pamela said softly, wondering at his sudden tenseness at the mention of Priscilla. But she shrugged off the wonder, for it could not mean a thing. "Not I. Nor shall I ever love him."

Easing from Robert's arms, Pamela turned and went to the window. She looked across the rooftops of the handsome, well-built whitewashed houses standing picturesquely along the riverbank, the fort walls obtrusive in their ugliness. Colorfully cultivated gardens close to the streets behind high picket fences displayed their autumn finery in assorted colors of orange, red, and purple.

She looked down at the long avenue of the river, seeing pirogues traveling close to the banks below the trading post. Something clutched at her heart when she caught sight of some Indian braves unloading their hides from the pirogues, carrying them to the trading post. Should Strong Bear combine trading with his search of her, oh, wouldn't that be just too grand?

Feeling the pain of loneliness, Pamela had to force back a choked sob before she turned to face Robert again. When she felt his comforting arm encircle her waist, she looked into his eyes.

Pamela smiled awkwardly, for he most surely knew the reason for her distance, and he most surely didn't approve. Though he was well enough for her to leave him to live her own life, he had grown used to her being there for him. He was becoming too dependent on her, and she was becoming too dependent on him. It would be better for them both if she could find some way to break this chain, and start healthier lives.

At times, Pamela felt like a bird lost from its flock, floundering . . . floundering . . . floundering. . . .

"You will go to the dance tonight, won't you?" Robert asked thickly. "Lucas is countin' on it."

"And you? Do you think you might try to go?" Pamela asked, wishing Robert could find a proper lady to help draw him further from the shell he had built around himself. She smoothed a hand across his cheek. "Robert, it would do you good to mix." She giggled softly. "You can't marry a book, you know."

Robert tore himself free and went back to his bed and climbed onto it. He picked up the book and opened it. "You spend your time as you please, so shall I mine, " he said, stinging Pamela with his sudden gruffness.

Clearing her throat nervously, Pamela went to the door and swung it open. She started to say good-bye but saw that Robert's eyes were already absorbed in his book. Though his health was much better, she doubted if he would ever truly be the same again.

Almost running, wanting to get away from all the memories of what had befallen Robert, Pamela left the rectory. She raced along the wooden sidewalk, past the crowded mass of wooden frame buildings that were cluttered along the riverfront, ignoring the men traveling on the dirt roads with their barrows and mules, the carriages carrying fine gents to the trading post, a boy sweeping out the stable yard, even a warder in dun-brown redingote shuffling toward the magazine and guardhouse.

Soldiers, wagons, horses, and people—many speaking foreign languages—filled the unpaved streets. Pigeons were strutting along the walkway, scattering at Pamela's feet, and soon she welcomed the solace of the shadows of the beautiful Lombardy poplar trees at the base of the falls.

Picking up the tail of her skirt, her shawl draped loosely over her arms, Pamela moved along the large and rocky dry riverbank, for the water table was low. While watching for pirogues she had discovered this place of absolute mystery.

Bending, she scanned the riverbank, seeing the many objects lodged into the rock. Walnuts, acorns and shells of the same, deer and buffalo horns seemed to rest loosely atop the flat stone. But as she attempted to lift them up, it was as before, they were immovable and petrified.

Straightening her shoulders, again standing fully erect, Pamela walked along the shoreline. Her eyes rested on boats at the wharf with their blunt prows, and on others approaching the docks, their steersmen straining against sweeps, oars dipping.

And then she tensed when she saw several pirogues approaching with Indians. She shielded her eyes with a hand, becoming breathless with anxiousness, for didn't one Indian in particular look familiar? Did he not look so dignified in his stance as he sat tall and straight in command of the other pirogues following his? Was his chin not bold and proudly lifted? Did his hair not shine so sleekly beneath the soft rays of the early morning sun?

Memories of times in Strong Bear's arms swept through Pamela, making her tremble with desire. Blindly, she ran from the riverbank, through tall bluegrass, her skirt whipping in the wind, her long, flowing hair billowing about her face, her anxiousness surging as she grew closer.

But when she arrived at the wharf as the Indian climbed from his pirogue, she felt the fool, for it was not Strong Bear at all. It was always as before. It was just her heart yearning for his presence that made her see Strong Bear in every copper-skinned man approaching the fort by river.

Turning her eyes away, tears silvering her cheeks, Pamela again began running, but this time away from the waters. She would never torture herself like this again! She would never come watching, each time tearing her heart apart as though it were a rose, its petals being plucked and tossed into the wind!

"I must go to the dance with Lucas," she whispered. "I must at least try to forget. I must!"

She wiped the tears from her eyes and pushed through a picket gate at one side and entered the brick courtyard of the town bake shop, from which now emanated a rich aroma of cinnamon apples, molasses, yeast, and the smoke of hickory and oak.

Moving past a garden of box and holly, Pamela entered the bake shop, seeing Lucas eagerly at work with his baking chores, his face flushed from the heat of the great ovens. He was pressing dough for a gingerbread man into an elaborate wooden mold shaped like a cavalier, while another lad raked hot coals from the waist-high oven and shoveled them into a great canister.

Drawing her shawl from around her shoulders, Pamela walked farther into the bake shop, smiling warmly as Lucas looked suddenly her way. "I've just stopped by to get some bread to take back to Robert," Pamela said, having let this become a daily habit, knowing how much Robert liked freshly baked bread.

She spied the gingerbread men being readied for the oven, causing a pang of sorrow to fill her being. Anthony had been murdered and Robert had been abducted the day she had been baking her own gingerbread men. It had also been the day Strong Bear had rescued her from her tragic plight.

She dropped her gaze so that Lucas could not see the sadness etched across her face at these reminders of the past, which always included Strong Bear.

She forced her most pleasant smile as Lucas pushed the gingerbread men into the oven on a long paddle, then came to stand before her, wiping flour dust on his apron. If her heart did not already belong to another man, it would be easy to love the sweet, softly spoken one who now smiled down at her. His golden hair was swept back from his face and secured with a leather string at the back of his head; his blue eyes were pleasant. . . .

"You know how I look forward to your daily visits," Lucas said almost clumsily, feeling his already flushed face color. She did stir him so! Yet he had given up hoping that she would ever see him as anything but a friend. If she allowed him to escort her to the dance this evening, he knew not to try to steal a kiss. It would endanger their special friendship.

"I have come for more than the usual reason," Pamela said, trying to sound convincing, though she did not want him to believe that her allowing him to escort her to the dance could mean anything but a continued friendship.

"And, that is . . . ?" Lucas said, stepping away from her to place more hickory and oak into the massive stove. His heart frolicked inside his chest, awaiting her next words. She had put him off each time he had asked her to attend the dance with him. She had only then suggested he go with Priscilla. But little did Pamela know that Priscilla had eyes for someone else.

Priscilla Taylor came bustling into the room carrying a small basket hanging over her left arm, her petiteness making her look quite vulnerable. Her paleness matched the delicate lace-trimmed, richly gathered dress and the bonnet she had tied about her angular face. Almost golden with the light slanting in them from the front window, her eyes were bright, her lips delicately shaped, the dimples in her cheeks adorable.

"Why, Pamela, I didn't know you were here," Priscilla said, her voice slight, yet firm. She cast her eyes downward, as though she had something to be timid about, though Pamela knew not what. So far, Priscilla had paid no attention to Lucas at all, except to treat him as her brother. So it must be Pamela who was causing such a timid behavior, but why?

"Yes, I've stopped to get my brother something fresh from the oven," Pamela said, lifting an eyebrow when Priscilla's head jerked up at the mention of Robert. There was something in Priscilla's eyes. Still Pamela did not understand this change in the baker's daughter.

Priscilla swallowed hard, then took her basket and handed it to Lucas. "Please fill my wicker basket with a fragrant baker's dozen,'' she said, smiling over at Pamela. ''Pamela, please don't bother with taking Robert anything from the bakery today.'' She fluttered her thick lashes nervously. ''You see, *I* plan to.''

Pamela was taken aback by Priscilla's words. She raised a hand to her throat. ''You are . . . going . . . to do *what*?'' she half gasped.

''This will not be the first time,'' Priscilla confessed softly. ''I usually call on Robert while . . . while you are sitting vigil beside the river.'' Again Priscilla dropped her eyes. ''Today you did not stay as long. So you must know about my interest in your brother.''

Pamela was speechless, wondering why Robert had not uttered a word about Priscilla's visits. She went to Priscilla and coaxed her eyes up as she placed her forefinger under her chin. ''Why have you kept this a secret?'' she said hoarsely. ''Why has Robert?''

''He did not want you to feel threatened by my presence in your lives,'' Priscilla said in a rush of words. ''He knows how much you depend on him.''

Pamela dropped her hand and laughed softly, shaking her head in disbelief. All of this time she had been so worried about Robert being isolated. Yet he had been having a woman caller!

But, oh, she was glad! She now knew that she was free to do what she should have done long ago. Too many weeks had passed since she had seen Strong Bear. But how would she go to him? Who would accompany her?

''I must run now,'' Priscilla said, her basket heaping with steaming hot bread that Lucas had piled into it. ''Please don't be angry at Robert or me, Pamela. It was done only in your best interest. ''

There was a strained silence in the room after Priscilla's departure. Lucas checked the gingerbread men, then turned his eyes back to Pamela as she spoke.

''How do you know when the oven is hot enough for baking?'' Pamela asked, trying to force small talk, he mind swirling with what she now knew she must do. She would no longer sit vigil waiting for Strong Bear. She would go to him!

"I just put my arm in," Lucas said, trying to lighten Pamela's mood. "If it comes out charred, the temperature is right."

Pamela stared dumbfounded at him, then caught the joke and laughed. "Lucas, it is so good to jest with you," she said, going to him to give him a hug.

"I could make many a jest on the dance floor tonight," he said thickly as she drew away from him to straighten the shawl back around her shoulders. "Let us forget everything tonight but having fun, Pamela. What do you say?"

Pamela thought hard for a moment, then nodded. "Yes, let's," she said, deep down knowing this would be a way to say good-bye to a favorite friend. She hugged him again. "Yes, let's!"

Then she rushed back to her room at the rectory and took a long, leisurely bath. She sat, in a copper tub of hot water with a fragrant piece of soap floating beside her, deep in thought. Who could take her back to Strong Bear? Who would know the countryside well enough?

Her eyes lit up. "My Lord," she whispered. "Why didn't I think of that before? Lucas! He could get a leave from his apprentice duties and deliver me to Strong Bear! Who could know the countryside better than Lucas? Lucas realizes that I could love no one else but Strong Bear, and he is not the sort to be a bad loser!"

She threw her head back with a soft laugh, letting her hair tumble down the back of the tub. "Lucas, tonight won't be a good-bye! Hopefully it will be the beginning of a brand-new adventure for the two of us!"

The great bell clanged the evening hour of seven from the slender tower of the church steeple and then quivered into silence. Pamela looked at the darkness outside the window, wondering if she was truly ready to enter the wilderness again. She had suffered much there. Yet she

had also found love. But could Strong Bear love her again?
Would he deny her entrance, even, into his village?

A chill engulfed her. She was so full of wonder and
doubt!

Twenty-Six

Who would not love you,
Seeing you more warm-eyed and beautiful through
the green grove.

—Eastman

The ballroom was paneled in dark oak, sporting high windows, round and uncurtained. The wide floorboards gleamed. A violin squeaked forth a minuet as dancers swayed and swirled. Pamela spent a moment fluttering her fan, watching.

Patting her breast with the straw fan, she smiled warmly at Lucas as he cast her a bashful smile. She had not yet told him her plans of leaving. Nor had she told Robert. The mere thought of traveling to that wilderness again gave her cause to be sorely afraid. What would *they* say when they knew of her determination to go there again? Could she convince them how strongly she wanted to go? Could they understand that to find and make amends with Strong Bear she would go to the ends of the earth?

"Pamela, would you like some claret punch?" Lucas asked, edging closer to her, seeing how she nervously fanned herself. He was not sure if she showed such nervousness because of the heat, or something else. Her eyes seemed to hold some secret within them this evening. They had a lustrous sparkle, and he knew that it was not because he was her escort. It was something else. But what?

"It's quite crowded and hot in here," he added, running a finger about his stiff shirt collar with its two points turned down over a large, brown cravat. He wore a suit of gray silk trimmed with silver braid, worn with a brocade waistcoat.

His black leather shoes sported plain, square buckles. His golden hair was curled in two rolls at the side, the back tied in a black, silk bag.

He had spent much of his savings to impress a lady: Pamela. But the wrong lady had looked his way more oft than not this night. Lucas had become flattered by these attentions, watching from the corner of his eye as a frisky young thing had fluttered her lashes more than once at him. He had desired to introduce himself to her, yet thought it would be too rude, since he had escorted Pamela to the dance.

"Perhaps some refreshment would make you more comfortable?" he said, looking away from Pamela, casting another glance toward the young thing across the crowded room who now fluttered her fan, then used it to shield her face and expose only her green, mysterious eyes.

Something was happening inside Lucas. His loins were stirring strangely. Though he had been fascinated by Pamela from the first, never had her presence caused his insides to become so wildly alive! He *must* meet the lady! But it would have to be later. Perhaps tomorrow? He would question around. He would find out who she was and how he could become acquainted with her.

Pamela was amused by Lucas and the young lady exchanging glances. She was nearing the point of taking

Lucas by an arm and taking him to the beautiful woman who had caught his eye. But it would not be proper. Pamela did not even know the lady, herself, but she knew that Lucas would find out. The look in his eyes when he looked at the lady was proof of that.

"Yes, I would love some refreshment," Pamela said, giggling to herself at how he stumbled when she locked an arm through the one he was offering her as he still looked across the room at the lady. Yes, he was fascinated and would in his own way become acquainted.

Knowing this made Pamela much more relaxed about not being able to return his affections, herself. When she left Louisville, both these men of importance in her life could be left in the hands of adoring women! First Robert, and now Lucas! It was just perfect!

Walking proudly across the room, feeling admiring glances from many gentlemen, Pamela was inclined to understand the attention she was drawing. Having been fussed over by the nuns whom had grown so fond of her in her short stay with them, they had seen to it that a proper dress had been borrowed for the special occasion this night.

Her lustrous, dark hair was combed straight off the face and plaited in a loop at the back, decorated with a blue silk and feather pom-pom. She wore a dark pink sack dress that was tight-fitting around the bodice, but had a pleated side fullness from the waist to accommodate a small hoop.

The sleeves were trimmed with a horizontal band of ruched silk above the treble flounces. The nuns had also acquired clip-on earrings called "snaps," made of paste, and on her arms she wore bracelets of black silk.

Pamela could not have helped but admire herself when she had looked into the mirror. She had not worn such finery since Williamsburg. But if her plans developed as she wished, she would never wear such again. If Strong Bear accepted her back as a part of his life, she would forever dress in buckskin!

Pamela clung to Lucas's arm, as he had now taken

charge and was guiding her toward a large table at the far end of the ballroom where a giant bowl of claret punch had been prepared for the ladies and a pitcher of beer for the men. The ladies of Louisville had baked and brought an abundance of food spread out now on the table for the upcoming midnight feast.

A grand silver candelabrum holding numerous tapers showered its golden light down upon a table display of bread and butter, cake and pickles, and a chunk of boiled pork from which to slice off what was desired, along with various pies and other meats.

Smiling at others who stood at the table pouring claret punch, Pamela was startled when she heard a loud commotion at the wide expanse of door just opposite from where she now stood. Turning, her skirt and petticoats rustling, Pamela dropped her fan when she saw who was standing so boldly, so handsomely, just inside the door.

"Strong Bear—!" she gasped, raising her hands to her flushed cheeks, unable to believe that she was actually seeing him, not a phantom. He was the center of attention. Even the violin had ceased its playing.

The whisperings in the room floated about Pamela, like waves washing in on the shore. But Pamela was speechless, in awe of this Indian who had left his people to enter the world of the white man. As far as she knew this was the first time he had been emboldened to do so. He had even refused to trade at the Miami Indian stronghold of Kekionga because he had not wanted to mingle with people whose skin and habits differed from his. And now? Had he because of her? Why else would he be there, his eyes dark with anger as they searched the room?

Pamela's eyes were fixed on Strong Bear, unable to move she was so stunned by his sudden presence. She swept her gaze over him, seeing how his six-foot frame of sinew and muscle was handsomely attired in fringed buckskin leggings and shirt. The beads were resplendent on each garment. His luxuriant black hair was slicked down with bear grease, perfectly groomed, and graced with a distinguishing cluster of turkey feathers.

His strong, copper face, with its hard, high cheekbones and flat planes, shone as though having been freshly waxed. His lips were sealed tight, his determination communicated powerfully by the steel set of his jaws.

And then his hauntingly dark eyes found Pamela. She could see them waver only a moment. Then they filled with fire when he recognized her escort. As he forged his way across the crowded floor, women gasping and fluttering their fans as they stepped back, making room for him to pass, Pamela's heart wildly thumped, and her insides grew heated with wondrous excitement. Strong Bear *did* love her. He had risked so much to come for her in this way. The soldiers could have stopped him. The men in this room could even now threaten his life.

But since this was such an unusual occurrence, no one was doing anything but watching . . . waiting. The silence was almost deafening. Strong Bear's moccasins made not a sound on the floor as his strong, striking figure moved steadily toward Pamela. His each and every step was filled with authority, as though he were the one who presided over all of these gawking people, their leader.

When he stopped to tower over her, looking down at her with so much in the depths of his piercing dark eyes, Pamela could only look up at him with silent wonder overwhelming her. When Strong Bear moved swiftly and swept her into his arms and began to carry her away, only then did the gentlemen in the room begin to clamor toward them.

But Lucas came to both Pamela's and Strong Bear's defense, fully understanding what was happening without an explanation. As before, when Pamela had been bound to the stake in the courtyard of the British fort, Strong Bear had come for his woman. And as, before, Pamela was willingly going with him. The truth showed in the way she clung so devotedly about his neck, looking adoringly up at him. She had done her duty for her brother and now that he was well enough for her to leave him, she was going to go.

To stop any sort of bloodshed that might erupt from challenging a powerful Miami chief, Lucas blocked the door as Strong Bear carried Pamela to the outdoors. In a thick voice, he tried to explain to the onlookers that Pamela was not being abducted by an Indian, that she was going willingly.

The moon was a perfect circle in the sky; stars jeweled the heavens. The cool autumn breeze rustled against Pamela's dress as Strong Bear walked boldly down the street carrying her toward the river. Out of the corner of her eye she saw warriors stepping out of the shadows and joining them, soldiers standing mutely by, watching. No soldiers' weapons were drawn, for the Indians' bows were notched with arrows, ready for firing.

Pamela now understood how Strong Bear had been allowed to enter the ballroom without confrontation. There were more Indian warriors than soldiers!

"Strong Bear, I can't believe you are truly here," Pamela said, her eyes wide as she looked up at him. "Don't you know the chance you took by coming? How did you even know where to find me once you arrived? And, Strong Bear, I thought you truly didn't love me at all. Why did you let me leave you without even asking me to stay, or at least asking to see if I had planned to return to you? I thought you let me leave because you didn't love me anymore."

Looking across her shoulder, now realizing just what Strong Bear had planned for her, that he was not going to let her have the chance to say good-bye to Robert, a quiet panic seized her. This was happening too quickly. Though she wanted to go with Strong Bear, she needed to assure Robert that it was all right! And she wore a borrowed dress! And she also wanted to say a proper thank-you to Father Joseph and the sweet nuns who had taken her and

Robert under their wing. How could she if she was swept so quickly away?

"My woman, you ask too many questions," Strong Bear said gruffly. "This is not the time for questions or answers. Too much valuable time has been wasted already in such trivials. You should not have been allowed to leave Strong Bear. It was wrong. You are now being taken back. If you do not go willingly, you will go by force, for I have been a man without a soul while separated from you. My heart has been lonely. I cannot guide my people well enough when so troubled by loneliness for the woman I love."

"But my brother? Father Joseph . . ." Pamela said, her voice weak. "I must see them. They must *know*."

"You speak of a Father Joseph," Strong Bear said, carrying her closer to the shine of the river. "He is this village's man of God?"

"Yes," Pamela murmured, seeing a throng of warriors ringing the beached pirogues where the river lapped softly at the banks.

"Strong Bear conversed at length with this man of God," he said dryly. "Do you not recall that it was a man of God who taught me as a child to speak in the white man's tongue? It was good to speak with such a man again. It was this Father Joseph's great dwelling with the bell that speaks in a musical way that drew my eyes to it as I neared the village. It was the only place I went to, in my search for you. A man of God knows everything, does he not? He is almost equal in knowledge to my Great Spirit. It is through Father Joseph that I knew where to find you tonight. I was even directed to your brother's room. He knows that you are not returning to him tonight."

"And . . . what was his reaction?" Pamela dared to ask, knowing how Robert felt about her love for Strong Bear. She clung more tightly about his neck when he moved swiftly down the riverbank toward the first moored pirogue.

"Your brother is wise, for he did not question my

decision to return you to your rightful place," Strong Bear said, placing Pamela on a thick cushion of furs in the pirogue. "He now understands that your rightful place is with the Miami."

Pamela removed her arms from Strong Bear's neck and spread her skirt about her on the fur-covered seat, marveling at how many hides lined the bottom of the canoe so she could rest her feet for the long return journey down the Ohio.

A thrill coursed through her when Strong Bear gingerly placed a blanket about her shoulders, his hand grazing the flesh of her cheek as he drew it away. She was trembling. Not from the cold, but from happiness!

She did not question him any longer about Robert, or anything, for he and several of his warriors were walking the pirogue into the water. Soon they were inside, paddling hard, and moving away from the land.

Straining her eyes, Pamela looked across her shoulder in the direction of the town of Louisville, praying that Robert and Priscilla *would* find some sort of happiness together. She knew that Priscilla could do more than a mere sister to draw Robert from his sickbed and books. Robert would surely soon learn that a woman was a much better substitute for reading . . . !

She listened and faintly heard the resumed playing of the violin in the ballroom and envisioned Lucas now dancing with the young lady who had looked so adoringly at him across the dance floor. Lucas. Sweet Lucas. If not for him, so much in her life would not be!

A mist rose eerily from the floor of the forest, yet beneath a lean-to built for the night the fire was warm, the smell of cooked venison pleasant. Pamela snuggled against Strong Bear as they sat before the fire after the meal.

"Had you not come for me I would have come to you," she finally confessed, tilting her eyes to look up at him. "I was going to ask Lucas even tonight to escort me back to your village. But I was not sure of my return to your village, Strong Bear. I thought you did not want me at all."

"As Strong Bear thought you did not want *him*," he grumbled. His eyes were two dark pits as he looked down at her. "It was your decision to leave. Strong Bear had already decided that if you chose the white man's world over the Miami, then no argument would be raised against such a decision."

"But, Strong Bear, you came for me in Louisville. You missed me so much, that you came for me." Pamela sighed. "I am so glad. I have been oh, so lonely for you."

"But you did leave Strong Bear. Why did you?"

"For my brother. Only for my brother. I had to see that he was taken care of."

"You chose a brother over the man you loved?"

"It was not that way at all," Pamela said in a soft pout, easing from his arms to move to her knees directly before him, the skirt of her fancy dress pressed beneath her. She gently caressed Strong Bear's copper cheeks. "How could I ever choose a brother over the man I love? It was only temporary. Only . . . temporary . . ."

Leaning, she moved her lips slowly to his, trembling as she felt his powerful hands on her waist, guiding her to him.

"*Me-tam-sah,*" he said huskily, just before their lips met in a soft, wondrous kiss.

And then Strong Bear surrounded her with his hard, strong arms, drawing her fully against him. With eager fingers he released her hair of its bondages, then found the snaps at the back of her dress and loosened them.

"*Me-lo-na,*" Strong Bear said, leaning away from her as he looked down upon her with a fiery glance. "You are like *wa-bah-shik-ki,* a bright, white stream, so beautiful, my woman."

Unable to stand the waiting any longer, having dreamed so often of being with Strong Bear again in such a way, Pamela peeled off her dress from her shoulders along with her underthings, her cheeks growing hot as she revealed her breasts to Strong Bear's hungry eyes. In almost mechanical movements she finished disrobing, as Strong Bear began to shed his clothes, while *she* watched.

And then they twined themselves together, their bodies joining as though one, their hands wandering. Strong Bear eased Pamela down onto the bed of furs beside the fire, his lips worshiping her as he rained kisses across her face, down her throat, and then to her taut-tipped nipples. Pamela trembled as she became totally alive beneath his lips. Her hands sought out the familiar hard, muscled contours of his body, relishing the pleasure that was consuming her.

"My love . . ." Pamela whispered. His mouth was sensuous, hot, demanding as he moved lower on her body. When his lips traveled to the triangle nestled between her thighs, she inhaled a quick breath; then she closed her eyes and let the euphoria claim her.

As his lips and tongue gently caressed her, Pamela felt as though she were floating. Never before had she felt as carefree, so totally at peace. As his fingers pressed urgently into her flesh, opening her to his urgent mouth, she emitted a low moan of rapture and let the warmth of pleasure spill over inside her.

Tears of pure joy sparkled in Pamela's eyes as Strong Bear now rose above her, seeking her lips with wildness and desperation. She shuddered and arched as he buried his throbbing hardness deep inside her and began his eager strokes. Passion weaved between them as he kissed her long and hard, his hands molding and caressing her breasts. She clung to him, her legs locked at her ankles, riding with him. Her heart sang, the golden flames of desire burning higher . . . higher.

Delicious shivers of desire rode up and down Pamela's spine. Magic in his caress, he tantalized her with his hands and mouth, over and over again. She moaned softly, her fingers pressed into his buttocks, anchoring him closer . . . closer.

Strong Bear moved rhythmically within her, feeling the warm tightness answering him in kind. His heart soared, he breathed in the sweet scent of her. His hands moved up and down her back, feeling how silken and soft she was. How fiercely he had missed her! His tongue explored the nectar of her lips; then when they parted, he probed gently within.

Then he drew momentarily away from her, seeing the blush in her cheeks, the passion in her eyes. Her dark lashes fluttered on her cheeks as she smiled, sighing.

"We will never again part, my woman," Strong Bear whispered, smoothing her hair back from her brow. He placed a gentle kiss there, then lay his lips against the delicate curve of her neck and thrust more eagerly inside her until he felt the familiar warm pulsating begin, knowing that his sought-for release was near.

"My . . . woman . . ." he whispered, stiffening, then releasing his love seed deep within her womb. Smiling to himself, he felt her sensual response as her body softly quivered against his.

His tongue brushed her lips lightly; his hands held within them the softness of her breasts. "Soon you will become my *wife*," he said hoarsely, looking down at her with a keen possessiveness. "My people will witness your transformation into *Miami*."

Pamela tremored with the thrill. Could it truly be happening? Was life finally going to be good to her? She had fought so many battles to get to this point in her life. She was almost afraid to believe that the ugliness was over, and that she *could* finally be Strong Bear's totally.

And then her eyes wavered with memories that she did not wish to recall. But it was a reality that Strong Bear could take more than one wife. He would possibly *never* be totally hers!

Easing from his arms, feeling a sudden chill come over her, Pamela drew a blanket snugly about her shoulders and scooted closer to the flickering fire.

Strong Bear's eyebrows lifted in puzzlement at her withdrawn behavior. He went to her and clasped her shoulders with his hands, causing the blanket to drop away from her. "Why do you behave so distant to me?" he growled. "What was said to cause this behavior? Do you not wish to be my wife? Was Strong Bear wrong to think that you truly wanted to become a part of my people? Should Strong Bear return you to the land of the white people? Tell me that is not what you wish, my woman. Tell me!"

Pamela's head jerked up, her eyes wide. "No, I never want to leave you again," she said softly.

"Then tell me what is the matter," Strong Bear urged, his fingers softening against her flesh.

Pamela cast her eyes downward, afraid to tell him of her fears yet she knew that she must! Again she looked up into his dusky eyes "Strong Bear, I have given up all of the customs of my people to be with you," she said carefully. "Perhaps you can give up at least one of your customs for *me*."

Strong Bear dropped his hands away from her, taken aback by her request. "Customs?" he asked in confusion. "You would ask that I give up one of my customs? I do not understand."

Pamela cleared her throat nervously. "Strong Bear, do you not know that I can bear you many sons?" she blurted. "Do you not know that only one wife is required to bear many sons?"

She flung herself into his arms, resting a cheek against his bare chest. "Oh, Strong Bear, I would simply die if I had to share you with another wife," she cried. "Please tell me that I will be enough for you. Please . . . tell me that?"

Strong Bear framed her face between his hands and looked down at her. "You ask this of me not only because of special gifts Strong Bear will give you because you are only wife?" he said thickly. "For you know I have promised you many special gifts whether or not you are only wife."

Pamela was struck almost dumb by his question. Then, recalling Snow Owl and what she had wanted of Strong

Bear, she laughed softly. "My love, I don't want *any* gifts," she said. "I want only you. Only you."

She rose up onto her knees and laced her arms about his neck. Softly she kissed him, then pleaded with her eyes as she leaned back away from him. "I will be your only wife?" she asked. "Only . . . I?"

"Yes," Strong Bear said, drawing her fully into his embrace. "You will be only wife. Now and forever!"

He settled her down beside him, where they both shared the same blanket draped about their shoulders. "Now let me tell you about marriage customs of the Miami," he said, looking dreamily into the fire. "You will dress in the most dazzling of finery. You will wear shoulder straps of glass bead, porcelain, and bells. Four days will be spent in celebration. Then you will not only be Strong Bear's woman, you will be his *wife*."

Pamela listened intently, her heart bursting with happiness. Yet there was one disturbing thought to spoil this shared moment with the man she loved. Should she not bear him sons, would he then keep his promise of having only one wife?

Twenty-Seven

One year later . . .

The first snowfall had covered the land in its silken white shroud. Pamela sat with the other women of the village beside a great outdoor fire while the men and boys were participating in the snowshoe dance. Pamela sat straight-backed, a heavy blanket tucked around her arms, watching Strong Bear lead his braves and the sons of his braves in the traditional dance that was required when the first snow arrived.

The snow dance was given in honor of the Great Spirit who had sent the snow to help the Indians track wild game for their food during the long winter months. Since their food was principally the flesh of wild animals, the snow was of great service to the red man, for it helped him find animals that could be killed.

The braves were now all ready to dance. Many drums beat in unison in the distance. The braves' spears, hunting knives, and bows and arrows were piled on the ground. Each Indian who wanted to dance this particular dance had to put on his snowshoes.

Attired in his buckskin leggings and shirt, with a robe of bear fur draped about his shoulders, Strong Bear started out dancing in a circle about the weapons lying on the ground. All of the other Indians followed their leader.

While dancing, each Indian, one at a time, danced up to the pile of weapons, chose the one he wanted to hunt with, then danced back to the edge of the circle. Not once did he stop singing his hunting song.

At the same time he had to go through the motions of catching the game he hoped to bring back to the camp as his spoil. If he was pretending he was hunting deer, he danced by leaps and bounds, throwing his head up in the air and looking from side to side. If he was imitating hunting a bear he ran at a pacing run around the circle. Each man tried to imitate the animal he hoped to catch.

The drums beat incessantly, the song and dance lasting for a long while.

Then Pamela was drawn from the celebration when soft cries were heard from her nearby cabin. Smiling softly as she excused herself, she went to her dwelling and saw that her tiny, three-month-old son was awake, ready to suckle from her breast.

Love filling her insides with a special warmth, Pamela set the blanket she had been wearing aside and leaned down into the wooden crib and drew White Feather up into her arms.

Her child wrapped in a soft doeskin blanket, Pamela looked down upon perfect features that were an exact replica of his father's. "You are Strong Bear's son," she whispered. She sat down close to the fire in the firespace and eased the corner of her buckskin blouse away from a breast and offered it delicately to White Feather's lips. "My son, will your brother be the same?"

While White Feather suckled hungrily, she held him against her bosom with her one hand, touching her abdomen with the other. Most would say it was too soon to be with child again, but for a wife of a proud Indian chief, she knew that it was never too soon. She had promised him many sons! It looked as though the good Lord was going to bless them by letting it be so!

"Did I hear you tell White Feather something about a brother?" Strong Bear asked suddenly from behind Pamela.

She turned her head with a start, then smiled devotedly at him. "The dance is over?" she questioned.

"Yes. And I come into my dwelling and hear my wife talking with my son. What is this about another son?" Strong Bear repeated.

"I do not have to tell you that I have again missed my monthly weeps," Pamela said, giggling, for they had not missed one night of lovemaking since she had healed from having their son. "My love, are you happy?"

Strong Bear eased down beside her and reverently touched his son's cheek. "Perhaps it will not be a son at all," he said. "Perhaps a daughter?"

Pamela's smile faded. "Would that make you so unhappy?" she asked softly.

Strong Bear shrugged. "There is much time for many sons," he said hoarsely. "A daughter would be favored for our next child. She would be as beautiful as you, would she not?"

"You would truly wish that she were?" Pamela asked bashfully, tremoring as his fingers grazed against her bare breast just above where her son's lips were suckling.

"It is what I would wish," Strong Bear said, laughing huskily as he leaned to kiss her softly on the lips.

He reached for his pipe and filled it with Indian tobacco, then lit it. Looking into the fire, he spoke proudly. "The wind grows cold," he said. "The leaves of many colors have left the trees. The animals are waiting for us in winter coats. It is time for the hunt. Strong Bear goes willingly!"

"You love this land, do you not?" Pamela asked, wiping a trickle of milk from the corner of White Feather's tiny, puckered mouth.

"It is land that I have brought my people to," Strong Bear said, drawing deeply from his pipe. "They are happy. I am happy. *You* are happy. This land is like a piece of my body. Sometimes I think I could melt into it."

Pamela laid a hand to his arm. "But at one time you had thought to take your people to another stretch of land," she said, her heart aching when she thought about the past and what she had lost. "Do you regret that you did not, instead, take your people there? You had said that the Great Spirit had told you in your special vision that you should settle there, on the land where my father and brothers built a home."

A soft smile lifted the corners of Strong Bear's lips. He placed his pipe on a stone beside the firespace. Draping an arm about Pamela's waist and drawing her lips to his, he whispered soft words against her mouth. "My woman, did you not know that my vision led me to *you*, not the land?"

Pamela's heart soared as he kissed her ever so sweetly. . . .

PASSION'S TIMELESS HOUR

VIVIAN KNIGHT-JENKINS

Bestselling Author Of *The Outlaw Heart*

Propelled by a freak accident from the killing fields of Vietnam to a Civil War battlefield, army nurse Rebecca Ann Warren discovers long-buried desires in the arms of Confederate leader Alexander Random. But when Alex begins to suspect she may be a Yankee spy, the only way Rebecca can prove her innocence is to convince him of the impossible…that she is from another time, another place.

_52079-6 $4.99 US/$6.99 CAN

Dorchester Publishing Co., Inc.
65 Commerce Road
Stamford, CT 06902

Please add $1.75 for shipping and handling for the first book and $.50 for each book thereafter. NY, NYC, PA and CT residents, please add appropriate sales tax. No cash, stamps, or C.O.D.s. All orders shipped within 6 weeks via postal service book rate. Canadian orders require $2.00 extra postage and must be paid in U.S. dollars through a U.S. banking facility.

Name _____

Address _____

City _____ State _____ Zip _____

I have enclosed $_____ in payment for the checked book(s). Payment <u>must</u> accompany all orders.☐ Please send a free catalog.

Flames of Rapture

Lark Eden

"Great reading!"—*Romantic Times*

When Lyric Solei flees the bustling city for her summer retreat in Salem, Massachusetts, it is a chance for the lovely young psychic to escape the pain so often associated with her special sight. Investigating a mysterious seaside house whose ancient secrets have long beckoned to her, Lyric stumbles upon David Langston, the house's virile new owner, whose strong arms offer her an irresistible temptation. And it is there that Lyric discovers a dusty red coat, which from the time she first lays her gifted hands on it unravels to her its tragic history—and lets her relive the timeless passion that brought it into being.

_52078-8 $4.99 US/$6.99 CAN